By Jorge Zepeda Patterson

MILENA

THE BLACK JERSEY

THE BLACK JERSEY

RANDOM HOUSE

NEW YORK

THE
BLACK JERSEY

A NOVEL

Jorge Zepeda Patterson

Translated by Achy Obejas

Translation copyright © 2019 by Achy Obejas

Published in the United States by Random House, an imprint and division of Penguin Random House LLC, New York.

RANDOM HOUSE and the HOUSE colophon are registered trademarks of Penguin Random House LLC.

Originally published in Spanish by Planeta, Barcelona in 2018, copyright © 2018 by Jorge Zepeda Patterson.

LIBRARY OF CONGRESS CATALOGING-IN-PUBLICATION DATA
Names: Zepeda Patterson, Jorge, author. | Obejas, Achy, translator.
Title: The black jersey: a novel / Jorge Zepeda Patterson; translated by Achy Obejas.
Other titles: Maillot negro. English
Description: First edition. | New York: Random House, 2019.
Identifiers: LCCN 2018043386| ISBN 9781984801067 (hardback) | ISBN 9781984801074 (ebook)
Subjects: | BISAC: FICTION / Suspense. | FICTION / Sports. | GSAFD: Suspense fiction
Classification: LCC PQ7298.436.E65 M3513 2019 | DDC 863/.7—dc23
LC record available at https://lccn.loc.gov/2018043386

Printed in the United States of America on acid-free paper

randomhousebooks.com

9 8 7 6 5 4 3 2 1

FIRST U.S. EDITION

Title-page image: © iStockphoto.com

Book design by Dana Leigh Blanchette

To Susan Crowley

Cast

THE SUPERSTAR: Steve Panata

THE DOMESTIQUE: Marc Moreau

THE COACH: Robert Giraud

THE RIVALS: Alessio Matosas, Pablo Medel, Milenko Paniuk

THE MECHANIC: Fiona Crowley

THE MENTOR: Colonel Bruno Lombard

THE JOURNALIST: Ray Lumiere

THE COP: Commissioner Favre

A Tour de France Glossary

Who

Peloton—From French, meaning "little ball" or "platoon." This is the main cluster of riders in a race. It's an ever-shifting mass, alive in its own right. Riding in a tight group provides protection from the elements, but can sometimes lead to spectacular crashes. The peloton can absorb a rider who's broken away just as easily as it can spit one out the back. Stay with the pack.

Domestique—From the French for "servant." Though the wearer of the yellow jersey may cross the finish line alone, it's not without the help of a team. Each team has eight or nine riders with one leader, whom the rest of the team works to advance and protect, like a quarterback. Domestiques—the nonleader members of the team—shield their champion from wind, ensure he rides in the safest position (toward the front), and give spare wheels or even their own bike if needed. The primary domestique is as crucial as the leader himself, though is not above the humble task of ferrying supplies back and forth to the team.

DS (directeur sportif)—French for "sport director" or coach. As it sounds, this is the person in charge of the entire team's sporting efforts, including team selection, rider strategy, and training.

Soigneur—French for "caretaker." Overseeing practically everything but the bikes, these staff members are like the camp counselors of a team: They provide daily massage treatments and physical therapy, make supply runs, shuttle riders to and fro, and feed them during the race as they cling to the side of the team car. Prepared for anything, soigneurs may even administer first aid.

What

Stage—A section of a race. The Tour de France is usually made up of about twenty-one legs of competition, comprised of both flat and mountain terrain, as well as time trials.

Time trial—It's you against the clock in this stage. Unlike a group race where you can trail another rider, it's much harder to gauge where you are in the standings when riding alone. Best bet is to put your head down and book it, as a good time trial could boost your standing in the general classification.

Time limit—All riders must finish every stage within a certain range of the stage winner's time. If not, they face being eliminated from the race.

Yellow jersey—The color of a rider's jersey—such as yellow, green, white, or polka-dot—designates a particular standing or distinction in the race. The yellow jersey goes to the rider with the best standing at the end of each stage. Each rider who wins a stage of the race receives from the race organizers both a jersey to wear the next morning in the race and one to keep for the memories.

How

Drafting—Also called slipstreaming. Riding in the back of the paceline—a line of bikers—in order to reduce wind resistance and therefore effort. Riders rotate through the line so that each gets a chance to rest at the back.

Crosswind—The kind of wind that plasters your hair to the side of your face and knocks you off your bike, a crosswind can be downright deadly and is commonly found on flat stages of the Tour, where bucolic expanses provide little blockage from the wind. Teams often plan for attacks on windy parts of the course to catch rivals off guard.

Breakaway—Also known as an attack or a jump, this is a move made by one or more riders in an attempt to get ahead, tire out the pack, or break it apart. Generally, the peloton won't allow a main competitor to get far ahead of the pack, but riders who pose no threat in general classification may be permitted to escape.

Blocking—When riders set a relatively slow pace at the front of a group to control the speed, often to the advantage of one of their teammates who may be in a breakaway.

THE BLACK JERSEY

Prologue

On Sunday, when the multicolored column of cyclists glides under the Arc de Triomphe and conquers Paris after twenty-one days and 3,350 kilometers, I could be either in a drawer in the morgue or wrapped in a yellow jersey. I've never stepped up on that winner's podium, I've never even won a stage, but now I'm a few seconds behind Steve Panata, my teammate and brother for the past eleven years. In order to wear the yellow jersey, I'll have to betray him at the last minute.

There are cyclists willing to die to win a single stage of the Tour, taking suicidal descents at more than 90 kilometers an hour; but now I know there are cyclists willing to kill for it too. There's a killer among us, and the police have tasked me with finding out who it is. A criminal has divided the peloton and must be stopped before he deals the final blow. I could be his next victim. But I also know that, thanks to his interventions, I could become the next champion of the Tour de France.

2006

Everyone hated him the minute they laid eyes on him, except for me.

He was chewing gum nonstop, and every three seconds he would push back a lock of hair as if it were an extension he was afraid of losing. But even without those tics, he would've provoked the group's ill will. He arrived at camp driving a limited-edition Land Rover and unloaded an aerodynamic bike that the rest of us had only seen ridden by the most elite professionals. It didn't help that he was American, that he had a face like a Hollywood actor, and that he flaunted the smile of somebody who always gets his way.

But I welcomed him with open arms. A new guy was the only way the others would leave me in peace. Ever since I had arrived at training camp two weeks prior, my teammates had made me the butt of their practical jokes, the hazing a product of the excess of anxiety and testosterone that you might expect from our vigorous training sessions. They had turned my first few weeks as a professional—if getting paid fifty euros a week had made me that—into a kind of lonely purgatory, so I was grateful for the chance to not be the solitary victim of their abuse.

Maybe that's what brought us together. We took the torments the others inflicted on us philosophically and chose to treat them as some kind of initiation ritual directed at newbies. Although, to be more accurate, Steve took it philosophically and I just went along with him.

"Don't eat the oatmeal," he said the first time he ever spoke to me. "I think they spit in it." And then he offered me a protein bar. He seemed more pleased than upset, as if the fact that he'd figured it out made him cleverer than the others.

After a few days, we understood it wasn't an initiation ritual. Simply put: Our new teammates were scared of us. Of the forty-six racers who had started out at training camp for the Belgian team Ventoux, the legendary breeding ground of professional cyclists, only twenty-seven would be kept, and only the best nine would make it onto the first team, the one they take to the trials that really matter.

A month later, when the training became more demanding and the races turned into 160-kilometer journeys that included steep expanses, we understood their fear was justified. We *were* better. Steve Panata raced with a natural rhythm and elegance I'd never seen before and never would again. He devoured kilometers effortlessly, at a speed that would have forced anyone else to bend over the wheel. I balanced him with a physiological anomaly that in other circumstances would have made me a circus freak. My father was a native of the French Alps, and his DNA must have had a very good time with the Colombian genes from my mother's Andean ancestors because they ended up gifting me a third lung. Not literally, but the levels of oxygen in my blood are such that, for all practical purposes, I'm high when I'm racing.

Once we were actually on the road, Steve and I began to take revenge for all the affronts we had suffered. We did it almost without thinking. When we got within twenty or thirty kilometers of the goal set by our coaches, he'd smile slyly at me; I'd give a gesture of complicity, and we'd pick up the pace. We'd do it subtly at first so the others wouldn't immediately surrender and would make more of an effort. Ten kilometers later, when we sensed the group had hit its limit, we'd speed up again and leave them definitively behind. But not before Steve put in his final touch: He'd start talking in a very calm voice about the last movie he saw, like someone who's chatting in a bar instead of climbing a slope that had taken everybody else's breath away. Resentment soon mingled with the fear we inspired in our teammates. Now and again I thought that, stuck up on those mountain retreats in Catalonia among dozens of spiteful contenders determined to become professionals at any cost, we might be vulnerable to the kind of beating that would put our own careers at risk. For a lot of those guys, myself included, making the cut and being on the Ventoux team was the only thing keeping us from having to endure a mediocre job at a farm or a factory. To be honest, a couple of them looked like they had nowhere to go but jail. That wasn't the case with Steve, for whom professional cycling was just one option among many, in a lavish and generous future. Yet another reason to hate him.

It also didn't help that he could be irresistibly charming when he wanted to be, especially when it came to women, directors, and coaches. Charming in a way that provoked more than one brawl with the locals on the few occasions the group would go out to a local bar, even if it was just to have root beer. A passing flirtation or an exchange of napkins with scrawled telephone numbers was enough to unleash a fracas that would often end in blows.

Despite so frequently provoking envy and resentment among

others, Steve was notoriously incapable of defending himself. All the poise he displayed on a bike or on the dance floor would turn into ineptitude the instant punches flew. We managed to get out more or less unharmed anyway, thanks to my military police training and some army experiences dealing with hotheaded drunks in dive bars.

Locals were one thing. But in the end, I had to neutralize the damn bullies on our own team, starting with the group's bruiser, a hard and rough Briton with the thighs and face of a bulldog. He weighed about twenty-five pounds more than I did, but he hadn't grown up in a slum in Medellín or spent three years in the army barracks in Perpignan. I'd developed a survival strategy that was, in essence, conflict avoidance, which fit my temperament perfectly. But it's a strategy that only works if you're willing to commit to violence on the rare occasions when conflict is inevitable. Such as the time I had to defend Steve from Iván, the bruiser.

Iván had punctured my friend's bike tires a few times during the night, which forced us to make frantic repairs in order to report on time to the coaches. One morning, we discovered Steve's bike had disappeared altogether, and the smirk on Iván's face made it obvious he was the responsible party. I supposed he assumed Steve would finally have to confront him. He never saw me coming. I threw my forearm with all my strength and hit him in the face with my elbow: right between his jaw and temple. That imbecile fell like a rock while his minions looked on, astonished by my inconceivable aggression. And they certainly weren't expecting what happened next. I kicked up a storm as the goon's body curled up into a ball, not stopping until he confessed where he'd hidden the bike. After that incident, they left us in peace.

It also helped that Steve began to extend certain courtesies to the other racers. He would generously distribute the contents of packages he received from the U.S.: gels, protein bars, sports shoes, and T-shirts. A subtle kind of bribery that soon produced dividends. By the time the training season was over, our teammates were treating us as if we were kings of the road.

Sometimes I ask myself if our deep friendship, which would end up defining both our lives, was forged by the mutual protection of that initial alliance. At least in my case, it was. Even considering what happened years later, I'm convinced there was something genuine and profound in that unconditional and absolutely loyal brotherhood we forged from the very first.

But beyond that, the two of us fascinated each other. When we met, he was twenty-one and I was twenty-three. Steve had grown up in privilege, the spoiled only son of prominent lawyers from Santa Fe, New Mexico. His parents supported his racing obsession and paid for semiprofessional coaches when he decided to participate in his country's junior competitions. He ended up taking them all by storm, although always surrounded and protected by a small troop of supporters, first financed by his family and then by his sponsors, all of them attracted to the potential oozing from the golden boy.

Now, in northern Spain, he found himself in hostile territory for the first time in his life. His coaches had concluded he could never reach the top heights of racing without first going through the toughening offered by the European teams and their impeccable training.

Steve seemed hypnotized by my ability to survive in scenarios he considered exotic and fascinating and that I considered the norm. I became what I am because of circumstances, which is the case for everybody not named Panata. I ended up a cyclist the way others become office workers or salespeople: because that's what I found to hold on to when I was trying to stay afloat in the midst of a raging current. Steve, on the other hand, was one of those human beings whose future is a consequence of inevitable design.

He interpreted the abandonment in which I grew up as a kind of wasted freedom. I hadn't even turned nine when my father, a French military man attached to several Latin American embassies for many years, separated from my mother, a woman from Bogotá of Peruvian origin whose family had fallen on hard times. From that moment on, I spent my summers in a cabin in the Alps where my father had decided to retire, and the rest of the year in a redbrick house on the outskirts of Medellín. I was more or less neglected during my childhood, because of the exhausting nursing shifts my mother worked at two different hospitals. In time, I understood a part of her was also looking for an excuse to keep her distance from me, the product of an unhappy marriage that came about only because of an unwanted pregnancy. In my adolescence, I became convinced she was hoping I wouldn't come back from one of those summer trips to France. I would've been happy to comply except that my father was just as urgently trying to get rid of me every time I visited. Paying for my plane ticket and welcoming me for five weeks was a duty Colonel Moreau strictly complied with though without the slightest enthusiasm.

It's quite likely I would've ended up recruited by one of the youth gangs that terrorized our neighborhood if bike racing hadn't come to the rescue. It was my mother who was inadvertently responsible. Her many extra shifts allowed us to move from San Cristóbal, on the city outskirts, to San Javier, a more central neighborhood in Medellín. Although it was a step up socially, it was a literal step down because it forced me to walk almost seven kilometers uphill to get to school. I had to get up at four-thirty in the morning to make it on time to my first class. She must've taken pity on me at some point because one day she showed up with a big, heavy secondhand bike that was most likely stolen. We used to call it the bricklayers' bike, but it changed my life.

Paradoxically, it was my laziness that turned me into a climber. My new mount allowed me to reset my alarm clock for five-thirty; eventually, I started to time my routes in order to prolong my lazing in bed. It ended up becoming an obsession. Every week, I'd try to shave one or two minutes from my trip to school. I lessened the weight in my backpack, I learned to take advantage of every curve, I counted how often I put on the brakes and decreased them to the absolute minimum. Some of my schoolmates made fun of the old torn boots I'd begun wearing to school, but I didn't care: Their thick soles allowed me to better reach the pedals and thus reduce my trip by three minutes.

One day a teacher noticed the force I applied to the brakes when I got to school, followed immediately by a pause to check the time and record it in my notebook. She asked what I was doing and read my annotations with curiosity. A week later she told me about a race for amateur cyclists; she was one of the organizers. At first, I thought the idea was ridiculous. My torn boots and my crude bike didn't fit with the images I had of Colombian cycling idols wearing colorful uniforms and riding aerodynamic machines. But there was no way to say no. Half the class, at least the half that had already turned thirteen, was in love with Miss Carmen. Her tireless enthusiasm, her warm smile, her green eyes, and, more than anything, the way her skirt moved when she walked made her the object of our wet dreams.

Even though all the other racers wore better shoes than me, I was comforted to see there were a few bikes like mine. I was determined to impress my teacher. I shot out quickly from the starting line, surprised by how easily I left everyone behind. I didn't even do anything different from what I was used to doing on the way to school. Soon I understood what had happened. The others were pacing themselves to get through the thirty-two kilometers that separated them from the finish line; I was drained by the tenth. Soon, the first racers began to pass me. When we were five kilo-

meters from the finish line, I was in last place. It was my first experience with the torment of racing. My legs were in shreds and I
could feel each pedal from my belly on down; I thought my guts
were unraveling. It was also my first experience with the enemy
that every cyclist carries inside, the one who begs him to put a
stop to the torture. It kept telling me I'd done enough, that I was
the youngest in the race, that it was better to quit than to come in
last. But I imagined Carmen's disappointment and decided not to
give up, and not to come in last either. I focused on the back of the
racer thirty meters in front of me and put everything I had into
each downstroke. I passed him and looked for the next racer's
back. Soon I forgot my exhaustion. When I got to the finish line,
I threw up and stayed doubled over for a long time because of the
pain stabbing my side, but I didn't move away: I wanted to count
the racers who came in after me. There were ten. Before I left,
Carmen hugged me and gave me a kiss on the cheek.

After that day, I dedicated my afternoons to biking around
the hills surrounding our apartment. I designed longer courses;
I read everything Carmen gave me about nutrition and racing
techniques. My legs grew and I retired the boots. Although it
would be a long time before I won anything, it was enough for me
to see Carmen's enthusiasm and to realize that, each time I stood
at the finish line, there were more and more racers who came in
after me.

The athlete I am today was forged in those long solo training
sessions. Strategy came later, but it was there I developed the essence of a professional cyclist: my ability to sustain pain, to hit
the limits and still go on. I would kill myself with impossible
goals, convinced my suffering brought me closer to Carmen and
made me worthy of her attention and affection.

When she left two years later, promoted to a private school in
Bogotá, it shook my tiny universe and filled me with despair. After
a few tormented weeks, I became convinced I could get her back
with my bike: My fame as a racer would reach the capital city and

bring us together. I doubled down on my masochistic training sessions. Pain became my best friend.

It was during that time I developed another habit for which I became well-known. Measuring, timing, counting, and registering everything.

Years later, my colleagues, including Steve, would laugh at me because of my obsession with numbers, and more than one of them would call me the calculator, wanting to get under my skin. And yet, sooner or later, every one of them would ask me how many goddamn kilometers it was until the finish line or the stats of a racer who had just broken away from the peloton. I never minded being their Wikipedia in places where nobody could use their cell.

It was also in the mountains of Medellín that I realized others didn't have the same strange relationship I do to my own perspiration. It's shitty luck to be allergic to the sweat your body produces when you earn a living making your body sweat. The weather where I come from had already given me all sorts of rashes, and I'd had to turn to powders and balms in search of relief. It's not that I hadn't realized it until the moment I climbed on a bike, but until then it had only been an annoyance, mostly on excessively hot days. Now the burns and chafing had become a flesh-colored tattoo on parts of my body that an adolescent shouldn't be embarrassed about, or at least not for those reasons.

Sweating and counting, I became a familiar figure at the weekend races around where I lived. At some point, I stopped counting the racers who came in after me and started counting those who got to the finish line before me.

Finally, I began to place and to climb the podiums. Even though I competed against adults, I won a few medals; these prizes and tips from the bettors kept me away from the voracious violence in Colombia during those years. Still, it wasn't a happy time: My bicycle weighed more than forty pounds, and the state of my tires led to inopportune blowouts that made me abandon about half the races I entered. I've never felt such impotent rage as when, standing on the side of the road with tears in my eyes, I watched the racers I'd left behind minutes before pass me by.

Drug money, from which I'd been running away, changed everything. One of the guys from the neighborhood started betting on my races. He must've been sixteen or seventeen years old, nothing more than a lowly foot soldier in the ranks of organized crime, but the money he flashed around seemed like a fortune to me. Once, when I came in third, he congratulated me with a lot of fanfare, celebrating as if I'd won. He must've been high because, in his euphoria, he grabbed my bike and threw it off the small cliff where we were standing. Before I had a chance to launch myself after it, he dragged me to a bike shop and bought me the best bike we could find. For months, I lived with the fear that he would want me to pay back the favor at any moment, but luckily he stuck to just betting on me. I want to think he recovered his investment grandly because, from that moment on, I began to win more and more races.

Shortly after I turned seventeen, I heard Carmen had come back to Medellín as the principal of my old school. My first impulse was to go see her and show her the racer I had become. But I contained myself. I realized I had nothing but medals from amateur races. I decided not to see her until I'd won a pro race. I managed to sign up for the Vuelta la Cordillera, which would take place in three months. It was a fierce competition in which fledgling professionals and veterans in their twilight years frequently participated. I trained obsessively until I reached the kinds of numbers that convinced me I had a real shot at winning.

Two weeks before the race I got a call from a former schoolmate telling me Carmen had been killed in cross fire between rival gangs. I kept my distance at the funeral and cried over the end of my adolescence. I never again got on the bike my narco friend had given me. And it would be a while before I got on any other bike at all.

When I turned eighteen, my mother accepted a marriage proposal from a doctor with a good heart and galloping halitosis. It was more an act of surrender on her part than anything to do with falling in love; in any case, I had no say. Two weeks later, I left her a note in the kitchen. Three days after that, I was on the other side of the ocean, knocking on my father's door without prior warning. He didn't seem particularly surprised; he offered me some lentils and set me up in what had been my room during my summer visits.

During the next few months I did what I could to earn a place by his side. If he asked me to cut wood, I'd chop down the forest until I tore my hands to shreds. I learned to make his favorite stew and to drive his ancient Ford so I could relieve him of weekly grocery shopping in town. After the first snows, I taught myself to ski with the same intensity I'd previously dedicated to pedaling my bike. My father respected winter sports and considered it foolish to wear yourself out on a bike when a motorcycle would get you to the same place with much greater efficiency. Or at least that's what he said when I tried to tell him about my modest cycling exploits.

It was by dint of many falls and bruises that, by Christmas, my skiing had ceased to be an embarrassment. I had just decided to work toward becoming a winter sports instructor when my father told me he'd enlisted me in the army, and had even managed to get me assigned to a regiment led by an old friend of his at the foot of the Pyrenees, close to Perpignan. This was possible because, eighteen years earlier, my father had demanded I be born on French soil, even if to do so my mother had to fly eight months pregnant with a medical certificate forged by the embassy doctor.

I marched off to the barracks convinced I was headed to a life as a galley slave, digging trenches and going on long expeditions in the Sahara. And it might have been that way but for an unexpected turn of events that put me back on a bike. My father's colleague died suddenly a few days after my arrival. He was replaced by Colonel Bruno Lombard, an odd man much more interested in athletic competitions between regiments than in army life or military theory. When he found out about my youthful adventures racing in the Colombian mountains, he made me a part of his beloved army cycling team.

"Take care of it as if it was yours," he told me ten days after his arrival, showing me a battered, scraped-up racing bike. I don't know what Lombard did to get the team's twelve bikes. They looked like something thrown out by a professional team from an inferior league, but they were definitely racing bikes, if a decade old.

The bike was technically property of the French state, but I felt as if I'd been gifted a Ferrari. For the next couple of weeks, I did everything in my power to not get off that thing. Even at the risk of neglecting my military duties and ending up with saddle sores.

Some official must have complained about my lack of diligence, because Lombard made a radical decision; it's the reason why today, I've found myself playing detective on the Tour de France. He assigned me to the regiment's small military police unit, directly under his command. It freed me from almost all the boring routines assigned to my troop, and put me in the hands of the unit's director, who also happened to be the coach of the cycling squad.

The coach was an old grouch, tough and uncompromising. I suppose it was his personality that kept him from working with professional teams, because he had more than enough talent and knowledge of the sport. He sensed my predisposition for the mountains and, in the following months, pushed my body to its limits racing the imposing peaks all around us.

In the next four years, our regiment won absolutely everything. Not only the races against teams from other French government institutions, but also all of the regional tournaments Lombard could justify taking us to.

His "boys" were basically me and twenty conscripts who rotated in and out over the years, more enthused about the breaks from military work than any talent we might have had for cycling. And Julián. Julián was a good racer and could have become a professional in time as part of a modest team, except that his past in the Marseille gangs reclaimed him when he finished his military service. But he had good instincts for racing and a savage capacity for enduring pain and maxing out on a hill. And that first taste of collaboration and competition was enough. It was all I needed to go up on the podium so many times that it ceased being fun for any of us, except Lombard. At twenty-two I was well-known in the regional press, which gave me the nickname Hannibal because I had conquered the Pyrenees and the Alps, though I didn't find out about that until later. Initially, I didn't understand the nickname until I was told about the Punic general who'd brought his army through the mountains on elephants to attack Ancient Rome. In time, I became fond of it, although I didn't like that my speed on the bike was being compared to Hannibal's elephantine march. I decided to tattoo a small dragon on my neck, which was our regiment's symbol, hoping it would squash any reference to those damn elephants. But Lombard loved the nickname and endorsed Hannibal as if it were the consecration of a legend.

At the end of my four years in the army, the colonel let me go, sad yet proud of his creation, but not before making sure I had a place with Ventoux, the pro team where I met Steve.

I don't know exactly when I decided to devote myself to a life of cycling. Perhaps it was on hearing the phrase my father used when I returned to his refuge in the Alps after my military service.

"You weren't even good enough for the barracks," he said

when I knocked on his door once more. He probably thought I'd become a high-ranking officer, like him. His words ended up helping me decide. In that moment, I told myself someday I'd enter Paris wrapped in the yellow jersey worn by the Tour de France champion.

Ten years later, the press still referred to me as Hannibal even though I hadn't managed to win a single stage in the Pyrenees, never mind any of the big races.

Today

The Tour, Stages 1–6

"And let's not even talk about sex," said Robert Giraud, our directeur sportif. We were on the team bus, making our way to Utrecht, in the Netherlands, where we would set off on the first stage of the Tour de France. It was a rhetorical recommendation. None of us would risk a race for which we'd been preparing for months just for a night of revelry. Making it to Paris was essentially about knowing how to manage fatigue for three weeks. When you're dropping eight thousand calories a day, sex is the last thing you need.

The only one who didn't seem to understand this was Stevlana. Yes, Stevlana. Wives and girlfriends were not welcome on the Tour. And none was less welcome than Steve's partner, a Russian supermodel almost as famous as he was. She had decided to make a stop in Holland on her way to London to surprise her man and wish him good luck, much to his consternation.

Earlier that same morning, I had gotten a call from Steve on my cell. He didn't respond to my greeting and instead let the phone pick up Stevlana's voice. I understood what he was getting at and went to rescue him. I knocked on his door and, in a loud voice, told him we'd been chosen for an anti-doping test that would take place in my room. The door swung open, and I faked surprise to find Stevlana there.

"But I just got here, Stivy," she protested. "Marc, don't do this to me."

"This doesn't have anything to do with you, Stivy," Steve said; his tone was so sad I almost believed him.

Stivy is what they called each other, which the other racers loved to make fun of. Although I think a lot of them did it to try to hide the envy her spectacular breasts induced.

Generally speaking, Stevlana believed everything revolved around her. That included the anti-doping test, a nuisance designed exclusively to ruin a morning with her lover. While Steve finished dressing, his girlfriend tried to kill the messenger with a couple of poisonous looks.

She'd never liked me. And she liked my girlfriend, Fiona, even less. Fiona was a mechanic and inspector with the International Cycling Union (UCI), the governing body that oversees international competitive cycling events. The few times the four of us had dinner together it had been funereal. The two women couldn't be more different, which Stevlana made sure to underscore for Steve. In the guise of fashion advice, she'd make fun of Fiona's brusque manners, her messy hair, her thighs, as thick and hard as if she regularly ran the 100 meters, and her hands, which were always calloused and oil-stained.

The way Fiona had become the director of technical inspectors for UCI was a curious story. For thirty years, her father, an Irish man with a long cycling lineage, had been the head mechanic for the best teams on the professional circuit. He had a legendary reputation in which the racers blindly believed. When her mother died, Fiona was only ten, and her father made her an "assistant" on the team. Friends and strangers got used to the sight of the little red-haired girl handling tools at her father's side, like a nurse assisting a surgeon. In time, she became an extension of the bike: Her ears and hands were capable of calibrating a perfect rotation of the chain or hearing the almost imperceptible grazing that could mean the loss of a thousandth of a second per kilometer. When the old man decided to retire at seventy, his mythic status on the circuit had spread from father to daughter. By then the little red-haired girl had become an explosive beauty, with strong arms and a back broader than most of the lanky cyclists'. An Amazonian bike whisperer, desired and feared by colleagues and athletes. This was especially true now that she was in charge of the legion of UCI inspectors who ensured compliance of a complex and sometimes capricious framework of technical regulations.

Fiona usually just nodded in a distracted fashion to Stevlana's jabs. Occasionally, when Stevlana's poking became particularly sharp, Fiona would look at her with the same curiosity she might have had toward an extraterrestrial. In the end, Stevlana's efforts to draw attention to herself were understandable: The three of us lived for cycling. And though Steve and Fiona could barely tolerate each other for some reason I could never fully understand, that could be set aside in the heat of after-dinner conversations when we would get tangled up in long and impassioned arguments over the advantages of a certain kind of pedal or the best way to climb the hill of the much-feared Tourmalet.

Of course it was superficially easy to understand why Steve and Stevlana were together: She was a lingerie model and he was one of the jet set's most famous bachelors. But I also sensed they both felt a certain pressure from the press, from their sponsors, and, more than anything, from the public, which expected that each would have a partner as glittering as they themselves were.

Steve's relief as soon as we left his room confirmed my suspicion that his desire for Stevlana was based more on appearances than reality. It was the first day of the Tour, and out on the streets of Utrecht, the cycling world was boiling over with excitement and impatience. We spent the morning holed up in my room, speculating about the design of the course and the real possibility that Steve would be wearing the winner's yellow jersey when we got to Paris three weeks later. At noon, when we finally confirmed Stevlana had returned to Amsterdam, we ventured out for lunch with the rest of the team, then dressed and got on the enormous team bus, our home away from home for the Tour, where we were made to listen to more endless admonishments from Giraud.

By then, all we wanted was for the damn race to start. It takes so many months of preparation, of revising the routes, of spartan diets devoid of flavor. The tension can be eased only when the cyclist gets on the road and lets himself enter the trance the whirlwind of the race induces.

This year like all the others, my task was, essentially, not to win. I was there to help Steve win. I'm loyal, that's for sure. For twenty-one days, I had to protect him from his rivals, from the crosswinds, from hunger and thirst, from accidents, and, above all, from that tall mountain where his enemies could tear him to pieces. I am what allows Steve to reach the last kilometer of the summit with as little effort as possible, even if it means I break down and place among the last racers. In the past few years, we'd become the best partners on the circuit, even though he's the only one who ever stepped up to the winner's podium.

The first day of the Tour began with what's called the Prologue, an individual time trial in which Steve didn't need anybody's help. He's the world champion. But in the following days, all our predictions went to hell. We quickly realized this Tour would be different from the previous ones although, at that point, we couldn't have even begun to guess why.

The first week is supposedly just a warm-up and a showcase for the teams and contenders. There are long stretches on flat roads in Belgium and in the north of France in which the whole peloton arrives at the finish line together, just behind the sprinters who fight over the last few meters. The real battle takes place during the second and third weeks, on terrible uphill climbs in the Pyrenees and the Alps in which only the finest athletes prevail.

But this year the action started during the very first stage. On day one of competition there were a couple of smaller accidents, and then a tragedy that kicked several important contenders off the initial peloton of 198 racers. Still, no one was alarmed. We were used to fate having the last word on the road: an unlucky puncture, a teammate who loses his balance and takes you down with him, a fan who gets in the way, a cold that overtakes months of preparation. We understood that every so often there would be an *annus horribilis,* a cursed year, for the Tour de France. By the time we finished the first four stages of the Tour, we would start to suspect this could be the worst of all.

There seemed to be an unusual tension in the air from the get-go. The Englishman Peter Stark, the Colombian Óscar Cuadrado, and my teammate Steve Panata were the three great contenders for the crown in Paris. For the past few years, they'd been taking turns winning the main races, and thanks to their heated rivalry, a greater-than-usual excitement had been awakened among the fans, who now feverishly followed the goings-on among the three racers striving to make their marks on cycling history. Stark, Cuadrado, and Panata had decided to make this year's Tour the setting in which it would be decided once and for all who was the best cyclist of their generation. The organizers were expecting a record TV audience and had acted accordingly, designing a bedeviling course, even for the first week.

The asphalt on day three was hell itself. Racing over cobblestones at 50 kilometers per hour will literally break your balls. Every jolt stabs your legs and sends shocks up your arms. These aren't Parisian paving stones, worn smooth over time by thousands of cars passing over them, but real pieces of jagged rock on narrow rural roads that hardly anyone ever uses. Few were as terrible as what we had suffered between Seraing and Cambrai, just before we left Belgium. The relentless rain that fell throughout the day turned the course into a minefield.

The only way to avoid being dragged down into a fall was to stay at the tip of the peloton. Making sure it became Steve's spot was my task. The problem is there are two hundred other cyclists trying to do the same thing, which can transform those tight paths into a real bottleneck. Trying to put another racer in the front under those conditions can cause tumultuous falls and the corresponding shattered clavicles, broken arms, and concussions.

Steve's, Cuadrado's, and Stark's teams all came out of the massacre intact because, without a word spoken between us, we had cooperated. Twenty-seven of us—nine racers per team—let our leaders go for the front and then blocked the way in so that the rest of the racers couldn't bother them. We weren't competing against one another in these initial stages; we just wanted to survive. But I couldn't let down my guard with the riders behind me. Over and over, I blocked the path to defend our position, using my elbows and teeth and, God help me, letting whoever fell be crushed by an avalanche of bikes and flying arms and legs.

By the end of the sixth day, fifty-two cyclists had dropped out, the most ever at this point in the competition. Even so, most of us continued to blame fate for the bad luck that had befallen us. One day later, we'd discover that the stars, or whatever it is that determines our fortunes in racing, couldn't explain all the tragedies we were enduring here. Unless you count murder as one of the tools chosen by fate.

Stage 7

Livarot—Fougères, 190.5 km.

"My son hooked up with his first bike when he was four," boasted Murat, the Fonar team's—our team's—muscular sprinter.

"What a perv," Steve said, joking, though no one else paid the comment any mind; it certainly wasn't new. Our teammate's sense of humor wasn't the best at breaking the ice or, really, for breaking much of anything except mouths and noggins.

We were having dinner at a hotel on the outskirts of Rennes, exhausted after the Tour's seventh stage. The day had once more been frustrating, rainy, and plagued by accidents. There wasn't a lot of energy for socializing. It also wasn't a particularly healthy idea to laugh at Murat. His back and thighs were as disproportionate as his temperamental outbursts.

But Steve was like that, unaware of the risks, completely oblivious to the feelings of others. I was the only one who knew his aptitude for hurting others was completely involuntary. Deep down, he had no malice; I might even say that, in his way, he was a generous guy. There are countless teammates whose careers or contracts were extended thanks to a spontaneous compliment on Steve's million-plus Twitter account or in any of his innumerable media interviews.

I've ended up believing that his inability to understand other people's fears and insecurities is because he's convinced everyone else is having as good a time as he is. A very convenient denial that allowed him to continue his privileged life with minimal guilt.

Still, the silence that fell on the table, pierced only by the sound of Murat's fork falling to his plate, let him know he'd inadvertently broken one of those unspoken rules he'd never bothered to assimilate. As he'd done so many other times when he sensed trouble, he looked for my eyes with the hope of finding a smile that would let everyone know his comment was innocent and that he wasn't making fun of Murat's kid. And like so many other times in the past, I went above and beyond for Steve.

"Yeah, that boy will go far. During our last training ride, he followed us for a stretch and almost caught up, remember? There's finally some hope of having a handsome Murat in the circuit." And now a few of the guys at the table laughed easily. Murat was nicknamed the Beast, which referred both to the mighty Catalonian's uneven face, sculpted by fists, and the ferocity of his rushes at the finish line. Murat was proud of his nom de guerre, and cracked a small smile.

Ten minutes later, meals devoured, the team dispersed to their rooms. Steve's bad joke aside, the racers were already feeling downcast. We had covered barely a third of the 3,350 kilometers we'd confront on this edition of the Tour, but in the first seven days the peloton had already suffered more accidents and scandals than we'd had in all twenty-one days of the previous year's Tour.

To everyone's surprise, because he had a reputation for being clean and upholding the honor of cycling, the Spaniard Carlos Santamaría had been accused of doping that morning. It had a huge impact because Santamaría, who led the Astana team, had been in third place overall.

But Steve was doing okay. His chances of winning the Tour had actually improved in the past few days. He told me to come hang for a while and share one of those ridiculous energy drinks named after him, but I was exhausted and told him so, heading toward the elevator. I noticed his frustration. Post-race, we almost always got together to review our day and discuss the challenges we'd face next. When we didn't hang out afterward, it was because Steve had something better to do: At the beginning of his career, women, and in the past few years, meetings with his agent, Benny, always accompanied by some new sponsor. But I'd decided today it was my turn to have something better to do, even if it was to just drop in bed.

He and I were the only ones on the team who had single rooms, thanks to a clause in his contract that generously extended to me. He followed me with his gaze for a few seconds when I turned to cross the lobby and then, as he did with everything that didn't jibe with what he wanted, he erased me from his mind. He probably didn't even notice I never made it to the elevators.

"Marc Moreau, could I have a few minutes of your time?"

The interruption sent my pulse racing in a way no steep hill or hours of pedaling on the road could do. And there was a reason: Nobody called me by my name. An elegant man now touched my arm as if he were gently trying to make sure I didn't get away. He didn't look like a reporter who'd snuck into the hotel. In fact, he looked exactly like the personification of a cyclist's worst nightmares. His impeccable suit and neatly trimmed mustache were those of someone who worked for an institution, and given the present circumstances, that institution could only be the much-feared WADA, the World Anti-Doping Agency.

Although I was convinced my body was free of banned substances, I knew the urine tests we'd taken on previous days could register illegal substances absorbed involuntarily, or that we could be victims of lab errors. This wouldn't be the first time somebody got kicked out of the competition because of a contaminated sample. I thought about Carlos Santamaría and I imagined my name in the headlines the next day.

"Excuse me?" I responded, defensive, and pulled my arm, trying to get distance from him.

"Could we talk in the lounge, Sergeant Moreau? I won't take up too much of your time."

During my short time in the army I'd never been promoted beyond corporal, but I wasn't about to contradict him. There was a room just off the main lobby lit by a faint artificial fireplace, even though it was 82 degrees outside. The hotels along the route aren't exactly bursting with luxury and comfort, never mind good taste.

I followed him to a secluded corner, feeling like I was walking into a trap. His reference to my military past aroused my curiosity but did nothing to ease my fears.

"Allow me to introduce myself: I'm Commissioner Favre." As he spoke, he quickly showed me an ID, his gestures those of someone who had done this a thousand times before. "Needless to say," he continued, leaning his head toward me, "I am an admirer of your athletic achievements."

His flattering words and, even more so, his manner, which was a tad unctuous, helped my curiosity surpass my fear. He didn't seem about to accuse me of doping, although he might still be interested in interrogating me about banned substances in circulation on the Tour. In fact, what he said next made me think that was his purpose.

"We need your cooperation, sergeant. Please, take a seat, make yourself comfortable."

I sat down on the tiny couch and felt as comfortable as if I were in a dentist chair. The commissioner seemed intent on inflating my military rank. I thought if there was a problem, it might be better to be a sergeant instead of a corporal, so I accepted the promotion and went on the offensive. "I can't help you with this issue. I keep myself away from everything and from anyone who has anything to do with that shit."

"We're not worried about that, but rather something much more dangerous." He paused and brought his face closer to mine and practically whispered, "There's a killer among you." Then he sat up and took note of my reaction.

I'm sure I disappointed him because I had none. The phrase was so absurd, my brain could find no way to process it. At least not immediately. In the light of the fake fireplace, I perceived the sheen of the wax on his fine mustache, sculpted atop thick wet lips. I thought it was the kind of thing some women might find seductive and others might find repulsive.

Disappointed by my silence, he began to explain as if he were reading a military report. "One: Hugo Lampar, the Australian and the best climber on the Rocca team, was beaten up two weeks ago as he rode alone on a practice course. There were no witnesses. He had multiple fractures and has no possibility of rejoining the Tour. Without his climber, Sergei Talancón's chances are few, if not null. He'll be unprotected and have to get used to someone else setting the tempo, which will disorient him.

"Two: Three days before the beginning of the competition, Michael Hankel was assaulted at dusk just a few steps from his hotel. Although he insists he didn't resist and offered his wallet immediately, one of the thugs became angry over how little cash he was carrying, knocked him down with a single punch, and then stomped his ankle. It's useless for the foreseeable future. He wasn't considered a major contender, but his unexpected third place at Il Giro in Italy at only twenty-four had made many people in the press think that if there was going to be a surprise on the Tour this year, it would come from the German.

"Three: The Englishman Phil Cunninham ran the first stage far slower than expected, because he was pumped up on antihistamines. He was the only one who could challenge Steve Panata in the time trial. Cunninham finished three minutes too late, which meant he ceased being a threat for the rest of the Tour. The doctors can't explain how he got sick. He ate the same things as the rest of the team and he has no allergies.

"Four: Just a few days ago, on the fifth stage, two fans stepped in front of the Movistar team, pretending they only wanted to wave at the camera on the motorcycle that runs in front of the squad. Óscar Cuadrado's teammates barely got a chance to react. It was a massive collision. Four of the racers had to drop out of the competition and the Colombian lost half his team with most of the Tour still to come. The 'fans' that knocked him down were discovered to be some hooligans from Marseille with no known prior interest in cycling. They're also hospitalized. We did get one revealing piece of information about them: One of them had recently deposited eight thousand euros in his bank account."

The commissioner paused again to see if I had grasped what he was telling me. None of those mishaps were new to me, although I hadn't known the details until now. The Movistar incident was the most disturbing. With only half his team, Cuadrado had practically zero chance of winning, and that changed the odds for the Tour. If what the commissioner said was true, someone had altered the history of cycling.

And yet, I couldn't buy into the idea of an attack against the tournament and, much less, that someone was physically assaulting the contenders. Every year the Tour lost a certain number of cyclists along its terrible journey, often in tragic circumstances.

"A mugging with mysterious circumstances and several accidents doesn't necessarily mean there's a conspiracy. In the ten years I've been racing on the Tour, I've seen plenty of stuff like this. Doesn't it seem like a bit much to talk about a killer?"

"Well, I haven't finished." He licked his lips and took a long pause, almost enjoying the moment. "Two hours ago we found Saul Fleming floating in the bathtub in his room, his wrists slit.

Whoever tried to make it look like suicide did a really sloppy job. That's why we decided to talk to you."

This time, the commissioner got the reaction he'd been look-ing for. My face must have reflected my shock as I imagined Saul drowning in his own blood. We'd never been close friends, but we'd had a profound respect for each other. Fleming was Peter Stark's primary domestique, his wingman in the same way I was Steve's. We'd gone through innumerable battles, wheel-to-wheel, defending our respective champions. Without talking about it, during the stretch up in the mountains, we'd developed our own competition within the overall race: Who would go further in protecting his leader? Knowing that the Englishman would never again challenge me on a slope made me shiver. Something had changed forever.

My second reaction was more reflexive although no less terri-ble. Without Fleming, Stark was lost. He was in fifth place, 16 seconds behind Steve, but until today he was confident he'd gain time on the mountain stages still to come. He was a better climber than my teammate. Without Fleming's strong defense, he would need a miracle to pass Steve.

"Surely you understand why we need you, sergeant."

"No, I don't understand." My brain was still stuck thinking about a bathtub too narrow to contain my rival's long, lean arms.

"We've concluded the killer or killers belong to the circuit. They've struck with surgical precision to maximize their effect on the results of the race."

"Anybody could have done that," I protested.

I found it hard to believe that a member of our closed commu-nity would attack one of our own. In spite of our rivalries, the peloton was a family, and that extended to the mechanics, the doctors, the massage therapists, the directors, and the coaches. Any cycling fan could point to a favorite racer and tell you his strengths and weaknesses, and I said as much to Favre.

"C'mon, Sergeant Moreau—you know no fan has access to the

team kitchens or to the tub in a hotel room for a member of a team as closed as Batesman."

The commissioner was right on that last point. Stark and Fleming's team was made up exclusively of British racers; all the assistants were also British. The rest of the teams were a small United Nations, with members recruited from every continent. But Batesman was an island unto itself, practically a brotherhood, which the other teams had nicknamed Brexit.

"You should check the betting companies. There are people who stake fortunes on these things," I said, resisting, although my argument sounded less than convincing. Still, I insisted: "There are also sponsors who risk millions, which could turn into a disaster or a boon depending on the race results."

"We haven't discounted any of those possibilities and we're investigating. But even if the motive is coming from outside the circuit, it's obvious there's material involvement, if not intellectual involvement, from within the cycling circuit."

"But why me?"

"Isn't it obvious, sergeant? You've got military police training. I checked your records myself and I know you closed about a dozen cases in your time."

As he said this, he placed a folder with an official seal on the little table between us. With a look, I asked permission to check it. I opened the folder and quickly scanned about a dozen pages about me, most of them faded with age.

I supposed the commissioner wanted to show me I was more than a cyclist, that I was a member of the French state and that this folder confirmed it. I only registered the passage of time on a lightly tanned face with blue eyes and wavy hair. Different versions of my image in those documents took me back to the time before I let the bike swallow everything up.

I remembered the three- and four-day seminars in Paris I attended a dozen years ago alongside police officers and provincial sheriffs, where I gathered vague notions about ballistics and forensic medicine amid so much cigarette smoke. And that reminded me of Claude, a pretty female agent from Biarritz with whom I'd shared some sessions dedicated to reviewing anatomy on our own.

"Something about this amuses you, sergeant?"

The commissioner had noticed my response to the memory. He was examining me like a mechanic turning a bicycle wheel in search of almost imperceptible damage. I supposed he wasn't particularly happy about having to confide in someone outside the police, and I assumed this hadn't been his idea. In fact, he was probably looking for reasons to confirm it was not a good idea. "No, nothing," I said. "I'm just not sure in what way I'd be able to help you. Or, in fact, if any of what you say is true. I don't know how much you know about cycling. The responsibilities a team has when it competes on the Tour are grueling and not just physical. It demands absolute concentration; it would be impossible to play detective when all I want to do is to stay alive for the next stage."

" 'To stay alive for the next stage,' " repeated the commissioner. "That's a curious choice of words, Sergeant Moreau. That's precisely what the authorities have been asking: Who among you will not be alive tomorrow? There haven't been any victims on your team yet, but until we know what's behind all this, you and your teammates are in danger."

His reasoning gave me chills. If the killer had wanted to get rid of Steve instead of Stark, that would have been me bleeding to death in that tub. I tried to remember where I was on the peloton when the fake fans blocked the Movistar team two days ago. Our team had taken over the front and we'd just gone around the curve when we heard the bikes crashing behind us. The Marseille hooligans had not come for us. An unsettling presentiment jabbed at my consciousness, but it was interrupted by the arrival of a man requiring no introduction.

"We need you, Hannibal. This can't go on," said Sam Jitrik,

the executive director of the Tour de France. "I hope the commissioner has explained the seriousness of the situation. We've gone over the police theories and we think they're right: The accidents have been deliberate, and if that's true, then we're looking at the most serious threat to the Tour de France in all its history. There are still two weeks to the finish, but the authorities could close it down if these accidents continue. That's something that hasn't happened in more than one hundred years." The solemn words from the most important man in cycling were punctuated by a long index finger, like a conductor's baton. He was an imposing figure in spite of his seventy-two years.

"They could reinforce security, limit public access on the road, seal off the hotels where we're staying," I responded, nervous in front of Jitrik. It was the first time I had exchanged words with the great man in spite of having participated in the Tour for more than a decade.

"It wouldn't do much good to seal off the public if those responsible are already inside, now would it?" Jitrik scoffed.

"Only you can help us: You were an officer with the French army and one of the best-known and most respected members of the peloton," said Favre, seconding him. "We can't trust anyone else. But you can't share what we just told you with anybody; you'd tip off the guilty parties."

"Let's not forget the media circus it would cause, the panic. The Tour itself would be at risk," said Jitrik, and then he cleared his throat and took on his solemn tone again before raising his index finger once more. "The Tour de France is one of the great institutions our country offers the world. Perhaps the greatest. We can't allow it to turn into a circus of bloodshed and scandal. Protecting it is a state matter. I appeal to your conscience as a French citizen, as a military officer, and, above all, as a cycling professional."

Jitrik ended up getting emotional over his own words, and I probably would have too if I hadn't been so worried. I wanted to tell them I wasn't a military officer, and not even really French, and that it was very difficult for me to admit the possibility that someone in the large family to which I belonged could be willing to kill a teammate to alter the course of the race. But I didn't say anything. I just nodded.

Under normal circumstances, it wouldn't have been a bad night. I was in tenth place in the race, which was unusually good for me and any domestique. But I slept very little, though I made sure the door was locked. The bathtub, its rust stains badly spackled over, played a starring role in the dreams I had that night.

GENERAL CLASSIFICATION: STAGE 7

RANK	RIDER	TIME
1	RICK SAGAL (PORTUGAL/FONTANA)	26:40:51
2	**STEVE PANATA (USA/FONAR)**	**+:12**
3	SERGEI TALANCÓN (ROMANIA/ROCCA)	+:13
4	LUIS DURÁN (SPAIN/IMAGINE)	+:26
5	PETER STARK (UK/BATESMAN)	+:28
6	ALESSIO MATOSAS (ITALY/LAVEZZA)	+:34
7	PABLO MEDEL (SPAIN/BALEARES)	+:36
8	MILENKO PANIUK (CZECH/RABONET)	+:52
9	ÓSCAR CUADRADO (COLOMBIA/MOVISTAR)	+1:01
10	**MARC MOREAU (FRANCE/FONAR)**	**+1:03**

Stage 8

Rennes—Mûr-de-Bretagne, 181.5 km.

"Are you worried about something, Mojito?" Fiona asked in greeting as I warmed up on the stationary bike just before the start of the day's stage. Although there were many things to love about Fiona, her knowledge of geography was not one of them. For whatever reason, she thought mojitos were Colombian in origin and saddled me with it as a nickname years ago. In private she usually called me Dragon, but in public she preferred Mojito. Luckily, no one had followed her lead; I don't even like the damn drink.

"Why do you ask?" My sharp and defensive tone surprised me.

"You haven't turned to look at the power meter one time since I've been watching you. Your warm-up isn't much good like that."

Fiona was right. The prep routine is intended to focus on a scrupulous method of pedaling, designed for the individual cyclist, and the point is to reach a certain number of watts per minute. To pedal without looking at the power meter is to throw energy away.

"I got distracted. I haven't seen Fleming all morning. The

Brexit team already did two sessions on the stationary bike but he hasn't shown up and my strategy for the day depends on what he does to put Stark in the front." I wasn't totally lying. I'd been waiting for the Englishman all morning, hoping his presence would reestablish some sort of normalcy in spite of what I'd heard the night before. Seeing Fleming would mean the conversation with the commissioner had been a nightmare, a bad joke.

Fiona hesitated, which was unusual for her. As the chief inspector of UCI, in charge of enforcing regulations on all the Tour teams, she was unaware of very few things. "Fleming won't be coming." She lowered her voice. "Supposedly the authorities are going to release a statement at the end of the day. Last night they took him to the hospital in critical condition. That's all I know."

My expression must have alarmed her because she rubbed her hand on my curved back. Generally speaking, she avoided making any kind of intimate gesture in public, even though the whole circuit knew we were lovers. Or—more accurately—that she had chosen me as her lover.

"Come by the trailer tonight and we'll talk, Mojito, and don't let this affect your plans for the race." This time her hand squeezed my neck softly as I took a quick glance at the power meter. It read 1200 watts, a number more appropriate to the final sprint of a race than a progressive warm-up.

I could tell that Fiona knew something else. But she wasn't about to tell me just minutes from the challenge that lay before us: 181 kilometers, mostly flat but not without risks. We weren't expecting any kind of assault on the leaders, who were mostly saving themselves for the mountain, but days like today, when the group stays together until the very end, are the most conducive for massive falls.

My task would be to keep my team near the front and to block any of the first fifteen in the standings from trying to make a breakaway. Should that happen, the pursuit would have to be relentless and the day could turn into an exhausting horror show.

And yet, the day transpired uneventfully. About a half-dozen racers, none particularly important, tried to get a jump ahead, but they were absorbed by the peloton. To be honest, the cyclists sensed something wasn't right: The average speed of 38 kilometers an hour that day was well below the 44 we had averaged in previous stages. During the ride my teammates asked one another if anyone knew anything about Fleming, and there were all kinds of rumors about the tragedies that had started to pile up. In spite of everything, the majority of us continued to attribute the bad luck that had fallen on us to simple fate.

Five hours of relative calm and few challenges allowed me to consider the information the commissioner had confided in me in a more detached fashion. Before we'd reached the fiftieth kilometer in the race, I'd already concluded that there were only two possible rationales for the attacks. One, to try to control the winner; two, to damage the competition, regardless of who ended up winning. If that was the case, we were dealing with someone who wanted to hurt us arbitrarily over and over until they forced a suspension of the competition or, at the very least, to discredit the institution, which meant the attacks were the result of resentment or some kind of economic or athletic interest contrary to the Tour. I remembered there were teams that had been suspended in the past few years and several racers who had ranted against the organizers for one reason or another.

My mind turned to Viktor Radek, the irascible Polish racer who was rolling just a few meters ahead of my team. Three years ago, he'd been involved in a fall he attributed to an erroneous maneuver by one of the officials on the motorcycles: It made him lose four minutes and place fifth in the general standings. The authorities had refused to compensate him for the time lost and Radek decided to leave the race, swearing he'd never come back. And yet to everyone's surprise, he'd returned this year, signed to the Locus team. I decided to make the Pole my number one suspect.

Almost without thinking about it, I found myself riding next to him. Every one of his gestures seemed to confirm my suspicions. Radek was the classic image of a villain personified. Although the race's rhythm today was relaxed compared to other days, he looked like a growling feline. I wondered if he was contemplating his next violent act that very second. I remembered the dusty tub in my room and slowed my pedaling so I could get some distance from him again.

Twenty kilometers later, I forced myself to think like a cop. Besides hate and resentment, the other great motive for committing a crime is greed. And when it came to a competition as glorified as the Tour de France, that could mean the purpose of the attacks was to modify the results of the race.

It seemed absurd, but it wasn't. The racers literally risked their lives in dizzying, nearly suicidal descents. If they were willing to die, why wouldn't they be willing to kill?

That line of thinking led me to come up with a list of those who had benefited from the tragedies of the past few days. Eight of the twenty-two teams that had begun the race remained uninjured, although only three of these, including Fonar, had been considered contenders before the Tour started. For all practical purposes, both Stark and Cuadrado had been eliminated. A look at them left no doubt about the state of their mood. Stark was pedaling out of sheer honor; it was clear his head was back at the morgue next to his friend's body. On two occasions his teammates had to pull him out of the back of the peloton, where he'd fallen without realizing it. I wouldn't be surprised if he abandoned the race before we got to Paris.

Cuadrado looked better, but we all knew he'd be screwed once we got to the mountain. He was a great climber and he could certainly win a stage, but nobody can do that day after day without teammates to protect him on the great slopes. And his Movistar teammates were in the hospital.

So the great beneficiary was Steve. Which led me to an absurd conclusion. I knew every one of his defects, but I also knew his virtues. My friend lacked the cruelty or ferocity necessary to hurt a teammate, and his own pride would keep him from seeking a win any way other than proving his superiority over his rivals.

In any case, we weren't even at the halfway point of the Tour. And nothing guaranteed that Steve, or myself, or any other key member of our team wouldn't be the next victim.

I turned my head to make sure Steve was where he was supposed to be: pedaling behind my wheel, making the least amount of effort until he was required to do otherwise. He smiled at me with the same complicity and intimacy with which he usually recognized my sacrifice. Genuine and affectionate, without guile or malice, his smile confirmed the pact that made us an unbreakable professional pair. I was ashamed of the suspicions that had run through my head and I told myself I would do the impossible so that neither he nor I would become one more name on the list of victims.

I spent the next 70 kilometers trying to avoid danger. I maneuvered so we would be surrounded by the squad but far enough away from the center to avoid getting dragged into any kind of fall.

During the last third of the race, I entertained myself by considering other suspects. Setting Steve aside, there were at least three other rivals who had a chance of winning. The Italian Alessio Matosas from the Lavezza team, a veteran who'd won the Tour six years before. Two weeks ago, he'd simply aspired to enter Paris as one of the first ten. But today, he was in sixth place, and if Steve should suffer a setback, he would be one of the principal aspirants to the podium. He was a valiant climber with an innate sense for reading his rivals' weaknesses and pouncing at the precise moment.

Milenko Paniuk, a Czech, was another possibility. Like Matosas, he was a good climber and was counting on improving his position in the standings when we got higher up the mountains. He was in eighth place, a little less than a minute behind Steve.

His team, Rabonet, still had all nine members, two of whom were excellent climbers.

Finally, there was the Spaniard, Pablo Medel, from team Baleares, who was completely unpredictable on an ascent. Actually, unpredictable in many ways. Medel is the only cyclist I've ever known who carries business cards, as if he were an insurance salesperson. I know because he gave me one. There was a title inscribed under his name: professional cyclist, as if he were afraid of being confused for a ballet dancer despite the racing jerseys he never took off.

But he was nothing like an insurance salesperson when it came time to get on a bike. He could keep the power going at more than 550 watts for half an hour. Translated into a breakaway on a steep road, that could mean five minutes over a rival in the last few kilometers. And that difference could help him leap to the lead at a decisive stage. Medel was one of the perennial champions when it came to the kinds of short races—three or four days long—that are held the rest of the year, though, to his dismay, his epic efforts in the longer, three-week competitions really took their toll on him. Even so, his DS had managed to contain his strategy, and he was in the top ten, making him a real threat on the mountains that end the Tour.

When the group reached the day's finish line without incident, my list was down to four names: Radek the resentful, Matosas the veteran, Paniuk and his powerful team, and Medel and his legendary climbs. I knew the four of them extremely well, especially Medel, with whom I practiced my Spanish and played dominoes during the less demanding races. Except for Radek, I never considered the possibility that any of them could be the criminal we were looking for. But because they were the beneficiaries of the tragedies, their coaches, mechanics, technicians, doctors, and soigneurs became my main suspects.

As soon as I got off the bike, I realized all this could also be said of Steve. There was one person who was actually more interested in my friend's triumph than Steve himself. Giraud, our team's DS, was willing to win at any cost.

In short, my list was composed of five possible lines of investigation. Three of them were made up of personal threats: If they wanted to be champions, they needed to get rid of Steve, or me, or both of us. On the other hand, Radek's resentment was like a Russian roulette that could take down anybody. And the last name on the list, Giraud, didn't present a threat to any member of our team, being Fonar's directeur sportif. Yet, if I had to pick a villain, part of me preferred that it be somebody in a suit instead of one of my fellow cyclists.

That night, I couldn't get away from Steve or from the commissioner. When we were finally done with our post-race routine of stretches, hydration, and massage, we gathered to eat on a terrace on the outskirts of Mûr-de-Bretagne. I was more tired than usual, although it's true that, as the Tour goes on, you think that same thing every single night. When you finish each stage, you're convinced you've hit rock bottom and that you have no fuel left in your body for the next day. Repeating that routine for three weeks is a challenge that ends up being impossible for about a third of the racers, who abandon the competition before the finish line. And that's without any killers or saboteurs.

But that night my fatigue was different. Even though the run had been simple and the cyclists had seen it as a kind of break, I felt as if I'd just crossed the Alps. I chalked the additional exhaustion up to the mission assigned to me by the commissioner. To imagine conspiracies, to inventory suspects and to fear being a victim of a double cross doesn't exactly make covering 180 kilometers in five hours a stroll in the park.

So I would have preferred to skip dinner and sneak off to drop into bed back in my room. A room with a shower and not a rusty bathtub, thank God. But I couldn't stand Steve up for a second night in a row, the commissioner was looking for me so we could talk as we had agreed to, and Fiona was waiting for me in the trailer parked a few meters from our hotel.

All I had to do was take one look at my teammates' faces as they arrived at the dining-room table to understand something had happened. Apparently the Tour had released a statement acknowledging Fleming's suicide, and everyone present, about fifteen total including cyclists and technicians, was whispering about it in trios and pairs. I heard words of praise for our fallen friend's career, alongside curses because of the mounting calamities. Guido, a Portuguese member of the Fonar team, filed his usual protest against the organizers, as if Fleming's suicide had been an act of rebellion motivated by the conditions imposed on the racers.

As soon as Giraud arrived, a silence fell over the room. Steve was two steps behind him. They must have been talking alone before joining the group.

"Few of you know this, but I was Fleming's first coach," Giraud said as he sat down at the head of the table. "It was thirteen years ago, in Liverpool, when I went to give a series of workshops and ended up coaching a semiprofessional team for a few months. He was a natural climber, and I helped him see he needed to leave the island to find mountains to meet his talent." He was talking as if he had made Fleming, although I knew him well enough to recognize that this was pure performance. Giraud always made everything about himself, including poor Fleming's life.

I looked over at Steve's anguished face and for the first time since I'd known him, I thought I saw a crack in his impregnable optimism. His chin was pressed to his chest, his eyes were wet, and there was a curl to his lip that made me think, also for the first time, that he looked an awful lot like his father.

"Today we lost a great man," said Giraud, seeming to take pleasure in his dramatic pauses. "His track record doesn't include a lot of trips to the podium nor record times, but everyone on the circuit knows the battle for the mountain will never be the same. Fleming didn't conquer a lot of stages, but he helped forge a lot of conquerors. He never wore the yellow jersey, but without his help, more than one Englishman would not have been able to wear it in Paris. Above all, he won the love and admiration of all of us who had the honor of riding at his side. Let us respect the reason for which he made this terrible decision; let us honor him with a minute of silence and dedicate every single kilometer we overtake on the road tomorrow to him."

Giraud managed to move everyone at the table, including a couple of racers who had had bad blood with Fleming; he had never been subtle when it came to blocking his rivals on the road. Steve choked up a little and several racers grabbed napkins to wipe their noses.

Giraud moved everyone at the table but me. Maybe because I had been ruminating over Fleming's death for hours, or because I'd found the manipulative sentimentality Giraud used a little shocking. I realized that I was not only unmoved but also irritated, and I soon understood why. What he had just said about Fleming could also be my epitaph. Maybe in three days in a hotel lobby or maybe in twenty years at a cemetery in Perpignan, but the words would be the same. "He never wore the yellow jersey, but without him . . ."

We finished eating and went over the strategies for the next day, then broke off into small groups. Steve took my arm and leaned his body on mine as if he were on the verge of fainting.

"Are you okay?" I asked, alarmed. "Do you feel all right?" I tried to remember if I knew anything about his past that might have brought him particularly close to Fleming but I couldn't think of a thing. We had always been the Englishman's heated rivals. Steve's reaction seemed excessive, even for a colleague who had died in tragic and unexpected conditions. I thought about the commissioner's words—a sloppy faked suicide—and a terrible idea crossed my mind. All the other incidents had been planned to perfection. It was possible those behind this one hadn't intended Fleming to die, but had simply wanted to hurt him and force him out of the competition. It was possible the Englishman recognized his attackers and tried to get help and they were forced to kill him. Was this what was tormenting Steve? Was he feeling directly or indirectly responsible for this death? Was this the reason why Giraud had taken him aside? Were they both involved in this?

"Don't you realize what's going on, bro?" Steve responded, a tad exasperated. He stopped me and took hold of my shoulders. "You could be next!"

"What are you talking about?" I asked. Supposedly only I knew there was a killer among us. How many of us had the commissioner talked to?

"Giraud has connections in Jitrik's office. He found out the organization called the police. They're convinced someone is knocking off the favorites. Cuadrado has no team left and Stark just lost Fleming. They weren't accidents but premeditated attacks. Now they'll come for us."

"Calm down, nothing's going to happen, that's all hearsay, rumors on the circuit. This is a cursed Tour, that's all. It's not the first time the race has taken lives."

"Sure, on the road, but not at night, not in the hotel rooms and hallways," he said as he checked out the shadows around us. There was genuine fear in his eyes. In spite of myself, I felt a shiver and turned my body to go back to the terrace from which we had come.

"But you don't have anything to worry about. I'll protect you," I reminded him while glancing around for one of the thugs who accompanied him wherever he went. A few years back, a million-dollar publicity contract had forced him to accept professional bodyguards, courtesy of a company that protected billionaires and Arab sheikhs when they traveled west.

"It's not me who's in danger," he protested, impatient. "They didn't go after Cuadrado or Stark, but after the guys who helped them win. They're not coming for me; they're coming for you."

I was on the verge of responding when Giraud reappeared; he said something about making an adjustment to Steve's shoes, since they had been bothering him the past few days. Steve's body and skull had been scanned in high resolution, and that data had been translated into a sophisticated mannequin on which they designed his racing kit with state-of-the-art materials and technology. But he had so many personal sponsorships, he couldn't always race with the brands he would have preferred.

I was grateful for the interruption and looked for the quickest door to the street so I could meet up with Fiona. But the commissioner intercepted me as soon as I stepped onto the sidewalk.

"So good you've come to meet me. Let's walk for a bit and share notes," said Favre. He took me by the arm and guided me toward a streetlight that illuminated the sidewalk. We stopped there. I was glad because we cyclists don't usually take walks between stages. We tend to limit all displacement, and when we move, we move like old people; our routines are designed to hoard the calories our bodies are in the process of recuperating.

"Do you mind if I sit down?" I said as I squatted and rested my back against the lamppost. The first commandment for any cyclist involved in a three-week race is to conserve energy: If you're standing, sit down; if you're sitting, lie down; and get as far away as you can from any stairway.

A soft sea breeze began to ease the thick heat that had been building all day. Favre squatted beside me, obviously uncomfortable with such an unorthodox arrangement. It seemed the commissioner behaved according to a Hollywood idea of what the police should be. Sitting on the ground in the middle of the sidewalk did not conform to a single cinematic convention.

"Any news? What kind of reactions did the squad have when

they heard about Fleming's death? Did anything catch your attention, sergeant?"

"Everything you might expect: regret, amazement, confusion. It had a strong impact, although I didn't see anything that seemed out of place." But as I said it, I couldn't help but picture Steve and his agitation a few moments ago. I wondered if Favre might have seen us from the bushes.

He looked at me carefully, like he had done the night before, and it was only then I realized he'd managed to engineer it so the light of the lamppost fell directly on my face but left his partially obscured. Not unlike the arrangement during our first conversation in front of the fireplace. Maybe the scene was more orthodox than I had first thought.

"I understand. I imagine that during the race there are few chances to chat with the other cyclists," he said. "But what did they say at the Fonar meeting? It had to have been the only topic of conversation, right? Did your DS speak?"

I felt as if I were being submitted to an interrogation. My face in the spotlight, contrasting with his in shadow, reminded me of a detective novel from the 1950s. Favre was just missing a black fedora.

"Just the usual condolences," I said grudgingly. The commissioner noticed my irritation and relaxed his body, apparently trying to activate some other facet of his personality.

"Do you mind if I smoke? The breeze will disperse it," he promised. He lit a cigarette and inhaled. "I'm not interested in your testimony, sergeant, but in your ability to observe, to find things out. I would like it if we could have a collegial relationship."

"I agree, commissioner, and hope it'll be that way. I understand what's at play and I promise to try my hardest, but I should've been resting already. If I don't, I won't be able to keep up with the group in the next few stages. The day I don't make the cut, I'll be eliminated. And, in that case, I won't be much help. Let me suggest something. Whenever I discover information I think could be useful, I'll get in touch with you. If I'm going to be undercover, then it's not a good idea that we should be seen talking." I thought this last argument would settle the matter once and for all.

"We traced the money received by the thugs from Marseille. It was deposited in cash and sent from a small bank in Warsaw."

I couldn't help but think about Radek the Pole and his unexpected return to the Tour. The commissioner kept talking, as if he were summarizing the case to his colleagues.

"There are no unusual movements in the betting circles right now to justify an attack of this nature coming from the outside. That leads me to the conclusion that one of the winners in Paris will surely be guilty or related in some way to whoever is guilty. The problem, sergeant, is that we have to find out who it is now, before there's another victim."

I thought the commissioner's words had more than a hint of pressure, as if every minute the killer was free was my responsibility. Maybe that wasn't his intention, but I'm one of those people who feels guilty whenever a police car drives by. So I got defensive: If Favre was light-years ahead of me when it came to criminal investigations, I had to make him see that, when it came to bikes, he was a novice.

"With all due respect, commissioner, you don't understand a thing about cycling. You're concentrating all your energies on the battle for the yellow jersey without realizing there are a hundred and ninety-eight battles on the Tour. Each cyclist is involved in his own war and most of them are willing to die to win it. There are twenty-two teams this year. Each team ranks their members from one to nine, and each and every one of them wants to go up on the scale. Each cyclist wants to bump off the riders ranked higher. The kid who comes to the Tour for the first time knows there are four even younger racers behind him waiting for him to fall, and does the impossible in order to come back the next year. The guy who has been on two Tours and hasn't finished either understands the next one could be his last. A climber will do what it takes to become the leader next season. And so on. The pressure is incredible, and not just for those on top. Name any racer and I can tell you at least three challenges he's facing. And we're not even talking about the competition between teams. So, no, this isn't just about the final three who step up to the podium after the last stage."

I was breathless when I finished, but satisfied. I knew the commissioner's hypothesis concentrating on the top leaders coincided with my own list of suspects, but I wasn't going to tell him that. I was a little sick of his barely veiled condescension.

"Every soccer or basketball player struggles to distinguish himself, but I don't recall murders in the locker rooms," he said, now a little defensive too.

"But that's precisely what you don't understand. Cycling isn't a game. We say *Let's play soccer,* or basketball or tennis, but no one says *Let's play cycling,* because you don't *play* cycling: Cycling is a battle; cycling is combat." The phrase wasn't mine, I'd heard some journalist say it, but Favre didn't need to know that either. "That we're talked about as a peloton isn't a coincidence, because we're a group on the way to war, except this war is among ourselves." I thought that finish was even better because I assumed it was my own saying. Though I wasn't entirely sure.

"Well, then, even more reason to apply ourselves; there are many possible suspects," he said, but this time without animosity, raising a white flag.

I nodded silently and thought about my list again. I wasn't ready to share it, not right then. I decided to take advantage of my small victory. If the commissioner wanted to play at being my colleague, he'd have to offer something in return.

"You say Fleming's suicide was faked. How do you know? What evidence do you have?" When Favre looked at me, I thought I caught a glimpse of surprise in his expression. He smoked half a cigarette in silence before he finally decided to answer.

"They drugged him, maybe during dinner, or with one of those drinks or energy bars you all never stop eating. The assailants expected to find him sleeping. That's our theory, anyway. But Fleming put up a fight at the last minute. There are bruises on his body, around the clavicles, as if they were holding him down. The truth is he died by drowning, not by bleeding out."

"The Brexit guys were at a small hostel, which they had to themselves. Anyone not with the team would have been noticed by the employees."

I was thinking aloud and a tad pleased with myself because I realized I had started to use police lingo. The Tour organizers chose hotels for each stage of the race and raffled them off to each of the teams. It wouldn't be hard to know who was assigned where ahead of time.

"Precisely, the Blue Galleon is so small, it only has one security camera; it's of terrible quality and placement. But, nonetheless, we were able to see a figure, apparently a man, crossing the lobby and going up the stairs at two fifty-four A.M. Fleming's death took place between two and four. The receptionist that night didn't see anything. He is also the hostel's bookkeeper, so when it gets quiet, he tends to work out of a small office where he keeps the books. Anybody with the slightest talent for opening locks could have come into the hotel and opened Fleming's door. None of the locks were forced."

Inevitably, my mind turned to the legion of mechanics who keep the squads moving, every one of them capable of taking apart a bike and putting it back together in an instant. For most of them, opening a lock would be child's play. I thought of Fiona. She would be waiting for me in her trailer, probably worried because of the delay. Well, maybe. There wasn't much in life that worried that woman.

I got up to let the commissioner know we were done talking but, as if he'd read my mind, he had one more thing to say.

"There's no need to let Mademoiselle Fiona know what we've spoken about. Of course, it would be very useful if you could find out if she or anyone from her office has seen anything unusual in the past few days."

I nodded in silence, held my hand out as a way of signaling farewell, and headed for the trailer. And, yes, the commissioner was right: Few things escaped Mademoiselle Fiona's attention.

In the same way the anti-doping office was in charge of making sure cyclists didn't give themselves an advantage by using banned substances, Fiona's office was in charge of making sure all racers on all teams complied with the strict regulations that applied to our bikes, instruments, and attire. The weight—six kilograms—and the dimensions of each bike were meticulously checked to make sure the competition didn't turn into a purely technological confrontation. Contrary to Formula One racing, cycling authorities wanted the wins to depend on the effort, strategy, and personal talent of the racers, not on technical expertise or the size of the sponsors' wallets.

Yes, it was possible Fiona already knew something. The challenge was trying to figure out how much of what she knew she would want to share with me. When I got to the trailer, I saw the lights were out and concluded tonight we would share absolutely nothing.

Back in my room, I spent another restless night on top of the sheets, going over two lists: that of the suspects and that of the general standings at the end of the last stage. Matosas, Paniuk, and Medel were on both lists. Steve too.

GENERAL CLASSIFICATION: STAGE 8

RANK	RIDER	TIME	NOTES
1	RICK SAGAL (PORTUGAL/FONTANA)	31:01:56	Not a rival, will fall in the mountains.
2	**STEVE PANATA (USA/FONAR)**	**+:18**	**He'll rise to first place working against the clock.**
3	SERGEI TALANCÓN (ROMANIA/ROCCA)	+:23	Has no team.
4	LUIS DURÁN (SPAIN/IMAGINE)	+:26	Weak team.
5	ALESSIO MATOSAS (ITALY/LAVEZZA)	+:34	Dangerous.
6	PABLO MEDEL (SPAIN/BALEARES)	+:40	Dangerous.
7	MILENKO PANIUK (CZECH/RABONET)	+:42	Dangerous.
8	PETER STARK (UK/BATESMAN)	+:58	Dismissed, poor Fleming.
9	ÓSCAR CUADRADO (COLOMBIA/MOVISTAR)	+1:05	They knocked his team over.
10	**MARC MOREAU (FRANCE/FONAR)**	**+1:07**	**I won't be able to make Fiona happy.**

2005–2016

I will never understand the reasons why Fiona chose me and not Steve, but sometimes I've asked myself if that wasn't the first crack in a friendship that until then had withstood everything.

Eleven years ago, during our first professional campaign with the Ventoux team, we both worked as domestiques, cogs in a machine in service of the team's historic leader, Bijon the Belgian, who was competing in his last season. There was all sorts of speculation about who would take Bijon's place the next year. The team didn't have the resources to recruit a star racer from the circuit, so it was a given that the DS would have to promote someone from within the team's own ranks. And the options came down to me and Steve.

For the Ventoux management, it wasn't an easy problem to solve. At that time we both had similar attributes when it came to quality and talent. Most of the experts leaned toward me. Historically, the Tour's champions are the best mountain climbers, and I had everything going for me to become one of them. Besides, I was twenty-four years old, and that seemed to make me a more appropriate team leader than Steve at twenty-two. The truth is we were both too young, but his age would turn out to be an anomaly in the circuit's history.

In the end, two circumstances did me in. The Spaniard Miguel Induráin had dominated cycling all through the nineties without being a particularly extraordinary climber. Half a dozen of his rivals usually beat him on the mountains. Still, he was a sublime stage racer and the best of his generation when it came to individual time trials. During those solitary races against the clock he usually managed to build up an advantage that cushioned him on the mountain days, when he was also helped by his team's defensive strategy; they had plenty of good climbers who were able to cover for him during the rough ascents. And that was precisely Steve's profile. An unbeatable racer, except on the mountains. Ventoux bet Steve would be the new Induráin.

The second factor was perhaps more decisive. The team needed new and more solid sponsors, and there was no greater promise than in the great American sports brands. If they could make the golden boy a star, the team's financial future was assured.

"The real reason was you," Fiona told me every time the topic came up. "Ventoux bet on Steve in spite of his weakness on the mountains because you were there to cover for him. They wouldn't have dared without you. They knew that, in terms of sheer power, they had the best climber in the circuit and decided to sacrifice him to benefit Steve. If, instead of the Induráin model, they'd used the Merckx or the Pantani model, you'd be number one in the world today."

Generally speaking, I appreciated the confidence Fiona had in that hypothesis, but I didn't take it very seriously. I imagined it had something to do with the grim but always unconditional love she had for me and the lack of sympathy she had toward my friend and his hangers-on.

Deep down I knew it wasn't just the Ventoux directors who

had been responsible for the decision that sealed our fates. During those months of doubt, Steve and I swore we would support the choice, whatever it was, and the loser would become the other's best squire. We completely believed in what we were saying. We faced the future with the conviction of two warriors who've sworn to fight shoulder-to-shoulder.

We were more than inseparable. Living in our own bubble, we grew into adulthood compensating for our weaknesses with the other's strengths. My presence and my temperament helped put a stop to my friend's outbursts; his desire to conquer the world and his limitless confidence challenged my shyness and the insecurities I'd harbored since realizing my parents found me a nuisance.

"We have a date tomorrow, buddy," he'd said just a few weeks after we'd met. Steve had managed to go out the previous Saturday night with one of the few young women we'd run into in the relative isolation of our training camp in Gerona. He tended to date girls who worked in nearby stores and restaurants. Even so, I never understood how he managed to engineer meet-ups during the few minutes we had free from training.

"We do?" I asked, surprised and a little worried. Neither my military service nor my shyness had been much help in developing an exciting love life. Women were magical and fascinating to me, while remaining inaccessible and the source of untold obsessions and anxiety.

"Susy is bringing her best friend and they'll come get us," he said, and then opened a drawer and pulled out a couple of condoms he threw in my direction. "They're my lucky brand."

I thought the possibility that a first date could end up in "that" was inconceivable; in my experience, sex had always been the result of siege-like crusades. And, in fact, our double date was a failure. God only knows what Susy told her friend Elena to get her to come out that Saturday, but it only took one look for her to let me know she had been expecting a second Steve.

Still, my friend wouldn't give up. He would do without Susy or any other solo conquest to make sure I had company. Little by little, I began to relax, to get caught up in Steve's spontaneity and to lose my fear about talking to whatever girl had been brought along. Even so, it took me four months to use the first of the condoms I carried, religiously and optimistically, on each date.

Deep down, I knew I was really responsible for Ventoux choosing Steve as our team leader. I realize now I regressed during those months. I don't know if I was afraid of the pressures a leader carries on his shoulders, including justifying the rest of the team's sacrifices with a win. It's also possible I knew, in spite of our mutual promises, that Steve would never stand to be relegated to second place. When the decision was made, I felt an unspeakable sense of relief. I assumed that was the best way forward for both of us, the only path that would allow us to continue together. I told myself I was the stronger of the two, the one who had the ability to endure adversity and keep standing. The truth is the Eddy Merckx who Fiona swears is in me died before he ever showed his face.

In the next few years, we both moved to the French team Fonar, and Steve became the circuit's David Beckham: His athletic feats were notable but his talent as a global celebrity who attracted multimillion-dollar sponsorships was even greater. And I became the best climber who never went up to the podium or wore a winner's jersey—the best, or nearly the best, domestique in the circuit. My only rival had drowned in a bathtub in a three-star hotel the night before.

Steve kept our pact impeccably. His triumphs made me rich, and I became a clause in every contract for any team that wanted him. He never failed to thank me from the podium, and I was always the first person he hugged when he came down. I still warmly remember how he tried to pull me up to the winner's circle when he won his first Tour de France, which the organizers didn't allow.

Does this mean I'm a loser? A wimp? Was this what my father had sensed? Did this explain his disdain? Was it cowardice or loyalty I'd felt for so long? I'd never thought about it like this, not until Fiona's insinuations that I was a better racer than I realized. Or, maybe, I only thought about it now because I finally had a chance to climb the podium when we got to Paris, even if it was thanks to the work of a killer. For the first time ever, being a domestique didn't seem enough.

But no. What Fiona and my father, while he was alive, never understood was how naturally the relationship between Steve and me evolved. From the very beginning, the two of us experienced our wins as mutual. And in many ways, they were.

By my side, he could conserve as much as twenty-five percent of his energy on a steep slope. I lived to save him during the half-dozen stages we ran through the Pyrenees and the Alps, where his enemies would otherwise destroy him. When the rest of our teammates lagged behind, I kept pace with Steve like a relentless tugboat until my lungs exploded and my legs gave out, which never happened until the very last stretch of the race. By then, his rivals could do him little harm. I didn't care about collapsing in that moment or being passed by dozens of mediocre racers. I never finished a Tour among the first fifteen spots, an anomaly considering I was the only climber in the circuit who could keep powering at 800 watts for more than ten minutes during a climb. The respect those stats inspired among my peers and the trophies won by my teammate thanks to my efforts were enough for me.

In time, we established our residence in a pair of houses next to each other among the hills of Lake De Como, close to the preseason training camp for the Fonar team. And, except for the brief vacations we took in December, him to Colorado and me to nowhere, we were together practically all year round. On more than one occasion, our routines were interrupted by some girlfriend of Steve's moving in, but they usually moved back out after a few months, overwhelmed by the abandonment a life dedicated to cycling condemned them to.

We became addicted to training, going much further than the

schedule established by the trainers. I'd go get him at five in the morning and we'd bike side by side for six or seven hours through the mountains of northern Italy, even in the winter cold of those preseason months. They were never relaxed rides: We talked very little, measured ascents and descents, modified our challenges and objectives every day, practiced strategies for pursuit and tailing. Basically, we aimed for extreme pain and fatigue. But we found something very comforting in the absolute exhaustion with which we concluded each day: the feeling that we had done our duty.

And we certainly had. We developed such synchronicity that, many years later, when the technicians made us race in a computer-moderated wind tunnel to optimize the angle and the distance where my body offered his the greatest energy savings, its findings coincided exactly with what we had discovered intuitively in our long, lonely sessions. We responded to changes in intensity or wind direction like a flock of birds—making small adjustments we were barely aware of that allowed us to keep going at maximum speed. We became the fastest duo in cycling history, and by quite a lot. We were a pair, a couple, in more than one sense, unaffected by the women who passed through our lives.

Until Fiona came along.

Stage 9

Vannes — Plumelec, 28 km. Individual time trial.

I woke up with the sense that I was missing something important in my list of suspects, like when you leave the house and know you're forgetting something, even though you can feel your keys, wallet, and cell in your pocket.

Up until now, my list had been limited to those who would benefit from the killer's attacks: Paniuk the Czech, Matosas the Italian, Medel the Spaniard; Steve's circle, including Giraud; and Radek the Pole, motivated by his hate and resentment.

But the night before, Favre had approached the matter in another way: to look for the guilty party based on the modus operandi of those attacks. His police logic took into account not only motive but also alibis and abilities. That made me remember certain loose fragments from the criminology seminars Lombard had made me take thirteen years back, although they were immediately erased by a smiling Claude from Biarritz and that small caiman tattooed on her belly. It had left a vague, salty taste in my mouth.

I forced myself to refocus on the damn modus operandi: the mechanics and their talents for opening locks, the doctors and their particular knowledge about sleeping pills and toxins, the soigneurs and their powerful hands that could've caused the bruises on Fleming's body. Dozens of faces passed through my mind, some well known to me, others anonymous participants in the vast personnel that surrounds the cyclists who race the Tour each year.

But I wasn't going to get anywhere by that route. The list of suspects could go on indefinitely. And, anyway, I didn't have access to the report about each attack, a description of the scene of the crime, the specific time or the precision with which it took place. Without that, it would be impossible to hunt down suspects or discard the innocent.

I tried to refocus on the day ahead. If I didn't dedicate myself to being a cyclist in the next few hours, I'd end up watching the Tour on TV in the next few days. For a lot of cyclists, the Tour's individual time trial is the real test: We run a shorter distance than in the other stages but we do it as if we were being chased by a tax collector. It's a solo battle against a stopwatch, without help, without domestiques, in which every pedal, every meter, and every second are decisive. This is where Steve was the absolute king. The question was not who would win this stage but rather with how much of a time advantage he would win. There were three or four great time-trial racers in the peloton, but none of them were team leaders or had a chance of winning the overall race, so we weren't worried about them.

For a lot of the climbers, this stage could become a real Waterloo. Especially because, for this occasion, the sadistic organizers had chosen an unusually long stretch of forty-two kilometers. If Steve performed at his peak, he could finish with three or four minutes over his rivals, which would determine this year's winner in one fell swoop.

In the warm-up area, anxiety flooded the air like a toxic cloud.

I saw Matosas, his two thick dark eyebrows fused into one; he was standing and stretching while his DS gave him loud instructions, but he wasn't paying attention to anything that wasn't coming from his earphones. I wondered if he was listening to that horrible Italian pop music he loved, although for all I knew he could have been listening to arias. I decided that was improbable: Matosas was an Italian pop culture cliché, although a good version of that.

A few meters away, Paniuk pedaled furiously, also completely consumed by his earphones. There was no need to speculate about what he was listening to: We all knew about the Czech's passion for metal and could hear the thundering noise with which he was punishing his eardrums. Of all the climbers, he was the one who might fare best during the day's trial. His time-trial stats weren't bad, and he had a good chance of getting distance from the other mountain specialists. I approached him in my detective mode, trying to think of the best way to start a casual conversation that could lead to an important revelation. I couldn't think of anything, so I just stood there two meters behind him. Even at that distance I got a sniff of the aromatic cloud around him. Paniuk was an extravagant guy: Who else would think to drench himself in cologne to race through the countryside? Although, on second thought, who among us wasn't extravagant, given we were all dedicated to this absurd profession? Just today, like on all racing days, I had covered my body in cornstarch with the hope of postponing the corrosive effect of my own perspiration.

I looked around and saw that one of the bikes next to the resentful Viktor Radek was open. I climbed on immediately.

"How's it going, Viktor? How is the Tour treating you?" I was trying to feel him out. As is the case with a lot of Poles, he was fluent in French.

"Bad, like everyone else. The Tour doesn't treat anyone well," he responded, sour. "Well, except for your pal," he said after a pause, although I pretended I didn't hear him. Radek's curly blond hair was quite a distraction, not only because it was wildly untamed, but because he didn't even try to comb it in the mornings. Among his many superstitions, and these weren't few, he considered seeing himself in the mirror before he got on a bike to be bad luck. He looked like a scarecrow trying to walk. A very ill-humored scarecrow.

"Steve isn't happy either; they've stuck us with more high mountain stages this year."

Radek didn't respond. I shouldn't have given him a counterargument if I wanted to see the depth of his rancor; I should have been on his side and let him vent his resentment. He was a strange guy, and not just because of his physique.

"But you're right: More than sixty people have dropped out so far, and this is supposed to be the easy part. The Tour is too demanding," I went on, as if there hadn't been two minutes of silence after his response.

"Easy part? It's a crime to have us go over those rock gardens on the first stages. I'd like to see Jitrik pedal over those wet and sandy rocks in those tiny towns they make us go through. And all so the Tour can make fifty thousand from each town. I got out of the first two scrambles by pure luck."

"And now, this thing with Fleming. Inexplicable . . ."

"Not so inexplicable when you consider the pressures we're under. You never know what kind of struggle Fleming was going through to make that kind of decision. They had disqualified Santamaría that morning for doping. We all knew he was clean."

I listened to him while watching his face, which was now flushed with indignation. If Radek was the killer, then he was a better actor than cyclist. There wasn't the slightest trace of guilt or embarrassment; he was stewing in pure hatred. A quick glimpse at his skinny arms also made me question if he could force somebody underwater against their will. If the Englishman had been drowned by a solitary killer, it didn't seem likely it was Radek.

A few minutes later, the organizers asked Radek to the exit

platform. The racers took off with two minutes between them to avoid running into each other. Steve would be the second to last, because he was second in the general classification, and I would take off six competitors ahead of him, as was determined by my ninth place. It was still a little under an hour before I'd be called. I stuck my earphones in my ears and surrendered to the *vallenato* I used to warm up.

I rotated my legs at a moderate rhythm as I edited my list of possible guilty parties. I moved Radek to the bottom, but I didn't completely eliminate him.

"Poor guy, his soul is tormented," said my old mentor Colonel Lombard as he greeted me by patting my back; his gaze followed Radek until he disappeared.

"Colonel, you scared me. Don't do that," I said, jumping off the bike.

"I've always greeted you the same way," he responded, surprised too.

Yes, but now there's a killer on the loose, I thought, although I didn't say it aloud. Lombard had retired from the military six years before and had made following my career his life's purpose, at least during the racing season. He had the resources, the time, and the relationships to win a place in the sprawling troupe that followed the cyclists. At first, his warm but obsessive presence had made me uncomfortable, but I ended up getting used to and being grateful for it. He was on top of all the advancements and technology in medicine and sports, and he followed my performance even more intensely than Fonar did. More than once, I adjusted my racing strategies and exercise programs based on his suggestions.

In time, the rest of the circuit had adopted him as part of the scene. He got his first accreditation as a consultant for Bimeo, the head of security on the Tour, so powerful and terrifying that he only required one name. And in the past few years, he'd become inseparable from Fiona, who ended up giving him a second accreditation as an inspector for something related to protocols and procedures. He used the two accreditations interchangeably to move like a fish in water up and down the competition. Lombard and Fiona were bonded because of their complete commitment to the cycling world, but that relationship grew into something like that of a father and daughter. Needless to say, they shared a conviction that I needed to free myself of Steve.

On this occasion, I was doubly grateful to Lombard. He had moved mountains to make sure Fonar gave me the same equipment my teammate had had the year before. Today, my clothes and bike were valued at more than half a million euros. The research in the development of Steve's new helmet alone had cost $250,000, an investment the manufacturer would recover as soon as they launched the prototype of what I was wearing into the market.

"The general standings are still very compact. If you manage one of your best times, you could be among the top five. And if that's where you're at when you get to the mountain, the rest is easy: champion or, at least, top three."

"Lower your voice," I said, looking around to make sure no one had heard us. A conversation like that between a domestique and his mentor was even more of a sacrilege than two cardinals speculating about how they'd look dressed in white and offering mass in St. Peter's Square.

"We already ran the races on the model, and only seven or eight cyclists can better your time trials. And it will help a lot that there are two hills on today's course," he insisted, whispering in my ear this time. Even though I couldn't see his mouth, I could swear he was salivating.

I worried we looked like two conspirators exchanging secrets— the cardinals discussing poison this time. Later, I realized no one was paying attention to us, but the clandestine meetings with the commissioner and now these intrigues with Lombard were making me paranoid. What he was talking about didn't have the slightest chance of becoming reality. My role as a domestique condemned me to finish the Tour after the first twenty racers no matter what kind of efforts Lombard put in. Still, Lombard's attentions were touching.

But that day he wasn't wrong. I finished the time trials with the sixth best time, 58 seconds behind Steve. Matosas also managed to sneak in with one of the ten best times. It was becoming clear the Italian would do whatever was necessary to enter Paris first.

That same night I discovered that could include killing me.

"I thought you weren't coming," Fiona said after the race, not turning around from grilling a salmon fillet in her little kitchen.

A few weeks before, she'd given me the key to her trailer, but I sensed she already regretted it. I knew she loved me; how could it be any other way after sharing this crazy life of ours for two years? Still, I knew she guarded her privacy and her space ferociously.

"Something kept me," I responded, contemplating the possibility of telling her about my new detective duties, but I decided to keep her out of it, at least for the moment. "Giraud was so euphoric after Steve's win he dragged out his speech before dinner."

"And he didn't say anything about your ranking? Last year Steve beat you by more than three minutes and you were in fifteenth place; now you're in sixth. You're the racer with the greatest improvement on the time trials. That bastard really didn't say anything?"

"Nope," I said as I went up to her, kissed her on the neck, and pulled her back against me. I was surprised to feel her tremble when I touched her sturdy body. I remembered we were off the next day, and I toyed with the idea of breaking the vow of chastity we subscribed to on the Tour.

"Son of a bitch. As far as Fonar is concerned, there's only Steve," she said gesticulating. I looked sadly at the silhouette through her thin Japanese robe. It was quite clear to me it would not be coming off tonight. Fiona got angry very rarely, but when she did, her anger could last for hours.

"Steve was happier than me about my sixth place. He celebrated like it was his own win," I protested.

"That's because he sees it as a win for him! He is so self-involved, he thinks you've gotten better at the time trials thanks to him, as if his talent radiated onto whoever was closest," she said.

I considered that if there was any possibility of getting that robe off tonight, defending Steve was probably not the best strategy. Still, I couldn't help it. She was being unfair to my friend.

"You're looking at it all wrong. You should've seen him yesterday. He was beside himself when he found out about Fleming's death. I'd never seen him like that before."

"I don't understand that reaction. They'd never been friends," she said, as if she knew everything about my colleagues. "And let's not be naïve: Unless there's some sort of catastrophe, Fleming's death essentially eliminates Stark. Steve and Giraud have the way cleared so they can be crowned in Paris. They don't have any rivals left."

"Well, there's Matosas, Paniuk, and Medel. All three are better climbers than Steve. They might get their chance on the Alps."

"You're the best climber! With your help, Steve can neutralize them," she said emphatically, finally looking at me for the first time that night. And then, in a very low whisper, she added: "In fact, you're the only one who can beat Panata."

As she had done so many times before, Fiona said the words I didn't dare articulate. A long silence followed her bombshell. My first reaction was to refuse to let the bomb go off. My loyalty to Steve was deeply ingrained. But instead of brushing aside Fiona's comment, my brain went straight to her use of a particular word. She didn't like Steve but she'd always called him by his first name. That she was now referring to him by his last name struck me as odd and vaguely threatening.

I was again led to wonder what the devil had happened between them, an inquiry I couldn't force myself to make for fear of what I might find out, and that, to be fair, they didn't seem willing to reveal to me. Fiona had been the chief mechanic for the Fonar team six years ago when Steve and I were both leaders. Like many others on the circuit before him, my friend tried to seduce her. She wasn't the only woman in our professional circle: There were soigneurs, nutritionists, doctors. Not many, but some. There was no question that she was the best mechanic in a trade that had up until then been exclusively male, and that made for an undeniable fascination among the racers. Her inaccessibility, her grease-stained hands, her large, unconfined breasts under her jumpsuit, her red hair, those green eyes and that surly expression they often held—in short, a strange and attractive amalgam had turned her into impossible prey for the wolf pack. And there was no greater alpha male than Steve Panata.

My friend tried every possible angle during the twenty months Fiona worked for our team. It must've become an obsession because I'd never seen him abuse his star power like that. He demanded personal checkups of his bike in order to force her to spend time alone with him. He'd make unannounced visits to her trailer at night. And he asked her to go with him to Munich in the off-season to supervise the new carbon components for his frame that a sponsor was designing. Something happened between them, or didn't happen, because at the end of the season, Fiona resigned from the team and left without saying a word. When she worked at Fonar, Fiona and I had two or three long conversations, but we were never intimate. I had long ceased being shy around women, but it was also clear this Irish Athena was way out of my league. And I imagine my close proximity to Steve made it impossible for her to relax in my presence.

Yet, months later, out of the blue, she sent me a message describing a meticulous program to adjust my posture, pedal, and bike seat to compensate for a difference of five millimeters in longitude between my left side and my right. This turned into a regular exchange of messages that slowly became more personal even after she took an inspector's job with UCI.

Two springs ago, on our way back from Catalonia, she knocked on my door one night and, after a brief greeting, stretched out on my bed, a bold and needy look in her eyes. In the following months, the visits became routine whenever our schedules allowed us to be in the same place, even if it was just to sleep holding each other. That inexpressive daytime Fiona disappeared at night. She would nestle close to me, touch me tenderly, and whisper sweet, senseless words.

I should say that my prestige in the circuit grew exponentially as soon as my relationship with Fiona was found out. For months, all my colleagues treated me with the kind of respect that only winning the Spanish Vuelta or the Italian Giro might have earned. All, that is, except Steve.

When he learned Fiona was in my life, something began to break in the nearly symbiotic relationship we'd shared for so long. In those first few days I caught him staring at me on more than one occasion, as if he was looking for something he might have missed. I imagined he was trying to figure out the reasons she'd chosen me. But that was a mystery to me as well.

He must not have found anything to justify her preference, so he figured it was some kind of revenge on Fiona's part: Getting involved with me not only showed her disdain but sowed the seeds of a discord that could threaten and affect his racing performance.

That's when he decided to destroy Fiona and bring me back around to his cause. At least that's my interpretation of the campaign he directed toward me and against her. He insisted on including me in some of his more lucrative publicity commercials, went overboard in his gratitude toward me in all his interviews, and introduced me to one attractive international jet-setting female friend after another. I suspect, based on a few troubling things I heard, that at the same time he tried to make Fiona's life impossible in the biking world, spreading damaging rumors, both personal and professional, that hurt me to remember.

Eventually, though, he realized the relationship between Fiona and me was here to stay, and he modified his attitude. Still, he seemed vaguely offended, as if he'd been a victim of some kind of betrayal on my part, even though he kept up appearances and didn't change anything obvious about the professional and personal codes we'd built up over the years. It was clear to me that his heretofore inexhaustible self-confidence had been shaken, especially because the hurt came from such an unexpected and mortifying place—his supposedly unconditional friend and domestique.

That's when he began to pay more attention to the demands of his agents and to devote more time to his agenda of celebrity events. He launched his courtship with Stevlana and erased Fiona and anything having to do with her from his life. I should note that during this period his obsession for training never diminished and he was never careless about the everyday physical discipline necessary, given the tough parameters this life demands. Nor did we modify in any way the work routine that had made us the most successful tandem in the professional circuit.

For her part, Fiona simply ignored Steve. First his hostility and then his absolute disdain. She treated him as one more variable in my life, without conceding him any more consideration than she would the weather or the kind of bike I was riding.

Or, at least, that's what I'd always thought. Just now, when she said I could "beat Panata," I realized that for the past few months Fiona had been weaving the most effective campaign conceivable against Steve: to convince me I was a better cyclist than him.

"Steve has an almost-two-minute lead, and to get over that I'd have to betray him on the mountain. Anyway, Giraud would never let me break away without dragging Steve with me. My own team would hunt me down."

"Not if you do it at the right moment."

I thought about Alpe d'Huez and the last long, steep twenty

kilometers we'd race on Stage 20, one day before we reached Paris. Technically, Fiona was right. If the rest of the Fonar team was exhausted at the start of the slope, and if it was just our champion and me, I could rid myself of Steve a few kilometers before the finish line and try to overtake the lead he'd have over me in the standings. I imagined my friend's surprised expression when I stood on the pedals and left him alone and paralyzed on a ramp with a ten percent incline.

"But I'm not going to do it," I said. "No win could justify a betrayal of that magnitude."

"It's you who's been betrayed, Mojito," said Fiona, exasperated. "I can understand that eleven years ago you accepted he was the leader and you were the domestique." She chewed on the last word as if it were nauseating. "The decision was made by the Ventoux directors and you were an unknown with few options at that moment. Three or four years later, any one of the intermediate teams would have been delighted to have you as a leader; I know you've had several offers in the last few years."

"They were never as good as the Fonar offers," I said in my defense.

"Fonar's offers were to keep you as the number two! Steve used money to squash any possibility that you could become one of the greats, and he did it because it was in his interest. You don't do that to a friend you love."

"I'm the best domestique in the circuit. What we've achieved together has already made history," I responded, offended. It was a weak argument, but it was compensated by my genuine indignation. We'd never discussed the subject so explicitly. My personal relationship with Steve had been a taboo subject between us until now.

"But you're not the best domestique in the circuit. You're the best climber in the circuit! Lombard and Bernard have spent months with their calculations and their models." Bernard was Lombard's only child, and a computer programmer. Although the two men were present in each other's lives, their relationship was more formal than affectionate. It was only in the past few years, and thanks to the programs Bernard had designed to analyze my performance, that father and son finally had something in common. Fiona continued: "If you competed protected by eight racers, the way Steve does, not to mention the state-of-the-art technology to which he's given priority, your time would be between three and five minutes better than his, depending on the kind of mountains you have to race through that year."

"Lombard and Bernard's programs, they're just obsessions, pyrotechnics."

"No, they're not. I've watched your technique and your numbers for years. Your progress as a cyclist has been better than Steve's, but that's buried because of the roles you play on the team. You've bettered your time trials when Steve hasn't been able to advance on the mountain. Pound for pound, you've become a better racer than him. At least admit it, even if you don't have the guts to do anything about it."

She said this as a challenge, with a furious expression and her arms akimbo. I'd never seen her like this. I wondered how much of this passion had to do with her love for me and how much with her resentment toward Steve.

Suddenly I felt the weight of the day's exhaustion. All I wanted was to get to my room, drop in bed, and forget about all these conspiracies and betrayals. Life was a lot simpler when it was just about making my teammate a champion. Maybe Fiona was right, and I'd spent years taking refuge in that complacent version of myself.

I started toward the door but realized I could not leave things like this. Fiona was now sitting on the couch in the front part of her living space, eating her salmon and salad, which was not allowed on my diet at that hour of the night. I approached her with the intention of saying goodbye with a long hug that might dismiss some of the demons that had been released. But I never got close enough to touch her. An explosion shook the trailer and a gale of heat hit my back. I wound up on the floor, dazed at Fiona's feet. When the smoke cleared I noticed a huge opening at the far end of the trailer, where flames were beginning to consume it. I looked for Fiona, who was still frozen on the couch. She saw the panicked question in my eyes and shook her head. Neither one of us was hurt.

"Let's get out of here, this could explode!" I shouted; my ears felt clogged.

"Whatever was going to explode has already exploded—that was the gas tank," she said as she took a couple of tentative steps to grab a fire extinguisher from the wall. When the first cops arrived on the scene just a few minutes later, the only thing left was a smoking hole and an unserviceable trailer.

It took us two hours to get back to my room, after the medical checkup and a rigorous interrogation by the local authorities. Miraculously, we'd both escaped without a scratch. The commissioner assured me he'd have an expert go over everything and come up with an explanation for the explosion, but he anticipated the conclusion: Although it had been unsuccessful, I'd become the target of the ninth attack by the killer of the Tour de France.

In spite of my team's rules against it, that night Fiona stayed in my room. She fell asleep caressing me while in my mind I added and deleted names from my list of suspects. I was fuming; not only was the attack personal, but Fiona could have been hurt or worse. I told myself any reconsideration of my podium potential had to take a backseat. The real priority was to find the killers before they attacked again. And yet, the last image that crossed my mind before I got lost in dreams was, of course, the general classification. I'd never been among the top six in the Tour de France before.

GENERAL CLASSIFICATION: STAGE 9

RANK	RIDER	TIME	NOTES
1	**STEVE PANATA (USA/FONAR)**	31:34:12	**My job is to make sure he continues to wear the jersey.**
2	RICK SAGAL (PORTUGAL/FONTANA)	+:58	No threat from Sagal, he'll lose on the mountain.
3	PHIL CUNNINHAM (UK/SAJONTRIP)	+1:04	He's good on the time trials, but not a threat.
4	MARTIN DENNIS (NETHERLANDS/COMPASS)	+1:26	A roller, he'll lose on the mountain.
5	ALESSIO MATOSAS (ITALY/LAVEZZA)	+1:42	This one is dangerous, and a suspect.
6	**MARC MOREAU (FRANCE/FONAR)**	+1:47	**Even if it doesn't last, nothing wrong with being in the top ten.**
7	MILENKO PANIUK (CZECH/RABONET)	+2:05	He'll be a threat on the mountain.
8	ÓSCAR CUADRADO (COLOMBIA/MOVISTAR)	+2:22	He doesn't have a team left.
9	PABLO MEDEL (SPAIN/BALEARES)	+2:35	Dangerous, unpredictable.
10	LUIS DURÁN (SPAIN/IMAGINE)	+3:01	No team.

Stage 10

Tarbes—La Pierre Saint-Martin, 167 km.

His personality may leave something to be desired, but there's no doubt Giraud is effective. Yesterday, when the whole circus around the Tour was taking advantage of the day off to travel from Britain to the Pyrenees, Giraud came to get me very early and had me fly to Toulouse in a small rented plane. I arrived several hours before the rest of the team at the little hotel on the outskirts of Pau, where we would be staying for the next few nights. The goal? To keep me away from reporters wanting me to make a statement about the trailer explosion.

Our DS's mission was to make Steve a champion, and no assassination attempt, no reporter or cop was going to keep me from doing what I needed to do on the mountain stages that would begin today. After all, that's why they'd brought me here: to be Steve's shield during the seven stages in which the other climbers would attack him.

I was sorry to leave Fiona alone with the media, although at least she didn't have sponsors to worry about. She could spit out a couple of sentences and then lock herself up in the UCI's mobile office until the storm passed. Still, to abandon her the day she'd lost what was essentially her home, at least during the racing season, left me with a guilty feeling.

I had woken up with a sore throat from the fire. I gargled some water, convinced I'd spit soot into the sink. Those damn pyromaniacs had at least been kind enough to attack on the eve of a day off.

In spite of everything, I enjoyed getting away from the Tour for a few hours. The isolation of the hotel provided a temporary haven. That's no small thing: The harassment of thousands of fans and the scrutiny of the cameras can be as draining as racing three thousand kilometers. I wondered what Steve did to relieve this pressure that, in his case, was exponentially greater than my own. He was now part of the rarified celebrity circuit chased by the paparazzi. His adventures with models and actresses were obsessively covered by the magazines that kept up with that kind of thing.

Calmed by my solitude, I decided to leave the hotel to sit under an old oak and imagine what life would have been like if I hadn't crossed paths with a bicycle. The oversized green leaves and their thick veins, reborn each spring and indifferent to whoever won or lost the Tour, put things in perspective. My father had died almost two years ago and I'd inherited his cabin at the foot of the Alps. On his deathbed, he made me promise that one day I'd move back to live there as he did, and his father before him. I agreed to his wish without the slightest intention of complying and with an urgent desire to get away from that decrepit and selfish man agonizing in a provincial hospital. But now, as I watched the swaying of the leaves at the foot of a different mountain, I told myself that a bucolic and placid life could have its charms. I imagined myself on a terrace overlooking those beautiful Alpine valleys, wearing a plaid flannel shirt and holding a huge mug of coffee in my hand. I later realized that was actually a childhood memory I'd kept of my father. If I ever lived there, I'd just be a shadow of Colonel Moreau.

No, the bike was my life, my way of facing the world, and whatever I did for the next thirty years would be a result of the first thirty, which I'd spent pedaling. I'd much rather grow old like Lombard, dedicated to his passion, than like my father, committed to cultivating his own bitterness.

I abandoned my Alpine daydreams and returned to the present and my beloved Pyrenees. What would happen if I gave in to Fiona and Lombard's desire and attacked Steve and my own team on the mountain? Was there a real possibility I could snatch the yellow jersey from him? I wasn't sure I could do it, even if I decided to. And the minute I went for it, I'd be a pariah, more alone during the competition than poor Óscar Cuadrado. If I *was* successful, was I willing to live with the pressure of the paparazzi and the constant media exposure, the astronomical expectations for the next race? I considered the enormous interests at play.

I was reminded that, because of those interests, there was a killer loose among us who had made an attempt on my life just a few hours before. I sat up, suddenly terrified that the thirty future years I'd been contemplating could be reduced to thirty minutes. I was alone and vulnerable on the edge of a wooded area. If the killer decided to try again, I'd made it easy for him. I quickly returned to my room.

That night, I texted Fiona to invite her to come and stay with me. My sudden disappearance must have upset her, because she said she felt tired after driving Lombard's trailer all day and that she would crash there until she found something better.

The next day, Giraud kept a solid barricade around me. He ordered that food, a soigneur, and a stationary bike be brought up to my room in the early hours. The idea was that the media wouldn't see me until I got off the team bus a few seconds before the regulatory signing in in Tarbes, the small town from which the next stage would depart. Later, a second stationary bike was brought up to my room with Steve behind it. After a day off, the coaches wanted us to loosen our knotted muscles.

"I told you they were coming for you!" he exclaimed as he came through the door. Then he hugged me tightly.

"It was just a defective gas tank," I said, freeing myself uncomfortably from his greeting. I realized that, in spite of the thousands of hours we'd spent together, our physical contact was usually minimal: brief and spontaneous hugs to celebrate a win and routine hugs on our birthdays.

"Defective, my ass," Steve said. "I'm going to ask my bodyguards to protect you as well from now on, at least until the end of the Tour." He climbed on one of the bikes and started his warm-up routine.

"It wasn't an attack," I said, mounting my own bike. "Fiona told me she was about to change the gas tank, that it had needed repairs for a long time. Luckily, it was practically empty." I wasn't lying. That's the explanation she gave the police after the incident. It was the same thing she'd said to the reporters in the morning when they caught her on her way to the UCI bus she used as her office. Truth be told, I didn't know what to think. It seemed too much to attribute a ninth violent incident to a mere accident. But I didn't want to feed Steve's panic, much less be in the constant company of one of his thugs. I wondered what the rest of the cyclists were thinking. Would they continue to believe that all these tragedies were nothing more than bad luck, or did they now realize there was something else afoot?

"Do you think it's Paniuk's people? Or Matosas's? That guy is desperate to win a second Tour before retiring," said Steve, as if he were reading my mind.

"They'll have to strike in the Pyrenees if they want another chance," I said, trying to deflect the conversation toward the kind of attack we were more used to: one on a bike.

"Seven stages on the mountain, three in the Pyrenees and four in the Alps. The rest is a piece of cake. But this year, the ascents are tougher than the four times I won," said Steve as we pedaled, staring at the deer-and-forest wallpaper that threatened to peel off the wall. "Not even the organizers want me to win this year," he added, worried.

I was about to say something when, after two quick raps on the door, Lombard burst in.

"Hannibal, you don't know how sorry I am," he said as a greeting. "It's my fault. Fiona had asked me to help her with the trailer maintenance, but the Tour overwhelmed us."

Lombard looked devastated, as if he really were responsible for the explosion. And yet, as soon as he registered Steve's presence, his expression changed. He hadn't expected to see him in my room at that hour. He greeted him with a nod, said something about catching me before the start of the race, and left the same way he'd come in.

"That old man gets crazier by the minute, bro. When are you going to get rid of him? He's a distraction."

"That old man is who got me started in this. Anyway, now you heard it: The gas tank was damaged, so forget about sticking me with one of your bodyguards, because it's not going to happen. Now, that would really be a distraction."

We turned to strategy for the next stage. Steve was nervous. It was the first day on the high mountain. Even though the steepest peaks were programmed for the following days, today we'd face the imposing incline at La Pierre Saint-Martin, after more than four hours of racing. The last fifteen kilometers were going to be brutal, long ramps with gradients of more than ten percent, the kind of incline that forces a car to go up in first gear and a cyclist to give up his kidney.

The first 150 kilometers went by quickly and without incident. A few second-tier teams without a chance of winning took advantage of the long stretch to try aggressive and prolonged breakaways. Grudgingly, the peloton sped up so as not to allow those who had tried to flee too much distance. We would have preferred to not get so worn down before hitting the tough test that awaited us at the end.

Although fatigued, the core of the group arrived whole at the foot of the long slope, but as soon as the ascent at La Pierre Saint-Martin began, racers began falling off. We were waiting for a sudden move from Matosas but instead got a concentrated attack from all three of our principal rivals—that is, the three that were left after the killer's purge. The domestiques for Matosas, Paniuk, and Medel sped up their rhythm from the very beginning of the incline, taking turns leading. It didn't look like an improvised strategy. Those sons of bitches were playing us—all three teams were colluding!

About halfway up the climb, only about a dozen of us were left. Three kilometers before the finish line, there were just five: Steve, his three rivals, and me.

Now without escorts, Matosas, Paniuk, and Medel did the same thing their assistants had done: They operated as a team. Over and over, the triad tried to get rid of us by pushing us into the crosswinds with devious moves on one side or another of the road. But on each occasion, I responded to the attacks by climbing up on the wheel of the last of them. I was afraid Steve would be unable to stay behind me during these changes in direction and speed, but the last reserves of his energy kept him just a few centimeters from my wheel. He pedaled without paying attention to any of the other racers, concentrating only on not losing the benefits of my slipstream: He knew I would take care of the rest.

It wasn't easy: In theory, kicking off is more demanding for whoever is at the front of the peloton than for someone who is two or three positions back; that person is well protected and can simply follow behind the other's wheel. It's just that the body doesn't react like that. The rider who speeds up abruptly to break away knows he has to make an extra effort and prepares for it; two or three seconds later, the rider behind finds himself obliged to transmit an urgent message—"Make a big effort!"—to his body that he may not be in condition to respond to. By then, the rider who has broken away has gained three or four meters, the benefit of the slipstream vanishes and the gap is much more difficult to close.

It seemed as if Matosas, Paniuk, and Medel had agreed to some sort of sign, because every two or three turns whoever was in the front would begin an attack and the other two would quickly follow. Luckily, I reacted immediately each time and was able to neutralize their moves. In that moment, fury was the best fuel. Steve was in a kind of trance and responded automatically to my improvisations, as if an invisible spoke linked his front wheel with my back wheel.

With only one kilometer to go before the finish line, I thought the danger had passed: The battering by our three rivals had lost its force and Medel appeared to have given up on the strategy. He stood on his pedals and pushed hard the rest of the way. I think the Spaniard just wanted to get to the peak separating his country from France; as soon as he crossed the finish line he'd be rolling on native soil. But this time, Matosas and Paniuk didn't follow him. I still had what was needed to catch up to Medel. But his takeoff was too violent for Steve, so I opted to let him go. I imagined Fiona shaking her head in disappointment, her hands on her hips.

That image made me move to take over the front spot. I wanted to keep Medel from gaining too much of an advantage. If I was going to be a coward, I'd at least be a coward with initiative. But with about two hundred meters before the finish line, Matosas and Paniuk blasted off and peeled away from Steve to grab the bonus seconds the Tour gives to the first three placers of each stage. I looked over at my partner; his face was a portrait of fatigue. I stayed behind and towed him until the finish line.

That day, Medel took 48 seconds from Steve, and Matosas and Paniuk each grabbed twenty-one. That wasn't easy to dismiss but we could deal with it. What was tougher to contend with was the strategy the three teams had used to collude against Fonar. If the peak had been longer and steeper, it would have been devastating. It wasn't necessary to have a catastrophic day to completely change the standings. Six more days like this one would do the trick.

When we got to the hotel, Giraud was losing his mind. Our DS wanted to blow the whistle on the three rival teams. Steve was in a frenzy too. For my part, I thought it was natural, up to a certain point. Medel, Paniuk, and Matosas were leaders of squads with more modest budgets and less acclaimed domestiques than the powerhouses headed by Steve, Óscar Cuadrado, and Stark. But, unexpectedly, the decimation of the Movistar and Batesman teams had made them contenders and put them in position to try to take out Fonar. So that's precisely what they were trying to do. And perhaps what the killer was trying to do as well.

Contrary to what I'd told Steve, I thought the explosion of Fiona's trailer fit that strategy perfectly. If the gas tank had been full, I would have found myself in a hospital bed instead of where I was now, on a massage table. Worse: I wouldn't have been able to protect Steve on the mountain and Matosas would be wearing the yellow jersey.

Lucky for me, the drama of today's race attracted the attention of the press, which seemed to forget about the explosion the night before. All the reporters' questions to the Fonar team were focused on Steve's defeat in the standings. No one, least of all the media, wants the leader to be determined midway through the race. Steve's dominating lead, and the collapse of Stark and Cuadrado, had threatened to make this year's Tour devoid of any suspense. But the offensive by Medel, Matosas, and Paniuk opened the way for a new rivalry and drama on the high mountains.

What was exciting to the press overwhelmed Steve. He didn't talk about the gas tank again or the need to protect me. The new challenge to him was too terrible to be ignored.

"It's an unacceptable conspiracy and the judges need to do something about it," said Giraud, who was indignant. He had called for a meeting of racers and technical assistants on the team bus a little before dinner.

"It's twenty-seven racers against nine. It's impossible to compete like that. We would have to look for alliances with other teams," Steve said.

"None of the smaller teams are going to help us. In fact, I think they're enjoying it. They'd love to see the powerful Fonar team bite the dust," I said, surprising myself. Generally speaking, I tend to avoid conflict.

"We have to at least file an official protest; it's not ethical for a part of this peloton to plot against its leaders. I've never seen anything like it," insisted Steve, put off by my resistance.

"But it's not like we can prove it. On the road, all sorts of alliances get made and, anyway, Medel competed against the other two on the final sprint, which undermines any accusation of some kind of agreement between the three," I said.

"We could make a deal with whoever's left with Movistar and Batesman," said our teammate Guido. "Cuadrado is in sixth. He doesn't have domestiques, but with our help, he could end up placing. Having him with us on the mountain would be huge. The British still have a couple of good climbers. If we support them so they win the white jersey, we could form an alliance." The white jersey is what the Tour gives to the most distinguished racer under the age of twenty-five. One of the racers with Batesman was now in second place in that category and a serious contender for the title.

Steve and Giraud looked at me, waiting for a response. In theory, Guido's suggestion seemed logical. But only in theory. I moved around uncomfortably in my seat and let the pause linger for as long as I could stand it.

"To ask Movistar or Batesman to help Fonar become the champion is the same as asking Real Madrid to help Barcelona. For the last four years, our three teams have taken turns winning the Tour, Il Giro, and La Vuelta. Even if Movistar and Batesman can't compete for the Tour, the last thing any of them wants is for Fonar to claim the championship."

"What team are you on?" said Giraud, exasperated by my objections.

"I'm with the leader and I think I proved that where it counts, on the mountain," I answered.

I was shocked by my defiant response. It's never a good idea to confront Giraud. The DS has all the power on a team and ours reigns over us with the pride of his prior successes. Not to mention the decisive role Giraud plays at the end of the season when we negotiate contracts for the following year. Tomorrow, he could easily condemn me to serving as the link between the squad and the Fonar car that follows it, going back and forth with water and nourishment for the rest of my teammates all along the course. It's a thankless task, usually left to the more modest members of each team.

Usually, I don't say much during the planning sessions for each stage, and when I do, I never confront the DS; if I have a suggestion, I present it respectfully. Although in theory Steve is the team leader, on the road I'm the strategist—I'm responsible for deciding if we chase after a group that has opted to break away, or whether to resettle our team within the squad after a sudden change in wind.

But it's true I'd grown impatient in the past few days. I didn't know if I'd be able to get up the courage or the cynicism to betray Steve in what was left of the Tour, but I was no longer willing to take Giraud's shit.

I stayed quiet for the rest of the session, wanting it to end. I really needed to see how Fiona was doing. I took off as soon as we were through, ate as quickly as I could, and went looking for her.

She told me she'd be in Lombard's trailer, which was parked no more than fifty meters from my hotel. I saw them through the window, sitting with their arms resting on the table, their heads inclined as if they were praying. I must have been the reason for their whispering because I felt a sudden stiffness in their greeting, as if I'd surprised them in the middle of telling a secret they couldn't share. What Lombard said next confirmed it.

"You could have gone after Medel, right? You had energy to spare," he said before I could even say hello.

"Let's not talk about that, not tonight," I protested, more tired than annoyed.

"According to my calculations, you could have reduced Steve's lead to a minute and won today: the first Tour stage win in your life!" Now he sounded indignant.

"You must be dead," said Fiona, coming to my rescue. "I imagine you didn't sleep much last night."

"I *am* dead." I nodded and then paused, wishing I had used any other words. Over the years I'd collected amulets and performed all kinds of rituals to bring me good luck on the road, but to fear using a particular phrase, that was new.

"I'm going to sleep here for a few days—the colonel has granted me asylum—but I'll go back to the hotel with you and make sure you get in bed," she said, getting to her feet.

I said goodbye to Lombard, and Fiona and I stepped out into the fresh night air, or what seemed like it after daytime temperatures as high as 90 degrees. The advantage of finishing a stage on a mountain was that sometimes the team would manage to stay at an empty ski lodge, where higher altitudes meant beautiful, cool weather. I'd put on a hat to avoid being recognized, although anyone who saw me walking like a medical patient shuffling down a hospital hallway would quickly identify me as a professional cyclist.

Fiona began talking. "Stark will drop out tomorrow because he doesn't have the spirit to go on after what happened with Fleming. Cuadrado wants to drop out too, but Movistar won't let him.

They have all kinds of sponsorship deals and only four out of their nine cyclists are left."

Fiona always found ways to get information about the other squads before it became public. Even though each team's mechanics compete against the rival mechanics, they inevitably make up their own interest group. Whatever gossip is circulating among them inevitably reaches Fiona, the queen of the fraternity. She ended her monologue with one even more important secret— Matosas was being threatened by his own team, Lavezza: If he wasn't among the top three finishers, they'd fire him at the end of the season.

Although she told me this without putting any emphasis on it, it struck me as an explosive bit of information. Lavezza had pinned Matosas against the wall; the demand was merely an excuse to fire him: They knew he didn't have a chance to place in Paris. Unless, of course, he got rid of the ten or so racers ahead of him. It was obvious then: Matosas and his circle were responsible for the tragedies on the Tour! Did Fiona realize this?

"Why are you telling me this? You hardly ever share anything about the other teams." It was true that she tried not to take advantage of her position as chief inspector for the whole Tour and give me any leverage over my rivals.

"First, because that information didn't come to me through my position. I'm not violating any kind of confidentiality statute. And second, because I see a unique opportunity for you and, if I may say so, for the good of cycling. You have three solid years left, which means there's still time for the leader in you to emerge. It would be enough if you did better than Matosas and placed in the race. Lavezza would offer to make you their leader next year."

"That is, if Matosas doesn't get rid of me first."

"What do you mean?"

"You don't believe there's a killer on the loose?" I couldn't help it: As soon as I asked, I looked over her shoulder, into the darkness surrounding us. Even though it was a starry night, the moon was dim, and I thought I saw two figures following us.

"I still don't know what's going on, but yes, there's something weird happening," she said, thoughtfully.

"It has to be Matosas. You've just given me the motive, and the facts are in plain view. And now he's second in the standings."

"Don't get ahead of yourself, *Sergeant* Moreau."

"You know about the commissioner?" I asked, alarmed, as we arrived at the entrance to the hotel. Although I was exhausted, I'd picked up the pace to try to lose the two shadows I'd seen, but right then I wasn't sure they were more than trees swaying in the wind, one more result of my spiraling paranoia.

"Let's drop the subject; I feel like even the walls are listening here," she whispered. "Try to rest, you're facing another high mountain tomorrow"—and, smiling, she added—"and another opportunity."

The walls are listening, but not just here, I thought. How did she know the commissioner addressed me like that when he wanted to get a rise out of me? Those conversations with him had always taken place in private. I watched Fiona carefully. There were times I felt like I was sharing my bed with a stranger. She could still take me by surprise with the rare moments when our intimacy broke through her reserves. Whenever I thought I'd finally gotten to know her, she would show a new facet that would tear to shreds the previous image I'd had of her.

But there was no version of Fiona in which I'd imagined she was capable of intrigue behind my back. On the contrary, I thought she was incapable of toning down her opinions to avoid a conflict. In general, she was up-front and direct, merciless but fair. There had to be a reasonable and inoffensive explanation for her comment. It would be easy enough to just ask her how she had found out about my conversations with the commissioner. But I didn't do it.

"Stay, don't leave," I pleaded as soon as we were in my room. I envisioned the dangers that awaited her on the short walk back to Lombard's trailer. But she interpreted my plea as an attempt at seduction and proceeded to undress. Although we tried to avoid sex during the course of exhausting trials like the Tour, we broke our team rule for the second night in a row. I didn't care.

With my face resting on her warm, freckled skin, I slept deeply that night. Before finally nodding off, I went over my two lists: the suspects, now led by Matosas, and the standings. About half the names appeared on both.

GENERAL CLASSIFICATION: STAGE 10

RANK	RIDER	TIME	NOTES
1	**STEVE PANATA (USA/FONAR)**	35:56:09	My bro, ever closer to his fifth jersey.
2	ALESSIO MATOSAS (ITALY/LAVEZZA)	+1:21	Main suspect.
3	MILENKO PANIUK (CZECH/RABONET)	+1:44	Matosas ally.
4	**MARK MOREAU (FRANCE/FONAR)**	+1:47	Fourth place!
5	PABLO MEDEL (SPAIN/BALEARES)	+1:48	Matosas ally.
6	ÓSCAR CUADRADO (COLOMBIA/MOVISTAR)	+2:58	He doesn't have a team.
7	LUIS DURÁN (SPAIN/IMAGINE)	+3:01	Weak.
8	PETER STARK (UK/BATESMAN)	+4:12	Will drop out at any moment.
9	SERGEI TALANCÓN (ROMANIA/ROCCA)	+4:16	No chance.
10	VIKTOR RADEK (POLAND/LOCUS)	+5:26	If he's not the killer, then what a waste of a face.

Stage 11

Pau—Cauterets-Vallée de Saint-Savin, 188 km.

In the middle of the night, I woke with questions. How to unmask Matosas? Was he working alone or was there a larger conspiracy to make him the champion? It was hard to imagine him as a killer. Matosas was a nice guy, always ready with a quick smile or a joke. His sense of humor is the kind that lightens everyone's mood. I remembered countless courtesies on his part out on the road and the more I thought about it, I realized Matosas could not be the criminal we were looking for.

Next, I considered Conti, Matosas's primary domestique, and Ferrara, his chief of mechanics, both tough guys from southern Italy who'd had wild, savage childhoods and who, in other circumstances, wouldn't be hard to imagine in the Neapolitan Mafia or another Mediterranean criminal organization. Maybe Matosas had accepted a plan that involved a few punches and bruises to open the way to victory in Paris and avoid a humiliating firing, but the struggle with Fleming in the tub got out of control. Yes, that all made sense: The killers on the Tour were Matosas and his people. I imagined the surprised expression on the commissioner's face when I told him who was responsible for the tragedies of the past few days. For an instant, I felt the tingling of vindication. I didn't know how difficult it would be to prove the Italian's guilt, but that was up to the cops. I fell back asleep, having thoroughly completed my task.

Fiona left my room as soon as day broke. It was still early and the race wouldn't start until one in the afternoon. If I hurried, I could talk to the commissioner before getting ready for the lap. It was imperative that he put surveillance on the Italian suspects and keep them from committing another crime.

I also wanted to talk to Jitrik, the Tour's patron, to hear his words of gratitude for having contributed to stopping the threat against his venerated institution. I shivered, remembering his invocation of responsibility: to protect the Tour de France at all costs in my capacity as a cyclist and a patriot. But unlike the commissioner, he hadn't offered me a telephone number.

I lingered over all the possible scenes of recognition when my colleagues eventually discovered my role in the case. Few would actually say anything to me although there would be a respectful silence when I walked among them. Or perhaps, for reasons that have to do with police protocol, there would never be a revelation about the details of the investigation. It didn't matter. The Tour organizers and the authorities would know and I'd make sure Fiona knew. That would help lessen the pressure she placed on me. She'd have to see me differently. I may never have won a stage, much less a place on the podium, but we would both know I'd accomplished something much more important.

"It's Matosas or his team, or both," I assured Commissioner Favre forty minutes later. We were meeting in my room shortly after breakfast. The setting didn't match the importance of my revelation. There were suitcases with their guts spilling out, towels strewn about, creams and dozens of containers of nutritional supplements opened throughout the room. We changed hotels every single night, so I never bothered to use dressers or closets; I just dove into my luggage to get what I needed.

"He's one of my suspects," responded a cautious Favre as he looked disapprovingly at the mess in my room.

"He's desperate. I found out his team is going to fire him if he doesn't place in Paris. That would mean an early retirement, losing his sponsorships, and probably the firing of two or three of his closest teammates. Lavezza is one of the few teams that hasn't been a victim of an attack and the casualties suffered by everyone else have made him a contender for the championship. If the race ended today, he'd be guaranteed one of the top three spots."

The commissioner looked at me with interest. He leaned his head back without taking his eyes off me, like a farsighted person trying to read without their glasses on. His forensic gaze made me hesitate. Spoken aloud, the signs around Matosas seemed less convincing.

"Everyone wants to be on the podium," objected Favre.

"A couple of the guys with Matosas have a dark past. In the circuit, we assume they had ties to the Mafia when they were younger; nobody wants to mess with them. It isn't a leap to think they could have gotten help to go through with their plan," I ventured. Suddenly I realized that, in my efforts to sound convincing, I too had started talking like a character in a TV cop show. And the commissioner's response to my big reveal wasn't anywhere near the gratitude I'd imagined. To the contrary, he had started to make me feel like a snitch, and not a particularly reliable one at that.

"He has the motive and the means," the commissioner conceded after a long pause. "I'll verify his teammates' records. Is there anything else?"

"Not at the moment," I responded as if I might be able to unravel another mystery the next day. I decided to shift to a strictly professional tone. "Is there any progress with respect to the investigation of the gas-tank explosion?"

"There's a preliminary report but it's not conclusive," he responded, while his eyes sent me a clear message: *Don't push it.*

"And what does the report say, commissioner?" I insisted. Pushing it.

He sighed. "That it was, in fact, an old tank, but according to the manufacturer, it's impossible for it to detonate without an external factor. It's never happened before. We'll know more when the experts are through analyzing the fragments and we can see whether there's any trace of an outside substance. In the meantime, I'm sticking to my thesis: It was an attack."

We agreed to speak again in twenty-four hours. I then headed for the team meeting. That day would be the second on a high mountain with a terrible ascent, this time to the legendary Tourmalet peak: seventeen sloping kilometers with inclines of 7.3 percent. Before that, we'd have to scale twelve kilometers to the top of Aspin. It was a day for climbers, even more demanding than the day before. If Steve's three rivals decided to join forces again, they could make us eat dirt.

And yet, we had a few things in our favor. The descent from the Tourmalet is almost as legendary as the ascent and much more dangerous. It's thirty kilometers of free-falling at 70 kilometers an hour on precarious paths that are at the edge of a terrifying abyss. But no one in the world can descend as skillfully as Steve. More than one racer has suffered an accident trying to follow him. Even I, who have trained with Steve for thousands of hours, usually lose sight of him on these interminable roller-coaster roads. My partner would be more than capable of compensating for whatever damage he suffered on the ascents.

As soon as we kicked off the stage, we saw our rivals' plan was a version of the day before's. The climb to Aspin broke the peloton. Matosas, Paniuk, and Medel burned their domestiques in their eagerness to tire out the other cyclists and, particularly, our team, Fonar. The pace was infernal from the beginning. By the time we got to the foot of the Tourmalet there were only a dozen of us.

From that moment, we all stabilized our speed and there weren't any stragglers for a good while.

At first, I thought the lack of assaults had to do with prudence or some kind of strategy, but later I realized it was all about fatigue. The attacks the day before had taken their toll, especially on Matosas and Medel. We were going up so slowly that I could take a leisurely look at the faces of the Italian and Conti, his somber domestique. They seemed to ooze guilt. I was staring at Conti so intensely that the baby-faced killer finally looked over and arched his eyebrows as if he were asking me what I needed. I thought about Fleming in the tub and couldn't help but shudder.

Our rivals' exhaustion was confirmed when we were five kilometers from the top of the Tourmalet and they finally began their attack. They didn't have the strength they'd had the day before. They'd stand up on their pedals to take off and sit down ten meters later. Still, the battering managed to get rid of four more racers.

As we climbed a little higher, Steve decided he had nothing to fear and, just two kilometers from the summit, asked me to go ahead if I had the strength for it.

"I'll catch up with you on the down side and we'll get away from all these guys," he said. His proposal went against Giraud's instructions, because it left him exposed and without my help if there was an assault from one of the other climbers on the last stretch of the mountain. And yet, he was right: The fatigue they were experiencing seemed to rule out the possibility of a threat. The pace of the ascent was painful and our adversaries were having a much worse time of it than us. And that's all you need. Up on the high mountains, realizing your rivals are worse off than you will give you a shot of adrenaline.

I confirmed it the instant I broke out. I positioned myself behind Medel and Paniuk, who were leading, and waited until we were on a curve, then changed gears and leaped ahead. The two rivals noticed Steve was not breaking away with me, so they let me go. Even though at that moment I was in fourth place, and breaking away meant I could pass them in the rankings, no team leader ever fears a domestique. Neither one of them was there to win the stage; they were there to destroy Steve. I wasn't who they were worried about.

It was a monumental mistake on their part, if understandable. It had been many years since I'd made a solitary attack, so they didn't have much to go on to guess what I was doing. They knew I was a natural climber whose job until now had always been to protect my squad leader. I always took the mountain at Steve's pace so that he could ride in my slipstream. Now, liberated, I accelerated on inclines of eight to nine percent, my heart filled with joy. When I got to the peak, the chalkboard on the motorcycle in front of me reported I'd advanced about three minutes over my pursuers. Maybe Fiona was right.

When I started the descent I didn't wait for Steve. I was the leader in the general standings of the Tour de France, an intoxicating sensation, even if it was just temporary. I came down at a suicidal speed, determined to widen the distance no matter the cost. A couple of times the front wheel touched the gravel at the edge of the road, just centimeters from the precipice. I knew there were still six kilometers to the finish line once the descent was over, the last few with a slight slope, and that my desperate pursuers would work together to diminish the lead I had over them.

I don't know how Steve did it, but when I got to the plain that leads to that last slope on the way to the finish line in Cauterets, my teammate had caught up with me. If my breakaway had been meritorious, the distance Steve created between him and our rivals on the descent was a real feat. Maybe Fiona wasn't right, after all.

We climbed the last few kilometers together, taking turns. Two thousand meters before the finish line, Steve took the lead. He pushed like he was trying to leave me behind. I assumed he wanted to take home the victory laurels and get those bonus 10 seconds for winning first place. I stuck to his wheel, grumbling bitterly about the thankless task of the domestique. I could have passed Steve if I wanted to in those last inclines on the final sprint. And yet, resigned once more, I understood that was not my role.

I asked myself if giving in to Steve yet again meant I could be losing Fiona. I'd never felt good enough to be her partner. Her insistence on making me the best cyclist in the circuit made me wonder if her love wasn't rooted in that conviction. For someone like Fiona, whose life revolves around the bike, talent is reason enough to respect, admire, and, lastly, love somebody. But what would happen if I stayed in second place forever? Would she disappear from my life as swiftly as she'd come into it?

I was so absorbed in my gloomy thoughts, Steve had to wave his arm. That's when I realized, just a hundred meters before the finish line, that he'd backed off.

"All yours, champ," he said with a playful look.

I didn't respond. I launched myself at the finish line and crossed it with my arms in the air to take my first ever stage win on the Tour. During those last meters, the fans—it seemed like thousands of them—were waving French flags along the way. That's when I remembered it was Bastille Day: July 14th, France's national holiday. For the next forty minutes, I floated on a cloud between the awarding of prizes, kisses from the assistants, microphones pressing into my face, frenzied interviews, and the inevitable anti-doping tests.

When I got to the bus, I found a euphoric Giraud. Fonar was in first and second place in the general classification. That's not an achievement that's seen very often. After the awards ceremony, he spent a long time next to the car, performing for the press. Later, on the way to the hotel, I saw him go up to Steve and whisper a few words. I knew him well enough to understand from his expressions that he was annoyed. A few minutes later, I found out why.

"He didn't like it one bit that I let you finish first," Steve told

me once we were alone after dinner. "Something about the sponsors and who knows what. But don't pay him any mind. It was
incredible to see you win that stage."

I wanted to say that if he'd let me go first it was because I had
previously relinquished the lead, but instead, I thanked him.

"Who would've thought, ten years ago, when we were stum-
bling around drunk in the bars in Catalonia . . ." he said, trying to
play down my gratitude. "If we take care of you, we can both
place in Paris."

*If I take care of you, you'll be able to climb the podium in
Paris!* I thought. But those enthralling words from my partner still
moved me. His joy over my success seemed genuine. I remembered the Jaguar coupé he drove up to my house three weeks after
he'd won his second Tour. He showed off the engine and the
leather and then forced me to sit in the passenger seat as he went
on and on about the elegant dashboard. Finally, he stretched out
his arm and handed me the keys, which hung on a green ribbon
with a bow. He was exultant, more excited at giving me the gift
than I was to receive it.

"Do you think Giraud will let me live long enough to get to
Paris?" I asked, intoxicated by his optimism. I wasn't naïve. If any
of our rivals put Steve's leadership at risk, the Fonar DS would
make me defend my leader, even if the effort screwed up my final
stretch on a hill. If that happened, I could lose ten or fifteen minutes and disappear at the bottom of the rankings.

"Matosas and Medel look tired," said Steve cautiously. It was
also clear he wasn't going to take any risks in his pursuit of a fifth
Tour crown.

I would have expected a different attitude from him, a call to
not surrender, to rebel against Giraud's designs. A promise to triumph together, shoulder-to-shoulder, with no thought to the consequences. Instead, I got his condescending generosity.

Steve sensed my letdown: Without saying a word, he hugged
me. His reaction disarmed me. I fell back to thinking I was being

unfair, that Lombard and Fiona's pretensions had distorted my perception of the natural order of things. A domestique is in service to his leader. That was the logic on which the Tour functioned: 198 racers making sure no more than ten fought for the yellow jersey. The Fonar team had been recruited and organized to make Steve champion, and he himself was a prisoner of that design.

We said goodbye without too much ceremony. I tried to throw off the sadness that shadowed me to my room. Today, I'd finally won a stage on the Tour. It should be the happiest day of my life as a cyclist, but I felt miserable. A domestique should not taste victory, for the same reason a boy in a refugee camp should not taste chocolate cake.

Not even Fiona could shake me out of it. She'd sent me a text: "Join us in Lombard's trailer, we're celebrating your win." I replied: "Very tired, tomorrow." I was exhausted, and I didn't want to see anyone. Least of all Fiona; the last thing I wanted to hear about was more chocolate cake.

Unlike Fiona, the commissioner proved indifferent to my wishes. He was waiting at the door to my room. Two stamped-out cigarette butts on the floor indicated that the environment and his health were not top priorities; neither was my rest. He followed me in, ignoring my lack of invitation.

"Any news, sergeant?" he asked distractedly as he scanned the room's usual disorder.

"None," I responded, irritated by the intrusion. I threw myself on the bed, resigned to his presence.

"What do you mean none? You're in second place in the rankings. Anyone would say the killer is trying to aid the Fonar team," he said sarcastically, as if he were making a joke. He attempted a kind of smile, a rictus that made me think of a barracuda. He was looking at me, waiting for any reaction to what he'd just said.

"Don't tell me I'm a suspect now," I said in the same sarcastic tone, as if I were joking right along. I didn't take my eyes off him either, also waiting for a response.

"We can't exclude anybody. As far as I'm concerned, there are one hundred and ninety-eight suspects along with their teams of assistants. You yourself told me: Each of the racers has his own agenda and is willing to die for it, right?" He threw that in my face with his infuriating half-smile. I imagined he must have been waiting for his chance to get me back for several days now.

"What about the part where I am your man in the peloton?"

"Well, let's leave it at one hundred and ninety-seven suspects," conceded Favre, "although certainly some are more suspicious than others."

"Did you check out Matosas's crew? Their ties to the Mafia?"

"Mmm, nothing conclusive," he said, leaning his head back while making a disdainful expression with his mouth. He'd used the same phrase when referring to the gas tank. I imagined even if there was something conclusive, Favre wouldn't tell me.

"What about Giraud?" Favre continued. "How desperate is he? Apparently, Steve's U.S. sponsors would feel more comfortable with an American DS for Fonar. They're already throwing around several names for next season. Giraud's in the same boat as Matosas: Only a win in Paris will save him. Or, at least, that's what he thinks."

I wasn't sure if Favre's information was right. I hadn't heard anything about it. Giraud *had* been nervous and irritated the past few days. Although the same thing could be said about him during any of the major races run under his supervision. I would have liked to tell the commissioner my DS was a real son of a bitch and that I considered him capable of anything in order to avoid failure. What kept my mouth shut was just a smidgen of loyalty toward Fonar and, by extension, Steve. To accept that our place in the rankings was a result of criminal machinations was a betrayal of the entire team's effort. And if Giraud had anything to do with the assaults, Steve and I, the two beneficiaries of his actions, would have to prove our innocence.

I wondered what the real reason was for the commissioner's visit. If I was a suspect, his intrusion could practically be considered forced entry. What he did next seemed to confirm it. He walked up to the nightstand and picked up one of the open bottles of supplements. He read the information on the back and sniffed the contents, as if he might find some evidence on my dresser.

"I wonder if I've already gotten to an age when I should start taking supplements," he said thoughtfully. "What were you saying about Giraud?" He turned back to me.

I hadn't said anything about Giraud, though my mind was buzzing. Favre's behavior was starting to make me nervous. I remembered the relief I felt during his first visit when I realized he wasn't with the anti-doping authorities; today I would have preferred he had been.

"Giraud has always been the same. Demanding and disciplined. I don't see anything different in him. Of course, given the plague of accidents and tragedies, he's worried about Steve. He already knows Tour management called the police. It makes perfect sense he'd be worried his racers could be the killer's victims."

"Worried? In what sense, worried?" A bloodhound, Favre didn't hide his excitement. His nostrils flared. He could turn the most slender piece of information into a bone to gnaw on.

"Simply in the sense of asking us to take precautions, to avoid unnecessary risks." Giraud hadn't said any such thing to me, but I imagined he'd said something very much like it to Steve, and just then, I was willing to make up almost anything to free myself of this police presence. I almost mentioned Matosas again, although I contained myself. Favre could have interpreted my insistence as an attempt to distract him from Fonar by incriminating someone else.

"I need you to concentrate your attention on Giraud in the next few days. He's our main suspect," Favre said, finally heading for the door, in his best imitation of an affable comrade. "Well, and Matosas too, but I'll deal with him. Your position within Fonar is of incalculable value right now, better not to distract you with something else."

The instructions did nothing to better my opinion of the commissioner. I had gone from being *his man in the peloton* to *his man inside Fonar*. The bastard was asking me to spy on my own team. Then he surprised me again. When he reached the hall, he half turned and put a hand on my shoulder.

"And congratulations on your second place in the rankings; I feel very proud," he said. "It's been more than thirty years since a Frenchman won the Tour," he added before quickly disappearing.

So a police officer, an ex–military man, and the chief inspector of mechanics—Favre, Lombard, and Fiona—all held out hope that I'd win the Tour, although I supposed each had their own reasons. I wondered if the killer also wanted me to win. And, if that was the case, was this psychopath sick with patriotism?

That night I tried to get some sleep while turning over the idea that I was less than a minute and a half away from the yellow jersey. A heretofore unknown sensation: excitement, in spite of the unease I'd experienced in the past few hours. I wondered if Fiona was as proud as the commissioner. Although the real question was if she would continue being proud once I disappeared from the top rankings. Sooner or later, Giraud, in his determination to take care of Steve, would make sure that was the case. And even if I managed to subvert his strategies, there was still the risk of falling victim to the killer on the loose. A fanatical French patriot? Matosas, a desperate Italian? Giraud, a ruthless narcissist?

The possibility that my own DS could be a threat ended up scaring away sleep. If I didn't manage to get some rest before confronting the rough climb that waited for me the following day, I wouldn't need a killer or a hostile strategy: Fatigue would do me in all by itself. Little by little, I managed to relax thanks to the sweet mantra I used every night.

GENERAL CLASSIFICATION: STAGE 11

RANK	RIDER	TIME	NOTES
1	STEVE PANATA (USA/FONAR)	41:03:31	Good and getting better.
2	MARC MOREAU (FRANCE/FONAR)	+1:43	Steve and I in first and second place. A dream.
3	ALESSIO MATOSAS (ITALY/LAVEZZA)	+3:37	We hit the bastard back.
4	MILENKO PANIUK (CZECH/RABONET)	+3:56	He failed in the conspiracy with the other three.
5	PABLO MEDEL (SPAIN/BALEARES)	+3:59	I don't understand Medel's betrayal, he was a friend.
6	ÓSCAR CUADRADO (COLOMBIA/MOVISTAR)	+6:02	
7	LUIS DURÁN (SPAIN/IMAGINE)	+6:41	
8	SERGEI TALANCÓN (ROMANIA/ROCCA)	+7:56	
9	VIKTOR RADEK (POLAND/LOCUS)	+8:21	
10	ROL CHARPENELLE (FRANCE/TOURGAZ)	+8:42	

2010

When I tell Fiona that Steve is my brother, she thinks it's just an expression; she doesn't understand that, in many ways, Steve *is* my brother. For years after I left Colombia, I barely heard from my mother Beatriz. In the first months of my military service, I sent her long letters in which I described the landscapes in Occitania and life in the barracks. I wanted to tell her I missed her, but I didn't know how. We were never close or affectionate, but amid all that hostile soldierly noise in which I was "the Colombian" in spite of my last name and my accentless French, my memories of Beatriz's brusque care transformed into a devoted expression of maternal love.

I didn't give up in spite of the silence that followed my letters, and the next Christmas, fourteen months after I'd left, I called home. She responded in a joyful and melodious voice that went mute the minute she realized it was me. The few monosyllables with which she responded to my awkward questions weren't angry or rancorous but, rather, bewildered, the result of surprise and discomfort. Maybe she was concerned I was calling to tell her I was coming back to Medellín. After a few minutes she said something about a pot on the stove and passed the phone to her husband. We dragged out a conversation that neither one of us was interested in and hung up quickly after wishing each other a Merry Christmas. At least his bad breath was inoffensive from eight thousand kilometers away.

In the days that followed, I tried to accept that—as far as her affection was concerned—I was dead to my mother. Although, to be honest, it wasn't entirely clear that I'd ever really been alive to her or that I'd ever been anything other than an obligation. She had me when she was seventeen years old with a forty-two-year-old man whom she initially found impressive but whom she ended up detesting just months later. It took them eight more years to separate, although toward the end they rarely saw each other because my father had been assigned to the embassy in neighboring Venezuela. I imagine my blue eyes and rosy cheeks reminded her of the man she loathed. She was all about gardens and flowers, music and parties; Colonel Moreau was jealous, controlled and controlling. It was a combination that made their time together unsustainable, and I became the proof that some bad decisions are irreversible.

In spite of this disappointment, I refused to give up. I refused to accept that the hoodlums from Lyon and Marseille whom I had to share my barracks with were more loved than I was. They had whole clans show up for calls and visits, and received boxes with cigarettes, nougats, or hard rolls baked by a fond great-grandmother. So I simply told myself my mother was forcing herself to reject me in order to have a chance at building a new life with the doctor and his two young daughters.

As I had done years earlier when my teacher left for Bogotá, I fooled myself into thinking the bike would be the way to bring back my mother. I would become a world champion, rich and famous, and one day I'd go to Medellín, pick her up in a chauffeured limousine, and take her to see the house I'd just bought her. That's when she'd realize how wrong she'd been to deny the calling of her heart.

But as the months went by, Lombard and the bike became my life, and not just the instrument with which I dreamed of recovering my mother. I embraced my French surroundings and ended up accepting that I might have been nothing more than some sort of divine punishment for Beatriz Restrepo. She did what she had to do to bury the memory of me once and for all. I tried to do the same.

Steve changed all that. When we decided to move together to Lake De Como, we shared a place the first year. My friend's parents were constant visitors and they soon adopted the grateful and cautious boy who had become their son's best friend. His mother, Diana, thought my measured temperament was a good influence on her son's rash impulses and optimistic naïveté.

On one occasion, Steve's father flew to Bogotá on business and the couple decided to extend their trip and turn it into a vacation through various South American countries. In part out of gratitude and in part out of curiosity, they built in a visit to Medellín where they'd meet my mother. I'd barely talked about her, and when I did, it was in the vaguest terms. Their inquisitive natures were piqued.

Beatriz must have felt honored to receive a visit from such fine people. They took her to eat at the restaurant in the famous hotel where they were staying, and they spoke glowingly about the son she had in France. When the meal was over, Mrs. Panata gave her an exquisite gold bracelet from a fashion designer in Santa Fe. It was probably a mix of pride and obligation that made her write the brief missive we received a few days later:

Steve and Marc,
How wonderful to know everything is going well. It must be very beautiful over there. Congratulations. Make your parents proud.
Beatriz Restrepo

Steve considered it a triumph, though to me, it was an affront more offensive than her silence. It was not a letter from a mother to her child; it seemed to me that it was really addressed to Steve and was fully motivated by her desire to not appear ill-mannered to his parents.

My friend got in the habit of sending my mother a postcard whenever he wrote to anyone in the United States, as if our coupling on the bike extended into our personal lives and that, when it came to the division of labor, he was responsible for dealing with relatives.

Not used to these attentions, Beatriz would respond with short notes addressed to Steve, greetings and thank-yous written in a very formal style with her round, schoolgirl scripts. My friend would show them to me; I'd nod my thanks and then try to forget them. Deep down, I knew nothing between my mother and me had changed; these correspondences weren't about me.

A few years later, we were living next to each other in the same neighborhood in Lake De Como. Steve came over to happily tell me that my mother was coming for Christmas. He was convinced he could bring parent and child into a reconciliatory embrace with a storybook ending. I later learned he'd spent months battling her objections and that he'd only managed to convince her after he sent her a first-class ticket to travel from Medellín to Milan. When I heard that, I knew he hadn't really convinced her of anything. For my mother, it would be bad manners to reject such a generous gift.

In the following days, Steve enthusiastically brainstormed things to do with Beatriz during her visit. The heated restaurant with the incredible views, the tea boutique, the best souvenir shop, the sophisticated chocolatier, the cashmere coat and scarf with which we would welcome her. I resignedly and nervously agreed to everything, knowing this could turn into a terrible ordeal for her and a cruel reminder for me of all the reasons we'd given up on our relationship.

But my mother took care of it in her own way. One day before she was to get on the plane, a neighbor sent a telegram letting us know Beatriz was in the hospital dealing with her sciatic nerve, which had been bothering her for months and had ended up immobilizing her. The telegram was addressed to Steve. Her lack of love turned out to be stronger than any desire for courtesy.

Steve was disillusioned but not defeated. He sent a bouquet of flowers to the hospital and kept up the postcards for several years, although he never again tried to bring us together. I received the news as a great relief. The experience made it clear to me I didn't have a mother and that, in the strictest sense, I'd never had one. But it also showed me I had a brother in Steve. That's something neither Fiona nor Lombard would ever understand.

Stage 12

Lannemezan—Plateau de Beille, 195 km.

I woke up, got out of bed, and opened the window in my room. The fresh morning breeze seemed like a good sign considering what was waiting for us that day. Seven hours of sleep had managed to pacify my demons. But the next half hour with my teammates sent them packing.

Generally speaking, breakfast with the team isn't the most lively activity of the day. A cockroach in a cloud of fumigation has more energy than the dazed and uncombed zombies that came down to the dining room a little after eight each morning. But today the Fonar table was downright merry: The four minutes Steve had over Matosas, who was in third place, had turned the Tour in our favor. We not only had the yellow jersey within our grasp, but we were leading the race as a team. Fonar was sweeping the scoreboard and the record books, and the team members' pockets would all benefit.

Steve was at the head of the table, following an unwritten protocol that assigned seats according to a hierarchy. I sat on his right, like I did every morning, no matter what hotel we were staying at. Several of my teammates patted my back, and members of the French team AG2R, who were staying at the same hotel, congratulated me from across the room. In the past twelve years, no Frenchman had won on Bastille Day, a real national humiliation.

Steve was happy for the team, for me, and for himself. His smile and his enthusiasm radiated over the table. When Steve's on, no one can be indifferent to my friend's emotions, least of all me. Everything was good now. He'd practically won the Tour, I'd won a stage, and, at least for a few hours, I was the second best in the whole peloton. Not even in our greatest fantasies in that training camp back in Catalonia could we have imagined a triumph like we were about to achieve.

I later realized Steve's euphoria was a little strident, a little anxious. More than happy, he seemed relieved. His exaggerated gestures seemed to belong to someone who's had a great weight taken off him. Maybe Fiona was right: Deep down he regretted the opportunities I'd lost by condemning me to be his shadow. But if we both managed to climb the podium in Paris, I too would become a part of cycling history and any grievance would be forgotten.

Before we went our own ways, he hugged me. "No matter what Giraud says, make us both win," he whispered in my ear before we returned to our rooms.

That day the starting line was just a few steps from our hotel, which let us rest for some precious extra hours. As I lay on my bed, eyes half-closed, Fiona knocked and edged into my room. I hadn't been able to see her the night before, because the UCI had organized a long meeting of inspectors that forced her to stay in another hotel in a nearby small town.

I thought she'd come to congratulate me. She looked beautiful. My body imagined various ways I might be rewarded. But Fiona limited herself to a quick hug and a fleeting kiss. She hadn't come for that. She pulled from her back pocket a folded piece of paper, which I imagined to be warm and slightly curved. My excitement refused to die down; when it came to Fiona, I was always an optimist. What she unfolded was a route plan.

"It's fine if nothing much happens among the leaders today, Mojito. Just make sure Matosas doesn't cut your time. If you make any move today, you're going to tip off Giraud, and you still have a lot of stages to go. It would be better if you left everything for the last two days before Paris."

Fiona's strategy was correct—that is, if I wanted to betray Fonar. Today was the last lap in the Pyrenees; next we'd have four straight stages of hills and valleys in which we should have no trouble controlling our rivals. The Tour would conclude with four extremely difficult days on the high mountains of the Alps, and those would be decisive.

"We're ready. We have better climbers than they do, don't worry; we'll be able to neutralize any attack," I said carefully, without mentioning Steve. "I promise you I'll still be in second place tonight," I said, giving her a kiss goodbye. I didn't know then that the killer would disrupt my promise just a few hours later.

At noon, we went to the team bus to get Giraud's instructions for the stage that awaited us. It was then I realized the uproar my win had provoked. There are roughly a thousand accredited journalists who cover the Tour de France, but today it seemed like two thousand squeezed around the pavilion for the signature ceremony before the start of the day's lap. They all wanted an exclusive statement or photo from me. In theory, reporters wait until the end of the race to ask the cyclists questions. They're supposed to respect the time before takeoff, when the racers are trying to relax their muscles and concentrate on the effort before them. But today, the press was shameless about ignoring protocol.

"It's been thirty-two years since a French citizen won the Tour," said Axel Simmon when I finally got to the bus and he showed me the headlines he'd been reading: *"France Comes Alive on the*

Tourmalet" gushed *L'Équipe.* Axel was the soigneur assigned to me, and one of my few compatriots on Fonar, even though the team was formally organized as a French organization. The soigneurs on the Tour have an unusual job. They're primarily massage therapists, but they don't work until the end of the stage, so before then they do a little bit of everything: They carry the racers' luggage to the next hotel, supply provisions for the competitors during and after each stage, and support the cars on the road. Axel continued: "You're the new celebrity. Even I got some of the rebound: French TV just interviewed me. They wanted to know all about you."

"What did you tell them?"

"That you'd won thanks to the massage. That since it was July 14th, I'd given you a special treatment," Axel joked. Though he looked like a gargoyle from Notre Dame, he was a good guy and an even better masseur. In fact, that was the reason we'd ended up together: The rest of my teammates found all sorts of reasons to avoid him, as if his ugliness was a contagious disease that could be transmitted through his hands. But I, on the other hand, had no problem recognizing another unloved soul.

"I hope you didn't tell them the massage has a happy ending."

"Don't worry, your secrets are safe with me. I didn't want to spoil their party; they were talking about you as if you were the reincarnation of Anquetil."

I thought about the legendary *enfant roi* Jacques Anquetil, as famous for his womanizing as for winning the Tour five times. My exploits in both areas were ridiculously lacking in comparison.

"You should have told them Steve is our leader and I'm a domestique," I said abruptly. I didn't want to continue the joke. "The minute and a half he has over me is a decisive distance, but even if it was only two seconds, it would be enough. There's no need to feed that kind of stupidity." Now in a bad mood, I climbed onto the bus to protect myself from the reporters in the few minutes before the start of the next stage. I felt bad for bringing down poor Axel: He only wanted to have a good time, but everything was starting to seem like a bad joke to me.

I wasn't going to betray Steve, no matter how much Fiona, Lombard, or the French press wanted me to. In fact, even coming in second place had started to seem like an outlandish possibility. We could probably contain our rivals' assaults today, but it would be too much to ask that we do it for the four days on the Alps. Especially if Matosas, Medel, and Paniuk joined their teams and worked together again. If that was the case, I'd have to do everything to protect Steve's yellow jersey, and that would mean finishing not in second place but in twentieth.

The bus turned out to be an oasis in the middle of the media tumult. The rest of my teammates were already rolling around on their bicycles and loosening their muscles in the parking lot, and their mechanics and assistants were readying the spare bikes that would be loaded into the three cars that follow us along the route. I thought about the 195 kilometers that lay before us and a part of me wanted to just say "screw it," to drop back fifteen or twenty minutes behind the leader and put an end to the absurd hope the press was stirring. The more they got people worked up, the more disappointing the final collapse would be. And I knew enough about this business to understand that the very same journalists and fans now praising my name would end up punishing me for the disillusionment they'd suffer.

Still, I couldn't resist taking a look at the copy of *Libération* that lay on Giraud's seat: a headline in big red letters. *"L'espoir"*— "Hope"—was branded across the page, on top of an image of me from the day before, arms raised as I crossed the finish line. About a dozen other newspapers lay at the feet of the DS's chair. I took another look at the front page of *Libération* and understood why Giraud had set that one aside. Under my photo there was another, smaller image of Lombard with a pull quote: "He's better than Steve." The article could not start in a worse way: "Colonel Lombard, Marc Moreau's personal trainer, is confident that, pound for pound, the French racer is a better cyclist than his team leader, the North American, Steve Panata. 'If Hannibal decides to, he could win the Tour.'"

I felt the world darken. Giraud would assume I was behind Lombard's public challenge. I now understood why the reporters had been so ravenous minutes before. My old mentor's statement had been interpreted as my declaration of war. I couldn't even blame it on a sloppy or ill-intentioned journalist, because the article was bylined by none other than Ray Lumiere, the most famous cycling reporter with the greatest credibility in the French press.

It was only now that I noticed the distance my teammates had kept from me in the last hours. The members of the Fonar team must have taken Lombard's comments as an act of disloyalty from me. And for Steve, they must have been like a stab in the back.

Fiona's hurried visit to my room now made a little more sense. She assumed Lombard spoke for me, and that meant I'd be making my first assault on Steve today. She had come to ask me to be careful and to wait until we got to the decisive laps. Apparently, I was not only a traitor, but my girlfriend considered me an imbecile too.

The call to the starting line interrupted my worries. One quick glance at the peloton was all I needed to know I was the target of the day. To my surprise, most of my colleagues from other teams were giving me friendly looks. For a lot of domestiques, the possibility that one of them could win the Tour represented a vindication against the monopoly the leaders had over each team. None of them actually thought I had a chance to climb the podium in Paris, but Lombard's statement probably struck them as stimulating and irreverent, an anomaly amid the rigid codes imposed on each team by its DS.

In fact, even our rivals were looking at me kindly. They weren't going to let me break away again now that they considered me an

aspirant to the yellow jersey, but they were delighted by the possibility of discord inside the Fonar team. Anything that could
deter Steve Panata was considered good news. An uprising by his
primary domestique was pure gold.

But the attitude among my Fonar teammates was the exact opposite. Their silence made it obvious they considered me a threat
to the team goals: that is, their bonuses. Certainly, more than one
of them was sympathetic to my cause, but today, I could blow a
hole in their pockets. With gritted teeth, they let me take my place
in the peloton.

I stared at the power meter screen as if I were seeing it for the
first time; an observer would've thought I was watching a movie
on that tiny gadget. Anything to avoid looking at Steve's face. A
slap on the back brought me out of my trance.

"You're my hero, Moreau. You're breaking everybody's balls,"
said a festive Radek. "If you need help on the mountain, count on
me because these cowards aren't going to do it." He amused himself by looking over at my teammates with disdain. If there'd ever
been a possibility to rebuild bridges with Fonar, this Polish scarecrow had just set them on fire. With his tiresome litany against the
Tour, Radek had become a pariah, a bird of ill omen from which
everyone fled. Well, maybe now he wasn't alone.

I felt better once the race started and the peloton began to
move. Everything's better when you're pedaling. As if my legs
were pumping oxygen to my brain, I tried to come up with strategies to show my team I was still one of them, that everything had
been just one huge misunderstanding. That evening, I would explain everything over dinner; that's where we talked about things
that mattered. But the most important thing was to show them
during the race. That's when it really counted.

There was no doubt the team would need me. The last stage on
the Pyrenees was the worst of all: two ascents of the worst order
and then, that brutal climb to the Plateau de Beille. According to
legend, the way the summits are classified comes from the way the

classic Citroen 2CV's clutch could climb the mountain. A category four summit, the easiest, was named because the old car could climb it in fourth gear, and so on, successively, until the toughest, those in category one, which could only be climbed in first gear. Those that were *hors categorie*—uncategorizable—required turning off the engine and using an ox to haul up the rattletrap. In this metaphor, I was the beast of labor that allowed Steve to conquer the peaks.

That's probably what saved me, at least for the moment, from Giraud's revenge. On a day like today, the other two climbers on the team wouldn't have been enough. We took it for granted that Matosas's, Medel's, and Paniuk's teams would repeat their punishing rhythm during the first two parts of the race to try to burn us out. Together they had about seven or eight decent climbers, and they didn't care about tiring out most of them if they succeeded in separating Steve and me on the final stretch. Alone, my leader would be easy prey for that trio of wolves.

So Giraud needed me. That's why he'd left that copy of *Libération* folded in his seat instead of throwing it in my face at the start of the stage. But the next day, when we would take off on the first of four relatively flat days, things would be different. He'd likely condemn me to the thankless task of passing out water, bars, and gels to the rest of the Fonar racers; at eight to ten bottles per cyclist, that would be a half-dozen visits to the supply car. The problem, of course, was not having to slow down to catch up to the car but rather getting back to where my teammates would be riding. It was usually a task performed by three or four racers, but Giraud could easily leave it just to me. A couple of days of this and the DS would have effectively drained me. After that, I'd be lucky if I managed to avoid being eliminated when they cut the slowest racers.

The race transpired as predicted. The three rival teams climbed the first two ascents as if there were no tomorrow. They lost most of their domestiques but got what they were looking for. At the foot of the last ascent it was just Steve and me from Fonar, six members from the rival teams, including three leaders, and four climbers from the other teams, none of them aspirants to the podium. To my surprise, one of them was Radek, who every now and again would bring his bike up next to mine, smile, and give me a thumbs-up. I would pretend I didn't know what was going on so I wouldn't inadvertently become an accomplice to any insanity the rabid Pole might be cooking up.

Whatever Steve might have been thinking about me, he put it aside for now. He attached himself to my wheel and together we did what we know how to do best on the mountain: resist. Our competition tried to get rid of us with every trick in the book: They exposed us to the wind by taking control of the curb. They pretended to break away while climbers protected the three leaders, no matter what team they were on. They even used a strategy that in any other sport would be considered the equivalent of spitting or biting: Over and over they tried to force a domestique between my wheel and that of the three rivals I was locked behind. If they'd succeeded they would have been able to block us so that the three leaders could get away without us being able to pursue. I defended my place with the desperation of a starving man in a ration line.

I'd positioned myself on Medel's wheel. He seemed to be in the best shape and most likely to attempt a solo escape. If the Spaniard got away, I'd have to make a risky decision. To follow him in a breakaway would mean abandoning the group with which we'd climbed relatively protected, albeit under attack. To bet on Medel would be successful if the three of us managed to crown the peak—I took it for granted Steve would stay on my wheel. But if one of us collapsed, the larger group would catch up and leave us behind because they'd been saving energy by staying together. The wrong decision could cost us the Tour.

But not making a decision could have the same effect. If we

didn't follow him, Medel or whoever of the three took off, there was still the possibility the group would slow the pace to let him get away. If I made the wrong decision, my DS would think it was an intentional error on my part to cause Steve's defeat. I realized my entire professional career depended on the decision I was going to make in the next few minutes. But, like on so many occasions all along this Tour, the killer decided for us.

As Paniuk, Matosas, and Medel faked a breakaway just to keep us on edge, Steve suffered a puncture. We all heard his cry, even though he immediately fell back. The other three pushed forward as if they'd just been whipped—nothing is more stimulating than realizing the leader has dropped out.

Steve pulled up to the curb and examined his bike. I rode up close and understood that the gods had given me a golden opportunity to redeem myself. Without hesitation, I leaped off my Pinarello and offered it to my teammate. It would be the end of my aspirations to the podium but also the end of any doubts about my loyalty. That a domestique would offer his steed to his leader is expected; but somebody in second place doing that to benefit the number one is unheard of.

Steve and I could hear Giraud screaming in our earphones, urging his golden boy to get back in the race as Steve took off on my bike. From the moment we paused, the stopwatch in my head had started counting: The escapees had already gotten 46 seconds on Steve. That distance would surely grow thanks to the teamwork they could wield against a solitary pursuer. Fonar's only comfort was that Steve had two flat stretches before him in which he could reduce the distance lost.

I assumed Giraud's car would come up at any moment carrying the spare bikes. With some luck, I'd be able to catch up with the leader and help mitigate the danger. Sure enough, I saw our blue-and-red vehicle coming around a curve, an enormous elk with a pair of beautiful antlers—our bikes. But that son of a bitch didn't slow down one bit. In fact, he sped up when he saw me, and I swear he would have hit me if I hadn't taken a step back. I lost sight of the car amid the pines. I couldn't believe it.

I heard our DS through the earphones: "Steve needs his spare bike, Marc, yours isn't the right height. Wait for the second car, they'll be coming soon." I could almost hear the taunting in his voice. Nobody would accuse him of acting deliberately against me. Giraud could say it was more urgent for him to get Steve the right bike than to stop for me.

Giraud had managed to get his revenge. The second car was about ten minutes back, according to the last report. For all practical purposes, my hopes of reaching the podium in Paris died right there. That night my name would not be in the top ten I'd recite before going to sleep.

The stopwatch in my head was still going. 1:25 . . . 1:26 . . . 1:27 . . . Technically, I was still in second place because my time had been 1:54, better than Matosas at the beginning of the day. But in a matter of seconds I would be displaced in the general classifications by each racer who had passed me.

I had just decided to sit down when Radek pulled up out of nowhere, pedaling in a furious state, alone, wasted and faint, although as resentful as ever. I remembered we'd left him behind one or two kilometers back. He stopped by my side, glanced at Steve's bike, and immediately understood what had happened. He scolded me without a word and then said something I didn't quite know how to interpret.

"I'm going to give you a second chance; don't blow it," he huffed and did something unfathomable. He got off his bike and offered it to me. It took me two seconds to react. 1:48 . . . 1:49 . . . I wasn't even sure what kind of penalty there was for accepting a bike from a member of a rival team. In that moment, I just wanted to stop the clock running in my head. 1:52 . . . 1:53. I got on his bike and climbed wildly, as if with each pedal I were crushing Giraud's face, my father's, that of the narcos who had assassinated

Carmen. I stood on the pedals and didn't sit until I made out our team's blue-and-red car just ahead.

I was surprised I'd caught up so quickly, but I immediately understood why. Giraud and two of the mechanics were next to the car, looking down. I got a cold chill up my spine. When I reached them, I saw my bike against a tree with the tube popped out of the tire. Then I saw Steve, trying to stand up at the bottom of a ditch three or four meters deep. He had scratches on his face and his yellow jersey was ripped. He moved one leg and then, very carefully, the other, as if he were afraid one of them wouldn't respond. His paleness contrasted with the deep green of the forest surrounding him.

Without thinking, I slid down to where he was. I later discovered a bad cut on my butt cheek. 3:49 . . . 3:50 . . .

"Are you all right? Can you move your arms? Your shoulders?" I asked as I checked him out like a frantic mother.

"The tube popped off your bike, and I hit the tree. These helmets are really great, aren't they?" He made like he was going to take his off to look at it. He must have still been in a state of shock, but we weren't in any position to worry about such things. 4:01 . . . 4:02 . . .

"C'mon, you're still the leader, let's not just give away the top spot," I said as I looked down at the bloody shreds of his jersey. The truth is, I knew as I pushed him back up to the road that we'd already lost that stage as well as the jersey, at least for the day. The two mechanics helped pull him up by the arms.

It took us another minute to compose ourselves, get on our spare bikes, and start to pedal. 5:02 . . . 5:03 . . . At that moment, Matosas was the new Tour leader, about a minute ahead, and that distance would only grow. As much as we pushed ourselves in the last four kilometers, ten racers taking turns up front are faster than a mere pair.

I ran ahead of Steve for the rest of the climb, not asking for relief. The image of a team of oxen pulling a broken-down Citroen reentered my head. There was something wrong with Steve: He was slightly off-kilter as he pedaled, with one arm closer to his body than the other, more bruised than we'd realized when we got him on the bike; I feared he might have a broken clavicle or a fractured rib. If that was the case, it was the end of the Tour for him. Several times I forced myself to slow down the rhythm so he wouldn't lose his way.

But I'd never admired my teammate more than in that moment. He was as pale as a cadaver and a strange grimace distorted his famous face. Yet he kept on moving his legs, like a windmill, as if he'd split the bottom part of his body from his useless torso and head. With a shiver, I imagined that once we crossed the finish line, we'd discover he was dead and it was just his legs pumping. I wasn't exactly right in the head at that moment either.

I don't know where that boy, raised in total comfort, found the strength to absorb so much suffering. With four Tours under his belt, he had nothing to prove, but there he was, ready to seriously hurt himself rather than admit defeat. A couple of times I had to shoo away the TV cameras on motorcycles, which kept trying to focus their lenses on his face to broadcast my friend's torment. He didn't even register when we crossed the finish line. Our assistants stopped him, grabbing the handlebars as he tried to keep pedaling, still in his trance. When he realized we'd finished, he fainted. I leaned against the fence and, without getting off the bike, vomited. What came up included thick, bright-colored substances I hoped were just food.

In the end, those three assholes took eight minutes from us and managed to reverse our roles: Now they monopolized the podium with a five-minute lead over Steve. In my case, the drop in ranking was worse because the penalty for taking the bike from another team turned out to be two minutes. Still, I hoped it had all been worth it.

The reporters who had watched our climb on the huge screen

at the finish line told us they had assumed we would lose about twenty minutes against the leaders of that stage. Both the media and the fans had given a cool welcome to the ten runaways, headed by Matosas, Paniuk, and Medel, instead focusing on the images of the two hurt racers dragging themselves to the summit. When we got there, I noticed a couple of our mechanics had tears in their eyes.

Suffering is the essence of cycling and not just because of what it demands from a professional; it's also what feeds the amateur's passion. It's no accident the spectators gather on the edge of the great summits, where they can be witnesses to the self-flogging their champions undergo in order to continue being their champions.

Later, after showering on the team bus on the way back to the hotel, I reflected that though Steve had lost the yellow jersey that day, he'd conquered something perhaps more important, something heretofore missing from his career. His victorious image, something à la Cristiano Ronaldo, was frequently confused for arrogance; his impressive physique and elegant style on the bike, that perfect round pedaling, and Fonar's overwhelming superiority contributed to the idea that there was nothing epic or heroic in his achievements. The jet-set celebrities that surrounded him didn't help either. All that made both the media and the public apt to ignore the discipline and effort behind his victories. Today, limp and haggard, he'd shown the world what he was made of and the world had liked what it had seen.

But my heart sank at the sight of Steve's empty seat on the bus. He'd been taken to the hospital for an examination. It was still not clear if he could continue.

Once we got to the hotel, I locked myself in Axel's room for an hour and a half to get my requisite massage. This time he kept quiet. I would have liked to apologize for being so brusque earlier that day, but I had no energy to talk. Given everything that had happened, this morning seemed like a distant memory. I needed to eat something and, if possible, to visit with Steve at the hospital.

When I left the soigneur's room, I found a police officer at the door. Even stranger, he followed me down the hall until I got to the room that had been assigned to me. "I'll be outside all night. Commissioner Favre's orders," he said in response to my arched brow. I wanted to protest, but my desire to throw myself in bed was much greater. My eyes closed immediately.

I don't know how much time passed before I was awakened by an urgent knocking. It was, of course, the commissioner. Something must have been really wrong in my head because I actually felt pleased that this time he would find the room in order: I still hadn't opened a single suitcase the assistants had brought up hours earlier.

"Steve is better," said Favre as a greeting and maybe also as a way of waking me up. "He's beaten up, but there are no fractures and no internal injuries. Your team says he'll be at the starting line tomorrow, although they would prefer he sleep at the hospital tonight."

"Good, very good," I said, grateful; so long as Steve could race, the Tour wasn't lost. The commissioner had finally brought some good news.

I continued standing, my hand on the door, hoping to signal that the visit was over. I vaguely remembered I had to ask him a question, but before I could figure it out, Favre squashed his good news.

"Your bicycle was sabotaged," he said abruptly, like somebody who could no longer keep a secret.

"What? How?" I said. Naps don't make me what could be called brilliant.

"They did something to the tube so it would come off the wheel. We'll know more tomorrow."

I recalled the broken wheel at the foot of a tree, the spokes bent like a plate of calamari. Steve's good fortune had allowed him to walk away from an accident that, as his dented helmet evidenced, could have been deadly. But the commissioner saw it differently.

"You were very lucky, sergeant. That hit was destined for you. You've managed to survive twice. I've put an officer outside because I don't want there to be a third time."

"It's impossible to know when a tube will come loose from the wheel. Today's temperatures were excessive," I insisted, but not too vehemently.

"At the very least, this crosses your DS off the list of suspects," Favre said, ignoring me. "Giraud would have been the least interested in provoking an incident to kick Panata out of the race." After a pause, he added thoughtfully: "Although, if the assault was conceived to hit you, he'd have no way of knowing Steve would end up on that bike."

"Hitting me at this stage of the Tour is the same as hitting Steve; I'm his primary domestique. He needs me. Giraud would have never tried anything like that," I responded as if making sure he understood two and two equaled four.

"Did he instruct you to give your bike to your teammate or was that of your own initiative? Did he say anything over the earphones when he realized Panata had a puncture?"

So that's what Favre had really come for: to make sure he could cross Giraud off the list. And what exactly was he asking when he inquired if it had been my idea to give Steve my bike? Was he contemplating the possibility I might have known the tire was tricked up? And even worse, that I had given it to Steve with the intention of having him have an accident?

"Let's see, commissioner," I said, going on with my own two plus two, "do you know who would go up to the podium if the race ended today? Maybe we should go back to your own thesis: Who benefits from these sinister acts?"

"Sinister! Very well, sergeant, now you're talking just like one of us," he said. If I'd had a razor then, I would have shaved off his goddamn mustache right there.

"Let me rest, all right?" I said, sick of him, sick of myself, sick of the Tour. He seemed to realize I could barely stand up, because he finally turned to leave.

"Very well," he said, trying to sound conciliatory. "Tomorrow I'll know the results of the tests on the wheel. I'll gladly let you know if we find anything . . ."

"Conclusive," I said, finishing the phrase for him.

"Just like one of us!" he repeated, although this time he didn't sound sarcastic at all. He half turned and made a gesture with the index finger of his right hand, as if he were lifting the brim of a hat.

I threw myself down face-first on the bed again, but now I couldn't get to sleep; I needed to eat, I needed very much to eat. With all the drama of the past few hours, I'd forgotten the cyclist's main obligation on finishing a stage: to replace calories. If I hurried, I'd still be able to meet up with the team in the dining room. The day's incidents had disrupted our routines; that was the only thing that explained why no assistant had come to get me. Giraud was probably at the hospital with Steve. I'd have dinner and then ask to be taken to see him.

But, once more, a knock on the door ruined my intentions. Fiona whirled into the room like a hurricane. She hugged me and gave me a long kiss. She hadn't been able to come earlier because one of her duties was to coordinate the technical team that evaluated the state of the bikes at the end of each stage.

"Why is there a cop at the door, Mojito? What, are they pissed because it wasn't you who got banged up on the bike?"

"Favre thinks someone sabotaged my Pinarello," I began but stopped. I realized I had never talked to her about the Frenchman. "He's a police commissioner who . . ."

"I know all about Favre," she said, putting a finger over my mouth. "And he's right. I just came from checking the tire myself. Someone used the wrong glue on the tube. Do you remember Beloki?" The image of Lance Armstrong came to mind, descending a hill while zigzagging around Beloki, who had fallen because of an imperfection in his wheel. It was later discovered one of the mechanics had mistakenly used a glue from when we still used aluminum wheels. The old adhesives look the same as today's, but they have no effect on carbon. It almost cost Beloki his life. In the end, it cost him his career. He had won second and third place on earlier Tours, but that fall caused femur, elbow, and wrist fractures. He was never able to distinguish himself as a cyclist again.

"If the wheel had come loose on one of the two descents, I wouldn't be here to talk about it," I said, remembering speeding down the second climb at more than 70 kilometers per hour.

"Honestly, I don't understand how the tube lasted as long as it did," she said, and I felt her shudder. She hugged me again, and in that moment I believed that, in spite of everything, she'd go on loving me even if I never made it up to the podium.

"The question is: Who did it?" I said, playing up my role of detective. Of course, she was the chief mechanic.

"It's very hard to imagine they could have done it without the complicity of a Fonar mechanic. Someone on the outside could have changed the jar of glue, but they wouldn't have had control of the bike once sabotaged. If they wanted to hit you, they needed to manipulate one of your tires. And only somebody on the inside can do that."

"How often do you use glue on the tubes?"

"It depends on how much wear there is per stage. It's not daily, maybe every two or three days. More frequently if it's hot or if you're racing on cobblestones."

"So it would have had to have been done today, right? Otherwise I suppose I would have fallen yesterday."

"Yes, it must have been today. On a stage like this, the bikes need to be lubricated and ready to go at ten in the morning before any of the cyclists do their stretches. That means the mechanics would have been working since seven o'clock at the very least. But it's really hard for me to believe this could be the work of a Fonar mechanic. They've been with the team for years. I know them all so well," said Fiona, shaking her head in distress.

I'd reviewed each of the five assistants in charge of getting the bikes ready, and like her, could find no reasons to doubt them. And yet, the facts didn't seem to allow any other possibility. It was hard to believe a colleague would have been willing to kill me, and even harder for Fiona to swallow that a mechanic would betray their trade like that. The devotion they have toward the machines they work on is practically religious. Now it was me who comforted her with a hug.

A call from Steve interrupted our embrace. In less than half an hour, my need to sleep, to eat, and whatever it was Fiona and I were about to do had been interrupted. We're talking three basic needs for any human, goddamnit. Hearing Steve's tinny voice, she untangled herself from my arms, and left before I could stop her.

I chatted with Steve, who was still at the hospital, as I walked to the dining room and served myself some fish, rice, and a thick chocolate shake. Neither of us brought up the statements Lombard had made to the press. We talked like two schoolboys making ambitious and improbable plans for the next summer. We promised we would physically recover in the five days we had before we got to the Alps and that, once on the high mountains, we'd make those three assholes pay. We didn't say a thing about the killer and his obvious goal of keeping us from arriving safe and sound in Paris.

I finished the call and devoured what was on my plate, fulfilling at least one of my three physiological needs. An hour later, I surrendered to the second, in spite of the fact that the mantra that night was not at all calming.

GENERAL CLASSIFICATION: STAGE 12

RANK	RIDER	TIME	NOTES
1	ALESSIO MATOSAS (ITALY/LAVEZZA)	46:50:32	The tire accident helped him. Coincidence?
2	MILENKO PANIUK (CZECH/RABONET)	+0:22	How complicit is he with Matosas?
3	PABLO MEDEL (SPAIN/BALEARES)	+0:26	I can't believe the Spaniard is a killer but . . .
4	**STEVE PANATA (USA/FONAR)**	**+4:49**	**Will my bro be able to continue the Tour?**
5	**MARC MOREAU (FRANCE/FONAR)**	**+8:26**	**This is the end of Fiona's and Lombard's hopes.**
6	ÓSCAR CUADRADO (COLOMBIA/MOVISTAR)	+8:42	Gotta give him props. I don't know how he can go on without a team.
7	LUIS DURÁN (SPAIN/IMAGINE)	+9:25	Has no chance but now he'll try for my fifth slot.
8	SERGEI TALANCÓN (ROMANIA/ROCCA)	+11:03	He needs a good domestique to be a threat.
9	ANSELMO CONTI (ITALY/LAVEZZA)	+13:21	And now it turns out the boy psychopath is in the top ten.
10	ROL CHARPENELLE (FRANCE/TOURGAZ)	+13:27	You're too far down, Rol.

Stage 13

Muret — Rodez, 198.5 km.

Today was supposed to be easy, one of the so-called transitional stages, but it was anything but. Especially off the road. If yesterday's headlines rattled my world, today's rattled the rest of the universe, at least the cycling universe. "A Killer in the Tourmalet" read *The Daily Sun*'s sensational front page. The story quoted the police speculating about the sabotage of my bike. Another three or four papers also wrote about the theory. There was no question one of Favre's colleagues had talked too much.

The representatives from the cycling union released a statement demanding "a thorough investigation" and considered the possibility of ceasing all activities if they judged that the integrity of the racers was at risk. The cyclists were the least interested in suspending the competition—except for those who were so tired they were at the point of throwing in the towel anyway.

"How's my Forrest Gump?" said Steve as he entered the hotel dining room where the rest of the team was finishing breakfast. When he talked, he twisted his mouth slightly, as if he'd just come from the dentist. He kept a folded arm close to his chest, which only looks natural on Napoleon.

"Forrest Gump?" I answered, happy to see him standing there. I would have hugged him if it hadn't seemed so ridiculous in a dining room full of cyclists—there were two other teams staying at that hotel—and, anyway, I wasn't sure if it was possible to hug Steve without hurting him.

"Three days ago no one could stop talking about the gas-tank explosion that almost killed you; yesterday you were France's salvation; and today you're the preferred victim of the Tourmalet killer. In other words, you're the center of everything on the Tour. The Forrest Gump of cycling!" said Steve.

"The hospital did not cure you of assholery," I said, moving my chair so he could pass.

"Asshole, me? It was you who gave me the tricked-up bike," he complained, laughing and pointing at me as he addressed the entire dining room. "Don't ever accept a bike from Marc Moreau unless you want to spend the night in the hospital: He sells the tires and exchanges them for secondhand ones."

The general laughter helped ease some of the tension, but I was not in the least bit amused. The pained face Steve made when he sat down belied the effort he was making to hide his injuries. Sometimes, self-denial is the only way you can complete the Tour.

For Favre, Steve's accident was a turning point. The commissioner finally had a list of probable suspects with which to work. He and his men had submitted the Fonar mechanics to severe interrogation all night long. He believed one of them had sabotaged my bike; sooner or later he'd confess and that would lead to the arrest of his accomplices. At this point, the police assumed the incidents couldn't be the work of just one person. At least that's what Favre told me as I boarded the bus taking us to the starting line in Muret, in the vicinity of Toulouse.

"We've decided to pause the interrogation for a few hours while the race is running; that will help the mechanics think." The truth was the commissioner had set them free against his will: Fonar had pressured the authorities to let the mechanics do their work, threatening to pull the entire team from competition. Favre's bosses agreed because they didn't want a scandal, but only on the condition that, as soon as the race was over, the suspects would be once more at the disposition of the police. "In the meantime, it would be very helpful if you could remember anything in particular about any of them. An embarrassing past, a deeply guarded secret. Those are the fissures that allow us to break a criminal during an interrogation."

"If it was a secret, I wouldn't know it, would I?" I said defensively. Favre was probably just doing his job, although I thought there were more subtle ways of asking me to be a snitch. What happens on a team stays with the team. Of course I knew things about a couple of the guys but I had no intention of making innocent people suffer.

"These are not your friends, sergeant. One of them tried to kill you." You had to give it to Favre: His lack of subtlety could certainly put things in perspective. I remembered my bike against that tree, the wheel still spinning ominously.

"Are you sure that tire was sabotaged? You told me yesterday you didn't have conclusive evidence." My question was genuine, but I couldn't help but exaggerate that last word. He looked at me like he wasn't sure if I was making fun of him or not.

"We know for a fact"—and now he pushed his jaw out defiantly, probably proud of being able to use that phrase—"that the adhesive used did not come from the jars Fonar had on its shelves. So it was no innocent mistake."

I knew that already, thanks to Fiona. But I got a strange pleasure from perplexing the meticulous commissioner. Right now, the rash of unshaven stubble intruding upon the sharp line of his mustache gave me tremendous satisfaction. Like the mechanics, Favre must not have slept the night before.

I told him I would let him know if I remembered anything in

particular, and I rid myself of the cop as quickly as I could—it had started to become a habit. Like every other time, I was left feeling a little guilty: After all, this was not a joking matter; Favre was trying to arrest someone who had already caused tremendous damage.

During the ride to the starting line, I went over what I knew about the five mechanics, trying to figure out which of them was most likely to be the guilty party. I started with Basset, a shy guy from the UK. There was also Marciel, whom we called "the Dandy" because of his expensive taste in clothes and accessories. Jordi, the Catalan, had barely been with us two years. Although not from southern Italy, Adriano was a compatriot of Matosas and his crew. And Joseph had five kids and a demanding wife. When you looked at them as suspects, not one was entirely without motive.

But what also came to mind was scene after scene of the family we had become, the jokes only we understood, the weaknesses we confided in one another, the shared joy when we won, the way we licked our wounds together at the end of a disastrous day.

To look for a killer in that group was really too painful, especially when we exited the bus and climbed onto the bikes, perfectly readied in a row by Basset, the Dandy, Jordi, Adriano, and Joseph in spite of the worry and lack of sleep still evident on their faces.

A few seconds before the start of the race, the Tour's grand baron, Sam Jitrik, went on TV to say the rumors coming from the press were nothing more than malicious lies, irresponsible and in bad taste. Already on our bikes, the racers watched the screen the sponsors had installed at the starting line as Jitrik's finger sculpted his phrases in the air. "Dozens of men have lost their lives during the history of the Tour and hundreds more have been broken in their desire to conquer these peaks with nothing more than a fragile bike and a brave heart. It's the essence of our sport. Tragedy is a by-product of our passion; to look for guilty parties is equivalent to insulting the valor of our athletes. Let them go to battle once more against the mountain ranges and hope the gods are generous to our heroes today."

Today we would not, in fact, be going to battle against any mountain, although Jitrik would never let geography destroy such a perfect phrase. He scurried into the lead car and started the race.

"He's a murderer," I heard Radek say; he'd pulled up to my side as we took off behind the car. I wanted to ask him who he was referring to. Did he actually know something, or was this just another one of his invectives against the organizers? I would have also liked to thank him for the gesture the day before. I tried to catch his eye, but he was already lost in the mêlée at the beginning of the race.

Once more, I experienced the relief that starting the race offered my tormented mind. Having to concentrate for the next four or five hours on the peloton's demands was the only thing that could make me forget about the killer. Steve came up on my wheel and the rest of the team surrounded us. I located Matosas and his people and directed our tiny float in their direction.

After the high mountains, which are tough on climbers and torturous for everyone else, the transitional stages are the days when most of the teams angle for a massive finish that allows their sprinters to explode. The teams that lack sprinters try early breakaways with the hope of getting a decisive lead and holding on to it to win the stage. For some racers, it's their only chance of getting fifteen minutes of glory during the Tour.

Fonar's transitional strategy is simple: to avoid escapes that might put the yellow jersey at risk. In theory, it was the same plan our rivals—Matosas, Paniuk, Medel—would follow. Yesterday's enemies would transform into today's allies to speed up the peloton and prevent any runaway from becoming a threat. We only let go racers whose position in the general classification didn't present a risk to our leaders, and even in those cases, we'd try to limit the distance they could get ahead on the road. Most of the time, the peloton would reabsorb them before they reached their goal.

That's what we were expecting. But what happened was something that had never been seen before in the history of the Tour. About thirty kilometers from the finish line, just as we were coming into the tiny town of La Baraque, our three rival teams took over the front. My alarms went off and I screamed to the other Fonar racers to wheel up to them. I didn't understand their strategy, but I knew a town's narrow streets were not the best place to get trapped. Only four of us could even get close to the front, although it didn't do much good. More than a dozen of Paniuk's and Medel's domestiques wrapped around us and bottlenecked our exits as Matosas's whole team jumped ahead, accompanied by two T-shirts of different colors: Paniuk's and Medel's.

The move was as astute as it was perverse. They wanted to give Steve a final blow before he'd recovered from his injuries. The eleven runaways garnered an advantage of several minutes before we could get out of the mousetrap in La Baraque, and even then it wasn't easy to break through the siege fomented by Paniuk's and Medel's domestiques.

When I finally broke the blockade, the battle seemed lost. It would take a few more minutes to get a group together to go after the breakaways. Half our teammates were scattered throughout the peloton, and their attempts to catch up with us were impeded by our rivals. I assumed the other teams wouldn't help; none of them had any contenders for the yellow jersey, so exerting the energy necessary to go on a chase would just mean losing the stage. The only one beyond recovery in the standings after this maneuver was Steve Panata.

We'd try our damndest, but I assumed we weren't any competition for the eleven who got away. The way our rivals had orchestrated the division of tasks was not coincidental. Matosas's squad was the fastest of the three against the clock; adding Paniuk and Medel made them as quick as a bullet. We'd be lucky if we managed to keep them from increasing the distance between us. Added to the five-minute disadvantage with which we'd started the stage, the Tour's fortunes seemed to favor the three who got away.

Then something strange happened. I assumed Fonar would be the only team trying to get ahead of the peloton and got ready to lead the effort. But, to my surprise, other teams began to pass ahead of us, and I silently cursed them because I thought they too were trying to take advantage of Steve's weakness. Soon I realized the entire peloton was overtaking us, and once more, it was Radek who shook me up.

"Let's go get those sons of bitches!" he shouted as he passed. "You guys, take it easy," he added, taking a quick glance at Steve.

What happened next was one of the most poignant moments in the history of the Tour de France. One hundred and fifty racers giving their all, legs and lungs, to stop a few assholes from getting away. Team after team took turns in the front and pedaled without mercy to pull the peloton up to its limit. Within minutes, we were transformed into a powerful missile hurled in search of the escapees.

The way Matosas and company had exploited Steve's accident had not gone down well with the rest of the racers. Though often violated, there's an unwritten rule that calls for not taking advantage of malevolent acts on the road, especially if the victim is the race leader. Our colleagues had taken note of Steve's courageous remounting yesterday afternoon.

When the peloton works together, it's a high-powered train, running over everything in its path. The avenging spirit that had come over the pack seemed to breathe life into the racers. Nothing feels better to a group than the sense that they're righting a wrong.

Grateful, I tried to cooperate with the effort by taking a turn near the front. I started to go up the line, but when Radek saw me, he courteously waved me to the back of the peloton. Apparently, they wanted to do us the whole favor: to neutralize the treasonous attack and help us compensate for the wasted energy the day before in the Pyrenees. I accepted the invitation and pulled Fonar to the rear.

"It's a trap, and if they bottleneck us again, we're fucked," thundered Giraud on our earphones. "Move up to the lead."

"It's not a trap," I responded.

"Let them pull, but you have to be on alert," he said, ignoring my comment. "And if they ease up on the pace, we'll get loose and attack. We need to catch up with the breakaways."

"We need to rest," I protested, looking over at Steve, who listened without speaking, "and it's being offered to us."

"Don't be naïve, Marc. Attack," shouted our DS.

After a long silence I said, "Giraud, there's such a thing as decency and you have to know how to recognize it when it presents itself." As I've said, pedaling helps bring oxygen to my brain.

"Luckily, I'm the directeur sportif," said Giraud, livid. "Attack, goddamnit."

I looked over at the rest of my Fonar teammates, who had heard every word of our dialogue without participating. They returned my gaze, waiting for a response. Years of conditioning makes racers respond to the instructions of their DSs without a peep, unless you're Lance Armstrong. But my teammates were as moved as I was by the solidarity of our colleagues. Like me, they considered it disrespectful to ignore the courtesy and show distrust by advancing to the front. Plus, all of us, except Giraud, knew Steve was not ready to make the chase. He was up on my wheel concentrating on the simple but incredibly tough task of compelling one pedal forward at a time, ignoring everything else, including the dialogue he had just heard.

So I did the only thing a racer can't do while on the road, according to his coach: I took my earphone out. I knew it could mean getting kicked out the next day. But I didn't have the desire or energy to keep arguing with Giraud. I could always say the gadget had come loose, although I knew it would be useless. The always-present TV cameras had captured the moment when my hand went up to disconnect it.

I kept riding, lost in thought, wondering if these would be the last kilometers of the Tour for me this year. I turned to see how Steve was doing; if he didn't recover, these would be the last for him as well. At that precise moment, without taking his eyes off my back wheel, he disconnected his earphone with an almost distracted gesture, as if he were scratching his ear. Nothing in his face gave away that he'd come out of his trance.

Subtle, but effective. I could be expelled from the team, but Steve never, and much less given what happened next. One by one, each of the members of Fonar did the same thing. I couldn't keep from smiling. Without trying to, I'd provoked a rebellion that would probably cause Giraud to be fired at the end of the competition. Even if the TV cameras hadn't caught all nine racers rebelling, they would soon realize all our earphones were just dangling useless.

Whatever the results of the chase and the final rankings of the stage, it would be the Fonar uprising that would be the talk of the day in the world of cycling. And, once again, without wanting to—well, almost—I'd been the protagonist. Maybe Steve was not so wrong when he called me the Forrest Gump of the Tour. I just hoped I wouldn't still be playing that role when the killer decided to attack again.

Lost in my thoughts, I didn't even realize what was going on until Guido pointed up the long stretch still before us. The escapees were about five hundred meters ahead. We still had eight kilometers to the finish line. We'd caught up with them thanks to my colleagues' savage efforts. I looked around and made sure everyone understood the profound debt we owed. What should have been an easy day for everyone had turned into a punitive stage with enormous sacrifices in service of righting a wrong. It was impossible that there could be a killer in that group of professionals. I wanted more than ever to believe he was among that little group of backstabbers riding up front.

We reached the three frontrunners kilometers before the finish line without any song and dance or smugness, except for Radek, who looked them in the eye provocatively, trying to start a fight.

On the team bus, Giraud didn't say a word about what happened. But the subject was like a pink rhinoceros we pretended not to see. From two seats away I could make out our DS's huge belly going up and down as he flared his nostrils. When we got to the hotel, on the outskirts of Rodez, I waited for Giraud to get off before exiting myself. The last thing I needed was to run into my resentful coach. I didn't wait long enough.

"You son of a bitch," he said into my ear as he pulled roughly on my neck just outside the bus. "If I do nothing else in my life, I'll make sure you never win a race, even if I have to throw you off the bike myself."

I started to reply, but it was clear his words were not meant to launch a conversation. He stormed away huffing and puffing.

His threat left me shaking. I tried to tell myself it wasn't like I'd won so many races before either. I didn't need his help to lose the next ones. Still, it's not easy to be cool when a guy who weighs a hundred pounds more than you leaves bruises on your neck and promises to punish you forever and ever.

Two hours later I told Fiona what had happened at the foot of the bus.

"You just killed his career," she said, with her usual implacable common sense.

"It wasn't on purpose. What he ordered us to do was crazy; the rest of the peloton would have thought we were total assholes."

"I know. You did the right thing," she said, lazily caressing my cheek with her knuckles, which were softer than the calloused palms of her hands. "Now I love you a little more."

That last part surprised me. Fiona could be physically very affectionate, especially when she was sleepy, but she rarely said anything florid and honeyed.

"Tomorrow, I'll start without the earphone," I joked, blushing a little and pulled up closer to her, a gesture based more in gratitude than flirtation. That anyone can love me still strikes me as an undeserved privilege. There was an hour before dinner. A quick look around the room made it clear we had gotten the short end of the hotel lottery today. The bed had a sunken mattress, the curtains had never been washed, and the shower had stains of dubious origins. Even Hitchcock would have rejected it for his films.

"Favre was right when he told you Fonar had been thinking about firing Giraud at the end of the season. I confirmed it. That's why he has such an obsession with winning this Tour; he thinks it could help them change their minds." Fiona had closed the tiny and unexpected romantic opening and returned to her usual analytical tone. "But even if they hadn't changed their minds, he assumed the other teams would compete among themselves to contract him. Now with that kind of defiance among his racers, anyone would think twice. So, yes, he thinks you screwed him over."

"The truth is I wouldn't be the least bit bothered if I never saw his face on the circuit again. If he ends up with another team, I'm always going to be afraid of suffering some kind of bullshit on the road. I swear to you, he would get revenge; he would make sure I never won another race in my life."

"Well, you have the best revenge within your reach . . . ," she said.

"What's that?" I asked, falling right into her trap.

"To win the Tour while you're still under his command!" she responded, elated.

I laughed along with her as if it were a good joke, although I knew she was deadly serious. So long as I had some chance at the podium, she would not drop that line. Since I didn't know what to say, I tried to hug her, a strategy that generally proved effective in my prior relationships; once more I discovered not everything worked with Fiona. She tolerated my arms the way a child accepts a hug from a relative wearing too much perfume. Then she pushed them aside with a serious look on her face, but I changed the subject before she had a chance to say anything.

"Do you know what's going on with Lombard? I haven't seen him today." The last few hours had been so intense I hadn't had a chance to talk with my old friend, although I couldn't ignore the troublemaking public statements he had given to *Libération*. I needed to make sure he didn't do that again.

"He's around somewhere," she said vaguely. "They're not letting him get anywhere near you," she added in a whisper.

"Did Giraud ban him from the Fonar hotels? As a question of security or something like that?" I said, trying to rationalize the situation.

"It wasn't Giraud," she said. "It was Steve."

"What? What do you mean, Steve?"

She just shook her head.

A few minutes later, after Fiona left, I sent Lombard a text telling him I wanted to meet that night. It wouldn't be easy, because I couldn't set foot outside without being surrounded by press or fans. And that's not even taking into account that I shouldn't have been wandering alone while there was a killer on the loose.

At dinner, we were like a soccer team that, having been down zero to four, manages to come back and only lose three to four. The last few kilometers of this stage, when the peloton had ridden at such a fury to catch up with our rivals, had become the stuff of legend. But all it really meant was our rivals hadn't improved their lead. When we got up the next day, we'd still be the same five minutes behind Matosas with which we'd begun. In sum, it had been an epic effort just to stay where we were. Now we concentrated on putting food in our mouths with as few words as necessary. There wasn't much enthusiasm but there also wasn't much sorrow. Exhaustion, more than anything else.

A little while later, I snuck out the back door, headed for the hotel parking lot, but as soon as I set foot outside, two of Steve's thuggish bodyguards came up and clung to me like dandruff.

"Easy, boys, I'm only going to the bus. I need a warm bath before going to sleep. The hotel shower has enough germs to supply a biological war." They silently followed me the ten meters to our enormous team vehicle.

I'd sent Axel a message asking him to let Lombard into the bus, since Axel was responsible for cleaning the vehicle at the end of the day, and he was also the only assistant whom I trusted. I don't know if he understood that this favor could cost him his job, but he did it without hesitation. The intimacy you develop with someone who works on your naked body for ninety minutes a day over several years isn't something even most lovers have. Axel knew my muscles and tendons the way a violinist knows his instrument.

"What the peloton did to those villains today was really incredible," said Lombard from the far end of the bus. The colonel actually talked like that. One time he told me he grew up with a nanny who made him read comic books. He could never get rid of the *Wow!* and *Bam!* in his speech.

"It *was* incredible," I repeated, not quite sure where to begin. I could never really scold him; I knew he loved me like a father.

"With a little luck, they'll keep it up and you and Steve will be back in the front. After that, the only thing left is to carefully choose the moment of your final attack."

Apparently, this was going to be a little harder than I had imagined. Far from being embarrassed or sorry about what he had provoked, the colonel was stuck on the same refrain as before: that I should betray Steve.

"No, it won't happen again. The peloton's support was just for today. It will be very hard for us to cut the lead those three have."

"You don't know the power and recovery you're capable of. If you'd only let me show you the numbers I have. But you never want to see them," he said, going from pride to disappointment, like a child. Lombard and his hacker son, Bernard, used my password to get into Fonar's database, which contained files on dozens of indicators the power meter documented each day during training or competition. Cross-referenced with other registers, it created indexes for recovery, fatigue, power, pedaling pace, and much more. All of this information was broadcast in real time during the race so that the technicians would know the potential performance of each racer during the competition. No one was as exhaustive in their analysis as Bernard, urged on by his father.

"Well, about that," I said after a long sigh, "you got me in all kinds of trouble after your statements to *Libération*. What you said about me being a better racer than Steve. First, I don't agree, although we're not even going to talk about that"—I raised the palm of my hand when I saw he wanted to interrupt me. "Second, everything you say to the press, or within the circuit, is considered to be coming from me, and that causes a lot of waves."

"But that was just the opinion of a simple old fan," he said in a hurt tone.

"Don't be naïve, colonel, and don't play with me. I gave you access to the circuit and Fiona accredited you as an assistant, because we assumed you'd be respectful and discreet about us, about me. You broke that agreement yesterday." Lombard hung his head, visibly hurt. I'd never talked to him like this. His eyes grew wet and he pressed his lips together as he blinked over and over, as if he was trying hard not to cry. I couldn't help but remember the moment when he, exultant, gave me my first real racing bike in front of the army barracks.

"Let's talk seriously, Hannibal," said the veteran, recovering himself. He straightened his torso, threw his shoulders back, and pushed out pecs he no longer had. "I have a son by blood and a son by circumstance, and what the two of them have done and might still do justifies my presence in this world. The rest is not worth worrying about, damn it." Lombard's comic book phrasing could sound a little kitschy, but he compensated with the intensity of his emotions.

"Thank you—" I started to say, but this time he stopped me with his hand.

"And for that same reason, I'm not going to let you commit a crime against yourself." His tone was now that of a commanding officer. "Even if it's the last thing I do in this life, I'll make sure you honor the gifts you've received and win one great race. I know you can win this Tour, you *should* win this Tour!"

It was a bit ironic that in a matter of one hour, two men had determined what was left of their lives would be dedicated to me. Giraud, to make sure I never won, and Lombard to make sure I did. I imagined the two of them, their sleeves rolled up, arm-wrestling across a table. And although my mentor's tone was decisive, I had no doubt about who would win that match.

"I am flattered by your words, colonel. And I'm grateful for them from the bottom of my heart. You're the father I never had; I can't adequately thank you for what you've done for me. But that and the yellow jersey are two different things: All the racers' fathers want their sons to go to the podium in Paris. You know that only three out of a hundred and ninety-eight manage that; the rest of us have the privilege of having run all twenty-one stages, which is no small thing. Taking pride in that doesn't make us unfaithful children. And if I can be the instrument by which the brother I never had wins, then I'll be the happiest person out there."

"You think of Steve as your brother?" he said in a tone of disgust. I remembered what Fiona had told me about my friend's supposed actions against the colonel.

"You may not like Steve, but he and I grew up cycling together," I responded. Lombard grimaced.

"You were already Hannibal when you met him. You were destined for greatness, but he got in your way."

The conversation was going nowhere. Lombard was convinced that I would have been Messi on a bike if I hadn't met Steve.

"I'm asking you to please not talk to the press about me again," I said, aware of the futility of continuing our conversation. "To the press or anyone else. Just stop. And wait a few minutes before you leave the bus," I added as I got up to go down the aisle and out to the street.

"Hannibal," he said, stopping me, "that man, the tall one"— and he pointed at one of the two guards who had escorted me to the vehicle. The man's shadow grew with the light from the hotel, large and heavy, like a sarcophagus carved into a human shape. The tinted windows allowed us to see them without them noticing us.

"What about him?"

"He's dangerous, a goon. He's who Steve was with when he came to talk to me."

"Steve talked to you?" Apparently, we couldn't avoid the subject whether I wanted to or not.

"Yes, yesterday," he said and then went silent. Now that he had me trapped, he wanted me to pluck out each individual word that he was nonetheless longing to tell me. "That bastard threatened me. Your *brother*," he said disdainfully.

"What do you mean he threatened you? What did he say?"

"He said if I didn't leave you alone, the least that would happen to me is that I would never come near cycling again. The least that would happen! That's an implicit death threat, you know?"

"Please, let's not exaggerate."

"Then, that guy"—he pointed again—"confused my foot with the floor as he was going out the door."

I didn't know if what the old man was telling me was true, but

I couldn't help but look out at the giant thug: He weighed at least three hundred pounds.

"This is all a misunderstanding. In his way, Steve is trying to protect me. Do you know how much damage your statement to the press did to me, colonel? After what you said, Steve must have thought your presence by my side could mean I believed your words. Giraud and the rest of the team looked at me as if I stank. And you completely ignored the possibility of a reprisal from Giraud. There are worse things than being a highly paid domestique, you know? For example, I could become the team's water boy."

"What about the way he stomped on my foot?" said Lombard, offended.

"That must have been his own initiative," I responded angrily. "You yourself just said it happened behind Steve's back."

"I doubt it. There are a lot of things you don't know about Steve. They say he and his agent have turned away more than one offer from other teams who wanted to make *you* their leader. They engaged in all kinds of machinations so those proposals wouldn't reach you."

"Do you have any evidence of this? I've heard these rumors too, and they usually come from teams we've beaten. Of course they'd like to break our bond."

"Evidence? Your friend always makes sure his image is spotless. I don't have evidence of his threats yesterday either. But my foot reminds me they were loud and clear," he said, and we both lowered our eyes to stare at his shoes. "In fact, I wouldn't be the least bit surprised if he and his crew had something to do with the tragedies that have been occurring over the last few days."

"Well, if it's him and his crew, they've done a terrible job," I said. "Matosas, Paniuk, and Medel are making us eat their dust."

We both went quiet. We were out of ammunition, like two boxers in the tenth round, more tired than belligerent. We separated without any real animosity, and I tried to believe that, though my arguments hadn't convinced him, the colonel would at least avoid making any more explosive statements.

Before I could exit the bus, Axel intercepted me.

I looked at him inquisitively. "There's something you need to know," he said.

I looked at the bodyguards waiting just a few meters ahead of us and Lombard, still on the bus, and shook my head. Today was determined to turn into Groundhog Day; it seemed like weeks since the last time I'd slept in a bed.

"Come up to my room in about fifteen minutes," I said. "One of those brutes will be outside; tell them I asked for a muscle relaxer."

Arriving at my door, I stopped cold when I saw Favre.

"Don't get angry, sergeant, it's just for a minute," he said, defensively, when he saw my face.

I didn't respond, just opened the door and waved him inside with a ceremonious pantomime.

"I didn't think I was important enough to take up so much of the police commissioner's time," I said, sarcastically.

"Well, Moreau, everything seems to revolve around you, which has intrigued me." He paused, reflective, and then continued. "But I haven't come to throw it in your face; not this time."

I took notice of the words: *Not now, but sometime soon.*

"Why are you here?" I asked, starting to feel impatient.

"We've continued the interrogation of the Fonar mechanics. You told me this morning you would look for something, some dirty laundry that would allow me to break one of them. You know how it is when it comes to setting traps."

I hadn't promised any such thing, but Favre seemed to enjoy putting words in the mouths of others. Using that method, I wouldn't be surprised if one of those poor mechanics ended up incriminating himself even if he was innocent.

"I'm sorry, commissioner, I couldn't remember a thing," I said, trying to follow whatever narrative line would get him back out to the hallway as soon as possible.

"Well," he responded lazily, as if trying to find another reason to stay. His eyes surveyed his surroundings, but my tiny hotel room had nothing for them to land on. This time, I'd been careful to keep everything in my suitcases. The only thing he could see were swollen bags with half-open zippers.

"If I remember anything, I'll send you a message. And, please, I'd be grateful if you would share anything you found out. These are my colleagues you're interrogating and . . ." After a slight hesitation, I added, "And it was my bike that was sabotaged."

"That's what I said: Everything seems to be happening around you," said the commissioner as he left the room.

I sat on the bed and sent Axel a text I would come to regret: "Whatever it is you have to tell me, tell me tomorrow, I'm drained." I turned off my phone and tumbled backward. I don't know what happened after that. It was the first night on the Tour de France in which I didn't go over the rankings at the end of a stage. I tried to find comfort by telling myself they were the same as the day before.

GENERAL CLASSIFICATION: STAGE 13

RANK	RIDER	TIME	NOTES
1	ALESSIO MATOSAS (ITALY/LAVEZZA)	51:34:21	Guiltier than ever.
2	MILENKO PANIUK (CZECH/RABONET)	+0:22	Accomplice #1.
3	PABLO MEDEL (SPAIN/BALEARES)	+0:26	Accomplice #2.
4	STEVE PANATA (USA/FONAR)	+4:49	He begins to recover but it might be too late.
5	MARC MOREAU (FRANCE/FONAR)	+8:26	End of my dreams, I'll be lucky if I can help Steve.

6	ÓSCAR CUADRADO (COLOMBIA/MOVISTAR)	+8:42

From here on down, no threat for the podium.

7	LUIS DURÁN (SPAIN/IMAGINE)	+9:25
8	SERGEI TALANCÓN (ROMANIA/ROCCA)	+11:03
9	ANSELMO CONTI (ITALY/LAVEZZA)	+13:21
10	ROL CHARPENELLE (FRANCE/TOURGAZ)	+13:27

2014

If Lombard was like a father to me, and Steve was the brother I never had, Diana Panata was the mother I'd been missing.

Diana died just weeks after Steve won his third yellow jersey in France, and just days before La Vuelta. She was killed by a sudden pneumonia that overcame her after a plastic surgery marketed as risk-free. Steve's father, a lawyer to his core, considered the possibility of suing the hospital, alleging she'd caught the fatal virus in its operating rooms. If anybody had seen us at her funeral, they would have sworn I was the mournful child and Steve was a friend there in solidarity.

We both suspended our training and flew to Santa Fe to get a glimpse of her body before it was cremated. I fell apart when I saw her in that wooden box, wrapped in a shroud, expressionless. That immobile face couldn't be hers. Diana was somebody who operated as if on a lithium battery, incapable of being still for more than three seconds.

What made me fall apart left them, father and son, utterly

overcome. They stared at her, numb, trying to understand what would happen to the rest of their lives without that woman, who illuminated everything she touched.

I had never been able to call her Mother, though she had told me to many times, but I ended up accepting the maternal attentions she gave Steve and me equally during her long visits to Lake De Como. From the first time she stayed with us for a season, she went on a crusade to end my orphanhood with a zeal the Templars would have envied. She corralled me into dental appointments, renovated my wardrobe, equipped both my kitchen and Steve's with all sorts of gadgets we never used, and watched over our girlfriends with the rigor of a warden looking over a harem. In short, she became everything Beatriz, my mother, had never been.

Steve's father, Robert, on the other hand, always treated me with a distant courtesy. Although, to be fair, that wasn't much different from how he treated Steve. He was a refined and cordial man; his condescension and impersonal ways did not feel disdainful—instead, he gave the impression his mind was caught up in something more transcendent than his immediate surroundings.

Instead of being jealous of his mother's attentions, Steve became her accomplice. He shared his belongings with me, his money—I think, if he'd been able to pull it off, he would've shared his girlfriends—and he did it all very organically, as if it were part of the natural order. It felt almost childlike. But there was a dark side to that intimacy. Take videogames. When it was my turn, he'd pass me the PlayStation, but he'd do it with a huff, like a child who has to share the swing with his brother even though he doesn't want to. Eventually, Diana bought me my own console and that was the end of our problems. Or at least that's what I thought.

We spent months engrossed in a cutthroat competition over a virtual soccer game for which I seemed to have an innate talent.

The first few weeks, I annihilated him so badly Steve would sulk, but insist on playing again and again, like a gambler addicted to his bad luck.

When Steve was in a good mood—that is, when he won—he was like the sun. Similar to his mother, he had the rare talent of making everything around him shiny. His enthusiasm and energy were like champagne to me, sparkly and intoxicating.

In victory, he was generous, expansive, and supportive. In defeat, he could be a kick in the balls. He would slam the door on the kitchen pantry, curse aloud over the tiniest thing, and dent the car pulling it out of the garage. He'd behave as if his losing were an act against nature, a sign there was a misalignment in the universe that had disrupted the order of things.

He practiced playing that soccer game on his own and, judging by the rings under his eyes, played late into the night until he began to beat me fairly regularly. It was only then that peace and happiness returned to our home and his fraternal love enveloped me again.

But, regardless of his moods, he never let me doubt I was more than an ordinary friend. During training camp in Tenerife at the beginning of the year, I got a strange fever that landed me in the hospital for four days. Steve raised holy hell because he wasn't allowed to sleep on the couch in my room. We weren't technically related, so he slept scrunched up in the backseat of his car in the parking lot. When I was finally released, it was hard to tell which of the two of us was achier. After that, he spent several months exploring the idea of a name change, so that situation would never happen again. His father finally put a stop to that plan when Steve asked him what legal steps he had to take in order to add Moreau as a surname.

Generally speaking, I was amused and flattered by these brotherly affections, but very aware that I was a transient figure in the Panata family. I took it for granted that sooner or later our destinies would diverge. When Steve won his first yellow jersey, he felt very badly that I didn't want to get a tattoo of a little bicycle on my calf, like he did, commemorating "our" triumph. But I thought it was excessive: It was one thing to accept that the Panatas had informally adopted me, but to brag about Steve's victory as if it were mine struck me as pathetic.

Lombard found the entire thing pitiful. He had originally sent me to try out with the Ventoux team with the secret hope they'd choose me to replace their star racer, Bijon, whose retirement was imminent. It must have been a huge disappointment to the colonel to realize the team had chosen Steve, and that I'd accepted becoming a domestique for the indefinite future. And worse yet, that I had found a family but not with him. In many ways, I was more his son than Bernard was. The boy had grown up living with his mother and had never had an interest in cycling, his father's passion.

As if in response to Diana's attentions, Lombard came over to visit more and more frequently. When he found out Diana called and talked to both me and Steve on Sunday mornings, he got in the habit of calling Saturdays after training or competition.

When he realized it was impossible to compete with Diana when it came to domestic advice, he opted to concentrate on the technical aspects of training and to churn out father-son speeches about the meaning of life that came straight out of a self-help book. At some point, I said something to Steve about that, and it became an inside joke between us. "Everything happens for a reason" was one of his favorites, and we began using it for just about everything. When we were out on dates or hanging with our friends and there was a moment of silence, we'd repeat the enigmatic, "You have to live like you think; otherwise you'll end up thinking like you live." We would say it with a very serious and absolutely convincing tone while trying to hold back gales of laughter.

I'll never be able to apologize enough for how hurt he was when he realized we were mocking him. One day when he called,

Steve got on the phone to ask him something about a power meter about to go on the market, chatted briefly, and then hung up, or so we thought.

"He told me early to bed, early to rise, makes a man healthy, wealthy, and wise," he said, laughing, turning around and stepping a few feet away from the kitchen counter, where the phone rested.

"It's true, the early bird gets the worm," I responded.

"Lose an hour in the morning and you'll be all day hunting for it."

"No, the devil is in the details."

We went on like that, cracking ourselves up with nonsense refrains until I went up to the kitchen counter to get a glass of water. A little green light on the phone let me know the line was still active, that Steve hadn't hung up properly. I picked it up and heard labored breathing on the other end. Then a click cut off the communication.

In the following weeks the colonel acted as if he hadn't heard anything, although I could tell from the stiff and measured way he treated me how offended he was. I never again made fun of his refrains. He himself went back to them a few days later. Lombard and Steve entered a state of mutual tolerance, but neither ever understood the importance of the other in my life.

Stage 14

Rodez—Mende, 178.5 km.

In the same way that I thought about the rankings before going to bed each night on the Tour, the first thing I did when I got up was visualize the stage that awaited us. Last night I'd broken my habit and that morning I did so again. Surviving two attempts on your life in four days would disrupt anybody's routines.

Instead of analyzing the course, my mind concentrated on how to stay alive for the next few days. I concluded I had two possible scenarios before me. If the killer was looking to have one of the three leaders—Matosas, Paniuk, and Medel—win in Paris, he was well on his way. With a little bit of luck, he would be satisfied with the lead they had and leave us alone. Of course, there was the possibility that, once Fonar was eliminated, the killer would concentrate his attacks on two of the three leaders to make sure his champion definitely won the yellow jersey. Matosas was still my main suspect. I felt sorry for Paniuk and Medel, although only a little, considering what they'd tried against us the day before yesterday.

But there was a second and much worse scenario. We hadn't gotten to the Alps yet; four days among those great peaks could change everything, including the five minutes they had over us. With the powerful English team, Batesman, and the Spaniards from Movistar crippled with injuries, Fonar was by far the strongest team on the high mountain. Precisely because attacking steep inclines was not Steve's strength, our team was made up of climbers. I figured if the killer knew even a little about cycling, and it was obvious he did, he wouldn't let us reach Ventoux and the other Alpine peaks in one piece.

I hadn't left my room yet, but I assumed there had been a guard all night at my door. I wouldn't die like Fleming, drowned by an intruder in the bathtub. Still, the imagination and the resources the killer had shown in making Fiona's gas tank explode and destroying my bicycle led me to conclude a third attack could come from anywhere. Today we would ride 178 kilometers of open countryside, which left us vulnerable for almost four hours.

Until now, whoever was responsible for these tragedies had been relatively successful in making them look like accidents. But if they decided to change tactics, there was no defense on the road against a sniper or a murderous motorcycle. After giving it some more thought, I set that possibility aside. That kind of killing would probably mean canceling the Tour, and I had long ago discarded Radek or any of the other race's enemies as the possible author of those attacks. No, whoever was behind this wanted to crown their man in Paris. And to do that, they needed to make sure their next incident looked equally accidental.

Favre was right: The only way to stop the next death was to find out who the killer was before he had a chance to attack. Instead of holding the commissioner in such disdain, I should have been working with him to find some evidence of guilt among the mechanics or eliminate them as suspects once and for all.

I went over the profiles of the five Fonar mechanics and decided to concentrate on the two who were responsible for preparing my bike: Marciel, aka the Dandy, and Joseph, the family man. In theory, any of the other three could have done it, but it would be difficult without the two in charge of my Pinarello noticing. I immediately set my sights on the first one. The Dandy was a little frivolous and tended to look down on his co-workers. Joseph was the opposite, a shy man dedicated to his numerous offspring and his wife. I set him aside for the moment. The mere suggestion of something risky would probably make him sick. If poor Joseph had been a part of any kind of sabotage, he would have cracked in the first hour of the interrogation.

I did a quick review of what I knew about the Dandy's private life, but I couldn't come up with any revealing facts. Then I remembered someone had recently mentioned he was suffering from heartbreak. The start of the race had buried the memory, but now I began to try to put it together, like someone trying to rescue a ring from a drain with nothing more than a fragile toothpick.

I knew there was something else, something important. Frustrated, I got dressed to go to breakfast, but I couldn't stop thinking about the matter. Now it was like something caught in a tooth I couldn't stop obsessively picking with the tip of my tongue. I went out in the hallway and said hello to the officer struggling to stay awake while sprawled out on a little bench. And that's exactly when I recovered the ring from the drain and got what was bothering me out of my teeth: The Dandy's sorrows were the result of a love affair involving Daniela, Di Salvo's sister. Di Salvo was an Italian cyclist who'd recently retired. Daniela was a beautiful woman with an explosive temperament that we all knew well because she'd gone out with half a dozen cyclists; apparently she didn't think much of going out with a mere mechanic and broke things off quickly with the Dandy.

I was walking down the hall when an even more pertinent bit of information hit me. Di Salvo was from southern Italy, like Conti and Ferrara, Matosas's men. If I'd been a character in one of Lombard's comic books, an imaginary lightbulb would have gone on above my head. I then did what no one ever does in those classic comics. I pulled out my cell and texted the information to the commissioner. When I finished I realized I had half a dozen messages from Axel and one from Fiona.

I still had the cell in my hand when I received Favre's response regarding the Dandy: "He's our main suspect. Today we confirmed he made deposits greater than his salary. That he has a girlfriend with ties to Matosas's people could be the key. Well done, Sergeant Moreau, please continue."

The commissioner's orders made the whole situation feel less like a game. To accuse the Dandy gave me a bad taste in my mouth; even though he wasn't a particularly nice guy, he was still a member of our team. I tried to shake off my discomfort by telling myself I was doing the right thing. In the end, if he was innocent, the whole incident wouldn't be more than a bad afternoon for him.

When I went into the dining room, I looked over at the mechanics' table and saw they were all there. A quick look at their faces made it clear none of them had slept very much. If Favre was trying to break them from sheer fatigue, it didn't look like it would take much more for them to confess to being responsible for Kennedy's assassination.

The Dandy was among them, wearing his little gold bracelet but without his usual poise, his eyes nailed on the cereal bowl before him. My teammates were rattled. Turning to me, Guido said the police had let the mechanics go at about five in the morning so they could do their work. Murat the Beast raved against the authorities and about the need for Fonar to protect its people against the abuse they were now being subjected to, slipping in a Catalan insult every other word. The rest of the table agreed and I nodded, fidgeting in my chair. It was touching that the cyclists stood in solidarity with the mechanics in spite of the sabotaged bike. Being a witness to this made me feel just a little shittier. And the worst was yet to come.

Minutes later, two of Favre's assistant detectives, followed by three police officers, walked into the dining room and went straight to the mechanics' table. They ordered the Dandy to come with them. It was clear that the commissioner had decided to make a scene. Three teams were staying at that hotel, among them Matosas's team, Lavezza. That means forty or so people started hitting their glassware with silverware to show their disapproval of the Dandy's arrest.

Several of my tablemates were standing now, and I could still see the backs of the police when my cell lit up next to my plate. Fortunately, no one was paying attention to me or my phone. "Your intuition was correct, sergeant. Daniela di Salvo and Ferrara are from the same town, Reggio Calabria. I will interrogate M. until he confesses. I can't set him free because he will flee."

I immediately looked around until I found the Lavezza team. Their chief of mechanics, Ferrara, was presiding over the table, the picture of someone who could blow your brains out without a pause in his breakfast. It was hard to imagine that man and the Dandy's ex, the exuberant Daniela, came from the same town.

Town. That's what Favre had said, but from what I remembered, Reggio Calabria was much more than just a town. I checked the internet and it turned out it was a city with a population of 180,000. Ferrara must have been around fifty years old and Daniela was maybe thirty; it was hard to imagine them as classmates. That didn't mean their families might not have known each other, although it was a stretch from that to any kind of evidence of complicity. If I trusted that line of thought, having grown up in Medellín, I would be a member of a drug cartel. But it's that line of thought—my line of thought—that had led to the Dandy's arrest. I felt like a Judas in disguise.

"Stevlana heard about my fall and wants to come," Steve said from his seat next to me. He seemed to be the only one not paying attention to the scene that had just unfolded, involved as he was in exchanging text messages with his girlfriend. Even at a distance, Stevlana could demand, and be, the center of attention, or at least my friend's attention.

"Tell her you're fine, that she should meet up with you in Paris. The Alps are going to be really tough and you don't need her all over you." Although it was just an expression, I couldn't avoid imagining her in bed, literally over Steve, shaking her breasts in the air.

"I know," he said, "but how do I make her understand that?"

"Tell Benny to distract her with something else, to earn his salary." Benny, Steve's agent, was an ingratiating kind of fellow who would lay his kid down in a ditch and walk over him in order not to get his fancy shoes dirty.

"She hates him right now because the tickets he got us for Bob Dylan's farewell concert were in the twentieth row."

"Who doesn't she hate?" My question was meant to be rhetorical, but Steve actually answered.

"I don't think she hates Margaret," he said. Margaret was the director of his foundation, dedicated to helping street kids. The foundation's efforts were focused in Colombia, something for which I'd have to be grateful to Steve for the rest of my days. They'd channeled millions of dollars into rough neighborhoods in Bogotá, Medellín, and Cali.

"That's it then: Tell Stevlana that Margaret is on the verge of resigning and that she is the only person to whom she would listen, or whatever. Plead with her to go to New York to talk to her, say you would do it yourself if you weren't in the middle of the Tour." Stevlana had traveled a couple of times to Colombia with Margaret to raise funds and visit favelas and had been very satisfied with her own good deeds. And, in fact, she had done a great deal of good: A number of millionaires had signed fat checks after she gazed into their eyes and said please.

"Perfect. Stevlana loves to save the day. I'll talk to Margaret so she can get her performance ready. That could keep her busy for a whole week," he said enthusiastically. "You're brilliant today, *Mojito*."

"Don't you dare call me that," I said, although I was pretty pleased myself. I only wish finding the killer and winning the yellow jersey were that easy.

As if he'd been waiting for the precise moment to reawaken my pessimism, Axel the soigneur came into the dining room, sweaty and agitated.

"Why aren't you answering my texts?" he complained. "Are you finished? Can we talk for a moment?"

"I'll leave you two alone; I don't want to know any intimate secrets," said Steve, laughing.

By that point most of the diners had left or were about to leave. Our own table had emptied. "I didn't get a chance to look at your messages yesterday," I said by way of apology. "What's going on?"

"The cops are killing the mechanics. They've had two sleepless nights in a row."

"I know, but there's nothing I can do," I said and felt my ears get hot and probably red. I'd never be a good poker player. Although Axel wouldn't be either, since he didn't seem to see anything out of the ordinary in my response. "Anyway, my sabotaged bike is the only clue the police have, so they can't actually charge anybody."

"It's just that the Dandy and the rest of them are all innocent," he said, contorting his body as if he couldn't wait one more second to pee.

"Come on, Axel, you're not going to tell me you think it was an accident. In 2008 it could be seen as a mistake, but not now. The adhesive for aluminum they used on my wheel has been banned for a long time on the circuit. Somebody was trying to mess with me. And that could only have been done by whoever worked on my bike just a few minutes before I got it."

"That's what I've been trying to tell you since last night. It was your bike . . . but it wasn't."

I stared at him, trying to figure out what he was saying. Axel could be a joker, although when it came to work he was sensible and responsible, and his anguished face didn't belong to somebody who was playing around.

I asked him to explain what he meant, and he did: At the beginning of the season each cyclist gets five bicycles; some, like Steve and me, get a few more. Over the course of several months, the bikes are cannibalized in order to create two or three with optimum conditions and those are the ones used in the competition. A hit here, a worn gear there, and you have to replace the handlebars or the pedals. Axel told me that, with a little bit of hustle, some mechanics on the circuit manage to steal enough pieces from the inventory to put together whole bikes that they then sell at astronomical prices. Steve's bikes and mine—although mine not as much as Steve's—are the most sought after from Fonar.

He reminded me that, during Il Giro two months earlier, I'd had two harmless falls. They had resulted in two rigged reports that exaggerated the damage. The result had been an impeccable bike sold on the black market for twenty thousand euros.

"That was the sales pitch: 'It's the one Marc Moreau uses on the Tour,'" said Axel, using air quotes around the last part.

"I can see where you're going with this. That black market bike could have been the one that was sabotaged. But that doesn't explain how I wound up on it, does it? It would have had to go through the Dandy or Joseph, who are in charge of my equipment."

"Not necessarily," he said, his eyes downcast, "and that's why I wanted to talk to you alone."

"What?" I asked, more intrigued by the minute.

"I had to take care of the bikes all that week," he said, and stopped, upset, hoping I would figure out the rest of the story.

And I did. The soigneurs on the Tour do a little bit of every-thing, including watch the bikes while the mechanics eat break-fast.

"It was just Pierre and me. But there are more than twenty bikes and you know how it is: journalists snooping around, tour-ists sneaking around, hotel staff. They take photos and ask you questions."

I did know how it was. The bus that carried the bicycles was usually parked on a hotel side street and always ended up becom-ing an improvised bike gallery. As the mechanics cleaned, greased, and prepared each bike, they left them somewhere near the vehi-cle: on the ground, against the wall, on their stands.

"You think someone could have come along and replaced the original in the full light of day?" I asked, incredulous.

"I've gone over it time and time again and I can't remember anything, but it's the only possible explanation. C'mon, you know Dandy and the other guys. None of them would ever do anything so vile. So it has to be someone from the outside who exchanged your bike."

"The police mentioned some suspicious deposits in Dandy's bank account," I said.

"Of course! It was for the bike sales he made under the table."

"Well, then, why doesn't the Dandy just say so?"

"He's not saying anything because that would mean confessing his theft: Fonar would fire him and maybe even press charges. Of course the way things are going, he may not have a choice."

"Then what's the problem?" I asked, impatient.

"If they buy the argument that the bike was exchanged, the cops will focus on trying to find out how the altered bike got to you. In other words, they'll interrogate whoever was watching the bicycles that day."

Now Axel was looking at me with arched brows and a crum-pling face, on the verge of tears. It was the face of a little boy sent to the school principal's office.

"Is that it?" I asked. I'd gotten scared; for a moment, I thought there might be something to really worry about. "We all know this is a circus and there are too many people around to take care of so many bicycles. The mechanics practically work in the street. Any one of us could testify to that, don't worry. They'll interrogate you for two hours, look at your past, check out your bank accounts. Then they'll let you go and that's that."

"It's just that, that's the problem," he said, lowering his eyes once more.

"What? Your past or your bank accounts?" I asked, more curious than anything else.

"It's just that . . . I was also involved in the bike sales," he responded in a barely audible voice.

"Fuck, Axel!"

"What we do isn't a big deal, Marc," he pleaded. "Fonar sells the bikes at the end of the season anyway. What's it matter if two or three disappear along the way? We never put the ones you use at risk. We always make sure they have all the pieces and replacements they need. Do you know how much we can get from a collector for one of Steve's bikes? Four or five times its market value. It's a fortune for us and it doesn't hurt anybody."

"But why are you telling me? You should confess to the police, or to Fonar at least, so they'll take you and any other member of the team off the list of suspects. It's better that you took advantage of a loophole than that you killed somebody, don't you think?" I was about to use the word "thief," but I stopped myself just in time; my soigneur was already feeling bad enough.

"I know. I wanted to ask your advice, because I heard you're consulting with the commissioner who's in charge of the interrogations. Perhaps you could put in a good word about me to him."

So he knew too. And to think I'd been convinced my meetings with Favre were a secret. Fiona always found a way to know everything. But if Axel was in the loop, the rest of my teammates probably were as well. They would see me as a collaborator. With the police squeezing our crews, it explained why so many of them were treating me coolly. I had attributed that to Lombard's statements in the press, which made me seem out to sabotage Steve's championship. Now I saw it probably also had to do with my closeness to the authorities. A collaborator on top of being a traitor—in the eyes of a cyclist, these are worse sins than being the inventor of cobblestones.

"I'm not consulting with the commissioner," I told Axel. "He's come to see me a couple of times because I was once with the military police. But, obviously, I didn't play along. I got him off me as best I could." I wished the whole team could hear me.

I wasn't lying to him. I *had* tried to get rid of Favre; I always said as little as possible. I was no traitor, at least not yet. And even less of a collaborator. Though if anybody took a look at my phone in the past hour, they'd think otherwise. Goddamn Favre, look what he'd gotten me into. What would Fiona think knowing it was my fault they'd arrested the Dandy? How would Lombard take it? Steve? Hell, all I'd wanted was to help put a stop to a killer who was hurting my community.

". . . incapable of hurting Fonar," I heard Axel say. The words brought me out of the black hole of self-pity into which I'd fallen. "Will you say something on my behalf?" he pleaded.

"I'll do what I can," I said.

He hesitated and, before leaving, turned and gave me a hug, as if he were saying a final farewell before being shipped off to Alcatraz.

When he pulled away he saw something on my neck and, with the confidence of someone who knows his territory well, pulled the collar of my sweat jacket aside to examine my skin.

"Where did those bruises come from?"

"What are you talking about? What bruises?" I asked, pulling away and crossing over to one of the large mirrors that tried to make this narrow room seem more expansive. In fact, I did have some purple marks on the side of my neck. They must have been the result of Giraud jerking me around outside the bus the day before. The combined genes of Colonel Moreau and Nurse Restrepo could be a blessing when it came to cycling, but they were a disaster when it came to many other things. In addition to my sulfuric sweat, my skin suffered from the sensitivity of Queen Marie Antoinette.

A little later, I saw Steve on the bus during the transfer to the starting line. I thought that he wouldn't give me a hard time for turning the Dandy over to the police. I could tell Steve I'd drowned a twin brother in order to be an only child; he would have shaken his head and attributed it to the incomprehensible characteristics of my French-Colombian nature. I had little appreciation for my friend's current celebrity lifestyle, and I supposed he looked down on my evenings of puzzles, jazz, and good novels. But the complete communion we had when it came to the bike neutralized any differences we might otherwise have had.

The objective for the day was the same as for the day before: to try to help Steve's recovery and to keep the leaders from gaining any more distance. Unfortunately, this was a much tougher stretch. We would race for 137 kilometers without obstacles and then have to deal with two climbs before the finish line in Mende. Our rivals were also keeping track of Steve's recovery, but with opposite intentions: They needed to get rid of him once and for all before he got completely well and Fonar launched its counterattack.

The stage began as predicted. Matosas and his gang set off at a dizzying rhythm, although without trying to break away or blocking in bad faith the way they'd done the day before. They were simply trying to get Steve to burn out before we reached the two final climbs, where they'd attack.

And yet I worried about a much more imminent danger I hadn't dared mention to Giraud or even Steve. Between kilometers 44 and 59 we would confront a fifteen-kilometer descent that was pure free fall, a modality my partner had mastered better than anyone else in the circuit. But only cyclists themselves know what goes on in the head after an accident. On the Vernhette descent, we would be flying at speeds of more than 80 kilometers per hour and it would be impossible for him to not relive the panic he'd experienced when he'd lost the tube, especially because at these speeds, an incident like that could mean death.

I'd seen real veterans become paralyzed facing a descent the day after a dangerous fall; it's similar to the panic experienced by an automobile driver taking the first curve after leaving the hospital they'd landed in after a car accident. I also feared the opposite effect: that Steve, in order to overcome his fear, would risk more than what was necessary to suppress the panic. That would be very characteristic of my friend.

"Let's go down slowly," I said when we began to toboggan at kilometer 44. He arched his brow, surprised, and I looked down between my right leg and the pedal, pretending to have some sort of difficulty. He looked at me worriedly and nodded toward the front, where the three leaders had gathered. He was afraid we would fall behind.

"Nothing serious, I'll change bikes when I stop to pee," I said, keeping up my deception. Starting at kilometer 59, we'd race over a long flatland in which the peloton would slow down for a few minutes while most of the racers pissed without getting off their bikes. This scene is never shown on TV, although it's as common as greased links and scrawny bodies: a Versailles-like fountain made up of one hundred colorful athletes emptying their fluids on both sides of the road.

My strategy meant losing a spare bike but it worked out. We went down with relative caution in the back of the peloton, and as soon as we got to the plain, we quickly recovered our positions just behind the leaders. Despite my anxieties, Steve's descent was impeccable. He seemed to have galvanized his spirit against the fear that haunts other cyclists; an accident was an anomaly that had nothing to do with him, a flaw in the bike, an incident that would not be repeated.

A few kilometers later, Giraud came up in his car and handed me another bike amid stares from the mechanics. I wanted to think the wary attitude with which they checked out my bike had everything to do with the sabotage we'd experienced two days before, although I couldn't help but notice a tinge of incredulity in the way they were looking at me. I understood that, after what happened, the mechanics had been painstaking in preparing my bike before the race, and when I asked for a change, they assumed I had had a puncture. Now that they saw that wasn't the case, they couldn't understand my reasoning.

I shook my head and emptied it of thought. I would confront every challenge that presented itself and only at the end would I try to compose a vision of the whole. We wouldn't survive this stage if I mixed killers and cops with the curves and slopes that awaited us.

The next kilometers went by at a frenetic pace, but without incident. Matosas, Paniuk, and Medel kept looking over at Steve's face, waiting for a sign of fatigue or surrender, while their domestiques brutally jerked the peloton around. They were like three impatient vultures waiting for the last gasp from a hopeless buffalo. Except that Steve refused to succumb. Only I, who knew him best, could see the tension in his jaw and the effort he was making to hide the pain he was suffering as he tried to keep his rhythm on the climb up the first of the two climbs on the last stretch.

The Sauveterre was not a particularly sharp peak, but it went on for more than nine kilometers. Steve held on, but I could tell he was bone weary. I had doubts he could get past the Croix Neuve waiting for us at the end of the stage: It was only five kilometers long, but three of these kilometers had a ten percent gradient, and he would feel that as if he were scaling a wall. I guessed that something in his ribs was bothering him; he was blinking strangely when he breathed, as if the intake of air was burning his insides. Giraud finally noticed it too. Since the beginning of the race, he'd been periodically asking Steve how he was doing and Steve had responded positively, if monosyllabically. In the past half hour of the race, though, he'd stopped answering the DS, as if he feared every word he spoke would steal energy from the next pedal.

When we started up the last hill, I prepared for the worst. If Steve collapsed at the foot of the slope, the three leaders would stand up on their pedals and end up with a two-digit lead. The Tour would be over for us. *Not for you,* I heard Fiona's voice in my head, or whatever ambitious beast Fiona had awakened inside me. The voice was right. If Steve was eliminated, I was the best positioned of the Fonar racers: fifth place in the rankings. In theory, the team would work for me and I could attack those hateful leaders. In fact, I could do it right now, in the Croix Neuve, as soon as my brother was officially dismissed from the race.

But we should never underestimate the devotion in the soul of a domestique. I swatted away my demons, gathered the team, and formed a kind of diamond around Steve. These noontime roads in the Pyrenees were where I was given the name Hannibal, and I knew every one of its summits from countless hours of training. I knew about the winds from the side that would buffet us during the first part of the ascent and I found a way to control the line by letting the mountain protect us. If our rivals wanted to pass us, they'd have to peel off the wall and do it against the wind. It may not have been much, but it was a strategy.

"C'mon, champ," I said to Steve, bringing my head close to his. "Just hold on for fifteen more minutes. Tomorrow's stage is all downhill and then we get a day off. Let's not let those sons of bitches cut us off today and I promise we'll take the jersey from them in the Alps."

He didn't respond. Just nodded his head, like an obedient child, although the pallor of his face gave me a bad feeling. He didn't even correct me: We had two more days before getting a day off, although right then I would have told him the moon was made of cheese so long as it got him to hold on a little longer. He managed to gather the strength to follow us when we snuck in between the mountain and our rivals.

"Defend your position even if you have to bash them; we're going into a headwind," I told the team over the radio or, more precisely, the four of us who were left. And it worked. In three hundred meters, when our competition felt the force of the wind, they wanted to get between us and the shelter provided by the mountain wall. But we closed ranks and they had no choice but to try to pass us, which was virtually impossible with all that gusting. They finally chose to get behind Guido's wheel—he was the last man in our formation—and share our shelter. They would wait until the playing field changed to attack Steve again.

A few seconds later we hit them back with one of the dirty tricks that they'd tried on us: Guido dragged out his pedaling so the rest of Fonar could take some distance from our rivals. They got frantic and tried to pass him, but as soon as they lunged forward, Guido would immediately accelerate, put his elbows out, and zigzag to force them into the middle of the road, exposed to the brutal whirlwind. This went on for more than a kilometer. Steve's weak state kept us from taking advantage of our teammate's ruse, but I still thought it had proven fruitful. Each kilometer that we weren't victims of an attack constituted a small victory for us.

Desperate because Croix Neuve was just ahead, Matosas consulted the other two leaders and they decided to go for it. If they didn't attack now, they'd lose any chance of taking over the Tour once and for all. They pulled away from the wall, sent their domestiques to take turns in pairs at the front, and stood up on their bikes. I knew that on the last stretch, just as we neared the peak, we'd lose the natural barrier, and I feared the worst. But it turned out that the rival domestiques were fried after a half-dozen attacks against Guido, and, even better, when the small group was finally at the point of catching up to us, Medel sat down, physically and spiritually spent. All you had to do was look at him to understand he'd been hit by the notorious and much feared bonking: that catastrophic moment when the cyclist's fuel tank is simply empty. Three weeks of riding had suddenly done him in.

Medel's teammates immediately slowed down to accompany their leader. Matosas and Paniuk lost their momentum and didn't know what to do. They had never considered the possibility that one of them would crumple before Steve. We took advantage of the situation to gain a few more meters. And that's how we arrived at the peak eight hundred meters later. After a slight descent, we reached the finish line. We were so concerned with what was going on behind us, we never broke formation to let Steve take the lead. It was only when we crossed the line that I realized I had once more won the stage. When we added in the bonuses for first and second place, we'd managed to take a few seconds from Matosas: I got 22 and Steve got 18. It wasn't much, but the psychological implications were enormous. Medel came in five minutes later, which let Steve knock him off third place in the general classification, something that, earlier that morning, we had thought impossible.

The gratifying sensation I got from our small and unexpected victory went to hell when I got to the hotel and discovered Axel and his hands were not there to receive me. I imagined my loyal soigneur stammering excuses and shaking before Favre's caustic phrases and disdainful smile.

I wasn't sure it would do any good to talk to the commissioner, but it was the least I could do for Axel. First, though, I needed to wait for Steve's soigneur to finish his usual session with our leader, so he could get his talons in me and help me avoid the embarrassing cramps typical of the day after a stage. The two-hour wait seemed eternal since I was used to getting a massage as soon as I got off the bus, but these were Giraud's instructions. Yet another small payback.

The thought of the Fonar DS made me run my fingertips softly over the dark bruises the bastard had left on my neck. That's when my brain made one of those connections that can only be the result of watching too much *CSI* on TV. Fleming's body had had bruises on its neck. Was it possible to compare the bruises and determine if Giraud's fingers had been responsible for both? My forensics knowledge wasn't that deep; in fact, it didn't go much further than the marvelous thighs of Claude from Biarritz. In spite of how inconvenient it would be for the head of Fonar to have been responsible for the crimes, I entertained myself with the image of our haughty DS being handcuffed and shoved into the backseat of a squad car. I decided to talk to the commissioner. I didn't even know if Fleming's body was still at the morgue or if he had been buried or cremated.

But now there was a more pressing matter I needed to take up with the detective. I had no idea where they could be interrogating Axel, and even if I knew, I didn't have the means or the pretext to just show up there. So I had no choice but to send the commissioner an urgent text asking him to come find me. I wasn't entirely clear what I would say, except to testify to my friend's professionalism and good heart, an argument about as useful as a thumbtack in the path of a bulldozer. Favre finally had the leverage he'd been looking for. He would describe the horrific prison where they would be sentenced for stealing those bikes, unless, of course, the Dandy and Axel were willing to tell all they knew about the other members of our circuit. And soigneurs and mechanics knew things: tricks and cheats, subtle forms of anti-doping, closeted homosexuality, adulteries, betrayals, and, yes, even felonies. In other words, the usual dirt that's part of any semi-closed society. In the hands of the commissioner, devoid of context and the mutual trust and solidarity involved in a team, that information would be a tool for extortion that could break wills and blood oaths. Favre might or might not find out who the killer was this way, but I had no doubt the process would ruin reputations and devastate lives. The ringing of the hotel room telephone brought me out of my worry.

"Monsieur Moreau," said Ray Lumiere's ceremonious and unmistakable voice on the phone. "Could I take up a few minutes of your time?"

I said yes and hurried downstairs to see the old journalist, even though experience had shown me that every time someone said that to me I ended up losing more than mere minutes.

The celebrated reporter was sitting on a cozy couch in the lobby of the lodge where we were staying that night. He was so famous his byline simply read "Ray"; he was the same reporter who had published Lombard's deafening declarations in *Libération* just days before. He was a romantic, cloaked in the hermetic shield of cynicism, and a legendary figure in the cycling world. He was almost seventy but looked almost the same as he had forty years ago, when he began to cover the Tour. When the dinosaurs disappeared and a bicycle emerged from the haze, Ray had been there to describe it.

But his fame wasn't entirely due to his apparent immortality. His pen had been responsible for many of the best lines ever written about cycling, or about any sport for that matter. For many of us, the finest reward that could come from winning the Tour was the possibility of being, finally, the subject of one of his articles. No racer could truly enter the pages of cycling history until they had inspired a legendary phrase from the poet of the pedal. The tennis star Rafael Nadal, a cycling fan, once said the only thing he regretted was that, after winning at Roland-Garros, there was no Ray to transform what he'd accomplished into a literary feat.

"Monsieur Moreau," Ray began on seeing me, "sorry to bother you, but you must understand that the circumstances demand acting with a certain poise."

I nodded, although I didn't exactly understand what he meant. Ray spoke in short phrases, but there always seemed to be more behind his words, like sharks or mermaids under placid surface water.

"There's someone among us who is causing havoc and it would be much better to find out who it is before the police do, don't you think?" Ray said.

"I don't know what to tell you; the information is quite confusing," I responded, trying to gain some time.

"The information is not confusing. The hits have been committed in plain sight. It seems to me that the only thing that's confusing is the identity of the person who's doing this."

I decided to be honest with the old journalist. Ray was a kind of cycling alter ego, a defender of the pure and epic nature of the sport. There were rumors he had tipped off the police about a cargo of drugs destined for the Festina team in 1998. It was the first great doping scandal. Although his role was never confirmed, many had assumed he did so with the hope of deliberately unleashing a purge to take out the trash his sport had been accumulating.

"Our mechanics are being run over by Commissioner Favre and that worries me. A lot of people could be hurt," I said, finally letting it all out.

"It has taken a lot of work to get over Festina and Lance Armstrong; I don't think we could survive a third scandal."

"And what do you suggest, Ray?"

"We were mistaken in how we handled doping. We should have never let the scandals play out in the press and in civilian courts. This time we have to figure out the problem and fix it ourselves."

Once more, I found myself imagining marine monsters under the surface of his words. What the devil did Ray mean by "fix it ourselves"? Up until this moment, I'd thought my responsibility was to help identify the guilty party and, once I'd accomplished that, to let the police know. They'd take care of it from there. But now, the reporter was proposing something terrible without quite saying it. To get rid of the killer? Make him disappear in a ditch and act like nothing had ever happened?

I stared at Ray, wondering if the old man had lost his mind. He was an odd guy, with hairy ears and a reputation as a wild and reckless driver, but with enough influence to terrorize the rest of the members of our circuit, police included. One character among the many in our circus. His parents had been killed in Treblinka and he had experienced great poverty during his postwar childhood. From a young age, he'd found a refuge from the horrors of the world in cycling, and he clung to the last vestiges of what he considered heroic in the sport with the desperation of a castaway. Now, it seemed to me, the demons from his childhood had come back to reclaim him.

"I don't see what we could do. We aren't cops and we don't have their resources. I don't see myself shaking up poor Dandy to make him confess who he sold the goddamn bike to," I said carefully, assuming Ray already had all the information I did. "I have a better chance of wearing the yellow jersey than I have of figuring out who is trying to kill me." I was disheartened to find I actually believed this, but there was a certain relief in talking to someone else who had been pondering this same question.

"You've always been able to wear the yellow jersey; you just never had it as a goal," he said with certainty. "But that's neither here nor there. What I've come to tell you is that we have something the police lack. There are few things on the Tour that could escape the combined forces of Fiona, you, and me."

I ignored the first part of his comment and focused, for a moment, on the alliance he was proposing. The old man was right. Among the three of us, we had strategic positions that were also complementary.

"What about Lombard . . . ?" I added, thoughtfully. My mentor had a lot of time on his hands and a talent for making friends with the mid-level functionaries of the organization, the officials who coordinated the patrol cars and the motorcycles, and the drivers and assistants who make up the daily framework of our spectacle.

"You know things, I know other things, and Mademoiselle Fiona must know more than the two of us put together," he said, ignoring my suggestion to bring Lombard into the group. "If we could exchange information about the strange incidents from these few weeks, we might be able to figure out what's going on. And let's be honest, Monsieur Moreau, the situation is limited to four teams: Fonar, Matosas's Lavezza, Paniuk's Rabonet, and Medel's Baleares."

"Let's suppose we find the responsible party, then what?"

"We neutralize them, we threaten to reveal their identity unless they stop, I don't know," he said, exasperated. "It really depends on who it is and what this is about. I'd do anything before I let another scandal destroy cycling's credibility."

In a way, the old man was right: A yellow jersey win because of the intervention of a killer could be the coup de grâce against the Tour. The race was just now starting to shake off the perception many people had that behind every winner there was a new illegal drug when, in fact, tough new rules had made drugs marginal. The overwhelming majority of cyclists raced without the help of banned substances or illegal transfusions, although many outside the sport continued to think that wasn't the case. One more scandal would send cycling's image on a journey of no return.

"All right. I'll talk to Fiona today. Just promise me one thing. If we find out who it is, swear you won't do anything unless the three of us decide together."

Ray stayed quiet for a moment and then nodded. It wasn't much but I had to live with it. Then I told him what I knew: that Matosas and Giraud risked being fired at the end of the season, about the bicycles sold on the black market by the Dandy and Axel, the summary report about the gas-tank explosion in Fiona's trailer, the autopsy report on Fleming's body, and, after some hesitation, about the purple marks my DS's fingers had left on my neck.

He listened, expressionless. I don't know how much he knew already. Neither did I know how much of what he told me in return was true or simply nonsense cooked up by an obsessed old man. He claimed that two of Medel's domestiques had had several nights of clandestine visits from women before Baleares's DS found out. It later turned out the women, who they'd thought were genuinely interested in them, were actually prostitutes sent by an anonymous benefactor. He'd learned that a very good climber with Partak, the Russian team, had gotten a generous financial offer to leave the race in the third week, and he imagined there must be other isolated cases. He said that the diarrhea that had affected various racers with the AG2R team the second week of the competition had been induced by a powder laxative used to spike their food.

A lot of these incidents struck me as the kind of stupid pranks typical of a college fraternity rather than the threatening designs of a criminal like the one the police were looking for. And yet. An orgy and its subsequent insomnia would affect a couple of domestiques enough that a mid-tier team wouldn't be able to surprise anyone. And the dehydration caused by a leaky stomach could be as effective as a leg fracture to unravel a rival. These were very easy, practical measures that could be taken by anyone in our circuit.

If what Ray said was true, the extent of the cases and the diversity of the resources pointed toward a well-planned conspiracy. Something thought out over a long period of time and executed by a network of collaborators. A group that had no problem murdering a cyclist in the tub or blowing my brains out by planting a bomb in a trailer, but that also didn't mind using a childish trick to get rid of a competitor. When you looked at the big picture, the killer had managed something remarkable: The ten or twelve most competitive teams had suffered some kind of setback that kept them from operating at one hundred percent, except for the squads of Matosas, Medel, and Paniuk. And Fonar, which survived thanks to whatever forces had allowed me to escape the two attempts on my life in the past few days.

I thought it might be good news that the attacks seemed so well planned. Maybe the criminals wouldn't be able to improvise a third attack on the seven stages that were left, especially now that we had been warned and that Giraud, the police, and Steve's bodyguards were all shielding the Fonar team. Right now, there were two thugs standing between us and the lobby entrance without the slightest interest in disguising their presence. Through the window I could see a patrol car in front of the hotel and several cops leaning on it.

Ray and I exchanged phone numbers and said goodbye. He told me he was staying at a hotel thirty kilometers away and that, as a precaution, he wanted to leave before it got dark. It being summer, we still had two hours before that would happen, but it wasn't a bad idea for the old man to be extra careful. I imagined cars, motorcycles, and pedestrians leaping to the side as Ray's green Renault lunged forward faster than his age and eyes should have permitted.

I checked my phone for messages. There were two. One was from the commissioner: "Impossible to see you now. Unexpected turn of events. I'll bring you up to speed tomorrow." Favre used texts like a telegram, as if each word had a price on it. I decided not to ask what an unexpected turn of events could possibly mean. On the contrary, I felt relieved at not having to see him that night, even if it meant not being able to intervene on poor Axel's behalf. I easily squelched my guilt by telling myself I had tried. And I completely forgot about my soigneur when I read the other message in my inbox. "Ask me to sleep over," wrote Fiona.

That night we did what we'd never done during three weeks of racing. We knew we had two of the least demanding stages of the

Tour before us and then a day off. Or maybe we just had a need to feel alive and together after the danger and the anguish of the past few days.

Fiona came from cold climes, but her body exhibited all the colors of summer. I started with the green of her eyes, then the cherry of her nipples, and wound up in the rose between her legs. In turn, she worked on my body unhurriedly, lingering over each moment, knowing it would be a long time before we could enjoy each other again.

We rested, grateful and silent, listening to the sounds of the Tour being dismantled. Little by little the voices of the mechanics and the assistants working around the buses under our window faded away. When the darkness and the silence were complete, I began to talk. I brought Fiona up to date on Ray's proposal as she caressed my chest with her calloused hand, attentive and quiet.

I described my experience of the past few days in detail—Favre's visits, my fears about the killer, and my fragile hope about the yellow jersey.

"Giraud or Matosas: One way or another, it has to do with one of them," she said with a raspy voice after a long pause.

"I feel the same way, but the attacks against me would have to eliminate Giraud," I said, almost disappointed. "He'd be harmed the most if Steve was beaten."

"He's the biggest son of a bitch in the entire circuit; I would expect almost anything from him. Although I agree, something's not right in all of this. The other person it could be is Ferrara; he's a total shit." Fiona talked like the mechanic she was.

"I guess he could have found out about the sale of my bike from the Dandy and Daniela, and gotten one of his people to buy it. He would know what to do with the tubular glue and how to stick the bike in with the others so it would come back to me. Do you think the mechanics who work with him might know anything?"

"I'll see. Although I'm confused about the gas tank in the trailer. Any mechanic would have realized immediately that it was almost empty: Once you open the hatch that protects it, the meter is right there. The only explanation is that they were trying to scare you but they wanted it to look like an accident. It doesn't make sense otherwise. And I won't dismiss Giraud or anyone else around Steve," she said. My chest flinched on contact with her fingers, as if they'd suddenly become live coals. "Your director and Fleming hated each other—you knew that, right? Back when Giraud was coaching an English team, he wanted to win at any price, like always, and he forced the guys to take drugs. Fleming refused and turned him in to the executives. There was a brief investigation and then the matter was discreetly forgotten. Giraud never worked with the Brits again. He spent months drinking and unemployed, and more than once he was heard saying that if he ever got his hands on Fleming, he'd kill him, that Fleming had made everything up."

I remembered the impassioned eulogy that Giraud had given about the dead man, and I felt an acid punch at the base of my stomach. I agreed with Fiona: Someone like that was capable of anything. He was the kind of guy who, if you saw him with red eyes at a funeral, it was only because he was allergic to flowers. I wasn't sure why she had said she wouldn't discount other people around Steve. I wanted to ask her but I didn't want to break the loving complicity we were enveloped in. If you ignored the deadly content of our conversation, we were talking like a married couple at the end of the day about the gossip in the neighborhood and the things that had to be done around the house. Moments like that were the closest thing to home I'd ever had.

I slowly started to fall asleep, but when I realized I had forgotten to ponder the state of the rankings, an image of them gradually filled my mind. Steve was in third place and I was in fifth. *Things could be much worse,* I thought, just before sleep overtook me.

GENERAL CLASSIFICATION: STAGE 14

RANK	RIDER	TIME	NOTES
1	ALESSIO MATOSAS (ITALY/LAVEZZA)	56:02:19	He's the killer, there's no doubt.
2	MILENKO PANIUK (CZECH/RABONET)	+0:22	Main accomplice.
3	**STEVE PANATA (USA/FONAR)**	+4:31	**So long as he's alive, there's hope.**
4	PABLO MEDEL (SPAIN/BALEARES)	+5:06	The Spaniard drops in the third week.
5	**MARC MOREAU (FRANCE/FONAR)**	+8:04	**I could overtake Medel, at the very least.**
6	ÓSCAR CUADRADO (COLOMBIA/MOVISTAR)	+9:56	
7	LUIS DURÁN (SPAIN/IMAGINE)	+10:25	
8	SERGEI TALANCÓN (ROMANIA/ROCCA)	+11:49	
9	ANSELMO CONTI (ITALY/LAVEZZA)	+14:38	
10	ROL CHARPENELLE (FRANCE/TOURGAZ)	+14:52	

Stage 15

I began the day with an optimism I hadn't felt in weeks, or at least since Favre's little mustache had come into my life. Fiona's body, which I was entangled with when I woke up, had the alchemical ability to transform shit into gold. It helped that the alliance with her and Ray made me feel as if I were part of a secret and powerful league rather than a simple domestique and fake detective being exploited by a manipulative commissioner.

And, besides, the course that day was for idiots. It had a minor climb in the middle of the route that barely counted, where the entire peloton would arrive en masse after many kilometers of subtle descent. It was a typical transitional stage as we neared the Alps. Our enemies wouldn't attack today no matter how much they wanted to. Or at least not on the bike, which made me remember that there was danger whether there were peaks or not. The very thought caused a spasm between my clavicles, and I invoked the memory of Fiona's body to get rid of it.

I tried to concentrate on the day's tasks. Making lists is a great tool to fight anxiety. One, to run the race as efficiently as Steve's physical recovery would allow. Two, to talk to Favre about Axel to avoid any unnecessary rudeness toward my soigneur on the part of the cops and, in the process, gather as much information as possible to take to the meeting with Fiona and Ray later that night. Three, to grill Steve to see how much he knew about Giraud's scheming. These past few days I'd seen them whispering more than usual. Until now I had assumed it was about technical things, but Fiona's and Ray's suspicions suggested Steve might know a little more about what was going on than I had assumed. I began with number three.

"Did you talk to Stevlana? Did she fall for the story about Margaret?" I asked as soon as I sat down beside Steve at the breakfast table. I wanted to immediately raise a topic that could bring us together. I was learning a little something from the commissioner's tactics.

"It worked like a charm," he said, pleased with himself, and he gave me a thumbs-up. "She's in New York now."

"And is your dad nervous?" Mr. Panata was already in France, but, being respectful of our wishes, he wouldn't show up for the Tour until we arrived in Paris.

"I calmed him down; luckily, he hadn't seen any of the rumors published in *The Daily Sun*."

"Did you hear that the cops suspect the accident with the tube was deliberate?" Up until that moment, Steve and I had not discussed the subject. The official explanation was that the arrests of Axel and the Dandy were a direct result of an investigation regarding negligence.

"Giraud brought me up to speed. You see? I told you something strange was going on, that we had to protect ourselves from something."

"What does Giraud think?"

"He thinks it's all coming from the Italians, that Ferrara and two or three of his people are playing out their entire repertoire of dirty tricks now that they've got the podium in sight. He says he's had run-ins with them for years."

"Listen, do you think it could be something between Giraud and the Italians? Could we be in the middle of a little war between them?" I'd finally taken the conversation in the direction I wanted. Steve thought for a few seconds.

"But then, how do you explain Fleming?" His response left me speechless. So Steve knew that the Englishman's death was a murder. My friend had not said a word to me to indicate he thought it was anything other than suicide. If I needed any proof that something had broken between us, there it was. He interpreted my surprised expression as an effort on my part to pretend I hadn't known. "I suppose the commissioner told you," he said in a scolding tone.

That meant Steve knew everything or almost everything. I preferred to think the fact that he hadn't told me was payback for my not having shared with him my conversations with Favre. He had a right to be offended.

"I didn't want to worry you," I responded sincerely. I remembered how sad he'd grown years earlier when we were told about my mother's sudden death. "I'm sorry," I added. He gave me a resigned half-smile.

"We can't forget that you and I were riding around together before any of these other people showed up," he said, moving his head in a semicircle, the gesture taking in everything that is the Tour. I thought that Lombard came before him, but I didn't say anything. "That includes Giraud, Stevlana, and Fiona," he added, scolding me yet again.

I was surprised. Generally speaking, he was even less inclined than me to talk about his feelings.

"Benny asked a private security firm called Protex to initiate an investigation parallel to the police's," he went on. He was clearly trying to be honest and signal that, from this moment on, we would be open about any secrets we'd previously been guarding.

"It's going to cost a bunch of money but, as my agent, he wanted to know if you and I are really in danger."

"What have they found out?" I asked, practically salivating at the idea that there might finally be a light in the darkness. Favre had infected me with his goddamned bloodhound tendencies.

"They're expensive but they're good," said Steve. "They have a way of getting into the police files. They've got two private detectives working on the case, although they prefer I not meet them or have any kind of relationship with them. They email me a report every night."

"Well, what have they found out?" I asked impatiently. Now, rather than a bloodhound, I felt like a dog in a butcher shop.

"The police found traces of a military-grade plastic explosive in the fragments from the gas tank from Fiona's trailer."

"That's in the police files?" I said, indignant.

"Didn't the commissioner tell you?" he asked, triumphant that his secrets were better than mine.

"No, that bastard didn't tell me anything," I responded, defeated. Apparently, I was destined to be Steve's domestique even when it came to detective matters. "What else?"

"Your bike was sold to an intermediary two months ago." He paused to consult an email on his cell. "It was a Dutch guy. He then sold it to a private collector, and that's when they lost track of it. They only know he was French."

"And what do they know about Matosas and his people?"

"Conti has a criminal record, and Ferrara was involved in drugs in and out of our circuit, but there's nothing to pin on them yet. They've already confirmed that for some of the 'accidents' before the Tour, they had alibis. In some cases, they weren't even in the same country. So, if they were involved, it's something much bigger than just the two of them."

"Do they have anything on Giraud? I know the Fonar owners want another DS for next year. He must be desperate."

"He can be a jerk, I agree, but you don't think he's a killer, do you? He wasn't even in Le Havre the night Fleming died. He told me he was going to Amiens because he was meeting some analysts coming from Paris. He ended up staying overnight and driving back early in the morning to meet us for breakfast."

The center where we did our biometric and performance analyses was just outside the capital. Every four or five days an expert would catch up with us wherever we were to discuss the progress of each racer and possibilities for the remaining stages.

"That's pretty convenient, don't you think? Do you know what time he drove back? Protex could find that out, right?" To be honest, I was mostly provoking Steve, although suddenly I could feel the purple spots on my neck, as if something had activated them.

"Giraud is an asshole but he's not an imbecile. If he wanted to kill Fleming he would never have done it personally. Everybody recognizes that belly of his a mile away. He could have used a hit man, though," he mused. He said this as if he were deciding whether to take a taxi or an Uber. Where was the innocent golden boy? We were now alone in the hotel dining room, accompanied only by waiters who kept looking at us, hoping we would get up so they could finish their shift. We said goodbye and agreed to meet two hours later on the team bus.

I still had time to see the commissioner about the second issue on my list: helping Axel. Grinning, I wrote Favre a note in his own telegraphic style: "I'm in my room until 11. I have new info. Urgent." The bloodhound would not be able to resist sniffing that.

On the way to my room, I thought about what Steve had told me. He was right about one thing: Our DS could be explosive and resentful but he wasn't dumb. He would never have taken the risk of being recognized. And yet, I still had a bad feeling knowing that he'd stayed in another town the night of Fleming's murder; it was too good an alibi. That's what I should have said to Steve, but this always happens to me: I only think of the perfect rebuttal when I can no longer use it.

Favre knocked on my door just a few minutes later.

"What did you find out, sergeant? What do you have?" he said, panting. He must've rushed up the stairs.

"Good morning, commissioner. Would you like something to drink?" In fact, I didn't have anything other than water and a few gels to offer him.

"Yes, yes, good morning. What is your news?" His poker face had been replaced by visible anxiety. There were pearls of sweat on his little mustache, all in a row. I wanted to drag out my response just to test his patience, but I too could barely contain myself.

"I found out the gas-tank blast was caused by a military-grade plastic explosive, according to a police specialist. I thought you should know." I congratulated myself for that last sentence.

"I do know. The information came to me late, and since we couldn't see each other yesterday . . ." he said, irritated, as if it were my fault. Then he looked at me as if trying to guess my weight. I could practically see a line of text on his forehead reading: *How the hell did he find out?*

"And have you found out anything else about my bike? Who was it sold to?" Now I was the one playing poker. He scrutinized me again, trying to figure out if the question was genuine. He decided not to chance it.

"It was sold for a brief time to a Dutch businessman, and he sold it to an anonymous buyer." He said it in one breath, like someone who wants to swallow a bitter drink as quickly as possible. "That's all we know." Obviously, the commissioner was used to receiving secrets, not telling them.

"Are Axel and the Dandy still detained? What you've just told me exonerates them; they didn't sabotage the bike, did they?"

"If it only worked like that," he said in the sorrowful tone that a carpet merchant might use because he can't lower the price. "That's not at all clear. And let's not get into the other offenses they could be charged with," he added, letting that veiled threat hang in the air.

"So long as Fonar doesn't accuse them of anything, and it hasn't and it won't, there's nothing to investigate. We both know that. We need them back to work; the team resents their absence."

"We're doing everything we can," he said, irritated once more. "These things take time." Our dialogue wasn't fun anymore for me either; I'd lost my initial advantage.

"Don't make me a double victim, commissioner. First a tricked-up bike, and now my soigneur detained. Axel has worked with me for years and he knows how to get me in shape. Yesterday I was numb during the race."

"I'll see what I can do," he said indifferently.

"Ray Lumiere visited me," I said abruptly, playing my last card. "He wanted to know what I thought of the incidents. I responded ambiguously, but you know how reporters can be. He kept insisting, and I ended up saying I too would *see what I could do*," I concluded, using his own phrase. This was the equivalent of opening my fly and putting the measuring tape on the table, and almost as tasteless, but I was done with subtleties. If he threatened to hold Axel indefinitely, I could try to bluff that I'd actually be willing to work with Ray to make the scandal public.

It worked. "I think Axel has already told us everything we could use," Favre conceded at last. "But Marciel still has a few things to tell," he added curtly, using the Dandy's real name.

"Is there any relationship between Daniela and Ferrara?" I asked now without any ulterior motive. Having dealt with Axel and taken care of my second goal of the day, it didn't make any sense to keep playing with the commissioner. My tone returned to that of a helpful colleague.

"Their families know each other. One of Ferrara's daughters went to the same school, although they were in different grades," he answered, embracing the cease-fire.

"This would begin to close the circle around Matosas's people," I said. "Of the three in front we might have to cross out

Medel. Two of the domestiques from the Baleares team got clandestine visits three nights in a row that lasted into the wee hours.
It turned out they were prostitutes sent by an anonymous benefactor. In other words, somebody was trying to mess with the
Spaniard. This leaves us with just two aspirants to the title who
have been untouched by any of these criminal events: Matosas
and Paniuk."

I don't know why I offered the commissioner this information.
I suppose I wanted to pay him back in some way after he shared
about Daniela. But I hadn't even finished saying it before I started
to feel guilty about being disloyal to Ray, who had given me the
information. My discomfort lasted even after Favre left and I
dressed for the race. But it vanished when I went out to the hallway and saw an exhausted Axel going into his room. Whatever I
had offered in the transaction with the commissioner had been
worth it.

On the team bus on our way to the starting line in Mende, I
asked Steve how he was feeling. He mimed as if he were the Hulk
ripping his shirt to ribbons, and although he grimaced, he gave a
thumbs-up. But once we got on the road I realized he was not well
just yet: His cadence hadn't recovered the elegance and efficiency
that had made him famous, and although it was less noticeable
now, the stiffness in one of his arms was inhibiting his style. The
doctors had said Steve hadn't broken anything, but it was clear
the bruising had an effect that would take a while to go away.
Nonetheless, his improvement had been noticeable over the past
two days and we still had three to go before the summits in the
Alps, where everything would be decided. I congratulated myself
on the ease with which we were tackling the 183 kilometers before
us. Or at least that's what I thought.

Nine out of ten stages like today's end with the entire peloton
arriving together at the finish line. When it doesn't work out like
that, it's because a little group of ten or more racers manages to

make an early breakaway, and if they manage it, it's because there isn't a contender among them to justify the extra effort a peloton would need to give chase. These are stages in which the leaders in the rankings don't move much. Matosas and company decided it would be different this time.

I was ready to respond to practically any escape or blocking tactic they might try. But I could never have imagined what they had in mind. Two and a half hours after we'd begun, just as we started to climb the only obstacle in our path, L'Escrinet summit, Matosas's teammate Alonzo approached Steve on his less protected side. Even though all of Fonar was riding more or less together, the tightness of the peloton made it impossible to keep a strict formation around our leader.

I noticed Alonzo's arrival—the Italians' green jerseys would set off alarms in me even if I were asleep—but his move didn't necessarily mean anything hostile. Inside the peloton, the riders mix like strawberry seeds in a blender. I began to worry when I realized Alonzo had stabilized his speed, staying right next to Steve, less than twenty centimeters away. I intuited what was coming: That bastard made a quick turn so that the part of the axle protruding from his back wheel hit the spokes on my friend's bike, as if he were a gladiator in *Ben-Hur*.

To break somebody's wheel in the middle of a race is a desperate measure. Its success is not guaranteed, and the result can be deadly. Especially if it happens in the middle of the peloton. As soon as one axle hits another, it can cause one or both racers to lose their balance and start a chain of accidents with unpredictable consequences. And even if those involved manage to keep their balance, the broken spokes force an immediate replacement of the bikes.

Clearly, Lavezza was willing to chance it, even if it meant sacrificing one of their teammates. Later, when I saw the scene on TV, I noticed the rest of the Italian team had moved to the front of the peloton before Alonzo made his hit. That way, they avoided the risk of being victims of a fall, and put themselves in position to attack as soon as it happened.

But, once more, the gods of the road took pity on us and our misfortunes. Alonzo attacked Steve on his right side, his hurt side, and the impact caused my teammate to inadvertently fold his arm and twist the handlebars into the Italian's way. Steve fell on top of Alonzo, right up front, and that's what saved him from the slaughter unleashed in the back. The Beast, who rode behind Steve, and Alonzo himself got the worst of it. Without intending to, they served as a containment wall against the rest of the riders, who collided against them.

When the incident unfolded I was riding on the other side of Steve. I had come up to ask him how he was feeling before we faced the slope. In that moment, I did what every racer does on sheer instinct when there's a fall: You keep pedaling to escape the avalanche but slow down enough to see how bad the situation is.

"Steve fell," I screamed into my mic. "With about half the peloton," I added after a pause. I later found out thirty racers had collapsed, although only a dozen were injured.

"Sons of bitches," I heard a furious Giraud say. "And the Italians? Paniuk?" he asked. I looked ahead and saw a good part of the green team standing on their pedals and trying to gain some distance. When it comes to accidents, the unwritten rules dictate that we should ride at the same speed or even slow down as a matter of respect for our fallen brethren. But Matosas and his group had long abandoned any code of ethics.

"They got away," I said, disappointed.

"I'm okay," Steve said in my earphone. In the distance I noticed he had stood up. A few other Fonar teammates did the same; the ones who hadn't fallen floated between my position and Steve, who seemed to be looking for something. I was afraid that, in shock, he had once more lost his sense of where he was. Later I found out he was just trying to find a Fonar bike in good enough condition to ride.

"Go after them, Marc. Don't let them get away, even if you have to knock them down," ordered Giraud. "Guido, get the rest of the guys and organize support for Steve."

I didn't wait a single second. I changed gears and leaped forward. Half a dozen racers—Paniuk and Radek among them—did the same. The three of us rode like madmen, taking turns leading until we saw the Italians. There were six of them, including Matosas and Conti. I was satisfied to see that two Lavezza racers whom I'd always liked weren't among them. From what I could tell, Matosas hadn't been able to get all his teammates on board with the dirty trick they'd just pulled.

The peak of L'Escrinet is only eight kilometers from the base, and the slope has a discreet gradient of six percent, but I still thought I could take maximum advantage. I had no way of knocking them down, like Giraud had ordered me to do, but I could certainly catch up to them. I decided I could also pass them.

"Will you follow me?" I asked Radek as we reached the Italians. He responded with a strange smile and then positioned himself behind me; a few others followed.

Most of the time, when a small pack reaches another, both stabilize their speed to recover their strength. When we caught up to the runaways, I felt the cyclists behind me begin to relax. We'd reached our objective, and they were taking a necessary breather. But Radek and I toughened our cadence and, to everyone's astonishment, kept going. We were able to put Matosas behind us a few meters, and we promptly extended that distance while his teammates organized a chase. I didn't mind towing Radek the rest of the climb; he'd earned it. He wasn't a bad climber, but I was stronger. For a moment, I thought maybe Fiona wasn't so far off in her estimation of my potential. When we got to the summit we learned we were 1:12 ahead of Matosas and Paniuk. The rest was a breeze. We got to the finish line 58 seconds ahead of them. I could've won my third stage of the Tour, but I let the Pole go first.

Unfortunately, Matosas had achieved his primary goal: to hurt

Steve. Maybe it wasn't that I was such a good cyclist, but rather that Matosas hadn't made much of an effort to go after me; I wasn't his target. That day he managed to take two minutes from my friend, and also from Medel, his ex-accomplice.

If I thought I'd seen Giraud furious before, what was happening now was epic. Sitting on the bus on the way to the hotel, the team simply listened to the DS explode, too tired or hurt to respond. Not that he was expecting a dialogue. Giraud is the type who considers a monologue a conversation. Nonetheless, in the end, he came at me.

"And you? Why didn't you do something?"

"Well, at least I kept them from winning." I didn't want to argue, but neither did I want to be crushed by the neighborhood bully.

"Don't be a fool! The idea was for you to slow them down, not make them go faster."

"You're the fool, Giraud," muttered Steve in a low, angry voice, although Giraud and a couple of racers heard him. Giraud went speechless, and maybe breathless, because he began to turn blue. Then he half turned and sat down. Our DS could be explosive but he was no fool. One word from Steve to the team owners and Giraud would be unemployed.

That night, Axel's hands ended up soothing my muscles and my ego. Although they were painful, his massages always put me in a better mood. When I got up after those sessions, the world always seemed a better place than the one I'd left ninety minutes before. To be fair, ninety minutes earlier I'd just gotten off a bus full of exhausted cyclists dealing with a furious and dissatisfied DS.

During the session with Axel, I tried to steer the topic toward the interrogation. Perhaps he had found out something useful that I could take to the meeting that night with Fiona and Ray, my new fellow detectives. But, though the soigneur's hands had not lost their magic, his gift of gab had been left behind at the local police station. The poor man was devastated, and all that tension and fatigue had not done much for the scarce beauty of his features. I decided to respect his silence. I didn't even know if he knew about my efforts to get him released, but that didn't seem very important.

I went to dinner a little before the scheduled time with the hope of finishing before Giraud showed up. I didn't want another harangue from our terrible manager. Apparently, a few others thought the same thing because most of the team members, including Steve, were already serving themselves from the buffet the chef had set up for Fonar.

"Don't be a fool, Guido, and serve yourself some salad," said Steve, in an exaggerated tone. Everyone laughed and that made me feel better. His sense of humor didn't take European sensibilities into account, and he didn't always understand what was funny to us. But this time he'd hit the target. Making fun of Giraud's insult robbed it of its sting.

We spent half the meal deploying the line whenever we asked for salt or Nutella, stopping only when Giraud showed up.

Luckily, that night we were sharing the dining room with the Dutch team, which imposed limits on what our DS could and would say. From what we could tell, it would have been stinging; he was furiously swallowing enormous bits of barely chewed food.

Fiona, Ray, and I agreed to meet after dinner in the room Fiona had taken that night in our hotel, a privilege afforded to only the highest level of UCI officials. I would have liked to spend a few moments alone with her, but we decided Ray should arrive first so the bodyguards Steve had put on me wouldn't see him. I had once again suggested that Lombard join us, but judging by the old man's absence, I'd been overruled.

As soon as I sat down, Ray began. "Given what happened today, it looks more and more like it's Matosas and his crew," he said. "He must be feeling desperate, to start playing gladiator in the middle of the race like that. I just got back from the hospital where the Beast and Alonzo are being treated. They'd put them in adjoining beds. Thank God, a nurse spotted the Beast dragging himself on the floor, trying to get to Alonzo. They changed their rooms before he could beat him to a pulp."

"Too bad that nurse showed up," I said. "Did the judges see what happened on the video?" I looked to Fiona when I said that; her UCI clearance kept her in the know. "Have they reviewed it yet?"

"I just got out of the meeting. They asked me to attend so I could explain what happens to a bike when the spokes are destroyed."

"And what did they decide?" Ray asked.

"Nothing. Alonzo chose the perfect moment. The helicopter that films them had just gone ahead, and all the video we have is from the motorcycles. The attack was in the very middle of the peloton. No matter how many witnesses say it was an act of aggression, there's no way to prove it, much less any reason to sanction Alonzo."

"Well, then, we're fucked," I said in frustration.

"Not entirely. At least you took that stage from them," said Ray, appreciatively.

My heart glowed. If only the journalist could be my DS.

"But there was something else of interest," said Fiona. "In the last of the footage from the helicopter, you can see the Italian team moving up front, because they know what's going to happen, but not Medel's or Paniuk's teams. Matosas screwed them over too."

"That makes sense; both of them are very close to the Italian in the rankings. I imagine they created the alliance to neutralize Steve with the idea that they would figure out the yellow jersey later, but Matosas got ahead of them," said Ray.

"Maybe that feud will take over, and they won't continue to join forces against us."

"That's what I think," said Fiona. "Which means the Alps are a golden opportunity for you. Those three are no competition for you there."

"Seven minutes behind and a killer on the loose," I said to Fiona. "That's a dangerous combination."

Ray watched us, amused. He could probably tell this was an old argument.

"Could be less than seven minutes." Fiona smiled. "I have good news for you. After the meeting, the members of the appellate commission stayed behind. They're trying to find a way to give you back the two minutes you were penalized for using Radek's bike."

"Why would they do that?" asked Ray, surprised.

"This is off the record, okay?" said Fiona.

"Yes, of course," he said after a painful pause. To ask that of a journalist is like asking a politician to pay his own expenses.

"Lombard has been hammering one of the Tour's administrators, complaining that you can't be punished, because your bike was sabotaged. Saying you can't apply a conventional penalty to an extraordinary case. They began to get worried when the colonel insinuated he could go to the press with his complaint, so they all turned to Jitrik. Now it seems he's pressuring the judges to come up with an elegant out."

"The rule doesn't allow for exceptions," said Ray skeptically.

"That doesn't matter to Jitrik. It seems they're considering saying they can't penalize Marc because he gave up his bike in a noble act of sportsmanship. But what's most interesting to me in all this is the lengths the Tour's leadership is going to in order to keep people from knowing there's a criminal taking out racers."

The old reporter shook his head in silence. He deplored that the judges would violate a rule, even if it was for a good reason. I certainly wouldn't put up an objection. I had already done the calculations. If they took away the penalty, I'd be five minutes behind the leader and in third place, ahead of Steve.

Fiona saw my expression and knew exactly what I was thinking. We couldn't avoid tiny smiles, and my hip imperceptibly moved a centimeter closer to hers. Suddenly, we had one reporter too many in the room. Then I remembered I had to leave first, so I could take the bodyguards with me and Ray could discreetly make his exit. But being in the same hotel meant nothing could keep me from coming back to her room later that night. I looked over at Fiona and it was clear she'd read my mind again, because she gave me one of those *Don't even think about it* looks. She was probably right, because if we made any missteps, those five minutes could become fifty.

I went back to my room and checked out the official Tour website. They still hadn't taken back the two-minute penalty, but I adjusted the positions in my head and I loved what I saw. I was ahead of Steve by a little more than a minute, something that hadn't happened since . . . ever.

GENERAL CLASSIFICATION: STAGE 15

RANK	RIDER	TIME	NOTES
1	ALESSIO MATOSAS (ITALY/LAVEZZA)	59:58:54	At least he's shown his true face. A killer. Everyone's enemy.
2	MILENKO PANIUK (CZECH/RABONET)	+0:22	Apparently, he was never a part of the criminal conspiracy.
3	MARC MOREAU (FRANCE/FONAR)	+5:12	It's not official yet but . . . Steve's behind me.
4	STEVE PANATA (USA/FONAR)	+6:30	How will my bro deal with this? Will he still be my bro?

5	PABLO MEDEL (SPAIN/BALEARES)	+7:05	You couldn't get to the podium even using dirty tricks, buddy.
6	ÓSCAR CUADRADO (COLOMBIA/MOVISTAR)	+11:55	
7	LUIS DURÁN (SPAIN/IMAGINE)	+12:24	
8	SERGEI TALANCÓN (ROMANIA/ROCCA)	+13:48	
9	ANSELMO CONTI (ITALY/LAVEZZA)	+16:37	What's this guy doing in the top ten?
10	ROL CHARPENELLE (FRANCE/TOURGAZ)	+16:57	

Stage 16

Bourg-de-Péage—Gap, 201 km.

I woke up indecisive, which is a very unpleasant way to start the day. I tossed and turned in bed, uncertain whether to surrender to the exquisite feeling of knowing I was ahead of Steve in the Tour de France—the Tour de France!—or concern myself with the terrible consequences that could bring. I was in third place, and better yet, I knew I could beat the two ahead of me on the mountain. I thought about the yellow jersey, and my heart responded with trumpet calls and palpitations.

A text from Steve cut short the festivities: "I have to see you before you talk to Giraud." I assumed my friend wanted to prep me for bad news. I imagined the worst: a warning of a positive report from the anti-doping agency, or Fonar's decision to cut me from the team because of my insubordination. After a moment, I rejected both possibilities. Fiona would have heard before my DS if there'd been any kind of anti-doping disqualification, and Giraud knew Steve had no chance of diminishing Matosas's lead on the mountain without my help.

Up until this point, I'd been attacked in order to harm my partner. Now that I could be crowned in Paris, there were double the reasons to eliminate me. Anything the DS was plotting against me seemed silly in the face of being killed. Armed with this precarious comfort, I knocked on Steve's door.

"He wants to teach you a lesson," he informed me as he let me in, "but it'll be symbolic, don't worry. Something that lets him show you he's still the boss, but harmless."

"And what's the lesson?" I asked, distrustful.

"To hand out supplies during today's stage," he said, lowering his eyes.

I can't say it took me by surprise. It was a humiliating task for a world-class domestique, forcing a chef to wash the restaurant's dishes.

Giraud must have been truly offended because, in strategic terms, he was playing with fire. Today's course wasn't transitional: Although we wouldn't be hitting any important summits, it was a journey of 201 kilometers, of which only 30 would be downhill. The rest would be a very long ramp—not too much of an incline but always uphill. Five hours of pure wear and tear that would leave us crying out for the next day's break. Going up and down the peloton's route would be an enormous additional strain if I wanted to finish at the same time as the leaders. It would be like running a marathon with metal weights on my ankles.

"Bastard."

"Don't worry, I convinced him to spread the task out among several people. Hopefully, he'll just ask you a couple of times. I told him I needed you fresh from Wednesday on so you were ready to help me whip Matosas." He said this in a conspiratorial tone, but in the end, his eyes fixed on mine expectantly.

In other circumstances, this would have been unnecessary to state; my role was taken for granted. But now Steve was looking at me as if his life depended on it. Suddenly the reason for his apprehension became clear to me. He knew the two-minute penalty was to be lifted and I'd start the stage officially ahead of him. He wanted to confirm my willingness to sacrifice myself for him. He wanted to make sure my third place in the standings hadn't changed the agreement between us: to make him champion.

"Thanks," I said, expressionless. I knew I would probably end up doing what all domestiques do, but for the moment I had that wonderful drug—power—flowing through my veins. I felt for my partner, but it was nice having things reversed for once in our lives. "Well, let's go get breakfast." I turned my back and left the room, leaving him to deal with his dilemma.

Not even Giraud's orders two hours later diminished my spirits. I nodded when he told me my task for the day, as if he'd asked me not to forget to adjust my helmet, refusing to give it importance. I didn't want to give him the satisfaction of seeing me enraged or humiliated.

When the riders grouped together to wait for the signal to leave Bourg-de-Péage, my bike was to Matosas's side. I took the position unconsciously, so used to seeing myself next to the yellow jersey. The leader ignored my presence.

I wondered if Lavezza would try something as outrageous as yesterday. They'd sacrificed one of their best domestiques in exchange for our leader, but Steve was still riding. On balance, they'd suffered the greater loss. And to top things off, their standing with the union couldn't be worse, even if they would never be officially sanctioned.

Once again, Radek spoke for our collective indignation. While Matosas avoided my gaze, checking his calf as if he'd found an inexplicably resilient hair after waxing, the Pole stuck his bicycle between us.

"If you do anything like yesterday," he told the Lavezza leader, "I'll kill you." Matosas shook his head and gave him a wry smile, as if he considered this just one more of Radek's amusing eccentricities. Then he turned around and murmured something to one of his teammates.

"I'll do it, you hear me?" Radek insisted, then looked at me defiantly, as if I'd also disrespected him. I nodded without a word, thinking anything I said could make him angrier or, worse, lead him to fulfill his promise. I recalled the initial list of suspects from just a few days ago, led by the Pole. Now, I'd conclusively ruled him out. I couldn't believe he was a criminal after all he'd done for me. Still, he was a weird guy, someone you didn't want to have as an enemy. I decided his warning to Matosas could be useful; the Italian would think twice before making another shitty move.

"Don't kill him," I said after a pause. "Just make sure he's not wearing the yellow jersey in Paris." I went for a festive tone, as if the whole conversation was nothing more than a joke. I hadn't finished my sentence when I realized my mistake. Radek pursed his lips and narrowed his eyes, like a Templar receiving a holy assignment. *I won't uncover the killer, but I'm going to end up creating one,* I thought with a shiver.

The next five hours were no less stressful. Giraud turned me into the pizza-delivery boy, carrying food and water from one end to the other along the peloton's route. It wasn't just a couple of times either, as Steve had promised. When my teammates realized what was happening, they stopped asking for drinks, bars, and gels and tried to limit themselves to what they could grab from the staff in the refreshment areas. Giraud decided to hydrate them in spite of that. I went up and down the ladder again and again, a miserable Sherpa carrying electrolytes on his back.

At least that day, none of the other teams tried anything out of the ordinary. Riders broke out from the bottom of the rankings, knowing it was their last chance to get on TV: Only the best climbers and the leaders in the standings would stay together through the four remaining stages on the Alps. Fortunately for me, the rest of the squads took it easy, turning that last lap before our day off into a Casual Friday. They made just enough of an effort to catch up with the runaways, so we all arrived in Gap together.

I crossed the finish line at the tail end of the peloton, although with the same official time as my rivals, Steve included. Unfortunately, I was much more exhausted than the rest of them. I cursed Giraud, and for a moment, while showering on the bus, I considered the possibility of persuading Radek to include my DS in his death threats. When I put on my pants I thought of something that improved my mood: I'd never go through this again. No matter how much he hated me, Giraud couldn't do without my strengths as a climber on the remaining stages.

The Tour was now over except for the mountains. We wouldn't be back on the road for another forty hours. Only two rivals separated me from the leader's jersey, and I knew that, in the terrible peaks ahead of us, I had the advantage. I imagined myself in Paris wearing yellow, the color of the Colombian national team. I would be the very first Colombian champion, and the first French champion after thirty-five years of drought. Fiona would love me forever and Lombard would fulfill his dream. Then a sudden shadow ripped through the rainbows: Steve. And then a much blacker and more foreboding stain appeared: the killer breathing heavily against the back of my neck.

During my massage session, I decided that tonight, I would at all costs avoid doing anything related to "Sergeant Moreau." Hannibal, the rider wearing number 22, the cyclist about to pull off a historic surprise at the Tour de France, was much more interesting and important. That meant avoiding Steve, who would likely want to share Protex's report; Favre, who was always optimistic about his ability to get information out of me; and Fiona and Ray, my partners in intrigue. I asked the loyal Axel to make my excuses to the rest of the team and bring me something to eat up to my room. Ending the day at eight o'clock at night was the best way to recover from the extreme weariness I was suffering anyway. And if I just locked myself in my room for four more days, except to race, I would deprive the murderer of any opportunity that could keep me from entering Paris with my arms up in the air.

That night I didn't need to invoke the rankings in order to sleep—nothing had changed during the rest day. But I did anyway.

GENERAL CLASSIFICATION: STAGE 16

RANK	RIDER	TIME	NOTES
1	ALESSIO MATOSAS (ITALY/LAVEZZA)	64:47:16	We'll see you on the mountain, you SOB.
2	MILENKO PANIUK (CZECH/RABONET)	+0:22	He's not the killer, but he's part of the plot.
3	MARC MOREAU (FRANCE/FONAR)	+5:12	I survived an explosion and Giraud—what next?
4	STEVE PANATA (USA/FONAR)	+6:30	He won't just sit there, but what will he do?
5	PABLO MEDEL (SPAIN/BALEARES)	+7:05	He won't either, and he might get desperate.
6	ÓSCAR CUADRADO (COLOMBIA/MOVISTAR)	+11:55	
7	LUIS DURÁN (SPAIN/IMAGINE)	+12:24	
8	SERGEI TALANCÓN (ROMANIA/ROCCA)	+13:48	
9	ANSELMO CONTI (ITALY/LAVEZZA)	+16:37	
10	ROL CHARPENELLE (FRANCE/TOURGAZ)	+16:57	

Rest

You don't survive twenty-one Tour stages without some sort of system. Each one of us develops our own ways to stay alive until that third week. It's not terribly different from the office worker who establishes a small ritual—making a cup of coffee, checking in with a co-worker—every day before officially sitting down at his desk for eight hours. My strategy consists of dividing the race into two different tournaments; I have other quirks, of course, like obsessively tallying my room numbers, the temperature, and the numbers on the backs of my colleagues, but this is the most important one.

I prepare myself emotionally for two races. The first one is two weeks long and the goal is simply to finish in the best possible position without sacrificing our team goals, whatever they might be.

The last five days are a different race, very different. Up until this moment the Tour has been hard; it always is, but it's also been something of a circus. But after Stage 16, most of the peloton falls back in the mountains, and those riders out of the race for all intents and purposes, having lost so much time. From this moment on, it's a war at breakneck speed between the two or three teams aspiring to the podium in Paris. It's the final battle of a long siege, and it is fought with knives between our teeth.

A day off separates these two races and I turn that day into a refuge from cycling however I can. I sleep late; I shower in the morning, which never happens during the race; I eat banned foods and watch movies—I even go to a movie theater if the town population and the circumstances allow it. I do whatever I can to feel like I'm on vacation, far away from the competition. The harm all this might do to my body is minimal compared to the benefits to my spirit.

Last year Fiona went with me to a double feature in Pau, and we stuffed ourselves with popcorn and Coke. But last year, I hadn't aspired to the yellow jersey and there was no criminal plot determined to knock me off my bike. I decided to enjoy my day off without my girlfriend. Her presence would be distracting because she would remind me of the demons stalking me. I'd lock myself in my room to eat junk food, kindly delivered by Axel, watch a Netflix series, and go up two levels on a game I'd downloaded on my PlayStation.

Under normal circumstances I would've had to negotiate this absence with Giraud, but it was clear he now considered me a lost cause. Whatever the results of the race, one of the two of us would leave Fonar at the end of the Tour; in the best but most improbable of all cases, he'd be handcuffed and I'd be wearing the yellow jersey.

Steve and Fiona were well aware of my rest day ritual, so they didn't put up any objections. Steve preferred to pedal a few kilometers to loosen his muscles, as the trainers suggested, but although he made fun of my pretend vacations, he respected them. For her part, Fiona—how could I not love her?—understood why, this time, I wanted to stay apart. Mid-morning she sent me a text, direct as always: "I'll keep Ray away, you keep away from shrimp and other seafood. I'll see you tomorrow, champ." I'd once gotten food poisoning two months before the end of the season, and I still looked on crayfish with a resentment worthy of Radek.

In contrast, it was much harder to keep Favre away. I decided to ignore a text he'd sent me at the break of dawn. But my silence made him anxious and he bombarded me with messages with the intensity of a lover. I answered laconically, telling him I was fine and that I'd be resting all day. That only made him up his efforts. I imagine mistrust is second nature to any detective; apparently, he was convinced that by refusing to see him, I was obscuring a dark secret.

If our texts had audio, you could say we ended up screaming at each other. "Come get me with an order of arrest or let me rest," I said in one of my last messages. A little later, he took back the upper hand: "I'm sorry to have bothered you, I wanted to bring you up to date about Ferrara's probable arrest."

The information startled me, causing me to screw up the level I'd reached in the videogame. What I'd just read would change everything. The Italian mechanic's arrest would free me to concentrate on the yellow jersey. Once more: rainbows and fanfare. Then I reread Favre's text. *Probable arrest* offered no guarantee. If the police had anything of substance against Ferrara, he would have already been arrested, or at least interrogated.

I decided the commissioner simply wanted to have the last word in our digital battle. "Good luck, you can tell me tomorrow," I typed and turned off the phone.

I tried to go back to the game, but I'd already been defeated by a multitude of satanic trolls, so I turned to sudoku and, later, to *Game of Thrones*. The commissioner had managed to ruin my special day. My eyes were on the screen but my mind kept imposing Ferrara's face on Tyrion Lannister's as he plotted new ways to screw me over.

I decided if I had to think about the Italians it was best to go over ways of beating them out on the course. There were only five of us left with any chance of winning the race. And I didn't need Fiona to know that, out on the mountain, I was in better shape than the other four, assuming we were on an even playing field. The problem was, each one of them had a team at his service, and I'd be alone. That meant I couldn't attack on any of the first three days on the Alps, because if I did, even Fonar would come at me. I'd have to wait until Stage 20 to betray Steve, if at all.

I got out of bed and stood up, as if I were trying to shake off a few imaginary crumbs. *To betray Steve* was a phrase that caused a short circuit in my neural system. I looked for another word, something other than *betray,* but none seemed to better define what I'd have to do to my friend.

A mirror above a small table reflected an unusually disheveled image back to me. I had my father's face and my mother's mane. Thinking about Beatriz brought me right back to Steve: He was the only family I had. In the past few years, he'd even been a more caring son than I had. No, I wouldn't betray him. A yellow jersey wasn't worth becoming a piece of shit.

My resolution made me feel like a better person. Fiona and Lombard would have to understand. Or not. Something tugged on my sternum. Maybe I could find an alternate solution. A compromise—to accompany Steve to the podium. And if he failed for any reason, I'd be there to rescue the yellow jersey. That was it: If my teammate wasn't up to being champion on the last day, I'd step in for him. But only if he faltered, and if he did, it wouldn't be because of me.

My resolution would not make Fiona happy. She wouldn't be content with second place, not if Steve was in first. I asked myself again if her hatred toward him was stronger than her love for me. I'd know next Sunday.

I fell asleep going over the times our rivals had on us. I didn't think about the killer again. From my hotel room cocoon, I had no way of knowing that during this time he'd attacked again.

Stage 17

Digne-les-Bains—Pra Loup, 161 km.

Fiona got me out of bed in the worst way possible: She was dressed and accompanied by Ray. I knew something really serious was going on when I opened my door to furious knocking and found them both in the hallway, not caring if they were seen by the sleeping cop posted there.

"Conti and Leandro were poisoned this morning. They took Conti to the hospital; he's in serious condition," said Fiona as she burst into my room. I'd seen her that agitated only a few times and her hair seemed particularly shocked. It was understandable. If I'd been told NASA had just reported the world was flat, it wouldn't have surprised me as much. Conti and Leandro were Matosas's domestiques, and, I'd assumed, his henchmen. How could they also be his victims?

"That's impossible," I said. "They're the—"

"The criminals? Apparently not," said Ray decisively. "We have to start from zero."

"Unless somebody's trying to get rid of their accomplices," interjected Fiona.

"What happened, exactly?" I asked, remembering the first lesson from my forensics classes: first the facts, then the interpretation.

"Your friend the commissioner will know better," she said, without hostility. "They drugged them, although I'm not clear on how or when. Somebody didn't want them to run this lap, but they overdid it with Conti. One of the Lavezza mechanics said that when they took him out on the stretcher the paramedics were trying to resuscitate him."

Conti's baby features no longer struck me as those of a psychopath but rather those of a young man who deserved to be in his mother's or his girlfriend's arms. I felt sorry for him and even sorrier for my theory that had now gone up in smoke. The Italians had seemed like the perfect villains, and now it turned out they were anything but.

"Do you know if the killer stole anything?" Ray asked Fiona.

Fiona shook her head. "They just got them out of the room less than a half hour ago. The police are still there."

"Why do you ask?" I said.

"I don't know, it reminds me of something," he said, turning to me now. "Could you find out how they were poisoned and if there's anything missing in the room?"

I could, I thought, although it would require a torturous session with Favre. And I wouldn't be able to do it until the finish line. I doubted the commissioner would see me before the start of the race, given the way I'd treated him the day before. But maybe Steve's Protex detectives knew something and would share it with me.

Whoever had hit the Italians had chosen a good moment because that night, there had been three other teams at the same hotel as Lavezza. The hotel was a big building in Le Lauzet, just twenty minutes from Gap. With so many guests coming and going, it would be impossible for the police to single out one sus-picious person from the lobby security video as they'd been able to do for the attack on the Brits ten days ago.

"If it's not the Italians, then who?" asked Fiona.

"Giraud," I suggested, although it was becoming more and more evident that a lot of things in this case didn't make sense; they only fit like forced puzzle pieces.

"Now there's just Paniuk and Medel left," said Ray sadly. "I would've never imagined this from them; they're both good peo-ple. But there's no other possibility. Without his domestiques, Matosas is lost in the Alps. The yellow jersey will go to the Czech or the Spaniard."

"Or the Frenchman," said Fiona, not looking at me.

"Or the Frenchman. That means the killer will attack again and probably twice: He'll attack one of those two and, yes, Moreau," said Ray, also avoiding looking at me. The French-Colombian, I was about to say, then decided it didn't matter. Pa-niuk or Medel were both on my original list, but I'd never given them careful thought, obsessed as I was with Matosas, Conti, Fer-rara, and their Sicilian connections. I had nothing against the Czech, but I preferred that the Spaniard be innocent. Although Medel had fewer wins than Paniuk, some of his escapades on the great summits were legendary, full of heroism and sacrifice, rec-ognized by pain professionals everywhere.

"Medel's never won a big race," said Fiona, busting in like a devil's advocate against my inner defense of the climber from Se-ville, "and he's close to retirement."

"Paniuk has always been a little strange," countered Ray. "He's never wanted to learn French or English and communicates with the rest of the peloton with about twenty words. His Bulgarian trainer is a little nefarious too, don't you think?"

Paniuk was a nice guy, quiet. It's true, I couldn't remember having exchanged more than a few words with him in all these years. But he read the race like few others could and, generally speaking, his intuition was right on. He was always on the correct side when it came to a chase or a breakaway. A proper and reliable professional in every sense.

It seemed to me we were trying to force ourselves to see people as killers who weren't, like a man in front of a mirror trying to tell himself the tight jacket he loves is perfect even if he has to stop breathing to wear it.

"Or it could be Giraud," I insisted resentfully.

"Giraud will probably want to kill you at the end of the Tour, but to do so before you crown his golden boy would be shooting himself in the foot. Let's not waste time on him," said Fiona.

Even though I wanted to insist on my theory, I didn't have anything to back it up. In Giraud's case, he fit the villain's jacket perfectly, except that the buttons were on the back. All my senses told me he was the culprit, but there was no way to tie him to the facts.

Quietly, the three of us immersed ourselves in impossible calculations. The silence magnified the knocking on the door, which startled us all, as if the murderer had come to introduce himself.

"You have to take care of yourself!" exclaimed Lombard, pushing through the door I'd barely opened. What he said had stopped being news ten days before, but he said it with such an anguished intensity that I felt it like a hoof stomping up my back. Involuntarily I looked out to the hall expecting to see a man with a scythe behind him.

"Hello, colonel," said Fiona, somewhere between amused and affectionate. She'd had more time to get used to the old soldier's senile outbursts than me in recent months.

Ray and Lombard greeted each other with a nod, neither of them seeming to want to look at the other. I wondered if those two had a past they preferred not to exhume.

"Damn it, you didn't need to be so violent, not unless you want a loser to win," Lombard said, and the rest of us were even more confused. He must have noticed our befuddled faces. "Paniuk and Medel are so bad someone had to knock down half the peloton for them to get on the podium," he added in the same tone you might use to explain that a bicycle is a two-wheeled vehicle. The three of us nodded in silence.

"Just as you were coming in we were talking about that. That Marc's in danger," Fiona said after a silence that was beginning to get awkward. I noticed that Fiona was speaking to the old man more slowly and clearly than usual, as if she were addressing a foreigner. Lombard looked slightly dazed; apparently he'd forgotten what he'd come for.

"I spoke with Bimeo," he finally said, lighting up at the mention of his friend, the Tour's head of security. Fiona's words had brought him out of his neural block. "Tour security will guard the hotel for the rest of your stay. I got them to agree to put another motorcycle with a camera to follow your movements exclusively. Nobody will be able to do anything to you without it being documented. And the rest of the time we'll have you surrounded. That's what I came to tell you," he finished, triumphant.

"During all the stages on the Alps you'll sleep at this hotel, right?" Fiona asked. "That'll make it easier."

We'd stay a total of four nights at the same hotel. The organization preferred to shuttle us to the starting and finish lines during the day so we'd get a better night's rest.

"Bimeo is a ruffian," Ray said scornfully. "He should be in jail and not in charge of Tour security." I had to agree. Years ago Bimeo had left Interpol under a suspicious cloud and was almost immediately recruited by Jitrik. Once the competition started, Bimeo was the real power behind the Tour's leadership. He coordinated logistics with the national police, the local police, the patrols, and the motorcycle cops, and he was surrounded by a handful of centurions who had his absolute confidence.

"I'm already more than taken care of by Steve's Protex crew and the cops sent by Favre," I said with a laugh. "If you add Tour security, there won't be enough room in the hallway for everyone."

"We're not going to find the culprit by piling guards at Marc's door," agreed Fiona. "Any idea who it might be, colonel? Bimeo must have a hypothesis. If this thing explodes, he'll be the first to lose his job."

"I've just come from talking to him," said Lombard. "He says these are pure journalistic exaggerations." And then he paused when he realized that there was a reporter among us. "The Tour is the Tour and there are always accidents, traps, and bad plays."

"Sabotaged bikes? Cyclists murdered in the bathtub? Poison?" Ray said. He was indignant.

"One hundred years ago, they'd throw tacks on the road to puncture tires, and they'd change the road signs to send rivals down the wrong path. They've gassed people before too," said Lombard, now seeming completely lucid.

"That was to rob them, not to send them to the hospital. And they were fine by morning. What's going on now is different," said Ray. Six or seven years ago, two soigneurs were knocked out with gas that entered their room through a small tube under the door. Someone took their money, their watches, and their laptops while the two were unconscious.

"Bimeo says it's the same motive," Lombard replied. "The room was sacked. The poisoning was just worse because the room was smaller and the thieves miscalculated. Anyway, it's a problem for hotel security, not the Tour."

"Which version of you should we believe, colonel? This guy who defends Bimeo and thinks everything is a journalistic exaggeration, or the guy who burst into the room trying to save Moreau from an imminent attack?" asked Ray, with the look of a prosecutor who's just laid out an irrefutable argument.

Ray's words must have shaken Lombard, because he looked over at my supplements on the nightstand and became instantly distracted, the overprotective parent making sure all his child's vitamins are in order.

"We can't take too many precautions. There are enemies everywhere," he finally said, returning from wherever Ray's question had sent him. "We all have to watch out for you, Marc, because, this year, you'll be the champion." He flung himself in my arms so awkwardly, he almost made me lose my balance. Then he walked out of the room without another word.

The strong smell of the mints the old man chewed made my eyes water, or maybe it was just hearing him say my legal name, which he hadn't used since my first months in the barracks.

Fiona's eyes were also moist. "He's sick, Mojito," she said, but, glancing at Ray, shook her head and refused to say anything more despite my inquisitive look.

Fiona, Ray, and I parted with our assignments, all three of us troubled. We agreed to meet again in the evening, to review. By day's end, I would have gotten through one of the four stages I needed to come out of the Tour alive. That was assuming, of course, that the danger ended in Paris.

Steve thought differently.

"I told Stevlana to meet us at Lake De Como," he told me at breakfast. "There's no point in her taking any risks by coming to Paris; let's see if she listens to me." At least he didn't call her Stivy when he talked to me. Our teammates usually let us talk with relative privacy during meals, sitting a couple feet away. It was a rule that no one had ever articulated but that even the newest members of the team adhered to. It allowed us to participate in the general conversation but also speak more intimately. We talked in a kind of argot, mostly French but mixed with whole English sentences and sprinkled with Spanish phrases he'd learned from his Mexican nanny. His vocabulary when it came to foods and parts of the body, both male and female, was admirable.

"Why? Do the Protex people know about a threat in Paris? Did you hear about Conti?"

"I heard, bro. They'll know more once they talk to their police contact, but they're worried, and they want me to double up on precautions. I'm getting sick of all this," he said, making a face and flinching slightly on his right side.

"I suppose we're down to just Paniuk and Medel as our last suspects, right?" I asked, just to check if the Protex professionals agreed with my improvised panel of detectives.

"That's what I said. But they said they don't discount anyone. And it looks like Interpol found the link between Ferrara and the Dutch businessman who bought your bike. That's why the whole thing with Conti is so weird. If the Italians came up with all this to make Matosas the champion, then what happened today makes no sense at all. Without Conti, Matosas is lost in the mountains."

"So, what are we going to do?" That was the subject neither one of us had dared to bring up. Would we attack Matosas today, when his teammates were hospitalized?

"Whatever Giraud says, I suppose," he said, wanting to avoid responsibility for whatever happened. There was no doubt about what our DS would order us to do, even if it was in bad taste. Codes of conduct, and ethics in particular, were not Giraud's strong suits.

"You really want to beat Matosas while he's down? The peloton helped us when *you* were in bad shape," I said, without animosity but firmly. I didn't want to let him get his way without at least first admitting we were about to do a very messed-up thing.

"Listen, if we lost time because of the bullshit the Italians pulled on your bike, it's only fair that we recover it now. It's not even an eye-for-an-eye kind of thing, because it wasn't us who shot the gas under the door." When it came to presenting an argument, my friend could be a cardinal in the Medici courts, especially if there's a yellow jersey at stake.

"Okay, then, let's do it like this. You lost five minutes from your fall. Let's attack to get those five minutes back, but just those five minutes. I'll talk to some of the other team leaders," I said.

"How are you going to make sure it's exactly five minutes? Are you going to talk to Jitrik about that too, like your two-minute penalty?" He said it lightly, but I felt it in my back like an ice pick. So he *was* hurt that I was ahead of him in the standings. I smiled and pretended it was all a joke.

"The question is, are you physically ready to take on Matosas?" I asked. "Without Conti, he can't attack us, although Matosas is still quite a climber. But he's already the leader. All he has to do is not lose sight of us. He's going to be all over you."

"Today's stage doesn't really lend itself to an attack," Steve replied. "Whoever hit Conti picked the wrong day to do it. They should have waited for the weekend." He was right about that. Today was the first lap in the Alps, but it was more of a warm-up. Matosas would have no trouble keeping up with us because there weren't any first-rate peaks, just an ascent to the low mountains. The tough climbs were coming up on the last two days.

"It doesn't have to be today. From what I can tell, Conti and Leandro are off the Tour entirely."

"Paniuk is going to be the harder one to beat. He's only twenty-two seconds behind Matosas."

"Even without taking into consideration that he or his people could be the criminals, we shouldn't cross Medel off that list either."

"It's not Medel," he said in a confident tone.

"How do you know?"

"It was in the report," he said, before explaining. "Protex isn't exactly bothered by legalities," he said, lowering his voice. He could see I was confused. "They have his phone tapped. It turns out Medel is sure he's the next one who'll be attacked. The conversations he's been having with his wife back in Seville suggest he's worried he might not make it home."

"They could also be the conversations someone who's afraid of going to jail might have," I said.

"Bro, he's terrified. He thinks they're going to kill him."

"Then it's Paniuk."

"No, there's someone else," he said, although he didn't sound particularly convinced.

I had the same instinct. It was hard to imagine Paniuk in the middle of such a complex mess. He didn't have close friends in the circuit and probably not outside it either. He was an unlikely person to be backed by a large network with a lot of muscle and resources.

But we weren't wrong about our predictions when it came to the day's strategy. Giraud was belligerently enthusiastic on the bus to the starting line.

"Attack with everything you've got, Steve," he said with the ferocity of a coach in a boxer's corner, although his gaze was directed at me. "Remember all the crap these bastards have been pulling on you. Fonar is much stronger than what's left of Lavezza, and Medel and Paniuk aren't real rivals without the Italians. I want Steve to be wearing that yellow jersey on Friday." His eyes dared me to disagree.

I hated myself when I realized I'd nodded without thinking, having given in to the force of his scrutiny. Yet another story I wouldn't tell Fiona that night. Then I realized he hadn't said anything about Saturday, and neither had I. It was Wednesday. Giraud was saying that he wanted to wrap up the Tour in the next three days, before the last, terrible stage Saturday on the Alpe d'Huez. That meant I could faithfully go along with my team's plans. Steve could sleep wearing the yellow jersey Friday night . . . and lose it Saturday, on the last summit. I suppose I could also be a devious cardinal.

As we squeezed together at the starting line at Digne-les-Bains, I went down the line of the peloton to talk to the squad leaders we respected. I briefly explained that from that day on, we'd be attacking Matosas to even out the time we'd lost because of his bullshit, but no more than that; if we succeeded, we'd let everything be decided on the last day. No one said anything, but I was sure they'd accept it as one more adjustment we cyclists frequently have to make in order to be fair in an organization that doesn't guarantee fairness.

I was right. No team helped or was sympathetic to Lavezza when Fonar struck with all our might. We imposed a suicidal pace, confident in our strength. The peloton followed us, including Matosas. As the race wore on, the peloton stretched out until it broke up into small groups just trying to survive. We broke the peloton's back when we reached the midway point and climbed Allos, a long ascent with an incline of only five percent. Under normal circumstances, most of the racers would have come out of it intact, but we'd set such an infernal rhythm that when we reached the highest peak, there were very few of us grouped together up front.

Although Matosas could be a bastard, he was a good cyclist. As we'd anticipated, he glued himself to Fonar's last man as if his life depended on it. Steve rode as protected as any leader could be at those speeds. When there were only forty-eight kilometers left, he decided to run it like a time trial. There were very few ascents, and a couple descents, but mostly it was just long, flat stretches. On one of those smooth expanses, he sped up to an impossible pace, stood on his pedals, and maintained that posture for several minutes. I followed him as best I could, but the others couldn't get up to such speeds. Now it was me who was following his slipstream, afraid every centimeter lost would turn into anguished meters impossible to recover. It seemed like Steve wanted to show the world he was, once more, in full control of his faculties, or perhaps he was simply infused with the desire for revenge.

My teammate had chosen the moment well; Matosas and Paniuk were riding alone and Medel had just one teammate left. All the others in the lead group were from Fonar, and they'd slowed down the moment Steve broke out. They, of course, wouldn't be contributing to any chase our rivals mounted.

When I glanced at my power meter, I realized I was going an

astonishing 65 kilometers per hour on the flat plain Steve had chosen to make his escape. In spite of being protected by his traction, I was still having trouble keeping my speed. I wondered if, after this showing, Fiona would still feel the same way about my possibilities.

Eight kilometers later, we began to climb a light but very long parapet. Giraud was thundering in our ears to go harder.

"Now you for a while," said Steve, his voice anguished as he let up. When I went by him, I noticed the tension and pallor in his face, but he gazed at me with bright eyes, challenging me with a look not much different from the one Giraud had given me just hours before.

I understood Steve wanted to do more than get back the five minutes stolen from us. His breakaway was a statement, a way for him to tell the world, and me, that he was the best. I limited my response to just pushing forward, as I'd done so often in the past ten years.

Soon, I began to feel fatigue overcoming me. I'd been going for several kilometers without him giving me a break, and I was now coming up on a small summit that seemed interminable. I was paying the price of having exerted so much energy in helping my partner with his brutal escape. The two times I slowed down, he simply said *más*. Even though he couldn't talk, it was clear he'd decided to eliminate Matosas once and for all.

Even in those conditions, we kept gaining distance. I'd learn later that both Matosas and Medel rode below their averages. I imagined the Italian's spirit had been broken by the morning's events. His friend and teammate—his version of me—was in intensive care fighting for his life. And if what the report said about Medel's phone conversations was true, then he was probably up until the wee hours the past few nights.

I was surprised we were still only five kilometers ahead when they told us we'd gotten our five minutes back. Our rivals were really underperforming. In that moment, I slowed down, and signaled Steve discreetly to do the same. I didn't want the camera or the mics on the motorcycle ahead of us to catch on to our agreement with the other leaders.

In response, Steve leaned forward uncertainly and pointed straight ahead with his index finger, his hand never leaving the handlebars.

"Now it's my turn," he said, and got in front of me as if he were simply taking a turn leading. Then he stood on his pedals and sped off. I wondered if this new breakaway was an emotional reaction or a strategy he'd schemed up in the past few kilometers.

I don't know if I would have had the strength to follow Steve, who'd raced the last thirty kilometers protected by my wheel, but I didn't even try. I preferred to respect the deal I'd made with our colleagues. On TV, to the rest of the world, the moment would register as absolute and implacable proof that Steve was superior to his domestique.

I got to the finish line exactly 4:58 ahead of Matosas and 2 minutes behind Steve. My friend was now the Tour's leader. Giraud had managed to meet his Friday goal on Wednesday.

Steve waited for me at the finish line, ignoring the inspectors who are required to immediately administer a urine test to the winner at each stage.

"It's bigger than me, Marc," he whispered in my ear as he gave me a hug. "I couldn't hold back. Those miserable assholes don't deserve it."

I deserved it, you imbecile, not them; that was our agreement, I wanted to say to him, but, like always, I didn't think of it until he'd gone on his way to the inspection pavilion.

I tried to ride my bike over to our team bus, but a mob of journalists blocked me. Everyone wanted an explanation of what had happened. I searched for an escort among the Fonar assistants, but the only one I saw was Axel, who looked at me helplessly. I responded with monosyllables to the questions machine-gunning at me left and right. Even the Protex bodyguards seemed more interested in my answers than in getting me out of this jam. Lombard finally came to the rescue with two Bimeo guards. Flashing their official badges, they surrounded me, and helped me make it to the bus.

I was just about to step inside when I realized the reporters had suddenly abandoned me. I looked around and understood why: At the foot of the Lavezza bus, Carlo Benett, the Italians' DS, was hugging Matosas, who was sobbing and heaving on his shoulder. Even the journalists pulled back and respected the moment. When he realized the press was watching them, Benett urged his racer into the bus.

The scene lasted only an instant but affected me greatly. Matosas was even more of a veteran than me, a leader on his team, and a cyclist who had gone through everything on the circuit. Seeing him cry like that was heartbreaking. Maybe he'd just been told about Conti's death, I thought. Or maybe Steve's slapdown on that last climb sealed the end of his career.

I forced myself to remember that Matosas had cooked up the attack that had put the Beast in the hospital with multiple fractures. The thought did nothing to improve my mood. All I felt was more sadness on top of my profound fatigue.

During the long ride back to the hotel in Gap, I had to put up with my team's party spirit. Giraud was celebrating as if the Tour had already been won and we'd be entering Paris the next day. Maybe he was right: Steve was the leader again, and with Fonar's superiority on the mountains and the collapse of the rival teams, there was no reason to think anything would change. Although less rowdy than the DS, my teammates were also having a good time. The conquest of the yellow jersey guaranteed them generous bonuses. I was the only one who wore a frozen smile. Steve didn't come near me the rest of the day.

"What happened, Mojito?" Fiona asked, halfway between worry and complaint, as soon as she came into the room where Axel was giving me a rigorous massage. She'd never interrupted a massage session before, but she was bewildered by what Steve had done.

I almost told her about the tense moment Steve and I had shared over breakfast, but I didn't want to feed her dislike for my teammate. Or maybe I just didn't want to look like more of an idiot to her. Plus, it wasn't something that could be discussed in front of Axel.

"It was a slump, something like that," I murmured, as if the pressure of the massage barely let me make a sound.

"That can happen to anybody, any day," she said, forgivingly. "And, let's not forget, he also wore you out by making you lead for almost twenty kilometers."

"At least we recovered the ground we'd lost, and Steve is in first place again," I said, more for Axel's ears than Fiona's. I trusted him completely, but I still didn't want to put him to the test. Going against Steve was tantamount to betraying Fonar, his employer.

"Luckily, there were no incidents on the road," she said, watching Axel, who was visibly uncomfortable with her presence. Fiona stared, fascinated with the way his hands roamed territory she considered her own. I stretched an arm and stroked her ankle. She said goodbye after thanking Axel, although neither of us understood exactly what for.

Back in my room, I found several messages from Favre on my cellphone. He told me Conti had survived, although he'd remain hospitalized. They expected him to recover enough to be questioned tomorrow about Ferrara and his role in sabotaging my bicycle. The commissioner hadn't ruled out that Ferrara might have tried to eliminate his accomplices, sensing the police investigation was getting close. He asked me to let him know about any background information that could help him in his questioning.

While I was thinking of an answer, a message from Steve came in: "Look at what's waiting for us at the lake"—the text served as a caption to an image of a spectacular sailboat. "Tell Fiona to get her swimsuit ready," he added in a second message. Steve must have been desperate to iron out our differences, because it was the first time he'd included Fiona in any of his plans. I held back the urge to respond. This time, I would not be so accommodating with my friend. We'd work together so that he could win his fifth Tour, but today, at least, I didn't want him to think things were okay.

My cell buzzed again; I had several messages from Lombard's son, Bernard. He asked me to call him as soon as possible. I assumed he'd already analyzed today's data and would have noticed that my revolutions per minute and the power of my pedaling were more than enough to have followed Steve during his getaway. No doubt he wanted to discuss it with me.

Instead of responding to him, I did something impulsive, inexplicable. I sent Matosas a text: "I'm glad Conti is out of danger." Then I turned off the phone.

That night I went down to dinner as late as possible, in order to avoid Steve and the rest of my teammates. There were only two mechanics left at the tables, and they told me Steve had left instructions to take me to a lounge in the hotel where Giraud had arranged a small celebration in honor of the day's triumph. I excused myself by saying I had a pulled muscle in my back and needed to rest, and returned to my room.

Fiona, to whom I'd given my room key, and Ray were already waiting for me. The reporter had news.

"I was talking to Havel, who published a biography of Paniuk some time ago," he said. Johanes Havel was the Ray Lumiere of Eastern Europe, a veteran journalist for whom cycling held no secrets. "The Czech is not as innocent as he seems. It's not clear if he's an orphan or if he was abandoned, but he went through several orphanages between the ages of fourteen and sixteen and was in and out of juvenile detention centers for gang crimes. Cycling was how his mentors got him off the streets."

I considered that my own youth might not have been very different if a bicycle hadn't crossed my path when I was thirteen. Far from being a reason to suspect him, I thought his conversion into a professional athlete was laudable, and that's what I told the journalist.

"There's one piece of information that particularly caught my attention," Ray went on. "It's from when he did time as a minor. He and another boy blew up the gas tanks in a cafeteria owned by some guy who they were having problems with. The explosion started a fire that razed the place."

With a shudder, I remembered a gust of boiling air on my back and the slight smell of ashes hitting my nose.

"But how would Paniuk have access to military-grade explosives like those used on the trailer?" I asked, trying to give him the benefit of the doubt.

"And where would he get the accomplices for the other ten or twelve attacks? He might be a squad leader, but the guy is a loner," added Fiona.

"I'm only passing on the information," said Ray, shrugging. "But Paniuk and his team are the only ones who haven't been attacked; one of them has to be responsible."

"Well, what about Medel?" said Fiona.

"Forget about Medel." I told them what Steve had shared with me about the Spaniard's phone calls.

"Let's suppose for a moment that it's Paniuk," Fiona said in a schoolmaster's tone. "That would mean his strategy has been a resounding failure. He's in third place, one minute behind Steve Panata, with the police breathing down his neck. Right now he has a better chance of wearing orange than yellow." I tried to remember the color of the prison uniform worn in France, but, like Fiona, I could only think of American movies.

"Paniuk's plan wasn't absurd," said Ray. "He'll beat Matosas and Medel, who are falling apart. If the gas tank or the sabotaged bicycle had worked, Fonar would be down too"—*and I'd be in a coffin,* I thought.

"And Paniuk would be the champion," Fiona finished, although she didn't sound entirely convinced. "Let's eliminate the Czech for a moment and look for another possibility that might fit the facts." Her proposition opened up the possibility of re-inserting Giraud to the list of suspects, but I restrained myself.

"Let's suppose it was Ferrara and his accomplices from the beginning, and that when they sensed the police on their tails, they decided to get rid of Conti and Leandro. That way they eliminated two potential witnesses and freed the Italian team of suspicion," I hypothesized.

"That makes more sense to me than poor Paniuk," said Fiona.

"But we can't rule out Giraud either," I said, encouraged by the success of my speech. "Using the same logic, we could assume he orchestrated the initial attacks to leave Steve alone at the top. He never believed Matosas and Paniuk would be serious rivals, because he didn't anticipate that the three teams would work as one."

"But how to explain the attack against you at the trailer?" asked Ray.

"He tried to get rid of Marc because without Cuadrado or Stark in the way, Giraud knew he was the only one who could beat Steve." Fiona spoke as if it were a revelation. "That does make sense: You're the only one who doesn't realize you're ready for the yellow jersey. Giraud is more afraid of you, Mojito, than anyone."

"There are less bloody ways to neutralize me, don't you think? I mean, a directeur sportif has many ways to influence and manipulate what his racers do."

"He tried that after the attacks on the trailer and the tire sabotage failed," Ray said. "Remember how he made you the water boy, trying to exhaust you before you reached the mountain?"

"The attack on the trailer came the night before the time trials, when you surprised everyone by coming in very close to Steve," said Fiona. "I think that's when Giraud realized you were a real threat."

"That would also explain why it failed: It was a hasty decision," said Ray. "They didn't know the gas tank was almost empty."

"'They'?" Fiona said, almost to herself. "Who could 'they' be?"

The three of us reflected in silence, trying to identify Giraud's allies. I realized who "they" were immediately, but I hesitated to mention them aloud.

"What's the name of the security company that protects Steve?" asked Fiona, arriving at the same conclusion as me.

"Protex," I answered, resigned.

"They seem vicious enough to do all that," Ray said in a low voice, suddenly aware one of their thugs was out in the hallway. I tried to remember what they might have overheard the night before.

"Could there be microphones in here?" Fiona asked in a barely audible voice. The three of us moved closer together, as if the night breeze were drawing us toward an imaginary campfire.

"Giraud would have the motive and Protex would have the muscle. Everything to guarantee Steve's win," said Ray.

"The question is whether Steve knows anything about this," said Fiona.

Something in the way she said it made me think she wanted an affirmative answer. It couldn't have been much different from the pleasure I felt just a few minutes before when we all came to the conclusion Giraud was our main suspect.

"In conclusion," said Ray, "it's Giraud or Ferrara."

"Ferrara is already being investigated by the police. Unfortunately, I don't think Favre is considering Giraud. Since I've been the object of attacks, it takes suspicion off Fonar."

"Even worse," said Fiona, "if Ferrara is the criminal, then you're no longer in danger because it's obvious that, by attacking Conti, he decided to cover his tracks and lay low. But if it's Giraud, then you're still in his sights, maybe more than ever, because he knows if you decide to, you can beat Steve in the Alpe d'Huez."

"Exactly," said Ray. They both looked at me: him with curiosity, her with urgency. They were waiting for my response.

"I'll look for Favre; maybe I can get him to reconsider investigating Giraud," I said, but I didn't have much hope.

"In the meantime, I don't think it's such a good idea to spend the night with a Protex goon at the door," said Fiona.

"Yeah," I said. "That's the same guy who stomped on Lombard's foot. But I have no way of getting rid of him; he's here on Steve's orders."

"I'll ask the colonel to send somebody," she said. "At least that way there will be eyes on Protex, protection against protection." She pulled her cell out to call Lombard. "I'll arrange it. And I'll stay with you tonight. It'll be much harder for them to come up with some sort of accident if we're together."

"And sleep with the window open, in case they decide to repeat the same little sleeping gas trick," said Ray. "Good luck, Monsieur Moreau. In and out of the race."

Ten minutes after Ray left, there was a knock on the door. I opened it. Two guys stood there who looked like anything but bodyguards.

"Bimeo sent us," said one of them. "We're going to be watching over you tonight." He said this so tenaciously, it sounded like he was talking about climbing Mount Everest. He was tall, slender, and gawky; I decided to call him Quixote in my mind. That meant the second man would be Sancho Panza. He'd clearly never turned down a meal in his life; without the mustache, he could pass for a woman in her eighth month of pregnancy.

"Thank you, I'm flattered," I said, somewhat amused. In case of any kind of assault, they'd be more useful as witnesses than as defenders, and only if they happened to turn around as they ran away. They settled in the hallway in front of the hulking Protex guy, sitting on a pair of high stools probably confiscated from the small hotel bar. The Sarcophagus, as I'd dubbed him, looked at

Quixote and Sancho with disdain and not a little indignation; their presence brought his occupation several levels down in terms of professionalism.

"At the very least the rumor will spread that I'm now also protected by Bimeo," I told Fiona when we closed the door. "Everybody's afraid of him."

"Bimeo's a bit of a bastard, although I suppose an organization as complex as the Tour needs somebody who will raise their voice and step on some toes," she said.

"But I'm not sure who those two out there could possibly keep in line."

"Bimeo recruits based on loyalty, not appearances. Protex's gorilla is a mercenary, but those two would kill for their boss."

We froze on those last few words.

"I suppose it's an advantage that they're on our side then, or at least on Lombard's side. How did he and Bimeo become such good friends anyway?"

"I think they've exchanged mutual favors over the years. Lombard spent more than two decades in charge of military provisions on the Alps and the Pyrenees. He knows all the local chiefs of police, and many of the politicians and the bureaucrats in the region are friends of his. Those relationships are golden when it comes to Tour logistics."

I thought about the old man with affection. Once more, I realized I'd been ungrateful to him in the past few days. It was thanks to Lombard that my two-minute penalty had been dropped. And now I had Quixote and Sancho outside my door protecting me from the beefy flunky who might be working on orders from Giraud. I decided to find Lombard in the morning and offer him a kind word. That made me remember the messages his son had left me. I searched for my phone and saw there were two new texts.

One was from Favre: "We detained Ferrara. Interrogating. I'll keep you posted." The commissioner's digital conciseness was getting worse; at this rate, he'd end up writing in shorthand. But I took it as good news. If the Italian turned out to be the killer and the detective managed to get a confession, everything would be over and I could focus on the race. Although, if Ferrara wasn't the killer, Giraud would have gained time to organize another assault against me. I decided not to think about that for the moment.

The other message didn't identify the sender, although I recognized the country code for Andorra, where Matosas lived: "Let's stop this, I need to talk to you. Tomorrow night at the hotel?" The text was in Italian, and I assumed Matosas's ego was big enough that he thought he didn't need to sign his texts. I shared it with Fiona.

"He must be scared if he's using a second phone. He doesn't identify himself because he probably thinks that would incriminate him. As if texting doesn't already do that."

"It's because they're interrogating Ferrara. Axel did the same thing when they detained the Dandy: He wanted me to intervene for him with the commissioner."

"You're probably right," she said. "Meet him. That way we can find out what he knows."

"Should I say something to the commissioner?" Before she responded, I already knew it was a bad idea.

"I think it's better to wait and see what Matosas has to say. First, though, we have to deal with things between us," she said, but I was no longer paying attention to her words. She'd started to undress, almost robotically, throwing her clothes over a chair without a hint of flirtation. She had a body that didn't need to employ tools of seduction. Her broad hips, her swaying breasts, her smooth belly, and that patch of red hair would have aroused me even if the Tourmalet killer, as the press had dubbed him, burst into the room.

That night, we fell asleep with me as the little spoon, and her holding me. She said it was because that was the best position to protect me from any attack; I couldn't tell if she was joking or not. It took me a long time to stop thinking about Fiona and take up the litany of the rankings.

GENERAL CLASSIFICATION: STAGE 17

RANK	RIDER	TIME	NOTES
1	**STEVE PANATA (USA/FONAR)**	**69:06:49**	**A fifth jersey looks inevitable.**
2	ALESSIO MATOSAS (ITALY/LAVEZZA)	+0:38	Is he looking for me to save me from the cops or to kill me?
3	MILENKO PANIUK (CZECH/RABONET)	+1:00	The hermit. Could he be the killer and I just can't see it?
4	**MARC MOREAU (FRANCE/FONAR)**	**+1:31**	**I may not win the jersey but I could be on the podium.**
5	PABLO MEDEL (SPAIN/BALEARES)	+7:43	The Spaniard is out of the competition, unless something crazy happens.
6	ÓSCAR CUADRADO (COLOMBIA/MOVISTAR)	+12:59	
7	LUIS DURÁN (SPAIN/IMAGINE)	+14:36	
8	SERGE TALANCÓN (ROMANIA/ROCCA)	+15:48	
9	ANSELMO CONTI (ITALY/LAVEZZA)	+18:12	
10	ROL CHARPENELLE (FRANCE/TOURGAZ)	+18:46	

Stage 18

Gap—Saint-Jean-de-Maurienne, 186.5 km.

Before I was fully awake, the summit at Glandon filled my mind. We didn't race it every year, but I always thought of the peak with affection, because it had been the key to Steve's first Tour win, part of a successful defense against the Batesman team.

Remembering the Brits made me squirm. I'd never again see Fleming pedaling between those lethal gaps. Now that he was dead, I thought of my fierce competitor's kind face, the meticulous way he checked his bike before getting on it, and the funny way he held his head as he rode, like a bobblehead on a taxi dashboard.

I wondered if he'd had someone like Fiona, someone who made him believe he could be more than a domestique. I compared Fleming's merits against his leader's: Stark was a superb climber, though he often faltered on the time trials. I don't think Fleming ever considered the possibility of replacing him, even in his wildest dreams; he personified the very essence of a domestique. He was probably rolling over in his grave knowing his death had denied Stark any chance of winning the race. Then again, maybe Fleming would have said the same thing about me.

I tried to empty my head of these thoughts and concentrate on the day before me. Our goal was simple: to keep Steve on top of the rankings, which meant ensuring that Matosas and Paniuk didn't get to the finish line before him. Medel wasn't a real threat anymore; he'd have to make some kind of historic comeback to catch up. I assumed Giraud would instruct us to race relatively conservatively today. There was no need to waste Steve's energy.

I thought once more about how disappointed Fiona would be when my teammate won; my coming out alive in Paris would have to be enough. If she loved me, that should be enough. I ran my hand over the space on the pillow where her head had been, idly searching for one of her red hairs; she'd snuck out of the room early in the morning after giving me a kiss on the shoulder. I spotted a tiny curl that was unquestionably hers and wished with all my might it was already Monday so I could make love to her unhurriedly, and without fear. But there were still four days and almost 550 kilometers left. Hopefully, there would also be a few arrests.

"Hey, bro, I just talked to the Protex guys," Steve said as soon as I sat down next to him at breakfast. He was solicitous and cheerful, well aware I was irritated by his bullying on the course the day before. I hadn't responded to any of the messages he'd sent yesterday.

"What did they tell you?"

"The cops have been interrogating Ferrara all night long," he said, "about the incident with your bike."

"Yeah, I knew that yesterday," I responded dryly but without hostility.

"They're convinced it was the Italians behind all these incidents."

"Who's convinced, the police or Protex?"

"Both. Given all this, Lavezza hasn't got a shot anymore. I

won't be taking off the jersey until after Paris," he said triumphantly. I stayed quiet, as if cutting up fruit and pouring milk on my muesli were as demanding a task as deactivating a bomb. "I've been thinking about your career, brother," he added. I froze, as if paralyzed by a decision about which cable to cut on the bomb. In general, we talked about his career, not mine.

"This is my fifth yellow jersey, but I'll need another one to break the record. I've been thinking about not competing in any other races this coming year and strictly concentrating on the Tour," he said. Steve's dream was to one-up cycling's four greats: Anquetil, Merckx, Hinault, and Induráin had each won five Tours and were never able to do any better. The sixth win was seen as a curse, always out of reach. Only Lance Armstrong had managed to get seven, but his wins were all taken away when it was confirmed he'd been doping. Steve wanted to be known as the greatest of them all.

"That's your career we're talking about," I said.

"The two go together, bro." He was very animated now. "If I don't do any of the other races, I can make sure you're the team leader. Lombard is right about that: Without me in the way, I'd bet my life you win them all." He paused for a moment. "At least one of the two big ones, I'm sure."

"Seriously?" I forgot about the muesli, the bomb, and yesterday's betrayal. To win Il Giro, the most important Italian race, or La Vuelta, the most important Spanish race, wasn't the same as winning the Tour, but they were the next biggest things in cycling. It meant leaving the anonymity of the domestiques and entering the pages of history. I hadn't been offered such a gift since my mother gave me a bike and Fiona slipped into my bed. Then I remembered there was an obstacle. "Giraud won't accept that."

"Giraud won't be here next year," he whispered, leaning over my plate.

"I'd heard the rumor, but I didn't realize it was true."

"Giraud won't be here, but neither will we. The guy behind

Snatch, that Silicon Valley health company, is a huge cycling fan and he wants to put a team together. Obviously around me." Only coming from Steve would such an immodest declaration sound, not vulgar, but natural. "The money men want my opinion about a couple of candidates for DS. Basically, I'm picking the guy. And whoever it is, I'll make clear to him he'll only have my support if he promises what I just told you."

"Il Giro," I said, exhaling heavily. To win it, and on the Italians' home turf, would be like a punch with a white glove after the attacks on the trailer and on my bicycle—although pronouncing the words made me pessimistic again. "Hey, and where are we going to get the teammates to win all that in just one year? The mechanics and the assistants?"

"Don't worry, we'll have an insane budget. The Snatch guy is obsessed with the possibility of an American making history with six Tours. He's going to open his wallet. The Batesman and Fonar budgets are peanuts compared to what they've been talking about. We can hire a dream team, if we want it. They just asked me to keep it clean. I promised I'd pee more transparently than a baby," he said with a laugh.

"I don't know if we'll be ready for Il Giro; next year Stark and Cuadrado will come with everything they've got after losing here," I said, giving the matter more consideration. "We'd only have four months of competition to create a totally new team before going to Italy in May. It might be better to bet on La Vuelta in August."

Steve looked at me for a moment and then spoke as if the truce were over.

"Don't get confused, Marc. We'll be in Il Giro and the Spanish Vuelta only to get the team used to three-week competitions. Snatch will be focused on winning the Tour and my sixth yellow jersey."

"You assume it's already won this year?"

"You don't?" he asked.

"The danger's still out there."

"The police and Protex are sure it was the Italians. My friends have Paniuk and gang wired: They can't watch Netflix without us knowing what episode they're on, and I don't see who else could take my jersey. Do you?" Once again, the intensity of his gaze made me think his question came from a long time ago, from back when he was left behind in those demanding climbs during our training in Gerona.

And what he said about surveillance bothered me. Since when did Protex spy on rivals? Was it after the attacks, as an investigative tool to protect Steve, or had they started before that? Were they spying on me too? Was he aware of the conversations Fiona and I had behind his back? My restlessness turned into a chill. Maybe that explained his generous offer to make me leader for some important races: He was trying to neutralize any possibility that I'd attack him on the Alps.

"No, sorry. This murderer's got me a bit paranoid," I said, backtracking. "Hey, does Giraud know anything about Snatch? I get the impression he's more agitated than usual."

"He doesn't know anything. Only Benny and now you. Not even Stevlana," he said, as if that meant anything. She didn't seem to be aware of much besides her own image in the mirror. "Although he knows the Fonar owners want to make a drastic change. Poor Fonar; they don't know just how drastic that change will be."

Steve's comment about Fonar seemed a bit ungrateful to me. As far as I knew, they'd been generous to him for years with all kinds of perks and privileges, some of them quite unusual. If his plans were finalized, we'd end up destroying Fonar by taking the best of its cyclists, mechanics, and assistants. A hell of a move.

If the moment came, would my bro do the same to me? Or was I being unfair? I wasn't on top of the details of his negotiations. Maybe there were recent tensions that justified his leaving the squad. And, anyway, wasn't I considering betraying him by abandoning him at the foot of Alpe d'Huez?

I shook off those thoughts and we both turned to the day's race. We reminisced about our climb to Glandon four years ago and ended by high-fiving with an enthusiasm that was more pretend than real.

My mind went back to the conversation with Steve about spying on Paniuk. A twinge made its way into my sternum. I wrote a quick text to Lombard: "Do you have a way to check my room for microphones or cameras? I'll leave the key with Axel." As soon as I sent it, I realized I'd just made a mistake; I probably *was* being spied on, but setting Lombard off on this mission was probably not a good idea, seeing as the old man was becoming increasingly unstable.

I appreciated the call of the road. I'd spend the next five or six hours focused on the race.

Only Paniuk and his Rabonet team could threaten us at this stage. The Czech had never been so close to a yellow jersey, nor would he ever be again. So for him, third place would be like drowning within sight of the shore. He'd do anything to get back the minute he'd lost in the general classification.

But once we began, Rabonet was no match for Fonar. Again and again we responded to their attacks, which were more uncomfortable than dangerous. Their domestiques were overeager and didn't have the legs to climb Glandon. When we got to the middle of the ascent, I placed myself at the head of Fonar, increased my speed, and quickly left the entire Czech team behind except for Paniuk.

Matosas and Medel accompanied Fonar without attempting anything. I noticed a couple of looks from the Italian but I couldn't figure him out. I remembered the appointment we'd scheduled for that evening and asked myself again what revelations he'd offer. It was clear that his plans no longer included the yellow jersey; perhaps he was just trying to save himself a spot on the podium. Medel didn't seem like a threat anymore either. He was the most obviously tired of all the leaders.

We reached the finish line in a group of ten riders, four of them from Fonar. Radek, my erstwhile ally, took flight a kilometer from the finish line but no one chased him. He could burn himself out today if he wanted to in exchange for winning the stage; he was 52 in the rankings, almost two hours behind the leader in the general classification. The rest of us had to save energy for the mountains on Friday and Saturday, before arriving in Paris.

I was happy for Radek. With his two stage wins, he seemed to have forgotten his old grievances. Or that's what I believed.

The bus ride back to Gap was long and tedious. Today we'd hit the 3,000-kilometer mark for the Tour, and our bodies showed the ravages of each and every one of them. In the third week of competition, our muscles begin to consume the little fat we have left. More than one racer could be cast in a film about refugees or extermination camps. Except for some extraordinary reason to celebrate, like yesterday, at this point in the competition the mood on the bus is funereal. Each person is locked in his fatigue, with his demons, thinking about what he did or didn't do on the road, hoping that the massage waiting at the hotel will ease the small pull that could become a sprain.

I was anxious about my meeting later with Matosas. It's one thing to listen to a confession from Axel, and another to have a tête-à-tête with someone you've considered a murderer the past two weeks. I thought it would be useful to know something about Ferrara's interrogation before my meeting with the Italian.

So while Axel worked on my body in his hotel room, I sent Favre several texts without response. Perhaps the commissioner had given up on his relationship with Sergeant Moreau, his "man on the inside," after my poor performance as a detective. In all honesty, when I took stock of the information I'd passed on to him, I didn't find anything that would justify dedicating one more minute of his time to me.

But when I returned to my room, a motorcycle officer—judging from the helmet in his hand—was waiting for me while talking to plump Sancho Panza. Favre's man looked like he'd been cut out of a recruitment poster for the French police, especially next to Sancho: He was at least six feet tall, with an athletic build, perfect teeth, and a pleasant but manly face. My bodyguard must have been telling some very funny stories, because the cop was laughing loudly. He got serious when I walked up, and asked to talk privately with me.

"The commissioner says he received your messages and he needs to speak with you urgently, but he can't come right now." The poster boy ceased being a heartthrob the minute he used his voice. His vocal cords corresponded to those of a thirteen-year-old, which explained why, even with that impressive figure, he was just a messenger. There was no way a criminal would take him seriously.

"I need to see him. Could he get free a little later?"

"Oh for sure!" he said in a key higher than what could be reached with a stretched arm on a piano. After a pause, as if my question had reminded him of the other part of the mission, he added: "He asked me to give you this." After looking in two different pants pockets, he took an envelope from his jacket. I guessed the voice was not his only problem; that splendid, broad forehead had a purpose that was more aesthetic than functional.

It seemed the commissioner didn't trust his envoy too much either because in the envelope I found a long explanatory note and a cellphone. Unlike his laconic digital messages, on paper Favre had a flowery script and the eloquence of a nun with a lot of free time. He explained that his people had detected a spy network on cells and emails aimed at different members of the circuit and he asked me to take precautions about what I said or wrote digitally. He begged me—those were his words—to call him from the cell I now had in my hands at the preprogrammed number as soon as I was alone.

I walked the agent to the door, in case he couldn't find it himself. Sancho gave me a sardonic look, and I thought I'd have to update my prejudices; in case of emergency, it was clear to me I'd rather be in the fat man's hands than the poster boy's. I went back to the room and called Favre from my new phone.

"Ferrara has confessed," said the commissioner abruptly.

"To everything?" I asked excitedly.

"No, just to sabotaging your bicycle. He says the Dandy is an imbecile because he sold the black market bikes for a pittance. Through an intermediary he began to buy them from Fonar without the team's knowledge, to resell."

I waited for the rest of the revelation, but the commissioner went silent.

"And when did he decide to undo the tube and exchange the black market bike for one of mine so I would break my neck?"

"He hasn't told us that yet. He had no choice but to confess about the Dutch intermediary because we showed him the record of his payments. But he's about to break, and once he admits the attack against you, the rest will come like water."

"So you're convinced Ferrara is responsible for everything?"

"I don't know if he's the brains behind the operation, but he definitely participated."

"And what do you know about Matosas?"

"It's clear everything was about making Matosas champion. Since yesterday, we're investigating each of the Lavezza team members and managers—without them knowing. We want to have all our bases covered the moment we start to question them."

"Do me a favor, commissioner. Could you tell me when Ferrara says anything else?"

"Of course," the detective said mechanically, and then after a pause: "Anything new on your side, sergeant?"

"Fiona is looking at the circle of the Lavezza mechanics to find out who's clean and who's dirty," I replied, trying to demonstrate my utility. "Two of them worked with her in the past."

"We are getting closer," he said.

There was a long silence.

"Tell me something, Sergeant Moreau." I noticed the hesitation in his question. "Is there a chance you'll win this weekend?"

"Why are you asking, commissioner? Are you planning to bet?" I said in a nervous, joking tone.

"I asked to be assigned this case. It didn't originally fall under my jurisdiction. I've followed the Tour since I can remember, and my father before me. In my house it was a religion. The family used to camp the night before at a summit in the Pyrenees to cheer on the French racers the next day. I won't let anything happen to you," he said with great feeling.

"I didn't know," I answered honestly, not sure whether that last sentence was about my well-being or the Tour's.

"I've been waiting a long time for a compatriot to win. In 1985, Papá and I saw Hinault enter Paris with the yellow jersey; my old man died three days later, happy. At least he was spared this long drought."

Because of the tone the commissioner used, I sensed we were touching on matters more appropriate to the therapist's couch than to a police investigation. God knows what outstanding issues Favre had with his father.

"We all want a compatriot to win," I said, suddenly saddened by him, by me, by French cycling.

"Indeed," he replied. "Sleep well, sergeant."

I hung up the phone and I tried to focus on the videogame mission, the only thing that helps me deal with my mental fatigue. But I lost miserably, again and again. I couldn't concentrate. The commissioner had released the snakes of ambition once more. I could picture myself in the yellow jersey at the head of the squad, responding with a warm nod to the jubilant shouts from the fevered crowds, including Favre, Lombard, and Fiona, who cheered me on the Champs-Élysées.

Then I remembered Matosas. He'd said we'd meet at the hotel, although he hadn't specified where or when. There was nothing that prohibited the leader of one team from visiting a rival's room, but the positions we had in the general classification would make any clandestine meeting a major scandal. Steve was in first place, the Italian was in second, and I was in fourth.

A call on the room phone interrupted my thoughts.

"Hello, Marc. Could you come to the kitchen? There's something I want to show you about your diet," Carlo, our Genoese chef, said in his lousy English.

"How? Now?" I said.

"The Italian supplement you asked me about. I have some samples and I want you to try them. If you like, I'll integrate them beginning tomorrow at breakfast."

"I'll come right down," I said, finally understanding, heading to the elevator, followed closely by my three custodians—the Sarcophagus, Quixote, and Sancho. Matosas had a real gift for intrigue, but I worried what my guards would find when they stepped into the kitchen.

I'd underestimated Matosas. Carlo met us outside the elevator declaring there would be no crowding in his kitchen. His actual kitchen, narrow and splendid, was on the team bus, but hotel chefs frequently shared their restaurant's space with teams that stayed more than one night, as was the current case. My shadows reluctantly agreed to wait.

Carlo took me back to a pantry, and told me he'd wait outside. When I entered, the smell of olive oil and exotic seeds hit my nose. A small overhead lamp illuminated a pair of legs at the far end of the room. I felt a sudden panic. I'd placed myself in the ideal situation for an assassin to kill me. Why did I even believe it was Matosas who had summoned me? Carlo could be working for anyone. It was not reassuring to remember that, in the strictest sense, Giraud was our cook's boss.

But it was Matosas's voice I heard in the dark. "We have to settle accounts," he said in Italian. I wondered if I could beat him in hand-to-hand combat and felt optimistic. I recalled enough of my military police training to subdue an aggressor in my weight class. But if Matosas intended to attack me, he wouldn't have come unarmed. As I neared, I could see his left hand hanging empty, but the other was out of range of the beam of light the lamp projected.

"How so?" I replied in English.

"Ferrara was arrested."

"I know. The bastard wanted to kill me." Responding forcefully was perhaps not the most intelligent course of action, considering my interlocutor could've had a gun in his hand. But without realizing it, I'd initiated one of the proven strategies to disarm a possible aggressor: physically approaching while being engaged in an intense, emotional dialogue. In theory, that allows you to surprise him when you're close enough.

"Nobody wanted to kill you. We just wanted to respond to your attacks; we weren't going to let Fonar beat us thanks to your underhandedness."

"Our attacks? What are you talking about?" Maybe I'd misunderstood Matosas's response and was experiencing an episode of what Steve calls "lost in translation."

"Three days ago, the night watchman at the hotel where we were staying saw someone fiddling with our team bus's engine at three in the morning. When he went to talk to the man, the guy ran. Turns out he'd filed the brakes so they'd snap on the road. The bus was supposed to take us to the starting line in Lannemezan over forty-two kilometers of potholed roads."

"But what has that got to do with Fonar? We've all suffered attacks. What about the explosion at Fiona's trailer?"

"The description of the guy sounds a lot like that Protex giant who follows you everywhere."

I stopped short: I could see now that Matosas had nothing in his right hand. His revelation changed everything. But I didn't say that.

"The watchman could be confused. Did he see his face? And what about Fiona's trailer? If it's Fonar, eliminating me makes no sense."

"We think it was a feigned attack to head off suspicions about Fonar. That allowed you guys to continue getting rid of rivals without anyone being under the police spotlight."

What he was saying made a certain amount of sense. His arguments had the additional advantage, from my perspective, of making Giraud responsible for the crimes, or most of them, since Matosas had admitted to sabotaging my bike.

"Why are you telling me all this? Why are we down here? According to you, I'm one of the murderers, right?"

"We don't believe that anymore. We heard about your deal with the other squad leaders, about punishing me just for the five minutes. You kept your word, even though Steve didn't. You've always been a decent guy. I don't believe you would've been willing to take out so many of our comrades." He hesitated, then added, "Besides, nobody's stupid enough to willingly let a gas tank be blown up two meters away from their girlfriend. We also know your DS isn't exactly in love with you. So if they were going to feign an aggression, might as well do it against you."

His words hurt me, but they were painfully true.

"Then why did you sabotage me?"

"Because we only had your bike, not Steve's, and at that time we still believed you could be part of the scheme. We needed to hit Fonar. We thought, with a bit of luck, you could take Steve down in the fall."

"Why confess it to me now? That accident could've killed me," I said.

"I want to take responsibility for what we did, but we aren't willing to take the blame on the other crimes. We were just defending ourselves."

"Then tell the cops."

"You could help us explain our point of view; they don't understand the rules of the road. Besides, we know the commissioner who interrogated Ferrara listens to you."

Our conversation was beginning to sound a lot like the one I'd had with a frightened Axel a few days before.

"Why should I help you after what you wanted to do to me?"

"Because now we're on the same side," he said in an English that took me even more work to decipher than his Italian.

"How so?" I asked, although I was beginning to see it perfectly.

"I've given it a lot of thought," he said, returning to Italian. "The criminals want Steve to be champion. The rankings show it, and it's confirmed by the description of the man who cut the brakes on our truck. At this point, no one can take the win from the American; Fonar is very strong and everyone else is very weak. The only way he loses is if you pass him on the mountain. And it's obvious Giraud or Steve, or whoever in Fonar is behind this, doesn't trust you. That was made clear with the gas-tank explosion. So they'll probably come for you. Maybe it'll be the guy who's out there right now." As he spoke he'd gotten closer, and now the light was shining on his face. His handsome Italian features were devastated: emaciated cheeks, deep circles under his eyes, drooping lips. Matosas seemed to have aged several years since the Tour began, and it was due to something even more traumatic than three weeks of competition.

"There's a lot of speculation in what you're saying. Steve doesn't need help to win the Tour. But you do," I said.

"I never believed I'd win it; I'm not deluded. I was content to be in the top ten. I only thought I had a chance when the big guns started to disappear. But then I became a target. And I wasn't going to let that happen lying down."

"The best thing to do is tell the commissioner. As long as the police continue to believe you're the culprits, the real criminals will have carte blanche," I said. I wasn't going to confess my own suspicions about Giraud to a rival, even a helpful one. "I'll tell Favre what we've talked about. Some of what you say might make sense."

"Thank you," he said, in Spanish this time. "And good luck this weekend."

We left the kitchen separately. I stared at the Protex guard, who was looking with disgust at Sancho, who sat nibbling a piece of sausage stolen from the kitchen. Matosas's words had made a dent in my attitude. I wouldn't turn my back on Protex's man now. If what the Italian said was true about the sabotage to Lavezza's team bus, then the Sarcophagus who followed me around all day was the criminals' executioner.

Lombard was waiting for me in my room. He jumped into investigation mode right away.

"We didn't find any hidden mics or anything like that. Bimeo sent some technicians over while you were running the stage. But it's very easy to tap a cell, so better take care what you say on that."

"How are you, colonel? These must have been three exhausting weeks for you as well. How are you doing?" We hadn't talked about him in a long time; all of our exchanges had to do with my preparation, my diet, my times, my rivals. It's no surprise athletes often end up turning their obsession with performance and body preparation into a suffocating narcissism.

"Me? Good," he said, as if suspicious of the question. "Or rather, never better: You're already in fourth place, Hannibal, and the yellow jersey is within reach. I knew it ever since I first saw you ride all those years ago. I knew I had a champion on my hands."

"I might yet become a champion, colonel, but not on the Tour," I said.

"I don't understand," he said, distrustful and confused.

I hesitated a few moments, then decided to tell him about Snatch. It was the least I could do. I thought he'd be reassured when he found out I'd be a team leader the following year, a contender for Il Giro and La Vuelta in Spain.

To my surprise, the idea upset him.

"You can't trust Steve; he's going to cheat you. He just wants to keep you from taking his jersey. He knows you have it at your fingertips. It's exactly what Wiggins did to Froome in 2012: He promised him that if he didn't attack, he'd make him champion the following year. Twelve months later, he tried to betray him."

"Wiggins and Froome weren't brothers like Steve and me."

"You still believe that? Steve is not your brother. Anything you think you owe Panata you paid a long time ago. It's him who owes a great debt to you. Your *brother*"—he said it with contempt—"has deprived you of victory; worse, he's kept France from regaining its glory."

I swallowed my protests. When the colonel spoke with "La Marseillaise" as background music, no argument would be heard. I thought it better to change the subject.

"Tell me something, colonel. Where did Bimeo find the guys outside my door?"

Lombard took a moment to process my question. He didn't get how we'd gone from the mother country to the ridiculously mismatched men standing guard in the hall.

"Well," he said, rewinding his brain. "The fat one was the chief cook at a prison that Bimeo ran early in his career. But don't be fooled; even hardened criminals are afraid of that guy. They say he poisoned someone who tried to mess with him; he disfigured another by pushing his face into a soup pot. The inmates found that out after they'd eaten the soup. The tall one is a total mystery to me, but I think he's the boss." He laughed, and I seconded him nervously. Now I didn't know which of my three guards was scarier.

"Thanks for checking my room, colonel; it makes me feel better," I said, trying to end his visit, although he didn't get the message until I got up.

"No, thank *you*, Hannibal," he answered, getting emotional.

"For what?"

"Because this Saturday you're going to make me the happiest man in the world. After that, I can die in peace."

"Don't talk nonsense, you and I still have a lot ahead of us," I said, putting an arm around his shoulders. "The best is yet to come." There was a vulnerability about him I hadn't noticed before. The colonel had always enjoyed a firm muscle tone, even in old age; now I realized his chest was a little less solid, and I could've sworn he'd shrunk a few inches.

"It has to happen now. Next year isn't in your hands, it's in theirs. But this yellow jersey depends entirely on you. Don't disappoint me, Marc, I beg you." I had to guess the last word because it had drowned in his throat.

I didn't respond; instead, I extended my half-hug and accompanied him to the door. Just before we reached it, he stopped and turned toward me.

"And don't trust the Protex fellow, he's a bad bug," he said, gesturing toward the tall man in the hallway. "Better to not relax when he's close, although Bimeo's guards will have your back."

That night it took me a long time to fall asleep. Lombard's reaction had confused me. I'd wanted him to be impressed and excited about Steve's offer for next year. Instead, he'd put me against the wall. I wondered what Fiona would think when I brought her up to speed. But that would have to wait until the next day: She'd be trapped in committee meetings until very late.

I resorted to reviewing the rankings in search of their somnolent power, but again and again the thought of Giraud made it hard to breathe. My intuition had been right: Everything pointed to my DS.

What role did Steve play in all that? I preferred to think Giraud had acted behind his back to make him champion. What my friend had shared with me today confirmed there was no alliance between them. By going to Snatch, Steve was also dumping Giraud. And he'd never dare do that if they were involved in a crime together.

Satisfied with my conclusion, I decided to call Favre again. I had to let him know as soon as possible about Giraud. I'd tell him about the talk with Matosas, the relationship between Protex and the Fonar DS, and my own conclusions.

I dialed his number on the cell he'd given me, but he didn't answer. It was 12:45 A.M. I sent a text: "It's Giraud, not Ferrara."

That finally allowed me to focus on the top ten times. Well, in theory. My mind only focused on one number: 1:31. The 91 seconds that separated me and Steve. I was counting down from 91 when I got lost in dreams of yellow.

GENERAL CLASSIFICATION: STAGE 18

RANK	RIDER	TIME	NOTES
1	STEVE PANATA (USA/FONAR)	74:13:31	There is no human power that'll deny him the fifth jersey.
2	ALESSIO MATOSAS (ITALY/LAVEZZA)	+0:38	I thought he was the murderer, but he's more scared than me.
3	MILENKO PANIUK (CZECH/RABONET)	+1:00	The only one who might be dangerous, and only on the road, I hope.
4	MARC MOREAU (FRANCE/FONAR)	+1:31	I'm a domestique... I'm a domestique... I'm a domestique....
5	PABLO MEDEL (SPAIN/BALEARES)	+8:41	He hasn't counted in days.

6   ÓSCAR CUADRADO (COLOMBIA/MOVISTAR)   +12:59

7   LUIS DURÁN (SPAIN/IMAGINE)   +15:22

8   SERGEI TALANCÓN (ROMANIA/ROCCA)   +15:56

9   ROL CHARPENELLE (FRANCE/TOURGAZ)   +19:37

10   RICHARD MUELLER (GERMANY/THIELEMANN)   +21:16

Stage 19

I dreamed about the yellow jersey, but woke up a domestique once more. It's what I was and that was that. Fiona and Lombard were convinced Steve had made me a domestique. But, really, it's what I had always been: never a protagonist, always a survivor. Steve was the one who, with his Snatch project, was giving me the chance to attain personal glory. Rather than betraying him, I should be thanking him. I decided to show him as much when I saw him in the dining room that morning.

"Eat up, bro, we're gonna get the fifth today, right?" I grinned at him, nodding toward his calf, which I knew was tattooed with four bicycles, though it was currently covered by warm-up pants.

"It's already tatted; I just have to ink it," he said, obviously pleased by my attitude. I tried to swallow my shock at his confidence. "Now we have to put you in second place, don't you think? That way you'll be the Tour favorite next year if I don't come." Steve was generous, but never humble. "How much is Matosas beating you by?"

"Fifty-three seconds. But Giraud isn't going to make things easy for me; he wants us to chill so we don't tire you out. Matosas won't have a problem keeping up. So I can't ignore him for a second."

"I feel pretty good. Hit him with a strong pace when we climb the Croix de Fer to tire him out, and we'll really test him on Toussuire." Today's stage, the second to last of the Tour, offered two huge peaks; one a little after the halfway point with an almost twenty-three-kilometer ascent and another just eighteen kilometers before the finish line. A true torture for our aching bodies.

"I bet Giraud will have me handing out water. It'll be hard to get on the podium that way. As soon as he thinks you're safe and there are no more threats, he can get rid of me." I thought that Giraud would surely do that or worse if he found out about the message I'd sent the commissioner the day before.

"He won't do that; it'll look good for him if Fonar makes it one and two. And anyway, at this point in the Tour we don't have to give a shit about what Giraud says."

"Just like that? If he sends me to pass out cans, I just ignore him?" I asked, loving the idea. My long training as a domestique didn't leave me with much of an instinct for rebellion, but if it came from my leader, I was happy to obey.

"Our team radio has broken before, hasn't it?" he responded with his most radiant smile. "The signal's terrible in these mountains," he added, and burst out laughing.

I laughed too and for a second it felt like it was ten years earlier, in the kitchen of our shared house, when everything was a game and the future was an Eden, rich with marvelous fruits within our reach. But a shadow suddenly took over Steve's face.

"But if you see me falling back, slow the pace, all right?" He shot me a mistrustful, almost resentful look. A look that also reminded me of the old days, when I'd managed to beat him at videogames.

"To make it one and two, we need you to be number one," I

said, with the attitude and pronunciation Lombard used when he delivered his terrible proverbs. Again, we laughed, although after a few seconds I felt ashamed for mocking the old man.

My guilt grew even heavier when I went to my room a few minutes later and found Lombard himself there. He was squeezing a document against his chest with the zeal of a rugby player carrying the ball.

"Bernard and I have been working on this nonstop. It's the comparative performance curves between you and Steve in the mountains over the last few days: power, heart rate, cadence. We've set them up against the Alpe d'Huez climb and determined the exact point where you have to pass him." He placed half a dozen color printouts on the bed around a huge sketch of the legendary climb. "Look, at exactly four-point-five kilometers before the finish, the slope rises to nine percent. At that point, you'll both be going twenty to twenty-four kilometers per hour. You just have to increase your speed to twenty-eight to pull away from Steve. It's possible for you, but not for him; he won't be able to keep up. You'll end up with a two-minute-and-twenty-two-second lead, with a margin of error of five seconds, enough to take his jersey by more than half a minute. Bernard has checked it over and over," he concluded, smug and beaming, as if waiting for applause.

The mention of his son reminded me I hadn't answered Bernard's insistent text messages. I'd have to find him later.

"Thank you, colonel, it's all clear. The red X marks the spot, right?" I'd determined to stay loyal to Steve, but I didn't want to be impolite to Lombard, not after all he'd done for me.

"Exactly," he answered. "On Wednesday I went down and took photos. Here, right after you pass this blue milestone, that's the moment to attack." He had enlarged four shots taken from the perspective of the highway so there could be no doubt about where the blow had to be delivered.

"Leave this with me; I'll take care of it. And we'll see how tomorrow goes," I said in a neutral tone.

"Think of it this way, Hannibal: For three thousand, three hundred fifty-six kilometers and twenty days, you were his domestique. You just have to stop doing your job for the last four kilometers, for fifteen minutes. It's not so much to ask, is it?" He smiled at me with the satisfaction of someone demonstrating a lighter to a tribe of cave people.

"That's a good way of thinking about it," I said without much enthusiasm as I picked up the papers. But my brain couldn't completely push what he said away. The numbers were clear: Fiona and Lombard were right when they said that, at that moment, I was a better racer than Steve. But the final decision had nothing to do with graphics or power meters but with decency. I wasn't going to betray my brother.

There was a knock on the door. Favre's arrival put an end to the colonel's final efforts to persuade me. My old mentor said goodbye with devastation in his eyes. I hadn't fooled him; he knew me well enough to realize I'd already made a decision. I watched him walk down the hallway with slumped shoulders, dragging his feet, all his military uprightness abandoned. I remembered what Fiona had said about his illness, but was interrupted by Favre's voice.

"What's this?" he asked, showing me his cellphone screen with my message: "It's Giraud, not Ferrara."

I told him about Matosas's visit, his confession about sabotaging my bike in response to what they thought were attacks from Fonar, the man from Protex who tried to strip the brakes on the Lavezza bus, the Italians' hypothesis that the blown gas tank had been a faux attack, Matosas's fear of being murdered. I argued that Conti and Leandro's poisoning overturned the notion that Lavezza was guilty. I said nothing about Steve, about the reports he received from Protex every night or the electronic surveillance network his private guards had set up within the circuit.

The commissioner didn't seem surprised, but he wasn't convinced either. His little mustache was immobile, his pupils bearing into me.

"A surveillance camera recorded a long-distance shot of the man who was messing with Lavezza's bus that morning," Favre said in the end. "A tall guy, with a long silhouette, maybe like that Protex guard outside. But the shot is inconclusive; one of the Italian mechanics would also fit the description."

Radek or Quixote would too, I thought. There were plenty of tall, ill-defined men in this Babel of races and nationalities.

Favre continued. "We can't discard the possibility that the Italians fabricated the attack on the bus themselves, and Conti's and Leandro's poisoning too, even if they went too far on that front. These are amateur criminals."

"Matosas wasn't pretending; he's scared." What Favre was saying might be true, but I was an expert in reading my rivals' expressions. The Lavezza leader wasn't lying.

"I will say that the breadth and complexity of the attacks," the commissioner began in a scholarly tone, "and remembering they began weeks before the Tour, seem to exceed the capacities of a group of cyclists and mechanics, especially if they're wrapped up in the demands of the race."

"Exactly," I said. The commissioner had finally taken a step in the right direction.

"But explain something to me," he said, and I could've sworn he was enjoying it. "You already said why it couldn't be the Italians; now tell me why it's Giraud."

"He has the motive: to win the Tour at any cost in order to keep his job as Fonar's DS. He has the means, thanks to his relationship with Protex. You said yourself this seems to be the work of a professional organization. And as far as I'm concerned, he has a requirement the other members of the circuit don't: an absolute lack of scruples."

"In my line of work, we learn scruples are to passions what a drop of perfume is to a shit hole." I tried to keep up with the detective, who was now in his philosophical mode. "Although you're right about Protex, and we are closely investigating them. I hope you know, sergeant, that if you're right, Steve will of course be under suspicion. Protex was hired by *his* sponsors, not by Fonar or Giraud. Not to mention that he's the one who's benefited from all these crimes."

"But it's not his fault Giraud wants to make him champion."

"That would have to be proven."

"I'll prove it, rest assured," I said, although I would have liked to have been able to say it with greater confidence.

"Which brings us back to the guards out there," he said. "You've been the victim of two attacks. One of them was clearly carried out by the Italians, when they sabotaged your bike. But the gas tank is still a mystery. If your theory is right and Giraud and Protex are responsible, then what's Schrader doing outside your door?"

"Is that the Protex giant's name?"

"Yes. He's someone you should treat with care. He was a member of the German army's special forces before signing on with private contractors."

"You think I should ask him to leave?"

"That would just show Protex we suspect them. Especially if it happens right after I pay you a visit."

"What about the other two? They're Bimeo's people."

"They're both shady, although Bimeo is the one in control there, and he thinks of you as his ally. Anyway, there are only two nights left. I'll put a couple of agents on the stairs," he said. "Nobody else is going to fit in the hallway," he added with a tired smile. "They'll be within shouting distance. And even so, shut yourself in here with three locks."

"Don't worry, if Giraud is really guilty, he already got what he wanted; I don't think there'll be any more incidents. Steve is going to be champion."

What happened the next day seemed to confirm it. From the peloton lineup at the start, I could tell Matosas had ceased to be a threat. His weary gaze seemed to be that of someone simply waiting for everything to be over.

We suffered a few breakaways in the first half of the race from lower-ranked cyclists who didn't want to say goodbye to the Tour without showing up on TV. We caught up with all of them at the terrible Col de la Croix de Fer; nobody had the legs to make their break in the middle of the climb.

I followed Giraud's instructions, running conservatively on just half power. Still, I made Fonar put some more swing into the climb than was absolutely necessary. Nothing to separate the peloton, but enough to start wearing it down. The long, twenty-two-kilometer ascent went in my favor. When we conquered that first peak, most of the peloton were far behind. Fonar kept six of our teammates in the pack, and practically all the top ten in the rankings made it. I had to respect my fellow cyclists. Their bodies felt dead and their legs were in torment, but their will to fight was undeniable. Whoever was in eighth place would leave his soul behind to unseat the man in front of him, even if he knew he would have to defend seventh place tooth and nail to keep the man he'd just passed from overtaking him. Everyone had something to die and kill for in the final kilometers—at least figuratively.

After the summit, Paniuk, third in the rankings, descended at suicidal speeds down ravines and gorges and gained a 25-second advantage over all of us. Steve, a powerful racer on descents, wanted to follow him, but I convinced him not to. If the Czech wanted to break his neck, he had every right to do so, but there was no sense in putting ourselves at risk when the championship was already in our hands. Or in Steve's hands. Which was the same thing.

Regardless of what Paniuk did, we'd catch up to him at the Toussuire, the second climb. Still, I couldn't help but admire my fellow athlete for the heroic attempt. Once every twenty years a cyclist scales Toussuire's fifteen kilometers on his own and gets ahold of the yellow jersey, to the surprise of the other leaders, who inexplicably can't reach him. For every one who achieves that feat, two hundred inexorably fail. But the craving for glory does not calculate probabilities. Paniuk climbed every hundred meters as if they were his last. At one point, he widened his advantage to 35 seconds; I could feel nerves shaking the group when we got the news from the screen on the motorbike that went in front of us.

That morning, I had set off in fourth place, 31 seconds behind Paniuk. After the lead he got on us, that margin doubled. I started to wonder if we were about to experience one of those legendary days, and I felt a numbness in my temples, as if I'd swallowed an ice cube too fast.

My only challenge of the day was supposed to be leaving Matosas behind, knocking him out of second place in the rankings, but now I was struggling not to fall behind third. I still hadn't forced the pace I'd planned to attack the Italian with, but I'd reached an accelerated rhythm with which I planned to wear him out. Two of our domestiques had burned out after taking turns up front, per my instructions, and another two would soon abandon the group for the same reason. Within three kilometers, only Steve and I would still be there for Fonar, and then we'd attack Matosas. That had been the plan at least, but Paniuk was tearing it apart.

A few meters later, the distance separating us from the Czech was 48 seconds. How the hell was Paniuk able to keep widening his advantage when he was on his own? I tried to calm down: We still had twelve of the eighteen kilometers to climb. I told myself the Czech was planning poorly, that he couldn't keep up his pace. In situations like that, you can't get desperate and set off on a pursuit that won't bear fruit. I couldn't leave before Guido, the last of our domestiques, was spent; that would mean wasting the energy reserves my teammate had to offer. But it was clear Paniuk was rolling faster than Guido, and that was starting to become a significant disadvantage.

If I struck out after the Czech, Steve might not be in good enough condition to follow my wheel, which meant, in practice, betraying the leader. But to do nothing would condemn me to losing second place to Paniuk, who didn't seem to be slowing down. Later, I'd see the images of his face in those last kilometers on TV: a frozen and unchangeable grimace of pain, a mute scream like that of a dead body at Pompeii. A dead body at Pompeii that was about to bury my hopes for the Tour.

I told Guido to fall back from our team's front spot, gesturing toward his power meter; he couldn't do it anymore. We still had eight kilometers left to reach the finish line, and Paniuk was 51 seconds ahead of everyone. That meant he'd beat me by 82 seconds in the general classification.

"Let's go," I said to Steve, but he shook his head no. He seemed to be on his last legs. I wasn't feeling good either. For some time, a pull in my hips had been shooting down the outside of both thighs. It was as if my legs were dislocated; I imagined this is what it might feel like after taking a turn on the rack during the Spanish Inquisition. But I wasn't going to let the first podium of my career get away from me because of my old friend pain.

I did the math again. At this pace, Paniuk could achieve a distance we couldn't recover from tomorrow; he might even unseat Steve. This last fact was key.

I had to wake Steve up somehow. "If you don't watch out, he's going to take your yellow jersey today," I shouted as best I could at my teammate. My lungs were growing ever more jealous of what little oxygen they could get.

Steve didn't react for a few seconds, and I worried my taunt had failed. But then he changed gears, stood up on the pedals, and started his pursuit. Even I was stunned he was capable of it. I looked at Matosas's resigned, empty face, like a sheep on the way to slaughter, and I set off alone after Steve. Later, I asked Steve what he was thinking in that instant, and he didn't have an explanation. I suppose his aversion to defeat was so deeply rooted in him that it overcame his physical limitations. I didn't have that extra fuel; after all, I'd been trained for defeat. Nevertheless, all those years of rolling in front of the leader wouldn't let me stare at his back as he climbed on his own. Not while I had an ounce of energy left in me. He obeyed his nature and I obeyed mine.

It took me almost half a kilometer to make up for the thirty meters I'd lost to Steve on his initial push. When he saw me at his side, he seemed to come out of his trance and understand where he was. I put myself ahead and we let our ingrained instincts replace our epic impulses. We ate up the following kilometers with no fuss but at a good pace, regulating the loss. Or that's what we thought: We ended up catching Paniuk a kilometer before the finish line. The Czech was on his last legs; he fell apart when we passed him. He came in 34 seconds behind us. This time, I let Steve cross the finish line first. I had to recognize he'd been the protagonist of the pursuit, thanks to his unearthly leap forward.

Most important, we'd knocked Matosas off the podium: He arrived, zigzagging and at death's door, almost five minutes after us. With bonus points added, I was beating Paniuk and ended up in second place in the rankings. With one day left until Paris, Steve and I were again one and two in the competition. And this time, we thought, nothing could change that. We came together in a long embrace that the photographers snapped effusively, even if we were essentially falling into each other's arms out of fatigue.

On the way back to the hotel, Giraud said a few words in his motivational team leader mode. Though I was barely listening, I stared intensely at Giraud. I saw his flabby mouth, his heavy paws, and that enormous belly, wondering if he had been directly involved in the tragedies affecting my fellow racers. Had he himself run over Lampar on that lonely highway a few days before the Tour? Had the money to pay the women who seduced the Baleares team for three nights in a row come from the silly fanny pack that hung from his gut? Had those fat fingers left the marks on poor Fleming's neck?

I wished with all my soul that Favre's investigation would close quickly and that it would end in this sick bastard's arrest. I fantasized about Giraud being handcuffed at the very moment Steve and I climbed up onto the podium at the awards ceremony in Paris. I let my daydream go even further. Fiona would stand at the foot of the platform, flanked by Lombard and Ray, and I would throw my championship bouquet into her arms.

Lombard's presence in my idyllic image stirred up an uncomfortable shadow. Then I remembered why: I still hadn't responded to Bernard's messages. I checked my cell's signal strength and called his phone directly. I supposed he wanted to talk about the graphics his father had spread out on my bed, so I lowered my voice and pressed the device to my ear against the window. Fonar knew Lombard and son were advising me personally, but they had no idea the two men were secretly accessing the team's database, much less preparing an attack on its leader.

Bernard and I spoke briefly about the results of the stage, and he told me the data confirmed that my physical state and competitive level were the best they'd been in my entire career. Unlike his father, Bernard said so with little enthusiasm, in spite of the many hours he'd invested in the matter. I soon understood why.

"But that's not why I wanted to talk to you," he said finally, his voice trembling. "I'm worried about my father." I remembered Fiona's comment and the feeling in my hand when I squeezed Lombard's shrinking stature. A sense of suffocation rose in my throat, not unlike the one a medieval farmer might have felt when he heard the rumbling gallop of horsemen approaching. I feared the worst.

"What's wrong? Is he sick?"

"Something's wrong, but we're not sure what. He only lets himself be seen at the military hospital by his friends, who won't tell me anything. But that's not what worries me most. I think he's losing his mind."

"I've noticed he seems distracted, but he's seventy-eight, right?"

"It's much more than that. He's doing ridiculous things," he said, impatiently trying to make himself understood. "He sold the Ramoneda."

"When? Why?" The revelation hit me hard. The beautiful estate, twenty kilometers from Jurançon, near Pau, had been in the hands of the Lombard family for many generations. A huge chalet, almost a castle, surrounded by famous vineyards.

"At the end of last year, it seems. I found out by chance a few days ago, when I spoke to the family notary. He mentioned it because he thought I already knew."

"I don't understand; he always talks about the Ramoneda like something that will pass down from generation to generation. That's why he bugs you so much about grandchildren."

"But that's not all. The notary didn't want to tell me how much he sold it for when he realized I didn't know what had happened. Which made me nervous. The market value for that kind of estate is over two million euros. I'm afraid the buyers tricked him into accepting less."

"Why would he sell in the first place?"

"He's always talked about how great it would be to find sponsors to finance a team built around you. I think my analysis of your performance set things in motion. For months, he's talked about all the huge races you'd win if you were a leader. Two or three million euros wouldn't be enough to start a team, but maybe he thinks he could lay the first stone and incentivize others to join in. Hasn't he said anything to you?"

"Absolutely not. All he's worried about now is me getting my hands on the jersey in tomorrow's race," I said, almost whispering, looking around. No one seemed to be paying attention.

"My father knows nothing about business. He would be easy prey for the sharks that circle the circuit."

"And you haven't talked to him about this?"

"I wanted to do it in person, but I couldn't get away from work. I'll be able to see him when you get to Paris this weekend. Can we talk to him together? It'd be easier to face him and find out what's happening."

I agreed, he wished me good luck on the Alpe d'Huez, and we hung up. I could never forgive myself for being the cause of such a loss for a family, all because an old man believed in me too much. We would have to talk to him and stop this madness; with a little luck, maybe we could reverse the sale.

I'd thought the only thing on my to-do list for Sunday night was melting into Fiona's body. That distracted me, and I entertained myself for the next few minutes with the memory of her sweet taste, the glaze that fell over her eyes at the moment her pleasure peaked. I got out of the bus still wrapped in her arms and bumped into Sancho at the foot of the steps. The rush of lust flew off me like birds from a violently shaken tree.

I followed the bodyguard to my room, marveling at the unexpected agility with which he trotted along, quite an achievement considering the mass he was moving with every step. I was surprised not to see the Protex goon in the hallway. His usual place outside my room had been taken by Sancho's companion, Quixote. I shut the door and left them exchanging words and laughter in some strange jargon.

A little later, Favre knocked on my door. If I'd known what he was coming to tell me, I wouldn't have opened it. I assumed, excitedly, that he was bringing an update about the Giraud investigation, some incriminating new evidence or testimony. But, instead, the commissioner brought a cadaver.

He told me that morning, they'd found Schrader, the German sarcophagus who had been my shadow for several days. His head was stuffed in a plastic bag inside a car registered to Protex, in an abandoned lot outside Saint-Jean-de-Maurienne. The slashes and scratches on his skin indicated the huge man had fought until the last moment. Remembering the table he had for a back and the tree trunks he had for legs, anyone who'd sent him to the other world demanded respect.

Favre could tell I had expected different news. "If Giraud and Protex are behind the crimes, as you say, then Schrader's death is absurd," he said. As on many other occasions, I had the impression the commissioner wasn't there to problem-solve with me, but rather to sound out my reactions.

"Unless they're covering their tracks. Let's suppose Schrader was the one who killed Fleming, following Giraud's instructions. If Giraud panicked once he realized the police were starting to investigate, it's possible he wanted to eliminate the actual perpetrator, the only one who could really incriminate him."

"Could be," he conceded, "but there's a problem with your logic. I'm sure it took at least two people to do in Schrader, if not more. In that case, Giraud is now dealing not just with the actual perpetrator but with two or three more killers who could squeal."

"He could have brought on hired killers from outside for that. Schrader was already in full view of the police: The Italians had pointed him out as the man who tried to sabotage the brakes on their bus."

"But how could Giraud have known that?" Favre objected, fixing his eyes on me, fully transformed into his bloodhound alter ego.

I paused before saying, "Protex has an informant in the police."

We shared a moment of silence. Then: "That would make sense," said the commissioner, in a tone of real anxiety. For the first time I felt he was no longer playing the role of heroic detective he had in his head.

"Steve told me. They send him a report every night, supposedly for his eyes only. But if Giraud is colluding with Protex behind Steve's back, I'm sure he gets a copy too." I don't know why I felt the need to tell Favre everything. Perhaps it was an act of generosity on seeing him so stricken by the betrayal of a fellow police agent. Or perhaps it was an act of vengeance on my part, a little payback for the way he had played with me over the past three weeks.

"We can't count out the Italians either," he said, trying to pull himself together. It was clear he wasn't going to argue with me about a leak within the police corps. It must have fit with the information he already had. "Ferrara was furious with the German for the attempt on the bus."

"Ferrara is under arrest, and from what I've seen of Matosas, it looks like he just wants to get away from this mess. Killing Schrader after talking trash about him during his interrogation wouldn't be so smart, would it?"

The commissioner took another long pause. We were both out of arguments. Fatigue and disappointment turned the silence stony and cold.

"Or maybe we're wrong about the murderer and it's neither of those two," he said finally. The commissioner was talking to me, maybe for the first time, as if I were a true colleague. I tried to live up to it.

"In which case we're screwed; the Tour ends in a day and a half. It'll be harder to find the killer once the platform comes down and everyone in this circus disperses."

"I have to agree with you there, Sergeant Moreau."

We parted ways in the hall with our spirits down by our feet. I felt a little bit sorry for the commissioner. After all, I had a podium to climb on Sunday; he would have to crawl back to Paris with his tail between his legs. A tough blow for his pride, surely. Nevertheless, when we said goodbye he told me with an unexpected sparkle in his eyes that all of France would be climbing the Alpe d'Huez with me the next day. I gulped down my ambition and anxiety.

When I was finally left alone, I saw two messages from Steve on my cellphone. I called him at once. He asked me if I knew what had happened, and when I started telling him about the German, he asked me not to give him any details over the phone, that we'd have to talk at dinner. We agreed to meet in the dining room fifteen minutes later.

I assumed Steve's insistence that we be discreet over the phone confirmed that my phone was tapped and that he knew it. It had probably been at his instruction. For some reason, I didn't care. It could even be interpreted as a measure taken in order to protect me.

I got a message from Fiona and forgot about Steve for a moment. "I need to see you." As always, her words registered in my crotch. I started writing a response that would live up to her provocation, but with her next text, a bucket of ice water fell over me: "Ray and I will come up after dinner."

Down in the dining room, I counted six guards posted around the perimeter, although none were inside, out of respect for the other teams, I supposed.

"I just spoke with Protex's lead investigator, bro," Steve told me anxiously as soon as I took a seat by his side. "They've reached the conclusion that the Italians didn't kill Schrader."

Of course it wasn't the Italians, it was them, it was Protex, I thought.

Steve continued: "The thing is, this opens up all the possibilities. Schrader's the first victim who isn't part of the circuit; up to now they've all been cyclists."

"I can't make heads or tails of it," I said. "Does Protex have a hypothesis? A suspect?"

"Nothing, just one strange piece of info. They talked to Lampar." Lampar was the star Australian climber who was hit by a car on a training route before the Tour had even begun. "He says he didn't usually ride where he was run over. He was there because he'd agreed to meet up with someone from the Tour organization at a restaurant down that way. They made the date over the phone. Protex thinks someone deliberately lured him into the accident."

"Anyone could have passed as a member of the Tour organization on the phone."

"The meeting was about a personal issue for Lampar. He wanted to race wearing the Australian national colors, as national champion, but there was controversy for some reason. He petitioned in a very reserved way because he wanted to avoid public embarrassment in case they turned him down. It seems only his wife and the organizers knew."

"Strange." The more I thought about it, the less sense it made. "If there are hired killers, poisoners, and saboteurs, that means we're talking about a big operation, with resources; they could have easily paid off a Tour employee, don't you think?"

"Yes, of course," he responded, distracted again. "But I'm sick of this. I told Giraud this is the last night we're spending in a Tour hotel. Benny booked a private flight from Grenoble to Paris tomorrow afternoon. We can go straight from the Alpe d'Huez finish line. Adidas has offered me an apartment in Paris with security. They maintain it for celebrities. Stevlana will wait for me there. There's a room for you too . . . and Fiona," he added. "What matters is that we don't give the culprit the slightest opportunity to hit us, because now we have no fucking clue where the attacks are coming from."

"I'm assuming the rules don't allow it, right? Staying anywhere other than the Tour hotels." I already knew the answer, but a luxury suite after three weeks of rustic hotels was an irresistible proposal.

"Benny says we shouldn't worry about that. They killed Fleming in a Tour hotel, so he's sure he can persuade the organizers to be flexible. They just want this to be over too. Imagine the scandal if something happens to the yellow jersey. We just have to let the WADA people know for the anti-doping test."

"It'll be a relief to leave all this behind," I said, casting my eyes over the dining room packed with cyclists. I generally enjoyed the living conditions of long races; they reminded me of the barracks.

But I'd never experienced them so full of traps and betrayals. "I'll tell Fiona," I added, although I already took her negative response for granted. Being a guest of the *Stivys* might be one of her top ten worst nightmares.

Satisfied with my response, Steve looked down the table, clinked a glass with his spoon, and made himself heard. "A toast to tomorrow's victory, my fifth yellow jersey. I'll never forget what I owe you all," he declared, raising a glass of milk; the rest of us followed suit with juice, coffee, water, and bowls of cereal, but without much enthusiasm. Unlike Steve, we were uncomfortable celebrating while among colleagues we hadn't yet beaten. Many of them would see it as disrespectful, or even a taunt. But I knew my bro had done it in good faith, blind to his surroundings, caught up in his own generosity toward the members of his team.

I went up to the room followed by Sancho and Quixote, my remaining guards; they chatted happily in a French so slang-laden it was barely recognizable—the prison variety, I guessed.

Minutes later, Ray and Fiona arrived. I let them know about Schrader's death and the role of the supposed Tour official in Lampar's accident. Ray took notes and nodded. Then he offered a piece of revealing information.

"The Lampar thing adds a twist to something I thought was unimportant until now. Remember the hotel where Fleming died?" We nodded in silence; we were both familiar with the Blue Galleon, where the Batesman team had been put up. Fonar had stayed there two or three years before.

The journalist took out his road book, the thick PR packet that press members receive at the start of the Tour. He looked for the section on Stage 6 and paused on the page listing the hotels designated by the organization and the teams assigned to them for the night, according to the results of the raffle that had taken place weeks before. The Blue Galleon wasn't on the list. According to the program, Batesman was meant to spend that night at the Madelaine, along with four other teams.

"I don't understand. Batesman wouldn't have been able to stay there if the hotel wasn't on the official list," I said.

"I thought the same thing," said Ray, "so I asked the Brits. Their press guy told me that, at the last minute, someone from the organization informed them the Madelaine had problems with the electrical equipment in one wing of the building and they'd have to move them to the Blue Galleon. Since Batesman has the most employees, the organization decided letting them all stay there was more practical for everyone."

"If someone wanted to attack Fleming, the Blue Galleon was the perfect place. Small, modest, and isolated; practically no staff at night," Fiona mused.

"Did you ask which official made them change hotels?" I asked. "And do you know if it's true the Madelaine had electrical problems?"

"I didn't ask, no," said Ray. "The explanation seemed reasonable, until you mentioned what happened to Lampar."

"But it's absurd. Neither Jitrik nor the organization would ever do anything against the Tour," said Fiona, confused.

"True," said Ray, "but whoever put this whole circus together has already shown they have the resources to pay off whomever they want, especially a small-time official."

"That doesn't let Giraud off, although I'm starting to think this is way out of his league," said Fiona.

"So the commissioner doesn't know anything about this?" Ray asked me.

"About Lampar, and now the hotel? No, at least, I don't think so. He seems like he's at a dead end. I'll have to tell him. If the police find out the official's identity, we could follow the trail of whoever was buying them off. It's the first real clue we've had since this whole thing started." I couldn't ignore the fact that I'd felt equally confident about Giraud and the Italians, but a little self-deception never hurt anyone.

"Don't call Favre. Not yet," said Ray. "I've stayed in the Blue

Galleon three or four times in my thirty years covering the Tour. I
like it for the same reason the murderer probably chose it. It's
quiet and out of the way. The owner is a cagey, grouchy old man
whom I've grown fond of. I can get more information out of him
than any cop." He checked his watch. "Give me until ten A.M.
before letting your friend the commissioner know."

My friend? I thought. I would have liked to tell him that Favre
had been as friendly as a blister on my ass throughout the Tour,
but I didn't want to keep Ray any longer. I needed to talk to Fiona.
I wanted to let her know about my final decision in private. She
wasn't going to like it.

When we were alone, I explained Steve's plan to create a team
with Snatch, his proposal to make me leader in all races other
than the Tour, my chance to finally stop being a domestique and
take advantage of the potential she saw in me. I spoke while leaning back against the headboard, between the pillows, and she listened in silence, sitting on the edge of the bed. At one point, she
stood up, turned off the room lights, and lay down beside me.

I talked for a long time, unhurriedly, with more confidence and
conviction now that we were in the dark. Finally, I told her that
tomorrow, I'd protect Steve against whatever came at him, and I
would make sure he got his fifth yellow jersey. Without intending
to, I said the last few phrases as if they were a challenge.

My words floated in the silence of the room until they took on
a physical, ominous weight. Fiona's head was barely brushing
against the left side of my chest, but all my senses were piling up
in the patch of skin touched by the threads of her hair, awaiting a
response as if the rest of my life depended on it.

After a few long moments, Fiona spoke.

"I don't have many memories of my mother, except that she
used to read me stories at night. She went to the hospital when I
was four and never came back. My favorite story was about Saint
George, who saves the princess from the dragon, but I felt sorry
for the poor animal. The scene on the cover was terrifying; it

showed the fierce face of Saint George as he thrust his lance into the dragon's belly and it writhed in pain. My father was named George too; I guess you didn't know that, because everyone on the Tour called him Koky. He was a hard man and I thought the face he made when he got angry was the same as Saint George's."

I listened to her without moving.

"You probably don't remember, but one day in your first year as a professional you visited the bus my dad used as a workshop when he decided to go freelance. He thought that because of his prestige, cyclists and other mechanics would flock to him as if he were some kind of oracle. The experiment was a failure, but on that day, you came to ask a question. You explained you had gone through all sorts of seats but none of them quite worked, and at the end of a ride you felt torn up. Then you saw me and suddenly blushed when you realized you were talking about the state of your ass in front of a twenty-year-old girl. You lowered your head, and I could see the little dragon on your neck, just at your hairline."

I made an encouraging sound, although I didn't have the slightest idea of what she was getting at.

"My dad suggested it wasn't a matter of seats but rather the padding of your shorts and that you'd have to find a pair that fit you better. I'd been taking courses on sports anatomy and physiotherapy, and I suggested that one of your legs might be slightly longer than the other. My father insulted me in an ugly, terrible way, angry that I'd presumed to disagree with him, especially in front of you. You blushed again, but agreed that might also be it. Two weeks later you came back with the results of an anatomical exam that said your left leg was five millimeters shorter than your right. You said so right in front of my father, with an innocent smile. I felt that, finally, the dragon had reversed the roles and put the terrible Saint George in his place, saving the princess."

"So that's why you call me Dragon sometimes," I said finally, vaguely remembering the scene she described. "I didn't know; I thought it was just because of the tattoo. Why are you telling me this now?"

"I don't know. I've been thinking about us for a few days; I miss that dragon."

"If you're saying so because of Steve and the jersey—" I began, but she put a finger on my lips. After a moment she started to run her hand up and down my chest.

We made love for a long time. Fiona guided me from frenzies to intense pauses in which she held my face and examined it attentively, as if seeing it for the first time, or as if she never wanted to forget it. A couple of times I felt her tears on my neck.

Somewhere in my head, an alarm went off: It was madness to make love on the eve of the mother of all stages, the ascent of the terrible Alpe d'Huez. It broke every single professional rule by which and for which I lived. I understood something important was happening, without quite knowing what.

When we finished, Fiona once again fell silent. She seemed to still be awake, but I preferred not to interrupt whatever she was thinking. After a while, I tried to get to sleep with a review of the rankings, but on that occasion, and for the first time in many years, I thought it didn't make sense.

GENERAL CLASSIFICATION: STAGE 19

RANK	RIDER	TIME	NOTES
1	STEVE PANATA (USA/FONAR)	78:37:34	The yellow jersey is his.
2	MARC MOREAU (FRANCE/FONAR)	+1:33	Second place! Why am I not celebrating?
3	MILENKO PANIUK (CZECH/RABONET)	+1:40	I can't let him get away tomorrow.
4	ALESSIO MATOSAS (ITALY/LAVEZZA)	+5:42	In the end, I feel kind of sorry for him.
5	PABLO MEDEL (SPAIN/BALEARES)	+14:26	

6	ÓSCAR CUADRADO (COLOMBIA/MOVISTAR)	+17:59
7	LUIS DURÁN (SPAIN/IMAGINE)	+20:31
8	SERGEI TALANCÓN (ROMANIA/ROCCA)	+21:12
9	ROL CHARPENELLE (FRANCE/TOURGAZ)	+27:59
10	RICHARD MUELLER (GERMANY/THIELEMANN)	+32:43

Stage 20

Modane Valfréjus—Alpe d´Huez, 110.5 km.

When I woke up, Fiona wasn't there, which wasn't unusual. But even in my sleepy state, I could feel this absence was different: The thick silence that had followed our revelations, the way she'd clung to my body, the absence of a kiss on my shoulder before going out the door. A note on the keyboard and some paragraphs on the screen of my laptop confirmed just how different. I started with the handwritten note.

> *My beloved Dragon,*
> *This afternoon while you climb the Alpe, I'll be flying to Dublin. I already spoke with the organization and I told Ray everything I know. I have matters to deal with there and many things to think about. I simply couldn't bear to see you come behind Steve again of your own volition; it breaks my heart to imagine the scene in Paris, with you raising his arm on the podium; the Dragon I treasured all these years would shatter. I thought I could live with this but I can't. I need to be alone.*

Lombard is ill, he doesn't have long to live. Don't be too hard on him. We were going to tell you after the Tour— we didn't want to distract you—but the end may come sooner than anticipated. I've already said goodbye; that's what he wanted, to say goodbye to me while he's still standing.

I'm sure you've never seen the emails Steve sent me back when he wanted to rip me out of your arms at any cost. And if you have, then you're not the man I thought I was in love with. I never showed them to you, because I didn't want to make you suffer. It doesn't make sense anymore to hide them from you.

I love you, Fiona

The world darkened, and something in my belly struggled to make its way to my throat. The room began to revolve around the small table. Lombard at death's door, Fiona saying goodbye to me—was it over? Steve stuck in some unforgivable infamy, at least in the eyes of my girlfriend. The first two were devastating: Losing my old mentor and Fiona condemned me to orphanhood again, to loneliness. Like so many other times, Steve's friendship would be the only thing I had to hold on to.

I considered the possibility of erasing what Fiona had left on the screen without reading it. Steve wasn't perfect, but who was? He'd been a brother in good and bad times.

I was terrified to find something irreversible, something that could make me lose him too. What would I have left? But, slowly, as if I were in a horror movie, my eyes ignored my will and shifted to the screen. I started reading.

December 3, 2012

Marc, I've been to the hospital many times in these months. A few weeks ago the doctors told me I'm full of cancer and

*there is nothing to be done. As a nurse, I know what awaits
me. The family I thought I had left me lying on a bed, abandoned. I know I deserve it because I was a bad mother. I can
never forgive myself for what I did to you. And I don't expect you to forgive me either, but I thought I should tell you
your mother is dying. I wanted to tell you a long time ago,
but I was ashamed after ignoring you for so long. I'm sending this to Steve's email, which is the only one I have.*

  Beatriz Restrepo

December 9, 2012

*Marc, dear son. The pains are terrible, they don't want to
give me morphine but my friends sometimes get me something. I want to die but I can't do it without first talking to
you, without you forgiving me. All these days I've spent tor-
turing myself with the memory of the many times I left you
crying, of the caresses I never gave you. I hated your father
because he ruined my youth and I took my revenge on you.
I don't ask you to understand me, only that you consider
you are flesh of my flesh and let me go in peace.*

  Beatriz Restrepo

December 13, 2012

*I haven't slept for two nights and I think the end is near. It'll
be a relief to leave but, without your forgiveness, I feel dirty.
Steve says he's passed on my messages to you and you don't
want to talk to me. Don't forgive me then, but just say
something to me. Don't let me go like this, I beg you.*

  Your mother

December 14, 2012

Marc, my child, please.

Underneath the series of emails, there was a note in a different typeface. My heart sank even lower upon reading it.

Fiona—I later learned Mrs. Beatriz died the night of December 14, shortly after sending this last email. Marc never wanted to answer. When I told him about his mother's death, he shrugged. I'm asking you: Do you still prefer that man, now that you truly know him? Or this one, who adores you?
    Steve

When I finished I was drenched in tears. I cried for Beatriz, agonizing and tormented in her bed, for Steve and his inconceivable double betrayal, for Fiona and the loyalty that made her able to hide this from me. And I cried for myself and the impossibility of running to a hospital in Medellín to hug my mom and tell her I'd never stopped loving her.

I thought of Lombard. I'd been denied a chance to say goodbye to my mother, but I had the opportunity now, in his time of need, to be with the man who had been like a father to me.

But I couldn't move. I felt drained, paralyzed by these revelations. I wanted to find Fiona and tell her nothing in my life was more important than her, and if I had to win the yellow jersey to convince her of that, no human power would stop me. I wanted to beat Steve to a pulp, right there in the dining room, and shout out the list of his sins for everyone to hear. If he could do that to his brother, what would keep him from killing, running over, or poisoning others in order to enter the list of cycling immortals? I wanted to talk to the commissioner. I'd suddenly realized it was not Giraud but Steve who had been behind the attacks the whole time. He was the one who had sent Schrader to watch over me, who had intimidated Lombard so he wouldn't come near me, and who had the phones tapped. Protex worked for Steve, not for Giraud.

I didn't do any of that, though. When I calmed down, I realized the only possible answer was to snatch the yellow jersey. It would be the best and most terrible revenge. And if I wanted to beat Steve I couldn't say anything to anyone. The police had been infiltrated by Protex; all my communications were surely under surveillance. If Steve found out about my decision, he'd probably have a contingency plan to neutralize or liquidate me. He'd only kept me around because he needed me on the mountain and because he took my subordination for granted, especially after offering me Snatch. As Fiona had once told me, he was buying my submission.

On the bike, I'm all about the game plan, a chess player who anticipates his rivals' movements before they even conceive of them, an artist who can detect the precise moment to feint an attack, or give a final thrust. But off the road, I let life happen to me, without strategy, calculation, or design, simply adjusting to whatever comes along. From now on, it'd have to be different.

I lingered in my room before going down for breakfast. I wanted to spend as little time as possible with Steve for fear of revealing the demons churning in my stomach. I could barely eat in the state I was in anyway, even though today, more than any other day of my life as a cyclist, I'd need all the energy possible for the sacrilege I was about to commit.

I went down to the dining room flanked by my two companions. Lombard's orders had them shadowing me every second I spent off the road. Their boss, Bimeo, had even arranged for a couple more motorcyclists to ride around the peloton; their real purpose was to protect me and, once on the summit, to open the way for me. The most vulnerable moments during a race are usually the last kilometers on a hill, when the crowd overflows onto the road to encourage and touch the cyclists, but ends up engulfing them like a boa constrictor.

Like many successful people, Steve is perfectly capable of floating above everything that doesn't concern him, but when his interests are involved, he has the critical eye of a fashion designer. It was enough for him to see me to realize something was up. He greeted me solicitously, brushed the crumbs from my place at the table, and patted my back, asking how I was doing. I could tell it wasn't a rhetorical question. He wanted to know my mood and, above all, to determine if I was still willing to take him to the finish line.

"It's Lombard, he's dying, I just found out," I muttered, my head down. I wasn't lying, although a part of me regretted using the painful news to rid myself of Steve's suspicions.

"How? Where is he? What's wrong with him?" he asked, seeming genuinely surprised and alarmed. Although he had no love for the colonel, he knew how much Lombard meant to me. For a moment, his gesture of solidarity moved me, and I began to ease the resentment I'd built up in the past hour. Then I remembered how Steve had mourned after we learned of my mother's death and my anger returned. At the moment my "bro" was crying, that selfish bastard knew he had made the last days of Beatriz Restrepo's life a living hell in a half-assed attempt to steal my girlfriend.

But, locked in my grief over Lombard, I didn't have to say much more, especially since the call to the starting line was early that day.

Once back in my room, I got dressed, then sent Lombard a message urging him to see me, and he replied that he would look for me at the signature ceremony at Modane. Then I tried to call Fiona. I couldn't get through, but I did receive a text from Ray that left me cold: "I spoke with the folks at the Blue Galleon, the Madelaine, and with the woman who requested the hotel change for the organization, and I think I know who's behind this. If something comes to pass, open the envelope I sent to Dublin. Don't talk to Favre for any reason. I repeat, don't talk to Favre for any reason." The journalist's message left me with more questions than answers. In fact, no answers at all. Had he confirmed a Tour official was working for Protex? Would they make an attempt on Ray's life? Had they intercepted this message? Could Fiona be in danger now that an envelope with the answers was on its way to Dublin?

Before I could throw more questions up in the air, another text from the journalist flashed on my screen: "Win this damn Tour, Moreau. That's the only thing that will reveal the guilty parties."

I didn't know what to make of that either. Beating Steve was, until a few days ago, the most terrible thing I could think of doing; today, it was the way to keep Fiona's love, a patriotic act for the glory of France, and, according to the journalist, a way to solve the case of the Tourmalet killer.

I looked at my lacerated and scraped-up legs, my tired thighs, my face etched with worry, and I wondered if I was ready to live up to all those responsibilities. I also had the demons of resentment working against me, consuming me, and clouding my ability to come up with a strategy. I feared the internalized reflexes of the domestique and, at the same time, the way the well-oiled Fonar machine could neutralize any challenge on my part.

I took Lombard's graphics out of my suitcase and spread them out on the bed. The route designed by the organizers was savage. The first climb was in the first 20 kilometers; then there was the legendary Col de Galibier in the middle of the day. After that, there were 45 kilometers of steep descent, Steve's turf, until the foot of the Alpe d'Huez, a 15-kilometer wall more suitable for goats than for bikes. That's where the Tour would be decided, assuming we were all alive at that point. The course was one of the shortest of the competition—just 110 kilometers—but almost five and a half hours long, which said it all.

I stared at the X on kilometer 106, four kilometers before the finish line. That was the place where I would separate from Steve and our lives would change forever. I visualized the image on TV: me on the pedals, my leader's face twisted by rage, the commentators' screams, the audience's frenzy at the unexpected turn of events.

I thought back to the colonel and looked forward to hugging the old man before starting the course. I remembered what he had said to me a few days before—*This Saturday you're going to make me the happiest man in the world. After that I can die in peace*—and now I understood it wasn't senile sentimentality, but his goal for his literal last days.

I kept trying, without success, to reach Fiona, all the way up until the signature ceremony. I managed to avoid any personal contact with Steve, using the pretext of having to attend to a couple of reporters. Finally, I was able to get to Lombard and dragged him around behind the team bus for some privacy.

"Colonel, how are you? How do you feel?"

"Very well," he said with a frozen grin he tried to pass off as a smile. Now that I knew the truth, I noticed the faint yellow color of his skin. "I couldn't be better, now that you'll be champion."

"Fiona told me everything. You shouldn't be here; you should be fighting this in a hospital. Why didn't you tell me before? Not even Bernard knows!" I scolded him.

"I'm where I should be. I wouldn't miss what's going to happen today for anything in the world. This is worth my life—many lives! You in the yellow jersey . . ." he said, spellbound, and for an instant his eyes seemed to be two fiery embers in the dry desert of his face.

"What I don't understand is why you sold the Ramoneda. If you needed money for treatment, you should've said so, colonel; we would've all helped out. There was no need for you to lose your house," I said, scolding him again, but lovingly.

"When you have kids, you'll understand what you're willing to do for them, Marc," he responded.

Getting rid of the family home wasn't exactly a way of helping your child. And using the money to create a professional team and launch me as a leader seemed absurd if he only had days to live. I thought of the episodes of dementia Fiona had warned me about.

Before I could get any concrete answers, Axel interrupted our chat and took me by the arm, saying Giraud was waiting. I said goodbye to the colonel as best I could and joined the rest of my teammates inside the bus, where they had gathered around the DS.

"Everything is cooking perfectly, but you have to know when to take the pot off the stove and serve the soup. Not too cold, not too hot," he told all of us, although his eyes didn't move from mine. Kitchen metaphors were his favorites, whether they made sense or not. Giraud was a glutton even when it came to talking.

I gave a sideways glance at my friend's long leg, stretching into the aisle of the bus. Four tiny bicycles ran down his calf, along with the outline of a fifth. Today I'd make sure he'd regret that confidence.

"Like yesterday, let's stay very conservative: a firm rhythm but nothing that will tire out Steve . . . or Marc," said Giraud after an obvious pause. "We're going for one and two. Except for Paniuk or Matosas, let anybody go who breaks away. It's not about winning the stage. If a big group takes off, say, twelve or fifteen of them, then two of you can follow. Preferably Guido and Tessier so that Steve will have climbers in front of him in case he needs to change up. Everybody else stay around Steve, protect him from falls and keep him away from the peloton. I don't want any heroism today. I want the jersey and that's it. Clear?"

It wasn't a plan that I liked. If Steve still had two or three domestiques when he arrived at the X on Lombard's map, it would be difficult for me to get the minute and a half I needed to steal his crown. On a good day, Guido or Tessier, our other climbers, could pull him almost all the way to the finish line. The worst of all worlds would be to launch an attack for all the peloton to see and come up short by half a minute.

When we got to the middle of the climb up the terrible Galibier, it was clear to me most of the teams were using the same strategy as Giraud. There were only a few battles, and these were personal, between rivals in the rankings. The rhythm was disturbingly slow. Two or three small groups, all ranked very low, had broken out earlier, including two racers from Fonar whom Giraud had encouraged to do so, but we'd catch up to them on the last mountain. If the day went on this way, a good portion of the peloton would arrive intact at Alpe d'Huez. That would be fatal to my plans.

I decided to risk everything for everything. I put Fonar in the front, as if I wanted to protect Steve by separating him from the rest of the racers. But as soon as Alanís, one of our remaining domestiques, went up to the head, I signaled for him to pick up the pace. He obeyed, but the change was almost imperceptible. I signaled again for him to increase his speed, and although he looked at me with curiosity, he only picked up the rhythm the tiniest bit. My strategy wasn't working. At that speed, we weren't going to drop anybody.

Five hundred meters later and still a few kilometers before we reached a peak, I got impatient and took over the front myself. In my role as the team's primary domestique, I would usually hold out for the last summit, but it was also not rare for me to relieve whoever was in the front at some climb along the way. Given that I was number two in the rankings, it was a move that didn't go unnoticed. I picked up our speed, and that seemed to wake up a couple of important racers who were afraid of dropping out of the peloton. There was a momentary frenzy in which several of them tried to move up to the front, worried Fonar was about to play another dirty trick.

My strategy proved successful, at least for the moment. The

peloton intensified its cadence, and what had been a compact mass began to stretch out: that famous multicolored serpent sinuously climbing the mountain.

"What are you doing, Marc?" Giraud yelled into our earphones. "Get back behind Alanís's wheel. Slow down the pace, goddamnit!"

"What . . . ? Yes, of course," I said, as if I had been distracted. I pedaled vigorously for another twenty meters and then backed off to position myself next to Steve. I never should have done that: My "bro" looked me up and down and read my intentions as if he could tap my neurons the same way he tapped my phone. The look of indignation and fury he shot at me was the same as when I scored a goal in the PlayStation game ten years ago.

Without me in front, we returned to a desperately slow rhythm. Things looked like they were going to go down exactly as Giraud had said they would. But instead, to everyone's surprise, they went down the way Steve wanted.

With about eighty meters before the Galibier peak, I heard him say "Now!" I didn't know how to interpret that. Suddenly, Alanís cut in front of me and two other Fonar teammates fenced me in against the outside curb, effectively blocking me. I knew what was coming next. Steve gathered speed and left us behind so he could crown the peak and begin the long descent. It was a masterful play. It would take me precious seconds to break my siege, and by the time I managed it, Steve would be long gone, starting down the nearly fifty kilometers that would take us to the foot of the last summit. With his talent for descents, he could add a couple of minutes to his lead, and once he reached Alpe d'Huez, he'd have the support of the two Fonar racers who'd been among the first to break away.

I was an imbecile. I had spent so much time analyzing where and how to betray him, I never considered the possibility I'd be the victim instead. Steve had played me completely, and probably without any help from Giraud. With my attempt to speed up on

Galibier, I'd shown my cards too early, and he'd put his devilishly efficient contingency plan into play.

Paniuk and a few others chased after Steve. When I was finally able to break the block by my own teammates and reach the summit, I'd already lost sight of their backs. But to my surprise, I heard someone behind me: Radek and Matosas had been following my route. The Italian caught up with me and said something about not letting those killers win. Radek passed me muttering incomprehensible psalms.

I figured my chances weren't good, but they could be worse. Matosas was still a great climber and Radek descended like the gods, at least in the sense that he thought he was immortal. He positioned himself in front of Matosas and me and began taking the curves like a motorcyclist, his body implausibly inclined, his knee to the ground, and his strokes almost perfect. His wheels hit the gravel at the edge of the abyss on more than one occasion, and his jersey had a sleeve torn from when he rubbed up against the mountain on the inside curves.

I dedicated myself to riding behind him, copying him perfectly, following every millimeter of his tracks, as if we were crossing a minefield in a straight line. Matosas did the same behind me. That's how we rode for more than forty kilometers at preposterous speeds. We passed a few of the racers who had been the first to break away, and we found the rest on the small stretch just before the ascent to Alpe d'Huez. But there was no trace of Paniuk, Steve, and his two domestiques. That was not a good sign. Not only had I lost the yellow jersey, but now it looked like I'd dropped behind the Czech as well.

A few meters later, Matosas told me Steve and his gang were 50 seconds ahead and there was no one between them and us. My earphone had been quiet for a good while; I imagined my team had found a way to cut me off. Without coming to an explicit agreement, Matosas, Radek, and I began to take short turns leading at a breakneck pace. A kilometer later, we passed Tessier—the first of Fonar's two guns had burned out—and there was now just Steve and Paniuk, as well as Guido. Their lead had been reduced to 46 seconds, but it was little comfort given the 2:19 Steve had on me overall. The enemy now was not just time but distance. We'd consumed 5 of the 13.8 kilometers on the Alpe d'Huez. There were less than 4 kilometers before Lombard's turning point, but the colonel had come up with that mark thinking Steve and I would be riding together as we crossed it; there was no scenario in which he foresaw I'd be three hundred meters behind.

And if that wasn't enough, Steve had one more advantage. While the three of us were taking equal turns, up in their group Guido was carrying all the weight in the front to preserve Steve's energy. I assumed all was lost. I could shoot out by myself and maybe—maybe—reach Steve before we got to the finish line, but overcoming the lead he'd built up would be impossible.

As if he'd heard me, Radek said something unintelligible, passed in front, and signaled me to follow.

"He said he's going to give you two kilometers," Matosas translated, and we glued ourselves to Radek's wheel.

The Pole is an unpredictable cyclist. Racers like him are terrifying because they compete exclusively to win single stages. They'll spend three days effortlessly riding along in the back of the peloton, letting themselves come in fifteen minutes after the winner of the stage, and then the next day, they'll explode with all their might, fully aware that after all that effort, they'll have to rest again on the following days. But the day they explode they can go harder than the Tour champion.

Giving me two kilometers meant he would climb as if it were the end of the Tour, more or less like what Guido was doing for Steve, the difference being that Radek was better rested. He shot forward with such force, I thought he had been too optimistic in promising two kilometers; with that kind of cadence he'd bottom out halfway through that distance. I had to ask him to pull back a little so as not to leave us behind. Finally, we got on his pace and I lost track of myself, concentrating everything on staying a hand span behind the Pole's bicycle.

I don't know if it was two kilometers, but when Radek pulled over to one side and unblocked my view, I could see the yellow jersey getting lost around a curve a little more than 100 meters away, maybe 130. There was still a kilometer left before Lombard's mark, and only Matosas was left for me. Or what was left of Matosas. The Italian had also paid the price of the brutal pace imposed by Radek. I looked back and saw that the Pole had stopped, his bike between his legs, trying to catch his breath. He had literally given me his last kilometers.

"I can't anymore," said Matosas, panting. "I'll never catch up to Paniuk for third place, but I'll give you what I've got left; you get that fucking *americano*."

Matosas stood up on his pedals, overtook me, and pushed a few hundred meters. It was true, he had no way to snatch third place from the Czech, who was four minutes ahead of him in the rankings. Even catching up to him before reaching the finish line would have been a useless effort. On the other hand, his fourth-place prize wasn't threatened. Medel, who was in fifth, had fallen back many kilometers ago. So the leader of Lavezza, whom I had thought of as a criminal for more than half the Tour, offered me his last supply of fuel so the real killers wouldn't get away with it.

He burned out a little before the fateful mark, and I left him behind. I recognized the rock Lombard had photographed; it now sported a stroke of blue paint. I wondered if he had painted it himself, or if he had taken advantage of a preexisting stain. Then I remembered that blue was the background color on the regiment's dragon crest. And, if there was any doubt, ten meters ahead there was the colonel himself, hidden under a straw hat.

"Twenty-five seconds, Marc!" he shouted. "He's only ahead by twenty-five!" He handed me, as best he could, a little radio with earbuds, and I hung them from the bike's handlebars; I had thrown my own silent earbuds away some time ago. Lombard tried to follow me, but he could only make it a couple of steps. By then, half the crowd was screaming my name. Finally I was French among the French.

If my calculations were correct, I was right on the threshold of the five-second margin. That meant I would have to catch up to Steve within the next kilometer and then beat him by 30 seconds in each of the three remaining kilometers. That seemed inconceivable, but I climbed on the pedals, aware of the fans piled up along the path. If I was going to lose, I wanted to show them it had been in spite of putting my all into the effort.

As I came around a curve among a mess of arms and faces, I almost ran straight into Guido, still rolling as hard as he could, completely exhausted. It was an unexpected boost to my spirits. It meant Steve was going it alone. That was confirmed an instant later when a clearing opened and I could see him twenty or thirty meters ahead. Paniuk, a better climber than him, had moved forward, hoping to win the stage and, why not, the Tour itself.

I finally had Steve right where I wanted him, with no defenses or domestiques and mid-slope. Alone with his soul. Unfortunately for me, there were only a little more than two kilometers left before the end of the race and I still had to make up for the minute and a half he held over me in the rankings, not to mention catch up to Paniuk. Fortunately for me, we were on a mountain. I shortened the distance that separated me from his bike, and when I passed him, I changed gears to push forward as hard as I could. I wanted to make him feel clumsy and helpless; I wanted the dragon Fiona saw in me to burn him with the trail of its fiery passage. I didn't have much energy left either, but the stimulation of leaving him behind could have pulled me out of a coma. "Beatriz says, 'Fuck you, prick!'" I yelled at him as I passed, and a meter ahead I shouted, "And Fleming!" but I don't know if he heard me.

I kept pedaling with vigor, still standing up, as if I had just started the race, until I assumed he had lost sight of me around a curve and I could sit back on the seat and catch my breath. I had boosted my pulse far beyond the norm and was burning watts of power I'd need later, but the insult to Steve had been worth it.

Paniuk rolled just seventy or eighty meters ahead, but I knew I had to pull myself together before even attempting to go at him. The crowd was closing in around my bike, trying to spur me on, but it was having the exact opposite effect. I felt like I couldn't breathe in those tunnels of naked torsos and the suffocating smell of tanning lotion and sweat. I thought that if Steve had a second contingency plan, this would be the moment for it. Anyone trying to slap me on the back or shouting at my legs could knock me over and say it was an accident. I shook my head and refocused on the kilometers ahead.

I knew I was running out of mountain, so I had to shoot forward after Paniuk. If I wasn't going to win the Tour, at least I would come in first today. I had no way of knowing how far I really was from Steve's numbers; all I could do was pedal like crazy and reach the last shirt between me and the finish line.

Only then did I remember the earbuds Lombard had given me by the blue milestone. I grabbed them off my handlebars and put them on. I heard Bernard's voice and felt less alone. More important, he started telling me about the progress of my push. The first thing he said was, "You finally put them on, you bastard! You've gained fourteen seconds on Steve; you still need eighty more. You've got a kilometer and a half."

I shook my head when I heard that. The numbers were unreachable given the state I was in. My lungs tried to pull in oxygen that didn't exist among the clouds of human heat and the penetrating scent of grilled meat and spilled beer. A cramp threatened to lock up my left leg, the shorter one. I thought with dread that I might be suffering the first symptoms of burnout. If that was the case, all would be lost. Steve himself could pass me at any moment; I imagined his look of mockery and scorn—the humiliation of the domestique who wanted to be king.

But: "Steve is doing worse," said Bernard. "His heart rate is hitting the ceiling and he's barely going nineteen kilometers per hour. You're going twenty-one; he won't catch you. But you need to get up to twenty-four at least. Let's go, Marc. You still got some more in you, I can see it from your stats." Apparently the colonel's son was watching the data transmitted from the power meters on our bikes in real time.

The information was a dose of adrenaline. It wasn't just about what I could win, it was about what Steve could lose. I clung to the possibility that he would be the one to suffer the bonk. I saw myself zipped up in yellow again, and I climbed on the pedals after Paniuk. The crowd bellowed with excitement.

"That's right, Marc, you have to pass the Czech to come in first. We're going to need the ten-second bonus. We're still forty-nine seconds from Steve, and there are twelve hundred meters to the finish line."

According to Bernard's equations, 24 kilometers per hour was enough for the stopwatch to somehow end up making me champion. But, since the mountains of Medellín, I had been chasing someone's back, and I was sick of it. I set my sights on some point between Paniuk's shoulder blades and followed him, a greyhound after a hare. I passed him eight hundred meters before the finish line. When I looked at my power meter, I saw I was rolling at 25 per hour. I had done it. I would be champion.

The audience seemed to think the same thing, because the path, now protected by fences, had become a channel flanked by thousands of blue flags, as if the churning water had broken free and was running over the banks.

It was strange to hear nothing from Bernard in the past few minutes, and I supposed he was having audio problems. The last thing I'd heard from him was "nineteen seconds," the distance Steve was still ahead of me in the rankings. But that had been three hundred meters ago. The difference was probably no more than 10 seconds at that moment, and I still had five hundred meters to go. I would get a 10-second bonus for coming in first place, and he would get 4 for third. That would put me another 6 ahead. I judged I'd have no problem eating up the rest of the difference, and I shot toward the finish line with everything I had.

When I crossed the 400-meter line, I finally heard Bernard's voice. I could feel his fear when he declared "thirteen seconds." It took me a moment to understand the consequences. Steve had recovered and was still ahead of me in the rankings. He was defending his advantage tooth and nail.

"He increased his speed to twenty-three kilometers, he's breaking away," said Bernard, and I noticed a hint of admiration behind his surprise.

I should have known. Behind me came the possessed teenager able to go without sleep several nights in a row in order not to lose at PlayStation. The furious rage provoked by being passed by his own domestique had topped off his empty tank.

"It won't be enough at this speed, Marc; you need to go twenty-eight and even then it's in the hands of the gods," said Bernard, rapidly calculating.

For a moment, the idea that Bernard was lying to me just to ensure a wider margin of victory crossed my mind. It's common for coaches to distort the data to draw an extra effort out of their racers on the last few meters. But the fear in Bernard's voice sounded real.

I wrung out all I had left, but the damn speedometer didn't climb over 26. I remembered my teacher Carmen and I thought about Fiona, trying to call on the energy I didn't have. Even though I was about to hit the wall, I couldn't cut off the seconds I needed. "Thirteen, twelve, eleven," announced Bernard with painful slowness. When I passed the 100-meter mark, Steve was an estimated eleven seconds ahead of me in the battle for the jersey. I thought of Lombard's suffering, and my mother, tortured until her death by my indifference.

I took the last curve and shot straight down, feeling my thighs and tendons shattering. I couldn't even raise my arms in triumph when I crossed the finish line. When I lowered my head, I saw the monitor showed 34 kilometers per hour. I stopped as best I could, but only Axel from the Fonar team helped hold me up.

The audience gave in to their own delirium, captivated by the end of the curse: Finally, a Frenchman might wear the yellow jersey in Paris, although I knew the second half of the battle was only just starting. Bernard confirmed it.

"Bravo, Marc, great effort." His tone in my earbuds was more resignation than enthusiasm. Axel handed me my cellphone and I called him immediately.

"How does it look?" I asked Bernard, blurting out the words through my panting, still bent over, although my eyes didn't leave the huge screen that showed Steve passing the curves I'd just navigated. A stopwatch added up the seconds that had passed since I crossed the finish line.

"It all depends on Steve. But the bastard's climbing fast."

"And the bonus?" I said, trying to cling to hope anywhere. I barely noticed Paniuk crossing the line and the TV didn't pay him much attention either. The eyes of the world were fixed on Steve, glued to his recovery, and it was clear he knew it. He was feeding on the admiration and even the hostility of the crowd, which he cut through like a hot knife through butter.

"Already included. At the pace he's going, he'll keep nine or ten seconds of advantage in the classification, minus the six seconds' difference in bonus points for first and third place. He'll take the Tour by a margin of three to five seconds."

At the start of the stage, Steve had an advantage of 1:33. He would just have to cross the line 1:26 after me to make up for my bonus points and beat me. I saw the stopwatch on the screen advance impossibly slowly while he ate up the meters on the last curve —0:59, 0:60, 1:01, 1:02—and prepared to conquer the final stretch. He must have been hearing something from his own earbuds, because he wore a big smile on his face. Giraud had told him the jersey was his. He knew he was the winner.

I saw him approach the finish line and I decided to walk away. I didn't want to see his defiant, mocking gaze. I knew it well. If I had the strength, I would've thrown a punch at the jerk behind the camera who'd projected my disappointed face on the huge screen, under Steve's triumphant image.

Axel put his arm around my shoulders to lead me to the exit. The cloud of reporters that had previously fenced me in was now entranced by Steve's imminent arrival.

The soigneur's hand squeezed my shoulder and interrupted my escape. He stayed static for a second, as if watching the wind. Then I noticed it too. A cry, almost a roar, was ascending from the base of the mountain toward its peak, like an inverted avalanche. We both turned toward the finish line and understood the reason why. Matosas had surged around the curve, pushed on by an elated mob, just five or eight meters behind Steve.

Steve didn't seem to realize what was happening, surely believing the uproar was caused by the crowd yielding to his feat. I didn't understand why Giraud hadn't warned him, but then I remembered that during his great wins, my teammate pulled his earbuds out before crossing the finish line so they wouldn't appear in the photos. As if he believed the fact that he listened to someone else's instructions made the triumph seem less praiseworthy, less his own.

I don't know where Matosas got his second wind from, but he looked like a runaway horse, his body and bike swaying like a true sprinter, standing up on his pedals. Steve must have sensed something, or perhaps he simply saw the fans' eyes were not on him anymore. He turned when the Italian was just a couple of meters behind him, with less than ten before the finish line. Matosas's face was frightening, a monument to fury and desperation.

Steve imitated the sprinter's movements and pushed his body forward like a track-and-field runner. But he had lost his momentum; they crossed together. The stopwatch stopped at 1:25.

For a few seconds the world stopped too, as if an explosion

had destroyed all eardrums and imposed a strange silence. I could have sworn that everything moved in slow motion. Then the image of the photo finish froze on the big screen. I heard a scream by my side; it was Axel. Matosas's wheel had crossed first.

A roar began to spread among the thousands who flooded the mountain as the implications of that photo sank in. Matosas got the 4-second bonus corresponding to third place, meaning I got 10 seconds of advantage over Steve, not just 6. The Italian had made the difference with his incredible attack. The 1:33 lead with which Steve had set off that morning had become 1:23. My bro had come in 2 seconds late. I had snatched away the yellow jersey.

I remember the next hour as if through a fog. An anti-doping test, a tumultuous, improvised press conference during which I stuttered who knows what, an awards ceremony in which my fingers were unable to open the bottle of champagne that traditionally bathes everyone around the podium.

Then, trying to escape the siege of reporters, I headed for the team bus, led by Axel and still escorted by Sancho and his slender comrade. There was no sign of Giraud or anyone else from my team. When I got to the vehicle, I stopped short. I wasn't even sure if Fonar *was* still my team, at least in emotional terms. The mere possibility of sitting down beside Steve, among teammates who had tried to block me an hour before, was inconceivable. A snowman on a beach in Saint Tropez would have been less out of place than me on the Fonar bus.

"Don't even think about it," Lombard said, taking me by the arm. "Ray will take you to the airport in Grenoble so you can get a flight to Paris."

"Colonel! Where were you? I was looking for you at the awards ceremony. We did it! You did it!" I corrected myself. "This jersey belongs to both of us. You know that, right?"

He didn't say a word. He hugged me tightly and I wrapped him in my arms. He had never felt so fragile. He began to shake with sobs; dozens of cameras pecked around us. For me, that was the real awards ceremony. Finally, the sound of Ray's car horn pulled us out of the hug.

"Everything we did was worth it, Hannibal. It was worth it. Now get out of here, go with Ray."

"There's no point," I responded with resignation. "I have to fly with Fonar. There'll be no plane tickets left; the whole circus is going that way."

"You have no idea, Hannibal. They're talking about nothing but your yellow jersey all over France. I told Bernard to buy you a ticket at any cost so you wouldn't have to travel with those back-stabbers. The airline said they wouldn't take your money under any circumstances, and that it would be an honor to fly you, even if they had to bump off the co-pilot." He beamed with pride. "Now go on, get out of here."

"What about you?"

"I need to rest awhile. I'll see you tomorrow in Paris."

I agreed and he said goodbye with a military salute. It was the last time I'd see him.

Traveling in Ray's car, I thought there was a good chance I wouldn't see anyone again ever in my life. The damn journalist took curves furiously, as if he hated existence. We were a little less than a hundred kilometers away from the Grenoble airport, half of which consisted of narrow, winding roads. While I held on as best I could with my fingers and toes during the long descent, I thought about the irony of giving the yellow jersey back to Steve due to an accident that would keep me from showing up for the final ride through Paris on the last stage, which was mostly cere-monial. A pang of fear shot through my sternum.

"Ray, when was the last time someone tried to take the yellow jersey from the leader in Paris?"

"In 1989 Greg LeMond took the jersey from Fignon on the last stage, the Versailles–Paris time trial."

"An American and a Frenchman, that's a bad sign," I said in jest, but not entirely.

"But it was a time trial, you had to compete even if you didn't want to. Don't worry about it; these days there's no precedent for someone trying to make up seconds in Paris. The ride is designed for the peloton to arrive together at the finish line as a single unit and for the sprinters to show their stuff in the last few meters. All you have to do is avoid an accident." After a pause, he added, "Or some trick on the route."

After skidding around a curve, I thought the only accident I needed to avoid was shooting into the abyss in the journalist's old car. But he was onto something: Nothing could guarantee Steve and Protex wouldn't attempt one final blow even before the last stage started at Sèvres, on the outskirts of Paris.

"Or off the route. Steve has already shown he prefers to attack his rivals at night. I'll have to sleep with a chair wedged against the door of my hotel room."

"I understand Lombard's son reserved a room for you at the Chantelly in Paris; I think they're getting the presidential suite ready. Anyway, you're not in danger anymore. Steve's not the murderer."

"What? What do you mean? Did you find something?" Only then did I remember the message Ray had sent in which he told me not to communicate with the commissioner. With the frenzy of the race and the awards ceremony, I'd forgotten.

"My friend, the owner of the Blue Galleon, gave me the name of the woman who called him to reserve a spot for Fleming and his teammates. She was really a technical secretary from the Tour organization. I talked to her, and she said she was just following instructions."

"From whom?"

"The tall, skinny guy in the car behind us, the one with the fat guy. They've been following us since we left."

"What do you mean?" I craned my neck to see out the window. "Those are my bodyguards from Bimeo."

"They were the ones who tricked Lampar to go alone to the highway so they could run him over."

"And with Fiona's trailer, to force her to park in an isolated place," I ventured, horrified. I thought about her again. I hadn't stopped thinking about her, somewhere in my mind, since the moment I was zipped up in the yellow jersey. I had tried to call her while they did my anti-doping test after the race, but her phone seemed to be off. I had to comfort myself by sending messages. I checked my phone in search of a response from her, but now I didn't have service, no surprise in these infernal mountains.

"When did you talk to Fiona?" I asked. "You know where she is?"

"I saw her this morning at the start in Modane. She told me she was leaving for Dublin tonight, with a layover in Paris. Maybe it's for the best, after what she found out."

"What did she find out?"

"Lombard," he said.

"What are you saying?" A sudden jolt shot through my abdomen.

"It's all conjecture, but everything adds up in the end. Since last night, I've been sure that Bimeo was the key player in several of the attempts, if not all."

"Why would Bimeo want to sabotage the tour? He's in charge of security."

"Two million euros. When I confirmed Bimeo's role, Fiona told me about the colonel's terminal illness, him selling the house, his obsession with seeing you win before he died."

"Lombard would never sign off on a cyclist's death."

"I assume that wasn't meant to happen. I'm sure it got out of hand when he involved those guys behind us."

"If this was about making me win, the bike sabotage doesn't

fit." I was trying to find some fissure that would let me save the colonel, although I knew the answer to my objection before I even heard it.

"The tube business came from the Italians. Matosas wasn't lying about that; they really thought the attacks were coming from Fonar and they wanted to respond in the same way."

"That's why Lombard came to my room so worried they would do something to me. He was afraid the Italians would retaliate," I ventured.

"I bet the tall man who tried to sabotage the brakes on Lavezza's bus wasn't the German, but the bigger Bimeo guy."

"You're right. He could've done the job for fun," I added, and shared the dark story of the former prison cook Favre had told me.

"I wonder what they hope to gain from following us now," said Ray with an apprehensive voice, his eyes fixed on the rearview mirror. I would have preferred for him to look ahead; on the last curve, only a last-minute jam on the brakes had kept us from crashing into an embankment. The only good thing about the journalist's suicidal driving was that the car carrying Bimeo's men had been left behind.

"Maybe they're watching out for their money; I doubt the colonel has handed it all over yet. They'll be charging until I get the trophy in Paris, I suppose."

Only then, when I said it, did I understand the magnitude of Ray's revelation. People had died and several of my teammates had been injured in order to help me win. The very fate of the Tour had been changed. I couldn't be champion like this.

"We have to talk to Favre, to Jitrik. The Tour can't approve this result. I can't accept this result," I concluded, devastated.

"You're not to blame. You beat Steve fair and square. Let's be realistic, the Fonar team was the strongest this year; with or without murders, Steve was the favorite at the betting houses. And you beat the favorite. Never devalue your victory."

"That's up to the authorities, don't you think?"

"Do you really want Steve to take the yellow jersey? Fonar's lawyers will jump on you as soon as something about Lombard slips out."

"No, I don't want that bastard to take the title," I said, remembering the emails I'd read that morning. I thought about the agonizing but genuine way I'd beaten Steve hours earlier, in spite of my teammates' blockade. I had caught up to him and left him behind in the stage that decided it all. Ray was right about one thing. That day, I had been better than Steve and, truthfully, I had been better throughout the Tour, except in the time trials. Then I thought about Fleming. "But it's not just a question of bicycles; there was a murder, at least one. The police have to make those bastards pay," I said.

"Let me talk to Lombard first; I'm begging you not to call Favre. Just give me a few hours. I'll meet him at a hotel in Grenoble after I leave you at the airport. Until I talk to him, all of this is just conjecture."

I was about to answer him when several text messages from Fiona showed up all at once; I finally had service again.

"Dragon, I saw what you did. It's the most beautiful thing that's ever happened. I love you," said the first, sent at 5:05 P.M., half an hour after my victory.

"I canceled the trip, I was confirming a hypothesis and didn't make it to the ceremony, I'm sorry. Talk to Ray. Losing service," she wrote at 6:15, a little after I'd gotten into the journalist's car.

"I'm with Lombard, I'm taking care of him. You rest, tomorrow's the big day. We're nearing Grenoble, I'm driving the colonel's RV, then I'll take a train. I'll try to get to Paris by midnight" read another, sent at 6:45, just ten minutes earlier.

"Dragon, I love you. I want to marry you. No, better yet, I want you to win every color jersey there is," she added a minute later.

I started writing a response, but then realized I was disconnected once more. Soon we'd be out of the mountains and I could write her more calmly.

"Do you think she's in danger?" I asked Ray after letting him know Fiona was with Lombard.

"As far as I know, he loves her like a daughter, but you know them better than I do. The only danger is that Bimeo might realize that she, or we, have found them out. But I don't see how. Just stay calm. Get on the flight; I'll wait for Fiona and Lombard in Grenoble."

We spent the rest of the journey almost in silence, each of us wrapped up in our own worries. Once we were on the highway, I wrote several messages in a row to Fiona. Then I turned off my phone to save power, as journalists and friends were bombarding me with messages and calls.

I said goodbye to Ray with a hug on the sidewalk outside the airport. He kept it going longer than I would've expected from a man who was so controlled.

"Thank you, Monsieur Moreau. Cycling owes you. The domestique's rebellion, it's a lesson for the future. You broke through the cold machinery and the web of interests, armed with only your talent and your effort. It's been an honor to know you."

I would have liked to tell him that without Radek, Matosas, Bernard, Fiona, and, yes, Lombard too, I could never have done it. But I didn't have the chance because dozens of people suddenly surrounded me. Only then did I realize I was still wearing the yellow jersey and I had no luggage, not even an ID. I didn't need it. The people applauded as I walked toward the departures desks.

I didn't need money for the taxi from Charles de Gaulle Airport either; a Chantelly limousine was waiting for me. Later, I sent a message to Axel asking him to send my suitcase to the hotel in Paris. I walked into my room at 9:30 P.M. and took a shower knowing I had a lot to think about, but my fatigue kept me from making progress toward anything except sleep. I shut my eyes and put an end to the longest day of my life.

A final image of the rankings fought to appear in my mind's

eye before I lost consciousness. I barely got past the second line. I smiled and fell asleep wrapped up tight in yellows.

GENERAL CLASSIFICATION: STAGE 20

RANK	RIDER	TIME	NOTES
1	MARC MOREAU (FRANCE/FONAR)	81:56:36	Take that, bro!
2	STEVE PANATA (USA/FONAR)	+0:02	
3	MILENKO PANIUK (CZECH/RABONET)	+0:37	
4	ALESSIO MATOSAS (ITALY/LAVEZZA)	+5:38	
5	PABLO MEDEL (SPAIN/BALEARES)	+15:46	
6	ÓSCAR CUADRADO (COLOMBIA/MOVISTAR)	+21:54	
7	LUIS DURÁN (SPAIN/IMAGINE)	+29:34	
8	SERGEI TALANCÓN (ROMANIA/ROCCA)	+37:51	
9	ROL CHARPENELLE (FRANCE/TOURGAZ)	+40:12	
10	RICHARD MUELLER (GERMANY/THIELEMANN)	+46:18	

Stage 21

Sèvres–Seine Ouest — Paris-Champs-Élysées,
109.5 km.

The light was barely blushing through the heavy curtains, but the yellow on my chest seemed to light up the luxurious room. I smiled—it hadn't been a dream. Fiona's arm, still asleep, lay across me, face pressed onto the jersey, as if she had wanted to make sure it wouldn't disappear while we were sleeping. I stayed still for a long time, treasuring the moment. Fiona and the yellow jersey: an unbeatable combination.

Then I remembered Lombard and Bimeo and the vision fell to pieces. For a few minutes, I clung to the possibility it was all a huge misunderstanding; I couldn't imagine my old friend had a part in Fleming's death. I told myself the prime suspect's identity had changed so many times, from Radek to Steve, from Matosas to Giraud. There was no reason it couldn't happen again.

Fiona had a lot of influence over Lombard, and she had spoken to him the night before. If the old man had something to do with the crimes, my lover might know more than me.

When she finally opened her eyes, a huge smile broke across

her face, and soon after it wasn't exactly the jersey she was stroking. In any other circumstance it would have been a memorable moment, but my distress defeated me.

"Fiona, what did Lombard say to you? Did you tell him about Bimeo?" I asked, hating myself for interrupting what was just getting started. To my surprise, she kept going.

"My Dragon," she whispered. "You're the Tour champion!" Her voice was a purr, an invitation to comfort and pleasure. She seemed to still be in the limbo between dreams and reality.

"Ray told me everything," I said. "What's going to happen with Lombard? We have to tell Favre, to let Jitrik know what his people have done."

"Shhhh!" she responded, moving her hand to my face and putting a finger over my mouth. "Don't think about that, at least for the next few hours. Steve will try something today, I'm sure. He's not going to want to lose a Tour by two seconds. You have to concentrate on that, my love."

"But we have to stop Bimeo; he could pull another dirty trick."

"Bimeo's not going to do anything. He's already played his part."

"And Lombard? What are we going to do about Lombard?" I exclaimed.

"Mojito," she said, while holding my chin to make me look her straight in the eyes, "do you trust me?" She said it with the solemnity of a marriage proposal.

"Yes," I answered, equally grave.

"Then all I ask is that you make sure the yellow jersey is still with you when night falls. This is the decisive moment of your career, maybe of your life. Leave the whole Lombard issue to Ray and me. Nobody's going anywhere for the next few hours."

I didn't know what to say. But something she'd said started growing like a tumor in my brain: Steve wouldn't let himself lose a Tour by two seconds. Facing that challenge would have to be my priority.

"Agreed," I said. "But promise me that when this is over, you'll tell me everything and we'll decide what to do together, okay?"

"Okay." She gave me a kiss, and then, smiley and naked, she walked into the bathroom.

We ordered a sumptuous meal from room service and ate it wrapped in our bathrobes, our hair wet, feeding each other pieces of fruit. We indulged in the exultation brought on by success, in the excitement of sex not yet consummated.

The start of the stage was scheduled for four in the afternoon, so we spent the rest of the morning reading the papers and watching old movies on TV. But our giddiness soon faded into the background. The look of worry fixed on Fiona's brow had nothing to do with the dangers faced by Kirk Douglas in his unrealistic portrayal of Sitting Bull; every few minutes she would turn on her phone, check her messages, then turn it off again. I could tell her tension was growing as the hours passed.

For my part, I tried to push everything that didn't have to do with the race out of my mind, but there was very little there to keep me focused. We'd eat up the 110 kilometers of flat ground in a little more than two hours. Easier than training. Even though some riders would attempt to break away in Paris, I knew the peloton would never let the escapees widen their distances; tradition had transformed this stage into a parade through the cheering crowds greeting the survivors of the 3,350-kilometer journey. We survivors wanted to reach the finish line together.

That was the idea at least, but a second-place rider had never reached this stage just two seconds behind. Especially not Steve Panata. He wouldn't quietly accept defeat.

But, as much as I forced myself to think like him, I couldn't come up with anything else he could do. Like the great time-trial rider he was, he might attempt a breakaway on his own from the starting line, but unfortunately for him, nobody runs faster than the peloton. For the same reason, any attempt by Fonar would be neutralized.

I concluded his only chance would be some sort of cheating. One of his cronies could try to knock me down or feign a fall and drag me into it. I made a mental note to be sure to ride far away from any other member of the Fonar team.

"Hey, what if they mess with my bike? If I break down, none of my teammates will lend me theirs," I whispered to Fiona at one moment.

"Don't worry about that, one of my inspectors is going to check all your gear down to the smallest detail; we have the authority and the obligation."

"What if Giraud kicks me off the team before the stage starts?" I asked half an hour later.

"I don't see how that could happen," she responded after thinking for a few seconds. "Fonar's sponsors must be happy to have another champion on the team, and a French one at that. Giraud's no fool; he'd be risking getting lynched by the fans."

I turned on my phone and looked at the long list of calls and messages. I lingered on two names that were repeated with obsessive frequency. The ones from Favre I didn't open. The first one from Steve said, "Why did you do this to me, bro?" I didn't read any further and turned off my phone again.

That bastard has no shame. After everything, he's still telling me off. Then I considered it might be a strategy. To make me feel guilty in the hope that I'd return his jersey voluntarily, like the disciplined domestique I was meant to be.

Five minutes before leaving the hotel, as Fiona washed her face, I couldn't resist the impulse to open my laptop and write Steve an email: "Why did I do this to you, you son of a bitch? This is why." I copied and pasted the emails Fiona had sent me from my mother.

When I got to the starting line, I didn't stop for any journalist, although they couldn't come that close anyway. Besides my two guards, at least four other guys from Bimeo surrounded me when I got out of the team bus. I participated in the signature ceremony amid the noise of the cameras and distant questions, took the bike Axel handed me, and hurried to take a spot in the center of the peloton.

The welcome I received from my fellow riders took me by surprise. A hundred hands slapped my back and I heard congratulations in many different languages. I wanted to think that, for most of them, my jersey was a sort of vindication of the underdogs, of all of us who rode year after year only to lose, sacrificing for the designated champions.

Before the race started, the organizers asked me to come to the front, along with the lead sprinters, climbers, and youth racers. As I moved through the cyclists, I passed two meters from Steve and our eyes met. From the look in his eyes, somewhere between offended and confused, I assumed he hadn't seen my email. His face was a pitiful personification of the betrayed friend.

But as soon as the race began, it was clear Steve hadn't given up on anything. The Fonar team took over the front and immediately imposed a breakaway pace. The peloton simply picked up speed. At this rate, it was going to become the fastest Paris stage of all time. Still, at such a short distance and with no slope in the way, nobody from the peloton was going to be left behind.

Even so, Fonar kept trying. I don't know what Steve promised his teammates, because with ten kilometers left to finish the race, he launched a violent offensive down the right side at a pace more appropriate for a sprinter than for an all-rounder. I had no choice but to launch myself forward down the opposite side. I didn't have a team anymore, so I thought I'd have to defend myself alone, but immediately Matosas and Radek slipped in front to protect me. Another two or three important racers filled out my lines. Seen from a helicopter, we would've looked like a scarab moving forward; one antenna formed by Fonar, the other by my improvised motley crew.

We kept it up for three or four kilometers, with neither antenna ceding an inch of ground. Then something unexpected happened, something that put an end to any attempt at rebellion. Guido stood up on his pedals, broke away from the Fonar team, and crossed the space between us. For a moment, I thought it was an act of aggression and I tried to take shelter among my people. But he placed himself by Matosas's side to give the Italian some much-needed relief.

I couldn't resist looking at Steve's face; he kept trying furiously for a few minutes, but Guido's move left Fonar exposed to their fellow riders. Most of my ex-teammates were now riding with their eyes fixed on their handlebars at a visibly slower pace than before.

The peloton pushed its right flank forward and Steve was absorbed into the mass. He didn't stick his head out again; I guess he preferred not to be singled out by the cameras in what must have been the most humiliating moment of his career.

Now, finally, I knew the yellow jersey was mine. For the first time that day, I started enjoying the beautiful spectacle of the sidewalks flooded with thousands of my happy compatriots, celebrating this victory with me. Later, I would find out almost half a million people were out in the streets. It looked to me like they were celebrating the second liberation of Paris. It was my liberation, at any rate.

The peloton decreased its speed and I let myself move to the front for the rest of the race, at least until the last five hundred meters, when, as tradition dictates, the sprinters shot forward to compete for the final stage. I crossed the finish line in a blur.

The next hour was an endless series of hugs, ceremonies, and harassment from reporters. One moment sticks out: When I climbed the podium over Steve, our eyes didn't meet and we didn't say a word to each other. I threw the bouquet of flowers they handed me into Fiona's arms, but she received it with less enthusiasm than I would have expected.

The press conference was full of obvious and repetitive questions, although there were also some juicy ones about the fratricidal relationship between Steve and me. I realized the press was going to transform our two-day battle into an extended melodrama.

But I didn't expect the question I got from the reporter from *El Periódico de Cataluña*.

"Any reaction to the accident that recently befell your friend and adviser, Colonel Lombard? You must be sad he's not here to celebrate your victory."

I'm sure the reporter asked the question in good faith, assuming I was already aware of what had happened. I immediately got up from the table, bewildered, asking everyone who was around me, even Giraud, what had happened. From their faces, I realized I was the only one who didn't know.

I left the room and found Fiona. She hugged me tightly and dragged me into an empty broadcast booth.

"It happened when the race was about to start. He and Ray veered off the road coming from Grenoble. The car went off a cliff, and neither of them survived."

The road had finally made Ray pay for his recklessness. Even so, I couldn't wrap my head around the idea that they were no longer with us. Then I was struck by an inconsistency.

"I don't understand why they were on the road at that time. Nothing would have made them miss the start of the final stage, especially this year. Lombard would have given his life to see me on that podium."

"He did," she answered. I remembered her anxious face that morning every time she'd checked her phone.

"Do you know something?" I asked, fearful.

"It was Ray's idea. The only possible solution—a final sacrifice for you and the Tour. Last night, Lombard confirmed our fears. He'd hired Bimeo; he let the explosion on the trailer happen, knowing the tank was empty, to avoid any suspicion about you or

Fonar. And, yes, Fleming's death was overzealousness from those two guys who followed you around."

"What the hell was Lombard thinking? He cleared the path to let me win? Where's the glory in that?"

"The glory was always there for your taking, Dragon. His whole operation was just meant to shake you up, to pull you away from the role of domestique."

Then she laid out her plan.

I sent Favre a message asking him to come to my hotel room. Fiona went to talk to Jitrik. Later, she told me she had shown the Tour's director a confession signed by Lombard, including Bimeo's involvement. Jitrik felt like his world was falling apart; it was a scandal that could bring professional road cycling to its knees and completely destroy the Tour.

When she felt he was ready, she made her proposal: fire Bimeo immediately and assist in the police investigations to charge him with corruption and other offenses. Everyone knew about the bribes and extortions the security chief used with mayors who wanted to be included on the Tour agenda and the shameless way he milked the budget and placed family members in key positions; in recognition of the official's effectiveness in security matters, the organization ignored these irregularities. In exchange for dismissing Bimeo, Fiona offered to bury Lombard's confession and make sure it never came to light. Desperate to protect the Tour, Jitrik jumped at her offer.

The commissioner turned out to be a much harder nut to crack. At one point I thought about using Fiona's strategy by appealing to his devotion to cycling. But I knew his self-respect as a detective would end up overcoming any other passion. Also, he wouldn't be keen on the idea of someone other than him righting the wrongs.

"In the end, you were the winner, sergeant," he said sadly.

"You say that as if you wish otherwise, commissioner. I thought you'd be happy."

"I am happy. You're a Frenchman and a friend, and that fills me with pride," he said, although there was a suspicious look in his eyes. We were meeting in the sitting room of my suite. Through the window, I could see the section of the Champs-Élysées I'd ridden down a few hours earlier. "It's just a little unsettling that all these incidents and Fleming's death have led to this," he added, shooting a look at the yellow jersey I'd hung over the back of a chair.

"I won by two seconds, commissioner, and the whole world was watching. Surely you're not saying someone could have planned it like that."

"And on top of all that, the tragic accident with the journalist and your friend the colonel. I know Ray was investigating the previous incidents. The manager of the Hotel Madelaine told me. He was very interested in Bimeo's role."

"Bimeo?" I said, as if I had never heard the name in my life.

"Bimeo, the guy whose henchmen have been protecting you these past days," he said, with a tone that said *Stop busting my balls*.

"I know who Bimeo is. What I don't understand is what he has to do with any of this," I bluffed.

The commissioner was about to say something, but he changed his mind. He threw me a baleful glance and showed his cards.

"From the start, I've thought everything centered on you. And now I'm more convinced than ever. It's not the Italians, and I don't think it was Fonar's people either. Your victory, the deaths of Lombard and Ray, who you were meeting with every night. Too many signals to ignore, don't you think, sergeant?"

I nodded as if I were considering it myself, and then, after shaking my head, I added: "All I can say is this has been the most competitive final in the history of the Tour, and these are the legs that won me the yellow jersey. If you have other explanations, commissioner, show me the proof."

Favre was about to say something when there was a knock on

the door and it opened, revealing Fiona with a key in her hand. Jitrik was behind her.

"Sorry, I didn't know you were here, commissioner," she lied.

"Commissioner Favre, I came to congratulate Marc again in private," said Jitrik. "But I'm glad I found you here. I just spoke to your boss. I asked him to stop the investigation we'd requested. In the end, things have been resolved without any major scandals."

"There was at least one probable murder," said Favre, uncomfortable.

"Oh yes, that. Terribly sad," Jitrik responded, dismayed. "The chief inspector told me they're thinking about assigning the Fleming investigation to the police in Le Havre, where the crimes took place," he added in a casual tone.

"Our investigation is already very advanced; there's no reason we should let it go," the commissioner objected.

"Well, it's what your boss decided. I don't know what to tell you. You all know more about that than I do. Although they did tell me the central office will process the complaint we're filing against Bimeo first thing in the morning; we've had it in our sights for a while, you know?"

Favre looked at Fiona, then at me, and finally at Jitrik. He realized he'd been the victim of a setup; Jitrik had made no effort to hide it. He probably thought, being the Tour director, that there was no need to invest too much time or histrionics on a mere cop.

"Gentlemen, lady," Favre said with an ironic smile, nodding his head in my direction. "Have a nice night." I didn't see him for a long time after that.

Fiona and I got rid of Jitrik as soon as we could and fell back into each other's arms. She slid into my jersey and then lowered herself on top of me. We made love with the abandon of those who think there'll be no tomorrow, then we did it again with the tenderness of those who know all the tomorrows are yet to come.

We dozed for hours. I finally made myself go to the bathroom, and when I returned, I noticed my computer screen lit up on my desk. An alert showed an email from Steve in my inbox. I opened it.

"Your mom never wrote those messages. Someone played you." I read the two lines again, moved the cursor to the trash can, and deleted the message. I closed the screen and went back to bed, where I held Fiona in my arms and fell into a deep and peaceful sleep.

Acknowledgments

This novel would have been impossible without the wise and generous tutelage of Carlos Arribas of *El País* and Sergi López-Egea of *El Periódico de Cataluña;* these journalists are true institutions of road cycling. They adopted me as an apprentice, introduced me to cyclists, crew directors, and mechanics, and even accredited me as a correspondent for the Tour, among other races. Above all, they inoculated me with a germ of passion for cyclists—these new gladiators and their heroic deeds—a whole universe that is now a part of my life. The fidelity with which this small and specialized world is reflected in the novel is due to the teachings of Carlos and Sergi; the errors are all my own.

I am grateful to Guillermo Zepeda for his companionship on the mountain routes and summits of the Alps in our hard-hit Audi rental. The research required to write a novel has never been so joyful. Thanks also to Camila Zepeda and Ricardo Raphael, my readers since day one, for convincing me rightly or wrongly that each unpublished book has been better than the last.

I am indebted to the Pontas Agency for their involvement since the beginning of this project. Ana Soler-Pont and Maria Cardona, were able to secure translations in a dozen countries, thanks to their enthusiasm and their talent, even as I was still writing—which is the best motivation one could have.

No less important was the support of Gabriel Sandoval and Carmina Rufrancos at Editorial Planeta, who did not initially love the idea of a cycling novel, but trusted me anyway. And, above all, Carlos Revés, expert editor and lover of stories that deserve to come into the world.

Thanks also to Caitlin McKenna and her team at Random House New York, who managed to make the English edition an improved version of the original, thanks to their perseverance and loving attention to detail.

Finally, this book is dedicated to Susan Crowley, my yellow jersey, my Fiona, my muse and intellectual accomplice, for transforming life into one happy, loving bike ride.

ABOUT THE AUTHOR

JORGE ZEPEDA PATTERSON is a journalist, novelist, and political analyst. He has been the director of several Mexican newspapers and was the founder of *Siglo 21*, a groundbreaking publication throughout the 1990s. He currently runs *Sinembargo*, a leader in Mexican news sites, and writes a weekly column that is published in sixteen different newspapers. His debut novel, *Los corruptores*, was a finalist for El Premio Hammett, and his second novel, *Milena*, won the Planeta Prize. His novels have been translated into more than ten languages.

jorgezepeda.net
Twitter: @jorgezepedap

ABOUT THE TRANSLATOR

ACHY OBEJAS has translated Junot Díaz, Rita Indiana, Wendy Guerra, and many others. She's the author of *The Tower of the Antilles*, which was nominated for the PEN/Faulkner Award, the PEN Open Book Award, and several other honors. Her other books include *Days of Awe* and *Ruins*.

achyobejas.com
Twitter: @achylandia

ABOUT THE TYPE

This book was set in Sabon, a typeface designed by the well-known German typographer Jan Tschichold (1902–74). Sabon's design is based upon the original letterforms of sixteenth-century French type designer Claude Garamond and was created specifically to be used for three sources: foundry type for hand composition, Linotype, and Monotype. Tschichold named his typeface for the famous Frankfurt typefounder Jacques Sabon (c. 1520–80).